W9-AED-279

BALISAND

BRYAN UNIVERSITY LIBRARY

BALISAND

JOSEPH
HERGESHEIMER

Author of
"The Three Black Pennys"

the best tryall of a gentle-
man in bloud is by bearing
of armes — LORD COKE

BRYAN UNIVERSITY LIBRARY

GROSSET & DUNLAP
PUBLISHERS
by arrangement with Alfred A. Knopf

WITHDRAWN

H
42b

Copyright, 1924, by
JOSEPH HERGESHEIMER

MANUFACTURED IN THE UNITED STATES OF AMERICA

16209

2113

DEAR ALFRED,

Balisand is yours; or, rather, ours together. That is what gives it, for me, an especial value. It is the sign of an attachment superior even to a shared material interest, an affair not of books on the public stands, but of a bond private and happy and permanent.

JOSEPH HERGESHEIMER

I

SWEEPING about the thrust of Ware Neck Richard Bale lost sight of the wooded shore of Balisand. The four negroes rowing his canoe sang, in low concerted voice to the rhythm of the oars, an Anabaptist hymn. God's children lost in the land of Egypt! The sound was muted, scarcely above the breath, but it had an astonishing power: Richard Bale thought that it must be audible across all the shining reaches of Mockjack Bay. The servants, he reflected, were singing well, rowing smoothly, because London, his headman, was there. A tall, strongly built negro, no longer young but narrow in the hips and flexible, he sat in the bow singing with an immobile rapt face. His hair, Richard Bale saw, was definitely grey, and he was sorry; but not on account of any depreciation in London's value—he was a part, from its beginning, of Bale's consciousness and of the life at Balisand.

They were turning to the right, toward the mouth of Ware River; soon Todd Hundred, where he was bound, would be clear; but now the sun blazing on the water made the far shore practically invisible. It was past the middle of June, noon lay hardly back of the canoe—he had heard the bells ringing from the plantations—and the scents of the gardens on the river, of heliotrope and roses and Cape jasmine, floated out in the still heat. Richard Bale, shifting the cushion behind him, thanked God that it was hot: he couldn't, actually, grow accustomed to summer; he had been unable to take it for granted since the winter of 'seventy-seven, when it had seemed that all life was frozen into a perpetual cold. Even now, in memory, a chill like ice invaded him. He saw ice bright with blood.

Somewhere beside him London had put a flask of peach brandy, and, finding it, he took a drink. He drank and swore in bitter retrospect. The negro nearest him, just beyond Richard Bale's leather box, looked up half dazed, startled out of his abstraction of song. What was it, London demanded. Richard Bale answered that it was nothing. The old familiar ache in his right leg crept up from ankle to knee, from knee to hip; and, as usual, it gave him a perception of the futility of both body and mind, a feeling of age not warranted by his thirty years. It was ridiculous, and he returned to the brandy, but the sensation persisted, the conviction that nothing was safe or permanent . . . except, yes—except General Washington.

That he allowed; but what, he asked himself further, had Washington's integrity secured, either for his country, his officers or himself? Nothing, Richard Bale silently concluded. But he didn't, then, want to recall things so gloomy—he wasn't in the Congress at Annapolis, but going to a long gay party at Todd Hundred. And no politics! Yet that, probably, was a vain declaration, with Gawin Todd back from the Virginia Legislature and Jasper Robine, the friend and supporter of Patrick Henry and of Jefferson, present. Just the thought of Thomas Jefferson, or, rather, of his principles, inflamed Bale's anger. But he admonished himself again, rigidly — no politics; he shifted his thoughts to Gawin Todd's announced engagement:

To a Miss Roderick of Henrico County. Her given name, he had heard, was Lavinia. In some way it suggested the perfume of the flowers, growing stronger as the canoe drew near to land. The Rodericks were people of consequence — her father, Peyton Roderick, was in the Virginia Council of State — although not one of the older families of the Virginia Colony; and its interests, Richard Bale suspected, lay with the new disaffection on the West. Yet that, of course, would be in perfect keeping with Gawin Todd's particularist fallacies.

Damn it, there he was again relapsing into a resentful and partisan spirit. Lavinia Roderick. Gawin had put off marrying a long while, he must be nearly thirty-five. But then he, Richard Bale, was past thirty, with no sign of an attachment of the heart. Absolutely none. However, he had been seven years away in the war, from his Captain's commission in the Sixth Virginia Regulars, at Williamsburg, to Yorktown; and not only had marriage been impossible through that time; it had, as well, left him in no mood or condition for tenderness. It would have been different, perhaps, if Balisand were less capably managed; as it was, he had never seen a young and personable woman who even promised to match later the ability, the wise active force, of Mrs. Patton, his housekeeper.

It was true that she urged him to go out, in place of sitting home over a bowl of lime toddy, to attend the balls at the tavern, where, she predicted, he would soon meet with a happier fate; she thought Balisand lonely and said so; but he had no inclination for dancing. At any moment the pain might flare up his leg. The girls about him, though they had come into their early maturity while he was away, he knew too well for the entertaining there of romantic illusions. And the women, the society, he had met at Annapolis during the early session of the Congress, were too gaily metropolitan to be thought of in the terms of his quiet plantation. Still he felt that, like Gawin Todd, he would eventually marry, since he was strongly conscious of his duty toward the Bale succession; however, it must come in its own way; it couldn't be forced or deliberately planned.

That much, at any rate, he knew about love, and he asserted to himself it was enough. He wasn't lonely at Balisand. God, he was too glad to be back there to allow any sense of emptiness whatever. And where the lime toddy was concerned, it was his habit to ask Mrs. Patton why, then, she prepared it so beautifully. Besides all this, Morryson Bale, his uncle, although aged, was an admirable companion. Only the nights, perhaps, with Morryson asleep in his deep chair, seemed sometimes long; they would be impossible without the toddy bowl; but his days were occupied in riding about the fields, parleying with Thomas Ekkes, his overseer; meeting the gentlemen of his neighbourhood at crossroads and the courthouse; playing whist at rather more than he could afford, and matching his horse Spadille against any others in Gloucester County. And now, in addition, he was a member of the Congress of the Confederated States.

Yes, as it was, he was well employed. In reality, he

had tried to avoid the party at Todd Hundred; but Charles Todd, finding him at the ordinary, had insisted that he would take his absence as an act of unfriendliness; and Mrs. Patton had prepared and laid out his formal dress without stopping to consult his wishes. Now, however, viewing the light painted walls of Charles Todd's house across the garden, with the live oaks and cottonwood trees beyond, the dark magnolias and taller tulip poplars, he was glad of his decision to go. He had no doubt Mrs. Patton was right and that it would do him good. That, naturally, hadn't been the end of what she hinted . . . but he had paid no attention to a mere feminine sentimentality.

It was so pleasant on the river, in the sunlight, that he ordered his servants to stop rowing. The canoe lost its way, it half turned and slowly drifted. The negroes sat motionless, with parallel dripping oars, watching him intently. Richard Bale removed his broad planter's hat, and the sun's rays fell directly into his eyes. For a moment he was blinded; he held a palm across his vision, and the river, the shore, returned through the blaze.

*

* *

Suddenly he didn't want to land, again to take up with that act the difficulties and burdens of living. They had multiplied and grown heavy beyond all reason. Not that they touched him intimately, or extended to Balisand to disturb its isolated peace; but in consequence of that they were none the less real. He wondered a little why he had consented to become a member of Congress; why, when he was so worn with struggle, he had gone back into a fight more hopeless, that promised to be more prolonged, than the War with England at its darkest. This questioning was only superficial; he was aware of all the reasons, or, perhaps, the reason, for his course. But for the moment he was annoyed at his further voluntary commitment. No one could have demanded it of him, for he had, certainly, discharged every atom of his obligation to Virginia:

When the thought of that, his State, flashed into his mind, he was conscious that a change of obligations had overtaken him — at the beginning his whole duty had been to Virginia; but somewhere, midway of the late past, his allegiance had been removed from the Commonwealth, a place, to a personage. He had begun by serving the State and he had ended by a jealous devotion to General Washington. Exactly that had happened! It was, apparently, a simple affair, and growing simpler at the last; but the reverse was true: what was now a passionate attachment to an individual had been magnified into the service of a cause with no more substance than a chimera.

The same change, Richard Bale realized, he had seen come over Washington himself — the growth of a fantastic belief in the possibility of a strong and honourable Federal Government for the Sovereign United States. Bale silently repeated those three words, sovereign and united states, with an utter savage contempt. If he could have remembered them all, he would have cursed the States separately. He recalled, in spite of his contrary determination, the negligence politics and selfishness had shown the Continental Army. The war had for ever killed in him any regard for the supposed sacredness of the individual. He had come to hate troops of men, the militia, and to detest the instruments of what was called self-government. On one side he had seen the Toryism of merchants, rich shippers, who wanted to keep their privileges and wealth at any cost to independence, and on the other the ignorant apathy of a poor who asked nothing better than a wild without responsibility and the game of killing or being killed by Indians.

There had been, he recognized, absolutely no connection between the body of the newly united states and the army that won its freedom. The federated Congress had been as bad as Pennsylvania . . . he chose a notorious example. During the war there had been forced upon him, and the officers he operated with, a feeling of complete detachment from the people for whom, ostensibly, he was fighting. Yes, his allegiance had been removed from Virginia, even from the inhabitants of the Tidewater, to a man who, by some process of magic, had lost his identity in a heroic ideal.

That, for him, was what had happened to General Washington — he had entered into an engagement where no loyalty or force or purpose existed, and he had created them all out of his own spirit. More than that — he was obsessed by the conviction that they could be made permanent. Such was the conviction which had carried him, Richard Bale, into his present uncomfortable position. It had all the aspects of a battle hopeless from the first; but, he reminded himself, he was accustomed to that. His mature experience had been made up of nothing else — forced marches, retreats in the night, lost engagements, guns without ammunition, companies without men, leaders who had no faith.

That had been impossibly bad, but this, the dragging inaction at Annapolis, was worse. In battle, at least, there were men to be confronted — he had slain deserters — but in Congress there were nothing but concealed and unendurable insults. There was hardly a member present, out of the scant twenty-five or so, with whom he would have descended to fight. That, too, the fact that he was consciously, obviously, a gentleman, had begun to add to his difficulties. He thought of himself, with a sense of the deepest right, more highly than he thought of the common multitude. There were privileges, just as there were duties, to which he had been born. And, while he would permit nothing on earth to limit him in their exercise, he realized that a lower order, as a body, was elevating itself into a place from which, sooner or later, it might easily dictate at least the material form of his living.

He had enlisted instantly against the appearance of an intolerable injustice; this, at the time, had been enough; and a stiff smile moved his lips at the memory of his beginning simple fervour. But it was in the establishment of a succeeding integrity that the real, the lasting, struggle began. That, of course, lay between what was essential, if there was ever to be a nation in America, and what the increasing ignorant mass temporarily demanded. It was to the latter all his power was opposed; and if the worst happened, he thought, he'd retire to Balisand and end his life as it had begun, in the manner of his family. Again he recalled Washington, who had returned to his plantation, to the life of a country gentleman; but that, in effect, hadn't continued; it couldn't last, Richard Bale reflected. A vision born at Trenton and Monmouth and Stony Point kept Washington bitterly engaged in the blunders of an immaterial country.

The same thing, in a lesser degree, had happened to himself —— the flask, Richard Bale found, was empty —— only strife for him on the shore; or, to be precise, at Trenton, in November. It was better here, floating tranquilly on the water. The fragrance of a flower was its most invaluable quality. There was still time to drift before he landed, before dinner. He heard, very faintly, the sound of music, of fiddles, and he realized that dancing had begun at Todd Hundred; probably it had started soon after breakfast; and it would go on through the afternoon and for most of the night.

There was a deeper reluctance than any he had grasped for going on shore; it was without reason, nothing more than premonition; yet it was acute, with the effect on him of a suspended grief. This, he told himself, was the result of the distant music and the peach brandy. If it got so that brandy made him sentimental, he'd have to stop drinking. He would, by God! "London," he said abruptly, "I think we'd better come in to the wharf."

"They'll go right along without you if we don't,"

the negro replied; " sweet sounds are in that house." The oars slipped quietly into the water and the canoe was swung about. As they drew near the long slight wharf of Todd Hundred, a servant in a white coat moved out to its end. " You had better take Little York up to the house," London advised his master; " I wouldn't trust those Todd niggers with your fine shirts and gold buttons."

" Mr. Todd's house is a damned sight better run than Balisand," Richard Bale told him. " Any servant that touches my things will get in chains." London laughed good-naturedly, and then he leaned out, taking hold of the wharf. Bale rose uncertainly, stiff from his cramped position in the canoe, and a number of hands assisted him to the steps. The music of the fiddles grew louder and he could hear a voice calling the figure of a quadrille. A mimosa tree was massed with a fragile white flowering.

*

* *

On the narrow way leading over the water to the land he recalled the fact that the wharf at Balisand needed mending. There was no proper covering at the landing. It occurred to him to tell London about this at once, and he stopped, bringing the Todd servant following with his box to a sharp halt. But the canoe was already out on the river. London had started for home. The negroes were singing again: Lost . . . in Egypt. And the minor harmony of their voices mingled with the strains of the fiddles. The sun was almost behind him, and the trees that formed the shore of Ware Neck rose bluely from the level silver tide except where lawns, cut from the forest, met the river. The man carrying his things shuffled his feet; he was unable to go on; and Richard moved forward with a slight limp.

On his right there were the trees and close grass, ahead was a dairy house, whitewashed, and a buttercup field, and on the left was the manor of Todd Hundred. The central part was in two stories, with a small portico and flattened roof, and there was a projection of one story at either end; the wing away from the river, which held the dining room, was connected with the kitchen by a covered brick walk; and beyond the kitchen — drawing the façades of low orderly brick into a long line — was Charles Todd's office. There were steps leading down from the drawing room to the lawn and river; the garden was now hidden from Richard Bale by the house.

He stopped at the main portico, but the negro at his back explained that Miss Ava had directed him to be carried to the room above the schoolhouse. She thought he would be quieter there and have more room to spread out. So he continued past the house, the kitchens and office, and then turned to the left. The schoolhouse was at the corner of a hedge that enclosed the small separate dwellings of the slave quarters. There were no windows on that side, but the room that Richard Bale occupied looked out, on two walls, over the garden and the river. There was, he knew, another room on that floor, where the tutor lived. Very comfortable he must be, Bale told himself aloud. A bed was small, but the linen choice, and it was carefully hung with mosquito net; there was a case of drawers, a clear mirror, a table and two straight chairs.

The leather box was put down as he directed; the servant, leaving, stood aside for a second, who brought a can of hot water and a tray that held a decanter of Antigua rum. "Miss Ava says I was to take care of you." The negro unfastened the strap of the box. "Dinner I heard was at three." He laid out Richard's things with the assertion that Mr. Robine — he was attending him, too — had brought seventeen waistcoats for the day or so he expected to be at Todd Hundred. There was still an hour before he would be expected in the dining room. He took a deep drink of the Antigua rum, and then, critically, tried it again. "That must be fourth proof," he decided.

"It catches right hold of the gentlemen," the servant admitted. "Whisky's good enough for a headman and Guinea whites, but Mr. Charles and his friends like rum."

Richard Bale had another drink. He sat on one chair with his legs extended over the other. Below him the flower borders were bright with colour, there were blue patches of Canterbury bells, and through the cedars that bounded the garden the river was no more material than the sky. A deep contentment settled over him, and he determined to stay here and not go down for dinner. He had preserved this anyhow, Richard assured himself, out of the chaos of past years — an acceptance, while it was momentarily possible, of whatever good offered. He dismissed the servant, and then, when he was on the stair, ordered him to return in two hours. "I might need something," he proceeded. It was the servant's opinion, lost below, that what he needed he'd need before two hours.

The decanter of Antigua rum was generous in size, but the space occupied by the brown liquor fast gave way to clear glass. Richard Bale drank evenly, with an abstracted manner and a steady hand. The flowers, at times, appeared to him to be moving in gay procession, the river puzzled him because it seemed to be higher than the cedars. What was there to keep it back? But for the rest he was practically normal. He frowned in an effort of concentration, of thought: had he brought his case of pistols? He wouldn't need them at Todd Hundred, at a party to celebrate the engagement of Gawin Todd to — to Lavender, no, Lavinia Roderick of Henrico County, but it was his habit never to be without them. He rose and, swaying, proceeded to where his box was half unpacked.

Almost at once his hand fell on the heavy polished rectangular case he was in search of, and he opened the lid, lifting out one of the pair of pistols. It had been made by Mortimore of London, with a thirteen-inch barrel carrying an ounce bullet and it was discharged by a flintlock. The pan for the priming was bushed with gold, the touchhole was gold, and the hair trigger set by a beautiful and delicate mechanism. With the pistol in his grasp Richard Bale suddenly grew steady. He raised it with a rigid sweep of his arm, and, fully extended, held the sights dead against a small stain on the plaster of a wall. The pistol lay perfectly balanced, almost, it seemed, without weight. It was like a dove, he told himself, like a rose with a stem.

When he had put it away and returned to his chairs, he found that the decanter was empty. There was a splintering of glass on the floor; in putting it back he had missed the window ledge. Well, the servant with a fresh decanter would be up soon. Charles Todd had plenty of them, unlimited Antigua rum. At intervals he heard the music from the house — the dancing, as he had realized it would, was filling all the afternoon. There would be a late supper, and the quadrilles, the reels, again. Probably a minuet. He wondered if Gawin would conduct Lavinia Roderick through a minuet. That was a dance not in keeping with Todd's opinions. Richard Bale couldn't understand how Gawin Todd, who was, of course, a gentleman, could have such opinions. At this he very loudly damned Thomas Jefferson. But he was in excellent humour.

The negro appeared, with more rum, and he gathered up the broken glass. However, now Richard Bale had a taste for toddy; lime toddy, he directed; and, with his compliments to Mr. Charles, he sent back the rum. But the toddy, when it arrived, he didn't like; he insisted that it was harsh; poured it out of the window. "For the flowers," he explained; "the darling thirsty flowers." It then occurred to him that he might send for Mrs. Patton, whose lime toddy was superlative. Again, his compliments to Mr. Charles Todd, and would Mr. Todd send a carryall to Balisand for Mr. Bale's housekeeper, telling her to bring her own limes? The servant hesitated and Richard Bale slowly rose, with eyes, deep-sunk in his head, like stone. Still the servant waited by the door: he only wanted to be sure Mr. Bale was serious. "Certainly not," Richard Bale replied, sliding back into a chair. "A damned discourteous idea." Privately he knew that Mrs. Patton would not have come.

*

* *

Footfalls, quick and light, mounted the stair and went into the next room. It was the tutor. Richard Bale had heard his name — he came from New Jersey — what was it? Parrot, or some such. Other steps, heavier and deliberate, followed, and Charles Todd entered. He was in riding clothes, his boots stiff with mud, and it appeared that he had been engaged with his terrapin pen: his canoe had swung into the stockade, breaking down a corner, and practically all the terrapin had escaped into the Ware River. Ava, he represented, was in a rage with them both for, in effect, deserting her party. "But she says Gawin's near as bad — talking nothing but politics with Jasper Robine." Richard Bale replied that Ava was, as always, right:

"But there's nothing to drink that in." He was gazing at the emptied toddy bowl, and murmured an indistinct period about the darling flowers. "I'll send at once, but I think, for the moment, you've had plenty. Richard, you must appear at dinner."

Richard Bale swore to that; he added he would drink practically nothing until he had eaten. But he needed the servant, in the interest of his preparations for dinner.

He was already, Charles asserted, very handsomely prepared. But the negro who had been attached to him came back with a fresh supply of toddy. How much, Richard speculated, was practically nothing. Obviously it was more applied to lime toddy — and not Mrs. Patton's — than if he had been drinking Antigua rum. A bowl of this, another bowl, he proceeded, would be less than, for example, a taste of brandy; and, rigidly intent on his agreement with Charles, he limited himself to such a diluted drink. Dinner, Richard learned, was ready; but the scientific aspect of his present investigation, he now asserted, demanded his whole attention. Later returning to the chair at the window, he saw with surprise that the light was fading, the garden was dimly rich, but the river was a sweep of pure liquid gold. He was aware of the beauty of the moment — a strange and unaccustomed recognition — and of the swiftness with which night followed day. In no more than a minute the golden river would be dull and then the flowers hidden. This disturbed him so that he went unceremoniously into the tutor's room to tell him about it.

The tutor, he found, was reading by what remained of the daylight; but he rose at once, putting aside his book, and said good evening with a courteous sir. He was young, tall and thin; a simplicity of red hair was brushed back from his forehead; and he had a determined gaze in a face pale but not without good features. "I know your name," Bale said; "Parrot, Garret!"

The second, he was informed. "You are Richard Bale, Esquire, of Balisand. I have often seen you riding the roads."

“And so you might.” Bale sat down. He had developed a positive antipathy to standing. “I came in,” he proceeded with a prodigious gravity, “for your agreement to a very great subject. I'll put it into a question — why is a sunset so soon extinguished by night?”

“That follows the law of the alternation of the earth's relative surfaces,” the tutor replied.

Richard Bale regarded him without favour. “Forget your employment,” he said; “speak as a man. A moment ago the world was like a piece of gilt lace and now it's as dark as a cannon's mouth.”

“I gave you the answer as it existed in fact,” Garret replied firmly. “I didn't know you had mounted to the heavens of sentiment.”

“You're paid to know.”

“I'm paid to teach Mr. Charles Todd's children,” Garret contradicted him. “Sallust and grammatical exercises and reading, writing and ciphering in subtraction. When I have done that I am done, and when I am reading in my room I am reading in my room.” He stood and spoke uncompromisingly.

“You're a tutor,” Richard Bale declared, “a tutor and that's all. A tutor tells people things they ask him. But, of course, you have never worn gold lace. You won't know the feeling.”

“And I haven't any wish to,” Garret assured him. “But if you think I am incapable of sentiment you're — well, you're drunk.”

“I am,” Richard Bale admitted at once. “That is something else you will miss. Since, rightly, it is the privilege of gentlemen. A tutor as a tutor can't be a gentleman, naturally; but a gentleman, I suppose, can be a tutor and a gentleman when he isn't tutoring."

"I am of plain parents," Garret stoutly explained; "and I like them better for it. I would rather be what I am than ——" At last he hesitated.

"Than me?" Bale suggested.

"That came into my head," he admitted. "But I dismissed it because of your services."

"Very good it was of you. I didn't realize people generally, even tutors, had heard about them. But to go back — the sunset. It was fine."

"It's possible that it was. They have been known to be. I didn't notice this one. I was reading."

Richard Bale picked up the book the other had laid aside, and, after some difficulty, he read the title, "Pictate's Theologica Christiana." Was that, he asked, sentiment or fact.

"Both," Garret answered. "It is God."

"I never argue about religion," Richard Bale said hurriedly. "And, besides, you can't keep a subject. Life is dark and light, like night and day. Why?" The tutor set a candle aflame. "Now," he asserted, "the night is a little brighter and that is your answer."

"But the candle," Bale objected, "what's that?"

"Maybe it's love." He had spoken, it seemed, without premeditation.

"I have never been in love," Richard Bale continued; "and I don't know. You say it makes sunsets last . . . for all of life."

"In your spirit, yes," the tutor replied without hesitation. "That is exactly what love does. I suppose, if you care for metaphor, it's like that gold lace you spoke of, on the dull clothes of — of reality."

"Garret," Richard Bale was solemn, "there is only one explanation for you. It is love. You have been fatally wounded."

"And if I have," the demand was almost passionate, "how can it possibly concern you? Can your position force you into my room with drunken questions? If that's breeding I am well out of it, the world will be better to be rid of you, for all your fighting. Go to hell!" he cried at Richard Bale.

"I've been there," Bale answered sombrely. "And you've lost your manners. It doesn't matter, though, not just now. I like to hear you. That was a surprising idea about love. If you're right I have been wrong. It's more, then, than having children, leaving a name?" But Garret wouldn't answer him. He was standing at the window, facing the gathering darkness. The pale candlelight showed only the tenseness of his back. His manners were damnable. "You'll want to dress," Richard Bale said at random; "go down to the dancing." At this Garret whirled about:

"I don't dance. It's a thing of the devil's. Hell is kept hot with burning fiddles. Girls that dance ——" Speech failed him.

"They dance," Bale put in. "There is no more to be said for that. I don't myself, but not on account of any connection with the devil. It has to do with my leg. But let me tell you this;" he was at the door; "if you are in love, a minute or two with him, I understand, won't hurt your prospects." Here he was interrupted with the information that neither had he, Garret, asked for advice. "I'll have to go," Richard Bale decided. "You are too much for fighting. My mind was full of sunsets. I believe there is toddy in my room, and, if you like, I'll see you get some." The tutor — but he was no more than a boy — came very close to him:

"Your filthy drinks I wouldn't put a mouth to. Thank God, I don't have to be a gentleman." He then executed a caricaturing bow.

*

* *

On reflection, once more in his room, it occurred to Richard Bale that the tutor had suffered a grave lapse in manners. He hadn't, really, been annoyed by this, but there was a question in his mind — if, in enduring such ill-bred shouts, he hadn't been negligent. It might be necessary for him to go back and instruct . . . what was his name, Parrot? His voice, however, had held a deeper feeling than a mere resentment at Bale's intrusion. Richard was aware of that: the boy was acutely wretched. He, himself, was none too happy. The toddy bowl, again exhausted, he put with dignity away from him. The stinging liquor recalled to him the fact that he must appear for supper, that Ava was already indignant at his absence. One more cup and then he would be done. For the present, oh, very much for the present!

He wondered if supper were ready now, and decided in the negative, since, very faintly, he could still hear the fiddles. Then, suddenly thinking of Charles Todd in the river mud, vainly clutching at his escaping terrapin, Richard laughed outright. From that he turned, erratically, to his horse Spadille, not only beaten but badly lamed in his last race. The truth was that he had been a fool to enter Spadille at five miles on sod. His folly had cost him three hundred pounds sterling and a good horse, for it was probable that the lameness wouldn't mend. He mentally reviewed the yearlings in his stable: one, Diggery, showed a promise of speed. And Richard Bale decided to take David, light and a very skilful rider, from whatever he was doing and attach him to the colt for his racing life.

He had lost entirely too much money through the past few months; his luck at whist, in particular, had been bad. Bradlock Wiatt and Beverley Mathews, perhaps the richest men in Gloucester County, had won everything. But it was like that with chance, and he had no inclination to complain or reduce the amounts of his gambling. Instead, he'd get it all back . . . with Diggery. Automatically he turned to the toddy bowl, but he denied his intention. There would be wine after supper and more Antigua rum, and — but he didn't just know why — he wanted to keep his head steady. Invaded by a sensation of extreme virtue, he wished that Mrs. Patton could observe him.

Outside, only a faint glow was left of the day, and a mocking bird began a hesitating and unbelievably sweet song. There was a note and then silence and then another. They flowed together and stopped, followed by a high transcendent melody. Finer than the fiddles, Richard Bale told himself; indeed, of all the birds in the world, including the English nightingale and the bulbul — whatever in hell that was — he was convinced that the one now singing was easily, by eleven lengths, the superior. He couldn't leave for supper with that going on outside his window. Ava would realize that, especially Ava; and he rehearsed, with soundless but moving lips, the exact speech by which he would explain to her what had delayed him. He wondered if the tutor heard the mocking bird, and, overlooking Garret's insolence, he went at once to find out. But the door to the other bedroom was barred, there was no reply to his demands.

The tutor, then, had missed the song, a thing Richard immensely regretted. It would have calmed him and relieved his feeling, made him a proper tutor again. The bird continued, rising, from beauty to beauty of sound, and Richard Bale listened with the greatest politeness. He couldn't leave, he reiterated, until it was over. His patience lasted a long while, long after his pleasure had actually vanished, and at last he rose. "I liked it at first," he said aloud, in a severe voice, "but there is too damned much of it. Singing has the best of you. Anyhow, she ought to know it all by now." This reference to the celebrated purpose of such song was, he thought, very learned and adroit. He felt that he had the advantage of the mocking bird.

That, too, he would tell Ava, and even if he were a little late, she would forgive him in consequence of the solidity of his advice. But he had better be off, and, with a preliminary misstep, he descended the narrow stairs to the schoolroom and ground. He walked rapidly, and it seemed to him that he was a long while coming to the portico, when he realized that he was going in the wrong direction — he was hurrying away from the house. On his right were the fields and trees of Todd Hundred, and at the left the houses of the quarters. Some of the open doors were lighted, and there was an obscure stir of small negroes in the gloom. Then he saw a group of men by a bright fire of pine splinters. The group stood in a circle, dominated by the bulk of Fayson, Charles Todd's Dutch overseer. Bale, recognizing the preliminaries of chicken fighting, went up to the overseer. That individual made him a civil recognition. "A nigger from Gloucester Point with a famous bird," he explained. "We haven't anything good enough, but we couldn't let him crow without an effort." A small negro was stooping and at once smoothing the quills and irritating the shorn rooster in his hands; and, opposed to him, were a number with chickens clamouring at a chance for their favourite.

"Be quiet," Fayson ordered them. "Ash, where's Ash?" A negro stepped forward. "Which one of these is best?" he demanded, indicating the Todd Hundred roosters. "Stilley's is the wickedest chicken ever I see," he replied, and the overseer called for Stilley. "I want this to start," he said in addition; "don't keep Mr. Bale waiting." The servant who advanced was, it was plain, a field hand; he was naked but for a pair of drill trousers precariously held by a cotton handkerchief; the light from the fire slid in quivering reflections over his deep black chest and heavy shoulders. His rooster was stripped of tail and wing feathers, it was tall and evil-looking, and one spur had been repaired.

"Which do you like?" Fayson asked.

"You will want to back your own bird," Richard Bale replied. "I'll put ten pounds on the Gloucester Point scoundrel."

"I'm not Mr. Beverley Mathews," the overseer reminded him. "This is what I will do — if the Gloucester pirate wins I'll let you have three niggers for a month at the corn, and if ours comes up you can tell Thomas Ekkes to do the same."

Bale nodded, and Fayson shouted a warning to keep the pine fire bright. It was, evidently, a spot used for chicken fighting, since the edge of a board just showed above the bare earth; and across it the two crouching men, the two infuriated roosters, faced each other. There was a moment's pause, a crackling of burning fat wood, and then the negroes flung the chickens together. An audible clash of spurs sounded, a whirl of dust rose, gilded by the flames, and there was a dead rooster on the ground. Richard Bale was contemptuous:

"You had nothing but a pullet," he told Fayson. "London has a duck that would chase all the roosters off your place. And remember — send me three young men."

Fayson, in reply, harshly cursed Stilley and Ash. "I have a damned good mind to get Mr. Todd to send you South," he told the servant picking up the slain bird. "You might learn what a chicken was on the Mississippi." The victorious negro from Gloucester Point was vainly trying to recapture his rooster. It evaded him, retreating by Stilley, who met it with an unguarded and wholly successful kick. An outrage, Richard Bale asserted.

*

* *

A concerted ominous silence followed. The face of the overseer was wooden. The owner of the successful bird examined its fresh injury. It was evident to Richard Bale that the fowl's leg had been broken. Then the negro dropped it and walked with hanging hands to where Stilley stood. The two men faced each other in the open, against the red flare of the fire. The shifting light here and there made visible a black face on the darkness. This, Bale thought, promised to be better. Fayson, however, spoke warningly:

"Take yourself back to Gloucester Point."

Stilley retreated a step, but the other negro was motionless, with an appearance of brooding remoteness from all voices and commands. "I warned you," Fayson continued; "you can stay at the price of what happens to you." That, Bale knew, would be a gouging. "I'll take that ten pounds with you now." The overseer addressed him. But he declined:

"Your servant is too heavy."

"Weight's not all there is to gouging."

The brightness of the flames rose and fell, it shone on the trunks of trees, on the low walls of the quarters; it seemed to bring into pink flower the mass of a crape myrtle. There were, now, other mocking birds singing. Neither Stilley nor the negro before him moved; neither, it appeared, had any consciousness of the other's presence or intention. There was an uneasy mutter, the stirring of feet, about them. In the distance a woman called for her children. It seemed to Richard Bale that, here, Fayson was at fault to permit — but he had encouraged it, really — the chance of a serious injury to one of Charles Todd's valuable servants. Stilley must be worth a hundred pounds . . . more than that, if he had any special ability. His thought might have been voiced:

"There's no danger to our nigger," the overseer assured him. "He has gouged twenty men." While he was speaking the fight had begun, the two bodies were joined, bound, in a desperate struggle. There were hoarse gasps, utterly degraded and hideous promises, and whimpers of pain. The voices lost what trace of humanity they had held, they became inarticulate in an animal rage. "He's doing better than I expected," Fayson said, in an interested but detached manner. "If Stilley gets hurt I'll lay it across his back."

A consuming dislike for the overseer possessed Richard Bale, and he moved away from him. Charles Todd must be ignorant of the man he employed. He, Richard Bale, would have no such attitude toward his servants at Balisand; and he thought it might be his duty to speak to Charles about Fayson. He was thoroughly annoyed because he had descended to betting with him. His thoughts were sharply interrupted by a scream of insufferable and clear agony, and the struggling men separated. Stilley, with a labouring chest, was wiping blood from his face, but the other stumbled, with his hands pressed to his eyes, across the open. As he passed, Richard Bale saw, on his cheek, a dreadful pendulous smear.

Fayson, in a satisfied tone, declared that he had known how the gouging would turn out, and Bale, filled with loathing, abruptly left. He was utterly hard, cold, to death and any form of maiming, but he was suddenly revolted at the useless bestiality of what had occurred. It was the overseer, rather than the negro, who belonged in the cotton fields. There was no moon, but the sky was clear, the June stars were tender. He stood, opposite the office, in a reflection the result of feeling rather than thought. He wasn't, as the night wore on, any happier. And now he was what he called sober. The desire to drink had left him; he regarded it all, even Mrs. Patton's lime punch, with a supreme indifference. He wouldn't go in to the bottles of Madeira, the decanters of rum. The idea of the talk he would have to endure sickened him; he determined to go to the stables and, with a horse saddled, return to Balisand; and he actually changed his direction again when he realized that what he proposed was an absolute impossibility. He didn't like Gawin Todd enough to demand such an improper liberty of action.

He was in a hopelessly muddled state. What, and be damned to it, was it he wanted? To be back in the canoe, as much as anything, on the silver flood of the River Ware, with his servants resting for ever on their oars. He had felt that the land held only more trouble for him. Fretfully he continued that he didn't understand it; listen as he might in Congress, practically all that went on was over his head; he didn't know what the men of the present were about, what animated and drove them on. He was a planter turned soldier, nothing more; both simple things. And Garret, with his eternal sunsets in the heavens of sentiment, and his candle . . . what was it he meant? It wasn't his fault that love had escaped the tutor, Richard Bale insisted.

The music had begun again in the drawing room, and he had missed supper. Probably Charles was looking for him. He would have apologies to make. Mocking birds and fiddles, but it was quiet in the quarters, and he wondered if the negro Stilley injured was stumbling about in the dark. Soon even his pain would be over, and, with a flattened eyelid, he'd be again fighting chickens. There was the whisper of a skirt and Ava stood before him.

"Richard," she exclaimed, "I had begun to be worried about you. Why will you be so strange? You've had nothing to eat for hours."

"But I had a great deal to drink," he replied humbly. "Ava, you must forgive me."

"I don't understand it," she complained. "And I wish you wouldn't give people so much chance to talk about you. They don't know you like I do. We're so fond of you, Richard, and you give us so much uneasiness. Why?"

"I can't answer that," he said moodily. "And to-night I'm worse than usual."

"You are lonely," Ava Todd declared; "living with no one but that old man and Mrs. Patton. Won't you stay with us for the summer? It would be easy for you to ride over to Balisand in the mornings."

"Thank you, Ava, but no. The Bales belong at Balisand. What I am I'll have to be. And don't let people bother you with their stories about gambling and drink. It's not as bad as you hear; I have a colt, Diggery, that's going to make me a world of money; and the plantation is kept up."

She came closer to him and, momentarily, laid a hand on his. "Richard," she said, "it's been in my mind . . . I'd be willing to have you marry Mary Todd."

"Why, Ava!" He was startled, confused. "Mary's so young. She wouldn't want an aged wreck from the war." There were tears on his face at the compliment she had paid him: Mary, their choicest daughter.

"If you could, Richard, you'd both be happy, I know. Anyhow, you'll come into the house with me."

"In a minute," he reassured her. "Let me get myself straight first." She left him with that promise, and he walked stiffly down the bricked walk, by the house, and his feet struck upon the hollowness of the wharf. He had a sensation of being suspended in illimitable space above a tide without bottom or horizon. At the wharf's end, under the roof that blotted out an infinitesimal number of the stars, he halted. Below, the river was black, and he swayed dangerously, when a voice directly at his side exclaimed: "Oh!" His surprise at this very nearly completed the threatened disaster; he recovered his steadiness of footing with the narrowest margin possible.

*

* *

“Never do that again,” he said severely; “it nearly had me in the water.”

“I thought you were.” The voice answering him was young, vivid — the voice of a girl. It was darker here than by the house, he could make out only the pale indefinite blur of a white dress. It would be safer, he thought, if he sat down, and he found the little bench facing the unexpected and obscure figure. “Do I know you?” he was asked; “I have a feeling that I don’t.” He rose, momentarily. “I am Richard Bale of Balisand.” Then, she replied, she didn’t; at least not until now. “I’m Lavinia Roderick,” she told him in return. Again there was a necessity of getting to his feet. “You will be very happy with Gawin Todd.” He spoke with a formal propriety. “Gawin is wonderful,” she answered serenely. “I suppose you think it’s very strange for me to be here, alone in the dark, at my own party. But I had to. Everything, all at once, was so packed. Mrs. Todd understood. She came most of the way with me; but, really, she was looking for you.”

“I saw her,” Richard Bale acknowledged. He fell silent at the thought of what Ava had suggested . . . Mary Todd. But Charles and Ava had always been fond of him. Why, God knew. Mary Todd! She was a charming child, with a wide soft mass of light-coloured hair that made her blue eyes seem very intense indeed; but, aside from that, and the fact that she was a Todd, he was totally ignorant of her. “I don’t mind pauses,” the voice opposite him said, “because I have a great many myself. They are often complained about.

BRYAN UNIVERSITY LIBRARY

And so there is no reason for you to talk." He told her, completely unoriginal, that he had been thinking.

"But that won't do," she protested; "oh, not at all." He had never heard tones so delicately and sharply vital. They sounded as though the impulse that gave them being almost hurt, they were, at once, so eager and wistful. "I don't care if you sit and are just here—I mean busy with the night or river—but you mustn't leave me like that."

"It was inexcusable," Richard Bale admitted. "But, after all, you came out here to escape being bothered, to get away. So did I."

"You never appeared," she reminded him. "Everybody kept wondering about you, and I thought it was very uncomplimentary."

"There was a great deal of toddy around," he explained, once more, "and a tutor and some mocking birds. Anyhow, Gawin Todd was all you wanted."

"Gawin Todd is wonderful. We think he will be Governor of Virginia."

"Why not of the United States?"

A little laugh answered him first. Then: "I'm sorry—you see, I've heard Gawin speak of that and you together. Of course, he thinks it's all . . . a pleasant dream. I wish you'd tell me about General Washington and the war." That, he replied sombrely, he would rather avoid. "It would be useless, for you would listen to Gawin Todd and come to the conclusion all I said was a—a pleasant dream."

"He has a splendid head," she asserted. "But I didn't mean politics, it was the war itself. Did you really cross the river at Trenton and take the Hessians, and was it freezing?"

"We did. It was," he briefly replied. The ache stirred in the bone of his right leg. "If you don't mind," he added, "something else. Tell me about your engagement — how long has it been and how long have you known Gawin?"

"Two months except a day, and since last June." She copied his limited speech. "The time that Mr. Jefferson was elected to Congress."

"I hope it will be happier for you than it was for Congress," he replied with force.

"You see," she instructed him, "if I know how you feel about General Washington, that is the way we think of Mr. Jefferson. And so your manners were very bad. Weren't they?"

That he couldn't evade, and, in the stiffest of terms, he made her his apology. He didn't like this Lavinia, Richard Bale concluded. He now found her voice to be without the acquiescent tranquillity, the placid sweetness, he considered appropriate to girls. And then, very naturally, she had absorbed most of Gawin Todd's opinions and theories. All her life she would listen to them, hear the praises of dangerous and futile and seditious men. For, while it was true that nothing yet existed to create sedition, by God, there would be a federal unity soon . . . he hoped. Even he couldn't be sanguine about that. His actual apology should have been for the introduction of the subject of politics at all. Girls, women, had no part in it. She was, he discovered to his surprise, singing:

"A lilybud, a pink, a rose
I send to you.
But you must bring me oceans more,
Be true, be true."

She sang in a low voice, and the quality that made it a little disturbing in speech was in song emphasized. There was a note of questioning — the wistfulness — that troubled him. It demanded reassurance.

"I can't sing," she remarked. "That was only another pause. You will find out I am very unsatisfactory. I explained it to Gawin over and over, but he wouldn't listen."

"How?" he demanded.

"I forget things; in the middle of them I do something else — reading instead of being dressed for dinner, or turning down the wrong street or losing my gloves or money or bouquet at a ball. Everybody, particularly if you're a young man, gets furious at me. A lilybud, a pink, a rose; I make up my mind to have one and then I pick the other. It's specially hard on Gawin, who's very reasonable and not like that at all. He'll be good for me."

There was still another pause. Richard Bale could hear the river murmuring by the wharf. There was a faint light, a packet, out on Mockjack Bay. God's children lost in Egypt. His impressions were scattered like that, without order, and dark. Lavinia Roderick, from her own admission, would never be like Mrs. Patton. But she had brought into his mind a new conception — a lilybud, a pink . . . a flower might be even more desirable than the utilitarian perfection of any housekeeper.

This was a revolutionary thought; and, considering it for no more than a moment, he dismissed it as folly. The girl he married, took to Balisand, would have a pleasant but endless round of duties; the lives of the admirably bred and situated women of Gloucester were made up of their husbands and children and of the servants and manors of their plantations.

"Marriage will change you," he predicted.

"It had better," she said lightly. "But are you sure it will?" Again her tone was disturbing, grave. He had an illusion that, all at once, frightened by the dark around them, she had reached out her hand to him. "It always does." This, the best answer he could make, struck him as vague to the point of cowardice.

"I don't know why, I thought you could tell me something important," was all she said in reply. Then: "I can't get used to being by myself. Only a short while ago there were a hundred people, and then I found that I was quite alone. Oh, quite. I mean I lost them from inside of me. Could love do that, do you think?

He was unable, it seemed, to escape from the problems and difficulties of love — in the tutor, the mocking birds and now in Lavinia Roderick, who was going to marry Gawin Todd. That latter fact suggested his reply. "You must ask Gawin." His remark was so obvious, he concluded, that it killed any need of recognition. He had an idea that she had nodded. He could see her more clearly — the general details of her girlhood and spread white dress.

*

*   *

He began to be conscious of the extreme unconventionality in his situation on the end of the wharf with Lavinia Roderick. But, then, he was the intruder; he should have gone at once. However, he had an insuperable objection to moving, leaving his place over water at once cooling and invisible. The absurd impression seized him that there was no wharf, no means of communication, between them and the land. He was certain that if he rose, investigated it, he would find the narrow walk of boards gone. That would be awkward, since Gawin Todd would have to come after them in a boat. Or, rather, the little covered place that held them had drifted out far beyond any communication with Todd Hundred.

"If it's a thought again," she warned him, "I'll forgive you only if you tell me."

"It is too silly to repeat. I've had a very muddled time. Rum never did this before. It must be old age."

"But that's sillier!" she cried. "Why, you are younger than Gawin." Richard Bale was, definitely, weary of that name. "But I suppose all the things you went through——" She broke off. Then she leaned forward, speaking impetuously. "I hate it because you won't talk to me about anything important, just as though being alive was nothing more than a minuet. It isn't that I want to interfere, or be unattractive; but when I try and try to satisfy myself about living, I'm told to keep dancing. I love it, and I dance beautifully, but I get tired of only that."

Here, probably, in one girl, he reflected, was every quality which in women he disliked. He was glad that

Todd and not he was marrying Lavinia Roderick. She belonged in the sovereign state hullabaloo. " Now I've pained you," she observed in a totally indifferent voice. " But you can't say you weren't warned, and you don't have to endure it." Only one deduction could be taken from that.

" I am sorry to have interfered with your pleasure." He was slow rising, and she was before him. " No, you must stay; I leave you all my right; and I should have gone long ago. Thank you . . . for the dance."

Almost immediately she was lost in the night. He listened, subconsciously, for the retreating fall of her feet, but it was so light he heard nothing. She faded, with her absence, from his mind; he sat staring at the images of his own perplexity. It, when he considered that principally its appearance had been made only that afternoon, had grown alarmingly; and he wondered if Mary Todd were the answer. Here, it was plain, he wasn't moved by love but by reason. Love might easily follow. Probably that was what it did, come with the actualities of marriage.

No one, for him, for this, could be more suitable than a Todd; as a family — different from Lavinia Roderick — they had all the traits and qualities he most admired. Their breeding was the full equal of his own; and, in this connection, idly, he recalled the old legal definition of a gentleman — qui gerit arma. Yet that was no longer valid, except in a coat-armour, since it would admit the militia. The conjunction of those ideas vastly entertained him. He must speak of it to Charles. But not to-night: the day was too far gone for any apologetic or effective appearance in the drawing room.

No, he would sit a little longer and then go to his room in the schoolhouse. There was none yet at Balisand. His house needed new carpets, too, fresh paint, outside and in; but that, Richard reflected, was natural, with only men and housekeepers living there. His house was showing its age. Beside Bradlock Wiatt's new manor on Carter Creek, his was unimposing, small; but already it had stood facing the North River for more than a hundred years, years, through, to be exact, five generations of the Bales of Balisand. No additions or repairs could take away from the stamp of those successive and identical lives.

His thoughts returned to Mary Todd. If he got married — if, that was, she would consent to him — he'd have to change his habits. He doubted if she would allow the hounds in the dining room, the one reform that Mrs. Patton had been unable to effect. His father had had them there and his grandfather, and that Captain Richard Bale, the Cavalier, who had removed his branch of the family to the Virginia Colony in 'sixteen-fifty. They did make an infernal clamour and dirt. He was thinking of the hounds. He couldn't, probably, gamble so late at the tavern; but for the most, he concluded, his life would go on very much as it was now. All this, naturally, was bringing the three facts — Mary Todd, himself and marriage — more closely together. Actually, he was seriously entertaining the thought of making her an offer.

In a way he was irritated, for it seemed to him that

he was being hurried into a decision. To-morrow, it might be, he would feel entirely different. Although his need, his situation, wouldn't be changed. The whole truth was this — that since his heart failed to help him, his head must. Love afterwards. Perhaps. It would be the devil if, with everything staked, it failed him. This wasn't, after all, simply an affair of housekeepers. There was a splash in the river, a fish had jumped. He wondered what report Lavinia Roderick had made of him, and then he realized that she would say nothing about meeting him on the wharf. Without reason he was certain of this. He knew, too, that at the end she had been even more annoyed at him than he was by her. It didn't matter. She didn't matter. Richard Bale was surprised that she had returned to his mind.

He moved, finally, in to the land, walking to the right, under the high trees, so that he wouldn't be met at the house. The fragrance of sweet grass stirred around him, he collided with a Cape jasmine; in place of the mocking birds, screech owls were calling. The stair in the schoolhouse was dark, precarious, but a candle had been lighted, protected with glass, in his room. The box was entirely unpacked, his clothes and toilet things in order; the case of pistols was on the table.

All at once he was as tired as he ever remembered being, he could scarcely get through with the effort of undressing; and yet, in bed, he could not manage to fall asleep. A difficulty that he couldn't quite distinguish, a problem, weighed upon him, drove his mind to fresh impotent inquiry. He told himself that it was the question of his immediate future. In the stillness of his heart his head would have to serve. He sat up, his hands extended on the mattress, and asked himself directly — what about Mary Todd?

"By God, I'll do it!" He spoke aloud, and he was so surprised at the sound of his voice, and at all it implied, that he dropped back on his pillow. Now he was committed — he felt as though all Todd Hundred had heard his declaration — and, realizing it, he was unaccountably depressed. He had no right to say, to decide, so much. There was no warrant, where Mary was concerned, for taking anything for granted. The discourtesy of this was what had disturbed him. Yet, in speaking, he had meant only that he would lay such an offer before her. No one could object to that, particularly after all Ava had said. Damn it, what was bothering him now? He made another effort to sleep, fixing his mind on quiet things — the murmur of the water moving by the wharf. A lilybud, a pink, a rose . . . the sense of trouble lifted from him; he was peaceful, far out on the river, with his negroes, his own.

*

* *

Sitting in a flood of morning light, with his head laid back to allow for the smooth passage of the razor of the negro shaving him, Richard Bale regarded with surprise, almost incredulity, his emotions of the night before. He was certain, to-day, that they had been all bred of the bottle. Or almost all — his decision to ask Mary to marry him was a sober reality. And that, he asserted to himself, he would follow. No more than that had lifted the load from his mind, he continued; the actuality around him banished what had been no more than fancy. Richard Bale felt more cheerful at once — if life, as he often thought, was a gamble, why, he was no stranger to gambling; he would turn a card with chance. The servant standing above him was exceptionally skilful, his touch was firm and light and soothing; he was altogether superior to Little York, and Richard wondered if Charles would sell him.

"Have you ever been to Balisand?" he asked.

"Yes, sir, I got some family in the kitchen."

He remembered now that Sarah Markoe, the cook, had spoken of a nephew at Todd Hundred. It would suit very well, then; he didn't indiscriminately buy negroes. For the most part the servants at Balisand were happy — Thomas Ekkes, who was suspected of Quaker sympathies, maintained a very successful attitude toward them, at once impartial and comprehending. The overseer was, privately, opposed to slavery, and, alone with Richard Bale, he often, with reasons both temporal and spiritual, condemned it. But that was a question Richard couldn't approach with his conscious intelligence. It existed together with other immutable facts, and discussion only made him impatient. He was an upholder, from the days of disaster, of a very strict discipline, opposed to any personal communication whatever between leaders and ranks; so his relationship with the Balisand servants seemed entirely unremarkable and right. He never, in their hearing or out, spoke of them as slaves; he didn't, in a rigorous sense, think of them as that; but as a part of his inheritance, an aspect of the plantation itself.

Perhaps, if Mary came to Balisand, she would bring William, the negro attending him. There were many pleasant possibilities in connection with her. They occurred to him one by one as he was dressing. He was a very reflective man, the result of relative solitude, and he kept things a long while in his thoughts, speculating on their meanings and probable results. This, in itself, gave his contacts with ideas a mental slowness of which he was aware. It had taken a long while, however, to form his thoughts, and he didn't propose to upset them in a minute. He spoke quickly, explosively, when his temper or a prejudice was contradicted, but ordinarily he was not adroit. His conversation with Lavinia Roderick, though — he couldn't remember another occasion when he had spoken so much or with such ease.

The darkness had helped him, he concluded . . . he was dressed and the bell, hung in the covered way to the kitchen, was ringing for breakfast. The morning was even more perfected, more sunny and softly perfumed, than yesterday. The Ware River was an untroubled expanse of utter blue; Mockjack Bay reached idyllically to the sea. Almost everyone was in the dining room, and, after speaking to Ava, he went at once to Gawin Todd. " This," Richard said of his congratulations, " you should have had last evening. I'm sorry."

" The best Antigua rum in the world was your excuse," Gawin Todd replied easily. " Lavinia is somewhere in the room." She came up as he was speaking, and Todd introduced them. After all, she wasn't as handsome as, on the wharf, it had seemed she might be. That was, her cheeks were a trifle thin. Her eyes were brown, her hair only notable for a tendency to escape from the bounds of fashion; and, slender, she was neither short nor tall. That was his first impression; but, even in the briefness of their hampered and conventional sentences, he saw that he would have to change, enlarge, his opinion. She was very handsome, principally because of the brilliant temper of her youth. The emotion he had got from her voice alone, that sharp vitality, was infinitely increased by her whole presence. Yes, it hurt her just to be alive. In addition he realized that, under the long rigidity of her stays, the young grace of her body was flawless.

He was amazed at himself for entertaining such an inexcusable and low thought; he was painfully embarrassed; and he stood stupidly silent, with, he felt, his face the colour of red flannel. It was as hot as that. "You ought to like Richard," Gawin Todd went on, "he is the sort of idealist you would approve of — he wants a happy world made up of privileges for himself and his friends."

Richard Bale was forced to acknowledge the humour of this insight into politics and women. "I never thought of it," he admitted; "but, of course, you are right. All charming women are Federalists at heart. More than that — they belong in a monarchy."

"Then if you're able to go on," Gawin Todd insisted, "you'll soon have those in America rightly placed."

This Bale ignored, although, for a moment, his gaze

challenged Todd's assertion. Gawin Todd was a large man, in well-ordered but carefully plain clothes; a fact that Bale, with an amused disdain, attributed to the celebrated preference of the Western public for all the marks of a rough frugality. It was too bad, Richard thought, that he couldn't wear the blue hunting shirt, the buck tail and scalping knife of the Upper Virginia Volunteers. Lavinia Roderick, he saw, was in the middle of one of her pauses. He had an unwarranted feeling of knowing her very well, intimately. She glanced up at him suddenly:

"I have a great deal to overlook, but I will . . . in a minuet."

"It's unfortunate, I don't dance." Why, already knowing that, had she put him in such an awkward position? "Then I am afraid —— " She stopped, leaving the rest to his inference. "I adore dancing, I could keep on and on, and never stop." That was a direct contradiction to what, resentfully, she had already told him. Damn girls, he proceeded privately. But, "You would do it beautifully," was what he said. "And it's admirable you aren't concerned with things that belong to men." Gawin Todd, surprised, remarked:

"I believe you are fighting, but I can't think why." However, Richard Bale found a note of approval in his voice. All at once he disliked Gawin, not his principles but the man himself. Certainly in nothing did he resemble his brother, Charles, who dressed and drank, raced and gambled, like a gentleman. Enormously to his relief Ava came up to them, and Richard spoke with a warmth of manner that, as he had intended, she ac-

BRYAN UNIVERSITY LIBRARY

cepted as highly significant. She put her hand upon his arm and led him away. "You weren't getting on with Gawin," she observed. "There's no one like you, Ava," he replied. "How did you hit on that in no time at all?" She made no explanation.

"Charles," she called to her husband, who had just entered the room. When he reached them he addressed Richard: "I believe Ava thought I had gone on another terrapin hunt. And if you don't stay unnaturally sober, I'm afraid we'll get no more toddy." She said serenely, "Certainly not. This is a party for Lavinia and Gawin. After all, Todd Hundred isn't the tavern."

What, Richard wondered, did she think of Lavinia Roderick? Then he changed the direction of his query — what did he think of her? But there was no need for an answer, none for an opinion. Bradlock Wiatt and his daughter spoke to him. There could never be a question of her good looks: even so early in the morning Eliza Wiatt was positively lovely . . . with her tranquil but not tranquillizing smile.

*

* *

Henry Dalney crossed the dining room to sit at Richard's side, but they said nothing to each other immediately. There was no need for them to talk. Like himself, Dalney had served through the War with England; but he had been on the water, on the coasts — among other seas and channels — of the British Islands with Lambert Wickes. There was, in consequence, a deep bond of sympathy and understanding between them. Dalney's small plantation was across the county from Balisand, up on the River York, and Richard Bale didn't see him as often as he would have chosen. "Who is that beside Ava?" Richard asked presently. When he learned that the individual he had indicated was Jasper Robine, he studied him with a dissembled and considerable interest. He was a man with great properties in the Northern Neck, inherited from the patent under Lord Howard; and, notable in family, he had added to an education in England the experience of a wide travel over the Continent. Robine, different from Gawin Todd, was clothed in the extremity of fashionable taste. But, in spite of this and of all the aristocratic influences that had so largely moulded him, he was not a supporter of federal principles and hopes. He was, Richard Bale held, faithless to his own world. Yet he was forced to admit that Jasper Robine was an impressive figure: his well-known ability in the composition of music was reflected in his narrow, self-absorbed, pale face; his blood was made clear by the intolerant carriage of his head, the assuredness of his speech.

The base of his friendship for Gawin Todd must be politics, Richard concluded, for Gawin had a strong personality; he was already — in a way that, for the present anyhow, he chose to deprecate — a power with the new and regrettable ferment in Virginia. Ava was laughing at a phrase of Jasper Robine's; he was touching a napkin to his lips; his hands were delicately narrow and white. On Ava's other side Bradlock was sitting, devoted only to his breakfast and the tall glass of brandy and water it was his custom to take with that meal. Rose Ann Marable was next, and then, beyond Gawin, Mary.

Her face was set in a frame of hair, loosely confined at the back with a ribbon, that seemed to have over it a sheen of frost; her eyes were a darker and more intense blue than usual; her cheeks were rose. He calculated her age and found it to be fifteen — that was young, yet it was suitable for marriage. She discovered him looking at her, and raised her hand in a momentary recognizing gesture. She was busy, really, in a repressed and earnest conversation with her sister Delia, who was three years younger. On Henry Dalney's left was Sally, the Todds' youngest child. Marable, their son, a year Mary's senior, was absent; Charles had put him at school in England.

"What do you suppose Mary and Delia are talking about?" Sally inquired of Dalney and Richard Bale. "They won't let me hear a word. I know a great many things they couldn't guess at." Her face was round, her eyes grey like Ava's, and her mouth had the amused quirk that was characteristic of Charles Todd's expression and attitude toward the world.

"I couldn't imagine," Henry Dalney replied. "But we can whisper about something."

"It wouldn't do for Mr. Bale to know," she asserted. She leaned over and laid the freshness of her mouth against the man's ear. "If you told him I can't think what would happen to me. I'd be sold South."

"Sally," her mother exclaimed, "if I ever hear you use that expression again I'll send you North until you learn better! You encourage her, Charles. I hope you are ashamed of the result. Where can she hear such dreadful things!"

"Naturally I wouldn't speak of it," Dalney reassured the child. "It's gone out the other side of my head."

"Then it will strike Mr. Bale."

"Do you think so?" He turned and seriously regarded Richard. "There could be happenings a great deal worse." And then he asked Bale how Mrs. Patton was.

Mrs. Patton was well enough, Richard replied in an absent manner. She had always said that she would leave him when he married, but — if it were Mary — she mustn't do that, not for five or six years at the soonest. Then his wife would take over the white wicker basket that held the keys of Balisand. "Lucia Mathews is coming to-day," Sally informed them further. "I am glad. If she would only talk about something else than horses! She says when she grows up she'll fox-hunt. She's jumped now, in the paddock."

That was like Beverley Mathews, Richard thought, to let his daughter, who couldn't be ten years old, ride horses over jumps and talk of fox hunting. It must be almost as lonely at the Mathews' as it was at Balisand, with only Beverley and that one daughter. His wife had died at Lucia's birth, and there was another ten years between her and the child before. And now they had all gone from Gloucester but those two: a boy in the French Embassy, another in New Orleans, one on a Georgia plantation and a girl intermarried with the Du Puys of South Carolina. Beverley Mathews had a great house at Welfield, with an imposing falling garden, and Richard had a momentary vision of them, the child and the old but vigorous man, sitting on their long terrace.

There was a movement about the table, breakfast was at an end, and Jasper Robine took the chair beside Rose Ann Marable. She was Ava's sister, twenty, twenty-five, years old; but, dominated by her head, or, rather, by a universally applauded wit, she hadn't yet chosen to marry. A part of the brilliant and fashionable gatherings at the famous plantations on the James River and on the Rappahannock, there, naturally, Robine had come to know and — it was evident — appreciate her, for, careful to keep from anyone else the subject of their mutual interest, very much in the manner of Mary and Delia, they were being enormously amused.

Rose Ann was gazing innocently at the goblet she was turning in her fingers. How ugly she was, Richard Bale thought; the life she led, suitable enough for men, had visibly damaged the colour of her youth. Robine leaned forward on the table. "Mr. Bale," he said.

"Of Balisand," Richard continued.

"Certainly that, with all it means. I have heard a lot about you from men you've probably forgotten but who remember you with — shall I say — respect." Richard Bale thanked him. "It isn't often that soldiers are willing to meet actually the consequences of their fighting, like Washington and yourself, although there are always plenty after easy posts. I suppose you will be going North at the end of October with Colonel Richard Henry Lee."

Yes, Bale assented, he would. The conversation suffered from a halt since he was as indifferent to making any advances as Jasper Robine, under his extreme ease, was toward receiving them. Altogether their meeting was a success. Richard Bale had recognized a man of patent good breeding and mettle, whatever else might be urged against him; and Robine's manner was wholly acceptable. He was joined by Gawin Todd. "You know Captain Henry Dalney, too," he said negligently. "Rose Ann, you are being wicked."

"She was," Jasper Robine answered for her; "but fortunately with me and not you, for it would have blasted your tender republican nature." Gawin Todd lightly added that the failure of the Established English Church to chasten their vanities would be corrected by the Methodist, an American institution. "Did you hear that?" Rose Ann Marable cried to Lavinia Roderick. "You had better have your wedding dress cut out of homespun and carry cow peas."

*

* *

One by one those at the table left, until only Richard and Henry Dalney remained. "What do you think of Robine?" the latter asked. He listened with approval to Bale's opinion. "But you have missed what lies behind all that — he is looking to be Governor of Virginia. His ambition is bottomless." The other dismissed that for sheer nonsense: "Unless it gets to be as secondary as we hope; then he can have it and be damned to him. Will you come to Balisand with me when this is over?"

" I would, but I sent word to Jordan Gainge I'd ride out and see him. He's been sick, his overseer told a man of mine." There was the bond of the sea, Richard realized, between Dalney and Jordan Gainge, who had been the master of packets throughout his early life and in command of privateers later. He had, in Gloucester County, a doubtful reputation; not a great many years before he had been tried at the General Court for piracy among the West Indies; but the charge hadn't been sustained, and Henry Dalney publicly supported him.

" I wonder if you have any idea what Sally whispered to me," Dalney went on. " I have the greatest temptation to break my confidence with her." Richard said that he was willing to make a wide guess. " It had to do with my possible marriage."

" Wide! " he was echoed. " That was the thing itself, and to Mary. It seemed serious to me, Richard, because it was about Mary and not you. Since we have gone so far, I might as well finish — it's Sally's opinion she's in love with you. If that means anything. It hasn't to either of us yet." Richard Bale was silent; the truth was he was a little appalled at the rapidity with which such a consummation was gathering about him. Yet he had consented to it. " What do you think? " he asked.

" Nothing could be better, of course. I'm only surprised I hadn't thought of it long ago. Why, it's ideal — a Todd and a Bale. Richard, this would be made in heaven."

They rose, in a silent and common consent, and walked through the hall to the portico. A number of saddled horses were tied to the rack opposite, ready for whoever might require them, and there was a stableboy to adjust the stirrup lengths or perform any other similar duty. " I am going back to Charles Todd's office," Dalney announced. And, turned the other way, Richard walked out to the wharf. Sitting in a row at its end were Mary and Delia, Eliza Wiatt and, beside Sally, Lucia Mathews, who must just then have arrived. She was a strongly built child, with a good nose, a calm gaze and black eyebrows that almost met; her whole colouring was as dark as an Indian's. There was a great deal of laughter as he approached, but, when he was discovered, as quickly as possible it stopped. There were irrepressible giggles directed, he felt, at Mary Todd. She was entirely undisturbed. " What do you think? " she addressed him. " Eliza Wiatt has another suitor. We all think she ought to be ashamed to go around making so many men unhappy." Eliza looked at them slowly. " It isn't my fault, if it's true; I don't do anything; I don't specially want them." At this there was a derisive chorus that she'd die without attention. " I saw you with him," Delia asserted, " and it was a shame. I wanted to warn him."

" It's the tutor, Mr. Garret," Sally put in.

Here, then, was the cause of Garret's profound and resentful melancholy. Well, he would have to recover from disappointment as he best might, for he'd have no success with Eliza Wiatt. Dancing formed the largest part of her deliberate activities, she would never come to regard fiddles as a combustible material for hell. " He told me," she explained; " that he was plain but honourable, and that he had a call for the ministry. He thought I would be a beautiful minister's wife." It was their concerted response that the beauty, at least, was a possibility.

Richard Bale sat above them on the bench — where Lavinia Roderick had been the night before — and listened, half detached, to the bright animation of the chatter. But Mary, he fancied, was quieter than the others. Sally had said that she was in love with him, and if it were true it would make his course easy; but what he meant was that it almost assured his success. It wouldn't be easy. Why, he didn't know, he couldn't discern. Lucia Mathews got up. "I am going to the stable," she announced. "I suppose I'll have to go, too," Sally added. "But I won't stay there all morning, looking at horses, with everybody else dancing."

They left, and, at once, Eliza said that she must change her slippers. "There will be more people, I expect," Delia informed them. "I'm going to see. We'll find Lavinia."

Mary Todd, gazing into the river, didn't stir. She sat with her arms extended, either hand on the edge of the wharf, and Richard Bale could just see the line of her cheek beyond a soft mass of hair. This he concluded, was an admirable opportunity for asking her to marry him; he would do it . . . in a minute or two. A fish jumped. There was a schooner bearing away from the land, into the Bay. Only yesterday he had come from Balisand, around the point of Ware Neck, in his canoe. Then he had proceeded to get drunk, or nearly drunk. Devoted, apparently, to that end, he had midway changed his mind. No, that had been done for him. He recalled the screaming agony which had ended the gouging in the servants' quarters, and the peace that had followed, the night serene with singing birds and stars.

Mary shifted her position, she leaned back with her hands clasped behind her head. It was time he spoke. But he waited, his mind possessed by other thoughts and sensations. He remembered Lavinia Roderick's song, and her explanation that it had only been one of her pauses. Then his attention was caught by a negro, busy over what was evidently an oyster bed. There were marking stakes in his boat, and a fishing line tied to a thwart. The line straightened out and the negro, his hands moving rapidly one over the other, lifted a large fish from the water.

"It was a rock fish," Mary Todd observed. She turned to Richard. "Yes," he assented, "you are right." That wasn't what was in his mind to say. He had an insuperable reluctance to pronounce the words that would commit him, and perhaps Mary, to all the future. The illogical feeling assailed him that there was a reason to the contrary. This irritated him, since he was entirely free. But it persisted, quite as though a shadowy and restraining hand had been laid upon his mouth. "Yes, it was a rock fish. A big one." At this inanity she glanced up at him. Blue eyes and a pure appealing mouth. Her breath quickened; he could see it in the sharper rise and fall of her immature breast. With an extraordinary sense of relief it occurred to him that he ought first — for the form's sake — explain his intention to Charles Todd. And that he could do almost at once.

The air, so far as he was concerned, was remarkably cleared, he felt at once at his ease. "No one could be prettier than you, Mary," he told her. She was standing now, close beside him, and she said simply that she was glad he thought so. Her voice was deeper than he remembered it, a still voice, if such a thing were possible, like the difference when a stream fell into a pool. In a moment she had grown older, if not in appearance, then in a way infinitely more important and moving. Yet, he saw plainly, it was the fact that moved him — he was sorry for her to have life sweep over her so soon.

*

*   *

They walked slowly in toward the house, but, as if she followed an idle impulse, Mary turned to the left and they entered the garden. Within low borders of trimmed boxwood the flowers were like gorgeous silk shawls, yellow and white lilies were heavy with bloom; there were honeysuckle and tall larkspur and massed roses; fig trees and pomegranate; and, walled from the north, apricots, nectarines. Mary Todd stood for a moment, lost in reflection, and then, in a decided manner, she walked toward the half-circular stone steps and door to the hall. She said nothing, but, just as they entered the house, she gave him a faint smile. At once, inside, he came up to Lavinia Roderick. There were other people close by, but, for the purposes of conversation, they were alone; and, looking away from Richard Bale, she told him in a voice low but clear that he was absolutely detestable.

He was so startled that, in an unguarded and loud tone, he demanded why. She didn't answer; without looking at him, she went to the door through which he had just come. "Why?" he asked again, in a more ordered voice. "All those lies," she said. They were outside, and suddenly, indignantly, she faced him. "Why did you let me tell them, and to Gawin? It nearly killed me afterward."

"But I had nothing to do with that," he protested, confused by the injustice of her attack. "I didn't know, I couldn't guess, what you were going to say. And when you had, did you expect me to contradict you?"

"There was no reason for their not finding out I had met you," she proceeded; "it wasn't disgraceful. But, somehow . . . oh, like that! Well, I didn't want them to."

"I can't see, then, why you blame me," he insisted. "It's unreasonable. You are making entirely too much out of it. After all, you didn't deny that we had seen each other, heard each other, I mean, before."

"I didn't blame you, I called you detestable."

"Absolutely detestable," he reminded her.

"You weren't very pleasant, at the end," Lavinia Roderick replied. She referred, he gathered, to the night before; and, with a curious surprise at himself, he recalled that he had been glad when she left. "But you practically sent me away, after complaining of what I was saying."

Her answer to him was that she had found out why he didn't dance. "If I loved you it would be for that more than anything else." If she loved him! A tremendous and unexpected quality in that left him breathless. He found himself staring blankly at a smoke tree on the farther border of the garden. There was a premonitory scrape of fiddles at his back. All his present existence, it seemed to him, was ironically set to dance music. He allowed himself a swift glance at her and was relieved to discover that she was calmly regarding a pink hawthorn tree. Beyond it stood an octagonal summerhouse. "You'll be married soon?" he asked at random, in an effort of general conversation. "Very," she replied. "Gawin has so many plans, he wants to begin with the least important." Her manner as she said this was consciously light, without importance. However, he chose to offer a conventional objection:

"Gawin wouldn't agree to that."

"Gawin is wonderful." This, he thought, she had adopted as a phrase to be issued at intervals like gold coins of the same denomination and stamp. It didn't need his confirmation. She went down the steps, out into the garden, and he walked behind her. Lavinia Roderick led him to the summerhouse, where she stopped and again confronted him. "Why did I come here?" she demanded. "I didn't want to. I couldn't have been asleep and waked up in a summerhouse, with you."

There was a floor of wood, and, on all the closed sides, there were narrow benches. A lattice of sunlight fell across her shoulders, and, streaming on into his face, for a second it dazed him. Instead of the world of Todd

Hundred, there was a searing flash that left dancing spots of black in his vision. They cleared away and again he saw the cedar trees against the river and a stiff file of hollyhocks. She was still gazing at him with an air of being at a loss. More than handsome, she was incomparably lovely, lovelier by far than Eliza Wiatt.

"The sun got in my eyes," he told her. Why, only God knew. "If you don't like it here we can go," Richard reminded her. "Don't." She made a gesture for him to be quiet. She stood motionless, her lips parted, an arm raised in an instinctive self-protection. Then her tension relaxed. "I had a strange feeling," she said, but what it was she made no attempt to explain. He heard Gawin Todd calling her name; and, in answer, she went out to where Todd could see her. He came quickly up to them. "Jasper Robine wants a minuet with you." It was clear that this pleased him. As they started for the house he dropped back with Richard Bale. "And Robine wants to talk to you," he proceeded. "It's evident he doesn't think you are hopeless."

"You ought to warn him that from your position and his I am," Bale replied. His dislike for Gawin Todd — in the hypocrisy of his plain brown coat — had grown acute. How could he have persuaded Lavinia Roderick to marry him? But women were notoriously bad judges of men. Gawin was wonderful! Hell. He wouldn't, he decided, go in and see the minuet, but keep on to Charles Todd's office, where he would speak to him about Mary and his pretensions. The door to the office was open, and, entering unceremoniously, he found Charles in a very earnest conversation with the tutor. " After a little, Richard, please," he said over his shoulder, and Richard Bale escaped as quickly as possible. He thought of it, the truth was, as an escape; and he went at once to his room, where surely nothing positive could happen to him. Then up the stairs came plodding feet and Garret stood in the doorway.

" I thought you might have some rum," was his amazing admission. He advanced and dropped on a chair. Marks of sleeplessness lay beneath his eyes. " A short passage with the devil? " Bale inquired. The quotation that followed, in Latin, Richard Bale took as referring to a descent into the infernal region. " You're even lower than yesterday," he observed. In return he was treated to an enigmatic period about scarlet women. And, at this, he told the tutor plainly that he was a gloomy young fool. " I gather," he went on, " that you consider yourself to be in love, and if you are it's your mischance. There is no scarlet about it. I'll admit to you I have heard enough to know who it is, and there is only one thing for you to do. Recover."

" I have given up my place here," Garret replied. " I've lost that, and my good prospects, and I think I have lost my God. Dance! Why, I'd dance naked at the courthouse, I'd play a fiddle in church." He bent over, with his face in the bend of an arm, and his body was shaken by long hard sobs. Richard Bale, since there was nothing to say, said nothing. He wasn't specially sympathetic with the suffering of Mr. Garret. It was a shade too unreserved. The servant, William, might come in at any minute. " You can't go on like that," he finally, sharply, remonstrated. The tutor rose, with a wet face, but his voice was steady. "Not in your world," he said. "I am sorry to have troubled you with my private affair. Remember that you came into my room first." When he had gone Richard Bale smiled. Descents into Avernus and the scarlet woman! But, by heaven, he had been brushed by an overwhelming emotion. Or, rather, he had been overwhelmed, in the manner, very probably, of tutors.

*

* *

At dinner — which, on account of the general gaiety and numbers present, was not announced until nearly four o'clock — Richard Bale sat on Ava's right. He counted eighteen at the board, and the children had a second table by a window. When the great soup bowl had been removed, the meat and fowls set at the head and foot, the vegetables on the corners, of the table, the confusion of voices settled into separate conversations largely interrupted by periods of attention to the food. Decanters of Madeira wine were constantly moved on their coasters from hand to hand; the men who preferred rum or brandy kept their goblets in the frequent need of refilling. This, he realized, wasn't a custom at Todd Hundred, where the wine was brought on at the masculine ending of dinner; but, during such a celebration as this, the usual habit was suspended. He noticed that Rose Ann Marable had a glass of Madeira, and that, in a society where women practically never drank in public, showed him how far the polite gatherings of the great world had gone.

Ava's manner with him grew more intimate, she spoke to him in a low voice about the marrowfat peas, which seemed to her to have been improperly cooked. " I'll send Mary out to the kitchen," she went on; " there are a dozen Todd dishes she might as well know . . . carry with her," Ava Todd decided. Lavinia, Richard saw, was silent, but not from any attention to the dinner itself. Another pause. The truth about her was that her thoughts went on journeys of their own . . . to what country? He wished that he might guess. She wasn't very firmly attached to what occurred immediately around her. She wasn't, it was evident, interested. Spoken to, she would smile instinctively, and all her brilliant being pour back into the fine shell of her body. That, for him, was a very elaborate and successful idea, and he went over it again in detail.

Yes, she was a little foreign to life, she appeared to have been put down in it without preparation or warning — always as she was now — and, in consequence, she had that air of surprise, the need of reassurance she had already, in a way, spoken of to him. But he hadn't said a thing to her that was wise or valuable; all his contact with her, so hurried and broken into, had been a failure.

However, he reminded himself, Gawin Todd specially existed to give her support. No one else was necessary, to be permitted; and he fastened his thoughts on Mary, sent to the kitchen to learn the processes of pickling, or, perhaps, the coddling of fruit. Sarah Markoe, the enormously fat cook at Balisand, would listen to her with a hundred exclamations of approval, and then proceed as she had been doing for the past twenty years. He mustn't forget to speak to Charles Todd about William, Sarah's nephew. An admirable servant. He provided himself with a deep glass of rum. Mrs. Patton could make the best lime toddy on the Tidewater, but the Todd Antigua rum was the finest in Virginia.

There was a scraping of chairs, a chiming of voices, the whisper of silk, and the women left the dining room. Gawin Todd shifted to a place by Robine, Henry Dalney was absent in thought, Bradlock Wiatt had a face already flushed with liquor, and Beverley Mathews was discussing fox hunting with the younger Doctor Ambrose, accounted the most daring rider in Gloucester County. Jasper Robine was drinking deliberately; he had already absorbed a large quantity of spirits; but it made no impression on him whatever. Gawin Todd was talking to him in a low but emphatic voice; Robine, carefully listening, made no comment. When he spoke he addressed the table.

"It's the old question of the English debts," he proceeded; "whether they should be assumed by the State where they were contracted, have the Confederation take them over, or an agreement reached to ignore them. Gawin thinks that is justified, and he intends to carry his opinion as far as it will go in the Legislature, but I don't agree with him. The honour of Virginia is up for consideration, and I think that, at any price, it ought to be held inviolate. In other words, the State must assume the debts she contracted. British merchants who freely gave us credit, ought to be protected to the last pound."

"That's well enough for Robine, everyone knows that he is a very rich man, but the Virginians of Fauquier County have a right to a very different feeling. They have every right!" Gawin repeated strongly. It seemed to Richard Bale that Todd was directly addressing him. "They are poor," he continued, "and it may be they haven't been as long in Virginia as the Robines, but they are none the less Virginians. In a way they are more, for they're purely American, they have no old attachment to England. For that reason alone their opinions are particularly useful."

"But, after all," it was Doctor Ambrose who was speaking, "it oughtn't to be charged to the rest of us as a fault that we came to Virginia very early. I have as much sympathy with the West as possible, but I can't see how that would operate against my own responsibilities. Mr. Robine is correct."

"Correct!" Gawain Todd cried. "That's a word I'm getting damned sick of. It's a stone in all our pockets. And custom is in the other pocket. We're too weighted down to move."

"By God, you'd thought Ambrose was moving on Tansey if you had fox-hunted with him," Beverley Mathews put in. "Fox hunting isn't politics," Todd objected contemptuously. "Why, look at these British debts — what are they, most of them? I'll tell you, bills gentlemen owed for satin breeches. Nine times out of ten they are just that. A load of tobacco would be sent to England with requests for twice the nonsense it was worth, and the difference is this obligation of Robine's. To hell with it."

"You are not on the floor of the Legislature now," Jasper Robine reminded him. "Here we take satin breeches more or less for granted. And it doesn't matter what the money was spent for, we spent it, and that's enough. A large part, I'll remind you, went to the volunteers in the war. And there's the Treaty — what do you propose to do with it?"

"Nothing," Todd admitted. "A time comes when it's necessary to change policies."

"Policies but never honour." Bradlock Wiatt pronounced this sentiment with a blurred gravity. In return Gawin Todd asserted that he was as familiar with honour as any man present. That Robine impatiently waved aside. "It's a question of the whole State," he said; "the burden on one county must be borne by the others, or there will be no equity, no State."

"It's a question in my mind," Todd admitted, "if the Tidewater really belongs to the rest; it might better be joined to Maryland."

"You're mad, Gawin," Charles Todd interrupted him. "This is the heart of Virginia; it wasn't very long ago when we were the frontier, please recall. We went through that and paid dearly for what property and peace we have."

"English, English, English!" Gawin answered him, with a rising inflection. "This was a colony, it is a colony, and will always be that in spirit. Why, goddam it, in 1676 we had to have a Bacon in order to breathe. And about Virginia — I meant that the East would have to come to the West; all the movements, the concessions, can't keep on the other way. You don't seem to know, any of you, how the upper counties have grown. It's got to be a question of men against property, humanity or plantations, and I'm for men." He took a long drink.

"How did you vote on the bill to give Thomas Paine some public land in return for his services to the country?" he was asked.

"In the negative. The land belongs to all the people. Let him apply to his necessary evil, since he called the government that. We're a State." There was muttered the familiar phrase, a sovereign State. Bradlock Wiatt, with a crimson amazed face, vanished under the table.

*

* *

Charles Todd called a servant. "Help Mr. Wiatt to his room," he directed. He would need, it was plain, assistance, and the two negroes disappeared beneath the board, straightening up with Bradlock Wiatt between them. They tried to lead him away, but he resisted them and faced the assembled men. He launched upon what had every visible appearance of a speech, his expressions were appropriate to a succession of emotions: he appealed to them, he challenged them, he waited for their approval; but, although he was greeted with a clamorous applause, nothing but a strained and unintelligible whisper came from his lips. After a graceful pause he began again; there were loud cries of complete agreement; and then, suddenly, out of his muddled effort, sounded the declaration that Henrico County had grown the loveliest flower of Virginia.

This, understood as a reference to Lavinia Roderick and Gawin's engagement, was a complete surprise; it had been taken for granted that his speech had been political; but, after a moment, its reception was rapturous. Impatient at restraint, he pushed the servants aside, and again, immediately, slid from view. Gawin Todd made a brief proper reply, and then returned at once to the subject of State obligations. Now he leaned toward Richard:

"There is nothing personal in this, none of us would rob the army of a particle of its due, but I must say that a discharged soldier is no more than a common citizen. No more and no less. He has the same privileges and duties as those who may or may not have fought; and I am opposed to all this agitation of post-war payments. I realize that in some cases I would work an injustice, but it must be met as a whole; and any payments discharged at least not sooner than Virginia is solvent."

"Why pay the men at all?" Dalney asked. "Forget the poor devils and give it to the General Assemblymen."

This Gawin Todd pointedly ignored. "If Washington's army thinks so cursed much of itself, why didn't it hold on to the Continental script instead of selling it for about what the paper was worth?"

"We have to live," Dalney spoke again.

Richard Bale had made no effort to enter the discussion, since his beliefs were totally opposed to those of both Gawin Todd and Robine. He felt that he was so markedly their inferior in argument and in the possession of widespread facts that he determined to keep still. He hoped Henry would say no more; his old sense returned of being bound with Henry Dalney in a service that no one outside its officers and a few men understood or cared about. How could they explain what they had endured, for what they had fought? He had listened bitterly to Todd's account of the breaking down of even a Virginia unity. There weren't, it appeared, to be merely sovereign States, but sovereign counties . . . districts, hundreds, townships. Soon every individual would be a separate nation.

"Nothing could better show the weakness of Congress than the lack of public confidence in it," Gawin Todd continued. "But, then, it has no confidence in itself. Ask Richard Bale, who is a member, how many States were represented the beginning of this year, and if he won't tell you I will. Six! And get him to repeat the sea letter granted the ship United States — the United States: most serene, serene, most puissant, puissant, high, illustrious, noble, honourable, venerable, wise and prudent lords, emperors, kings. I got that much before it made me sick. Past the middle of January there were only three States attending, and Virginia wasn't one. But I haven't a doubt that Mr. Jefferson, at least, had something more important to attend to."

"That can be as true as you like," Beverley Mathews asserted. "But I'll be damned if it's any better in the Legislature, with everybody laughing and spitting and calling out at once. Yes, and the town mocking them through the windows. I remember in the fall of 1782 it took eighteen days to organize the House. I've heard James Madison damn it hotly enough."

" It's practically a new body," Gawin explained. " At least it has life and convictions. But Congress: it will spend a day wondering whether it would or wouldn't allow a foreign captain who was in Pulaski's regiment the money to sail home with. In spite of all I said, I'd have given it to him and thought the riddance cheap; but they condemned him to stay in America."

" I knew him," Richard Bale spoke without premeditation. " Paschke. A very brave and capable man." This was in violation of his decision to be still, and he went no further. " We can get along now without hired soldiers." Charles Todd quietly told his brother that he had said enough. " We understand you mean nothing personal, but your tone is the reverse of — well, hospitality."

" It goes back to Washington's ambitions," the other Todd still declared. " He wants a monarchy where he's monarch; he doesn't seem to realize that his service — and it was very creditable — is over. He has no ability for public affairs; he can't fathom a free people. He's after power and a crown."

" That is an opinion I have heard," Richard Bale answered, " but I can assure you it is wrong." After all, he had been forced to speak. " General Washington is in favour of a government strong enough to be fully responsible for its members."

" Not members, subjects," Gawin corrected him. " He wants a military boot set on them."

A familiar sensation overtook Richard Bale; it was one he had had cause to regret, but before which he was powerless: it seemed to him that all the elements of his body were congealing in the intense cold — like water in the act of turning into ice — of a black rage. He was sitting with his legs thrust out before him, his hands idle on the table, and he spoke without the shifting of a muscle:

"After this, Mr. Todd, when you speak to me of General Washington, see that it is at least with the form of respect."

Immediately the men about the decanters lost their indolence in a close attention to what might follow. "Do you mean that I'm not at liberty to say what's in my mind about a public character?" Gawin demanded. "Because if you do you're worse than drunk."

"Say what you like to who will listen," Bale replied; "I am speaking for myself. Don't calumniate General Washington to me."

Gawin Todd laughed, but Robine laid a hand on his sleeve. "You don't seem to understand," he said quietly; "this is serious."

"What if it is!" the other exclaimed. "If he thinks he's serious, do I, does anyone, have to be bound by his opinion of his own importance?"

"Yes," Jasper Robine said shortly. "You do. All men of your position would."

"You think you can force a duel on me," Gawin had returned to Bale. "That may be the custom in armies and with gamblers, but it's not outside of that. You'll have no shot at me on any ridiculous field of honour. But take this with the rest — if you get it into your head that I'm a coward I'll damn soon beat it out."

Charles Todd, suffused with anger, rose. "Then I'll speak for you, Gawin," he said harshly:

"Mr. Bale, yes, and Mr. Dalney, I offer you the fullest apology for what I consider an assault without excuse or manners. If this is politics, I thank God I am past the time for taking a part in it. And I give you my word," he addressed Richard Bale, "that no member of my family will ever again disparage General Washington to you." Gawin violently started to his feet, but Jasper Robine sharply silenced him. "Any more of this," he declared, "and I'll have to do without the privilege of knowing you. The world hasn't gone to the devil yet." He turned and bowed profoundly to Charles Todd.

*

*   *

There was a general slackening of tension; a high china bowl of toddy had been put on the table, and the business of drinking was taken up with renewed vigour. Charles Todd had left the dining room, but no one else — the application of the phrase was Ambrose's — was a deserter. Richard Bale was sunk in the mental depression that always followed his rages; physically, too, he was inert. Most of the talking that followed was by Robine; it was temperate, smooth and extraordinarily persuasive . . . and dangerous, Richard automatically recognized.

"Naturally," Robine declared, "there will have to be a reorganization of the States; everyone is agreed about that; and it's only a question of the form it will take. There was some truth in what Gawin began by saying — that there was no general confidence in the present Congress, and I think there never would be in a body of that sort. We fought for quite the opposite. And the men — like Colonel Lee — who would be drawn to a strongly centralized government, we need at home."

"The trouble with Congress now," Beverley Mathews asserted, "is that it doesn't know what it's there for. It isn't as useful as a negro stableboy."

"Exactly," Robine agreed, "and its duties must be fixed and its power defined and limited. But it ought never to assume the responsibilities which belong to the States. I suppose it should exist to control our relationship with foreign governments. Hardly anything more."

"Very well," Dalney said, "then how about the effort to regulate our commerce with powers who won't make treaties with us? The States wouldn't let Congress pass a bill to take care of that. If Massachusetts won't trade with England, then Virginia will and damned glad of the chance, and, with all the stinking jealousy, it's getting to be almost as bad among the States themselves." It was Gawin Todd's opinion that exactly that condition stimulated trade. "And no State will ever allow a federal excise," Robine proceeded; "the day for it, on this continent, is over. You all saw how the proposed imposts were met. The State must continue supreme," he insisted. "That is what we are and what we came from. A friendly body of equal powers."

"The small States are specially friendly with the large." Richard, from his lassitude, hugely admired the determination and intelligence with which Henry Dalney remained in the controversy. "Maryland was in a glow about our lands in the Ohio Valley." But Robine made it clear that he was not regarding the present. "I am showing you what must happen," he said positively. "It is because of Virginia's great future that we require an immediate State assumption of debts." He would be an able governor, Richard Bale realized; he would decorate any office of public dignity. Gawin Todd moved up to him unexpectedly. "There is no need for us to go on from where we last stopped," he addressed Richard very fairly.

"None," he agreed. He had no inclination to talk to Gawin Todd, and he attempted no civilities. Instead, he rose and went out to the main portico. His legs, he observed, were unsteady, but that was the result of the Madeira and rum and toddy. However, they hadn't touched his mind: that, abruptly, was concerned with Lavinia Roderick. Perhaps, except in throngs of people, he would never see her again, never again have an opportunity to speak anything but commonplaces to her. That, in reality, was all they had said now; and he went back over what, together, they had expressed, in order to discover what had been so significant in it. But he failed; the phrases had been hardly more than conventional.

There was a light step behind him, and he turned with such a sudden hopefulness that he collided with a pillar. But it was Eliza Wiatt. She paused, meeting him with her slow smile. Her manner always intimated a greater interest in men than she thought it was prudent to show.

" I couldn't think where you were." She conveyed the impression that she had missed him . . . perhaps even that she was here on his account. " Why have you kept away from — from the party? "

" But I haven't," he objected. " I have been very much in it. You have been too engaged to see me." That wasn't so, she assured him. " Do you say things like that to make me unhappy? Because they do."

" Mr. Garret told me he was leaving."

" It was dreadful," she confided to him; " I don't see how he came to misunderstand me. The way he read poetry was what I liked." Her voice hadn't an accent of regret. " Tell me, Eliza," he asked, " what is it that happens to the men who fall in love with you? "

" They just will without a reason."

" What is it in you? " he insisted.

" Well, I'm not too bad-looking."

" That hasn't a thing to do with it." At least he knew that much. " I'd like to know." He remained leaning against the pillar while she sat on a marble step. " If it's love, what does that explain? Absolutely nothing," he answered his own question moodily. " It might even be a sort of poison, and very deadly, instead of how it is regarded. Garret, for example — he thought he had lost his God." She admitted that she knew what he meant:

" I don't understand it myself; and you musn't think it makes me specially happy or that I try to upset anyone. Really, I behave quite well, Mr. Bale."

He replied impatiently that he hadn't dreamed of questioning that. She could tell him nothing, he saw.

"But I really did miss you." Richard thanked her absently. He was occupied with the thought of Lavinia . . . experimentally he stopped there, without adding Roderick. Lavinia. Her name sent a tide of delight through him. This would have to stop. "You are thinking of Mary," Eliza challenged him. Of course he was, he lied. Then, at once, he filled his mind with the image of Mary Todd.

A lilybud, a pink, a rose.

Richard Bale hadn't intended to repeat that; it had come of itself. But you must bring me oceans more. How could she marry Gawin? He wished, with a hardened mouth, that what had begun after dinner had gone on to the end. In imagination he felt the perfect balance of the pistols in his room. The set screws of the hair triggers could be moved to the weight of less than a hair. Yes, he'd have welcomed a shot at Gawin Todd. One. No more would be necessary. Strangely enough, he was convinced that he would kill Todd. In all this he recognized the justice of his reputation, which wasn't peaceable. He, Richard Bale of Balisand, was regarded as having an ugly disposition; of being, perhaps, too ready to fight. That, however, was the history of the Bale temper; in the past it had been a mark of honour. Men who bore arms.

"You are getting more impolite every minute," Eliza Wiatt complained. "I hate men who are in love . . . with someone else."

"Am I in love?" he demanded. "Do you know that or have you just been listening to the talk?" She rose, laughing:

"Terribly. I have never seen it more and plainer. You are finished, maybe for life." She went down the steps, pointedly leaving him; and her words, her half-disagreeable laughter, echoed and echoed in his consciousness. Maybe for life. But that was ridiculous; with him love was to come after marriage, through association and passion and birth. It was an actuality, like the other relationships of existence. Eliza Wiatt had been affected by her own nature and inclinations, the poetry read to her by the young and desperate Mr. Garret. He walked out by the house to the wharf, the sun was behind him, the river veiled in a tender and transparent haze; the shore opposite was immaterial. A mood appropriate to the hour swept over him, a happiness subdued in melancholy: afternoon had overtaken him without the compensation of a morning.

*

* *

The night, it seemed, came swiftly, although he had spent a long time dressing; supper passed unremarkably; and the interminable dancing was in progress. He had remained at the table, there was no one else but a servant in the room, and his thoughts were uninterrupted. They weren't gay; actually, they were not thoughts, they hadn't sufficient continuity for that; and yet neither were they emotions; at least he was not able to recognize them; his state more nearly resembled another depression. But it wasn't that . . . it might be that premonition described it. However, there was nothing before him; nothing but emptiness, he specified, and then he reached a painful knowledge — he couldn't marry Mary Todd.

This was so disastrous that he sat upright, appalled; yet there was no escape from a truth that apparently had been shouted at him. It was an impossibility. The reason was that he didn't love her and he never would. Never! He would only condemn her to a long wretchedness of the heart. No, it wasn't an affair of engaging a housekeeper; if that were all it would be easy; yes, desirable and pleasant; he'd have infinitely preferred an arrangement of that kind, amplified, certainly, but in the main calm. What, in addition, disturbed him was the recognition that that was possible for other men; they had, on the most equable ground, made marriage a success. Why, then, couldn't he?

There was a chance, as well, that he was already bound — his understanding with Ava had been complete without confirmation — and he remembered Mary's expression as she looked up at him from the edge of the wharf. Sally had said that her sister was in love with him. Anything he owed was to Mary and not to her parents. But she was so young that it could not be serious with her. Part of it would have come from suggestion, implication. Anyhow, he was unable to ask her. In planning, consequently, his action, he decided to speak to Ava, tell her briefly the cause of his failure, and to no one else. Ava Todd, if she had consulted him, could account for Charles' opinions. All this was unpleasant, but not impossible; and, on the whole, he was relieved.

However, only in a minor way; his lowness of spirit continued; but, intent upon that, he realized that he couldn't go on indulging it like this, alone in the dining room. His actions were becoming so peculiar that they would be noticeable. In the hall he was stopped by Jasper Robine. "There's some talk about a table of whist," he said; "if it's made up will you be one with Mathews and Bradlock Wiatt and me?" He had to agree, and he left Robine determined to lose himself in some dark and inaccessible corner. How could he play whist, he asked himself . . . with, naturally, no reply.

Following that illogical decision, he turned to the right, leaving the brilliancy of the drawing room for the garden. Red roses were black at night: a thing he had never before noted. There had been no late frosts in the spring, and, as a result, the apricots would have a long season and come to ripeness. Lost in the contemplation of nothing at all, he found himself by the summerhouse. He entered. It was intensely still, so silent that he heard a minute stirring of a leaf on the honeysuckle that climbed the lattices. Then there was the low sound of a passage, and Lavinia faced him dimly in the enclosed gloom.

He said her name, but not in any accent of surprise; it was all very familiar. She swayed slightly and he moved forward quickly and took her into his arms. She neither avoided nor sought him; she was entirely passive; her head was lowered, one hand outside his embrace, resting lightly on his arm. For a measureless time it was like that, and then she lifted her face and he kissed her.

It didn't, as he would have supposed it must, fill him with ecstasy. Rather he was conscious of a joy that might have been the far-approaching murmur of an overwhelming tidal wave. At first her lips hadn't answered him, but suddenly — the realization appeared to suffocate him — she kissed him in return.

The effect of that, as though it were a soundless but potent explosive, was to drive them slightly apart. He could see the line of her cheek, the slim whiteness of her shoulders, her grace of bearing. Richard hoped that she would speak, yet, beyond the audible unsteadiness of her breathing, she was still. It was he who should speak, who must say something, but when he did end the silence he was totally chagrined by his words. "This is serious," he said, and he repeated the word, "serious." Lavinia replied, "I had better sit down."

He found a place beside her, but not touching her, on the narrow bench. "It couldn't be helped," Richard Bale went on. "If you expect me to say I'm sorry you'll be disappointed."

"I'm not sorry." Her voice was level, clear. "I am much, much worse. Mr. Bale, I am a bad woman ——" He interrupted her, protesting against that; but she restrained him with a hand laid, for an instant, against his mouth. "You don't know — I wanted this to happen. The only thing left is to be truthful. I didn't realize what it was I wanted, but I encouraged it and kept it warm. Yes, I am bad. I've always been bad, because I have always waited for just this. Oh, what will you think of me? " she cried.

" It has nothing to do with my thoughts," he answered. " I love you. This is serious."

" If it is," she told him, " you must be everything. I depend on you. Explain what I will do." It wasn't easy enough to put into a sentence, to compress within a phrase or more of advice. One thing, however, he was certain of. " You will not marry Gawin Todd," he said quietly. " I couldn't, now," she assured him briefly. That, at least, was a fact they had gained. " You will have to go in," his voice sounded at random. " I'll decide about it all to-night." Her hand fell into his and he held it very gently. How serious it was, he must keep her, as long as possible, from knowing. She would never marry Gawin Todd, not Gawin but him. " After some arrangements we will be married and go to Balisand. There is a very old wicker basket to hold the keys." She wouldn't be put off:

" You would have to kill Gawin."

How was an answer, a denial, to be made to her? " We had better not discuss that," he said. " Whatever happens will be over very quickly. A time comes when life isn't very valuable, when it doesn't matter if it lasts a little longer or not. If I had to pay by death for these minutes . . . who would hesitate? " Midway in his period he was deep under the tidal wave of his incredible joy.

" You must go," he insisted, when he felt himself again to be on solid earth, but she answered that she was always leaving him. " Never again." Their hands tightened together. "My heart hurts me;" she moved his hand and pressed it against her body. She stood up. "Richard —— " she began. But she had gone. He had missed what she might have said. The wave in a tumult receded from him. He sat with his chin on his breast, his palms held out and open: he was no more than a shell turned over and over, driven by the sea; a grain of sand crushed by timeless immensity. In the silence the minute sound among the leaves recommenced. It was lost in the faint strains of the fiddles. Lavinia Bale who had been Lavinia Roderick, Lavinia . . . lavender. Sweet lavender, with a scent which lasted for so long after it was dead. That comparison, all such eventualities, he thrust hurriedly away from him.

*

* *

Jasper Robine caught Richard as he was walking with a stumbling quickness to his room. "We are waiting for you," Robine said. "Yes?" Bale replied blankly, suddenly called out of the miracle that had fallen upon him. "The others are at the table." It was the whist. He stood, trying in a swift desperation to think of an excuse that would make escape allowable; but none occurred to him; and he turned and accompanied Robine back to the house, feeling that he was wholly impotent in the arbitrary grip of events. The whist table was set in a corner of the hall, convenient to the toddy; and, cutting, he found that Bradlock Wiatt and he were partners. Robine, as it might have been predicted, played with great skill and an air of total detachment. Both Mathews and Wiatt were indifferent to the actual material results of the game — the stake was ten shillings a point — but Richard had a distant recognition of the fact that he ought to be careful. In the first place, his money was limited; and, in the second, now he would need it all. However, a hand was opened, the trump turned. Eight points in the lead, he demanded of his partner, "Can you one?" Bradlock had the third honor necessary for game. Someone moved up behind him . . . it was Gawin Todd. He stood intent at Richard's back, with a hand on his chair, watching the play.

That, Richard Bale thought, must be the last time Gawin and he would be peaceably, quietly, together. He had, he knew, terribly wronged Gawin Todd; he had outraged the hospitality of Todd Hundred; but he felt no remorse. Richard had no sense of embarrassment with Gawin standing beside him. He could have no regret at what had happened. Actually he managed his cards rather well; he did this consciously, even with a little pride, as a mark of his utter coolness and command over himself. He was specially glad, for Lavinia's sake, that his character was what it was, hard and sure, and accustomed to immediate dangerous decisions. The tragic necessities of the years in the army had assisted all that in him.

He heard Lavinia's voice — it was, but only as usual, a little breathless — she didn't come up to them, and Gawin turned away. "I hold a quint-major," Wiatt complained, "and Richard is as grateful as he might be for five loose cards. That's a bumper, too." In the end he was moderately successful, a question of a few shillings, but Beverley Mathews had won heavily. "If you'll come to the Northern Neck," Robine told him, "we'll get something done. I mean worth our while, in gold. Your hands ought to be more valuable than your plantation." But he added that Mathews' skill was equal to his luck. He might go now, Richard Bale decided. Of all the places in the world, his room over the schoolhouse seemed the only one that offered any security or relief from events.

The candles were lighted, the bed prepared, but he had no chance of sleep: he must meet the situation immediately before him. The main course of his action was comparatively simple, plain; the execution, the details, were difficult to decide upon. He wanted, beforehand, to know exactly what he was going to say. Up to a point he would have to speak, and then the rest must be left to Henry Dalney. Probably Dalney would confer with Robine, a very satisfactory arrangement.

However, should he speak at once to Gawin — this seemed no less than Gawin Todd's due — or ought he to confer with Henry Dalney. The important thing was the protection of Lavinia from all public and common talk. Then he saw that, with careful management and faultless discretion, the entire affair might be charged to his difficulty with Gawin Todd the night before. There wasn't a loyal Federalist officer who would not have resented, in the completest manner possible to honour, such reflections upon Washington. Yes, that quarrel could be easily and apparently revived: any motive, compared to the secret actuality of what they fought for, would be at once trivial and sufficient. It might be necessary, in connection with this, to put off his marriage with Lavinia for, perhaps, a year. A certain logic, a deep-shared interest, indeed, a responsibility of his own, would then exist to bring them naturally together.

His mind slipped away from the task before him and returned to Lavinia. It seemed to Richard that there was a flash of sunlight in his eyes; for a moment he was dazed. Where was she? But not in his room; not yet. He felt again the straitly confined perfection of her body in his arms, she rested against him and her lips returned his kiss. It surprised him that they hadn't kissed each other again, again and again. That, too, would follow. In the summerhouse they had been overcome by the sheer discovery of love. Even what he had said seemed in memory meaningless, futile; a few sentences and then he had hurried her away. What a fool he had been, what a damned uneasy fool. He heard her protesting against leaving him — she was always leaving him. But she went, with his name, Richard, the beginning of a phrase, on her lips. Later he must ask her what she had intended to say; he couldn't lose the most trivial of her words. Then he realized that he had practically seen her only in the dark, on the wharf and to-night: and adorable voice, an immaterial presence. Hardly anything more. Night and then day, he assured himself; long days at Balisand.

Richard brought his mental wandering to an end, he came resolutely back to what, first, confronted him. Well, he had decided to consult with Henry Dalney, and it should be at once, so that, to-morrow morning, he could proceed without hesitation or mistake. It must all happen immediately, before Lavinia had time to realize what was going, what had gone, on. She must be spared all the agony of mind possible.

Nothing could save her wholly: the texture of what had happened to them was too dark for that; yet, while she would never forget, years and happiness would soften the memory of what he would have to do.

It was a fortunate chance that he had almost entirely refused the toddy bowl through the rubbers of whist — his hand was steady, his head clear. Gawin Todd drank very little. William, the servant, came into the room with a can of hot water, and Richard Bale sent him for Dalney. "Tell him very quietly," he instructed the negro; "if he is engaged ask him to step aside. Mr. Bale would like to see him at his convenience in Mr. Bale's room." William went, and he told himself that another step toward Lavinia had been taken. Henry Dalney didn't come at once, and he grew impatient. He had been sitting, but he rose and walked across the small room from wall to wall, from wall to wall. He wasn't agitated, but only in a hurry to have it all done with. He didn't want his thoughts of Lavinia, of happiness, to be interrupted.

Perhaps, with some of the party — the night was immaculate — Henry had gone out on the river. Richard Bale looked at his watch and found that it was exactly midnight; he tried to decide how long he had been with Lavinia in the summerhouse . . . hell, what did it matter? He was getting to be no better than a cornet in his first affair of love and honour. The cover had slipped from the hot water, and he stooped to replace it. The black suit, he muttered, with a coat that buttoned up to his throat. Under the circumstances Gawin Todd would have to challenge. It wasn't really conceivable that he'd refuse. How could he? Just the same, it was a shade hard on Gawin — to be killed in a manner he detested because he had lost the girl he loved. This recognition, in Richard, was purely philosophical; it held no accompanying emotion of pity or regret. Qualities, where the world was concerned, he was bare of. There was a footfall, Henry Dalney, on the stair.

*

*   *

Yet, when he entered, Richard was silent, uncertain how best to explain what was in his mind. "I had thought of going to bed," Henry Dalney admitted. The other replied that he would have to put that off. After all, he had better be as explicit as possible, and he said abruptly: "Henry, I am in love with Lavinia, Lavinia Roderick." Dalney's expression was merely incredulous. "Then you are an idiot," he managed to pronounce. "That, of course, is evident," Richard agreed. "But it doesn't happen to change or lessen the fact. Serious," he added, largely to himself. Henry Dalney exclaimed:

"How can anything so wild be serious! And you don't look drunk. If you sent for me to say this, you must be moonstruck without the moon."

"I am going to have the moon," Richard Bale replied fantastically. "You'll help me get it."

Dalney studied him, plainly at a loss to account for the discrepancy between his grave manner and incomprehensible speech. "What is it?" he demanded impatiently. "You say you love Lavinia Roderick, well ——?"

"Lavinia loves me."

Immediately Henry Dalney's look changed to a deep and shocked concern. For a breath he was silent. "That," he said finally, "is the devil. What frightful bad luck! It's hard on you, Richard; for, of course, you can do nothing."

"On the contrary," Richard Bale answered him, "I am going to do everything."

"But that," Dalney protested, "is wrong. You are wrong." Richard reminded him that it wasn't necessary for him to hear any more, he could go on to bed. "Don't be worse than usual," Henry begged him. "You'll have to tell me, as much as you can, what has happened. I am obliged to remind you that it will affect us both. So far, nothing can be said for you."

"Well, there's nothing to add," he admitted. "Lavinia and I love each other, and we are going to make every other circumstance fit that."

"I suppose," Dalney spoke satirically, "you will have no trouble making Gawin Todd a part of it." He was seated, and Richard Bale stood over him frowning. "None." His voice was steady. Dalney's gaze met his and kept it with a dark interrogation. "Accidents turn up," he reminded Richard; "the wrong men get killed."

"This time it will be the right man. Of course I sent for you to see if you'd act for me. I never thought you might object, on a formality." Henry Dalney replied that formalities were often of immense weight . . . particularly in such a situation as threatened to develop. "It's my duty to get you out of this," he agreed; "but, perhaps, without the moon, and in a way you won't appreciate."

"I'm in it for ever, Henry." His hand gripped the shoulder before him. "Nothing can stop us. There's no one to blame."

"You will find plenty to blame you — Ava and Charles, all your world."

"Lavinia is my world," Richard Bale said.

"You're insane," Dalney told him.

"Naturally," Richard assented. "The thing is I am never going to recover. I wouldn't if I could. We are both mad. Why, it happened in a minute. There we were — two separate people with different lives, and then the difference was gone. Up to the moment it happened, nothing was further from my mind. If I had had an hour's warning, Henry, if any suggestion of it had come to me, I would have stopped it. After all, I'm not a seducer of women. Nobody knows better than you that I don't care for them. I always liked lime toddy more. If you can point to anything dishonourable in my past, I'll do whatever you ask." But that he couldn't let stand. "With one exception," he added, bringing his offer to less than nothing.

"You've been honourable enough," Dalney allowed. "I believe the general opinion is that you were a little too exacting, too disagreeably honourable. And the rest you said was true, as well. That's why I am so . . . good God, I don't know what I am or what to tell you."

" It ought to be clear enough."

" Gawin Todd will fight, at last," Henry Dalney asserted. " Certainly Jasper Robine would be his second." That, Richard agreed, had been his opinion. " I can depend on you, then."

" I don't like it, Richard," Dalney insisted. " It's as black as hell. No one will support us. You will lose, even if you are successful, more than you realize."

" I'll gain everything," Bale contradicted him.

" I thought you were in love with Mary Todd," Henry Dalney admitted. " It must have hit you like lightning." He repeated gloomily his remark about bad luck. " Bad for us all." He looked up. " The ideal thing would be to let him hit you." He was visibly relieved. That, he declared, was the perfection of honourable conduct. It was the only course open — to fire in the air and pay fully for the blessing — or the curse — of his passion.

" I am not an idealist," Richard Bale answered shortly; " and firing in the air is forbidden under every circumstance by the code. So far as he touches me, he's only an obstacle. I wish he could be moved out of the way quite differently. On account of Lavinia. Personally, I'd have a shot at him with pleasure." Henry Dalney pointed out that Richard had made that unmistakable at the table, the night before. He rose and, taking out one of the pistols from the case, he inspected it carefully. " A beautiful weapon," he said. " Todd couldn't ask finer. There is this to be decided;" it was clear he had accepted the responsibility Richard Bale asked; "would it be better for me to approach Jasper Robine, not yet as a second, but because he was Gawin Todd's friend? The whole proceeding might be arranged without your seeing Todd. It could be a very regrettable meeting, or even turn into murder."

This, Richard reflected, would be, for him, unexpectedly simple. There was a great deal to be said for it under the formalities of the code of duelling. Nothing would be more improper than a premature difficulty between Gawin and himself. And, as Henry Dalney had indicated, Gawin's conduct was unpredictable. He might easily — as, indeed, he had already threatened — use a stick, or even his bare hands. But, reluctantly, he was forced to give up that particular suggestion:

"I will have to tell him personally, and perhaps Charles, at the same time."

"You are dealing with a woman's name." Henry Dalney inevitably expressed the position already taken by Richard Bale. He continued, as well, with a reference to the fortunate disagreement that gave them a sufficient reason and excuse for all the consequences of a fatal meeting. "It won't be necessary for Gawin Todd to make his charges again," Henry concluded. "Everyone who knows you will believe that you couldn't, finally, swallow his contempt. Then there'd be no need for even Charles to know. A guess, remember, isn't a fact. He'd never be sure."

"It isn't like that," Richard Bale said stubbornly, "I have to take every responsibility for what happens. The situation can be met for Lavinia. If Charles Todd didn't understand the circumstance he wouldn't know how to treat me. He'll have a very definite idea about that. No, he should have an opportunity to speak, to — to do without me in the future."

That, Henry admitted, he had overlooked. "Then there is nothing for us to do to-night. You are shooting well, Richard?"

"I don't need to practise." Richard Bale spoke precisely. "Gawin Todd has hunted a lot with a gun," Dalney commented. "But that's different. The odds are not in favour of a wild turkey. Anyhow, I don't want you to sit up later or talk more. You ought to have coffee in the morning and nothing else. There won't be time or I'd have you empty of food — flat bowels if he happened to rake you there. But, probably, there's nothing but Antigua rum in you now. It's remarkable, Richard, you are so steady; if your hand did shake, no one with you would ever mistake the cause."

*

* *

Waking sharply at the presence of William in his room, Richard Bale had an instant memory and comprehension of what was before him. There was no need for hurry, and so, from minute to minute, he put off getting up. Instead of the sunlight there was a soft rain falling; it sounded on the shingles above him and there was a constant musical drip from a gutter. A tray with coffee William put on a table beside the bed. The tray held hot bread, as well, but he ate nothing. Then slowly he dressed. The servant, watching him with a critical interest, declared that he appeared very gloomy for a gentleman at a party, more like a gospel preacher.

What he had explained to Henry Dalney, Richard reflected — the necessity for Charles Todd to be fully acquainted with the motive of his act — this morning he approved. He would have to get Gawin and Charles Todd together . . . in the office. And, rather than subject their ignorance of what had occurred to any further friendliness, he didn't go to the house for breakfast. He sat again by the window overlooking the garden and, against the cedars at the river's edge, the summerhouse. Suddenly he recalled that he had been there with Lavinia before last evening — earlier in the day; followed by him, she had wandered there and stood confused, at a loss. If only he could have known then what was to follow! Then certainly, at any cost, he could have avoided it all. Even Henry Dalney had been severe, unsympathetic, toward him.

He could never, he realized, explain to anyone or justify what he had done. But, then, he was equally powerless to do this for himself. Richard hadn't — beyond the single and largely unsatisfactory word love — the faintest conception of what had happened to Lavinia and him. A kiss wasn't ordinarily fatal; a woman, naturally, like Lavinia, who was engaged to be married, didn't kiss other men; yet, granted that, she might very reasonably have hidden the memory in her heart — very much the way rose leaves were kept in a pot-pourri — and returned to duty. However, such a course hadn't restrained them for a second. All that had gone before fell away from them like a ribbon dropping from Lavinia's hair. Inconsequential. She hadn't picked it up; she was done with it. Neither had there been any argument or persuasion; no shadow of a question had been cast across their common and inescapable destiny.

Charles Todd went to his office early, Richard knew; the time, he decided, had come for what he was to say. He would first ask Charles to have Gawin called. Deliberately walking down the stairs, he could find no trace of excitement in his bearing or feelings; he wasn't nervous; but he was cloaked by a heavy sorrow as he looked across the lawn of Todd Hundred. It was familiar to him since early childhood, he adored Ava and had an endless affection for Charles; and very soon, some time that day, it would all be closed to him perpetually.

"Richard" — Charles Todd turned his chair from the desk to face him — "what is this about your getting too particular to appear in company? It's an idea of my own, but damned if there isn't some truth in it! I have to remind myself that you are on the plantation."

"I am glad you miss me, Charles," Richard Bale replied. "Perhaps you will again some day, a long time later. Charles," he repeated the name, lingering over it, "there is something I want to say to Gawin and you together, and I'd be obliged if you will send for him."

Charles Todd was obviously surprised, he paused for a moment, with a hand on either arm of his chair, and then he rose, proceeded to the door. "Ask my brother to come to the office," he called to someone invisible to Richard Bale. He returned to where he had been sitting; and, clearly intending to question Richard, he abruptly changed his mind and remained quiet. Gawin Todd reached the office very quickly. "What is it?" he demanded, glancing from one of the two seated men to the other. "Richard has something he wants to say to us." Gawin found a third chair.

"It's at once very hard and easy," Richard Bale told them; "easy because it is so plain and unavoidable, and hard because I can't make you understand it. You will think it is horrible and find me beneath contempt." He paused and drew a deep breath:

"Gawin, Charles — Lavinia and I love each other." His throat was dry but his voice steady. Gawin he watched, and Richard saw flare into his face a shocked and congested anger. Gawin Todd was on his feet. "What was that?" he demanded. "What in hell did you say?" Bale repeated his simple phrase. "But it isn't so! It can't be! They don't know each other." Gawin was interrogating the elder Todd. "I tell you it's a lie and this — this major is still trying to force his fight on me. We'll have him ridden off the plantation backwards." Charles Todd made no reply, he was studying Richard. His face was older, it was more lined, than Richard had remembered. Gawin had crossed the floor, he stood before him:

"Couldn't you arrange it except by a girl's name? There wasn't, really, anything to prevent you from shooting me in the dark. In the back. And though that would have been low, this is lower. Oh, immensely! It's so low in hell I didn't think even you could reach down to it. But I won't fight you; now — and this you didn't allow for — I don't have to. You have killed yourself without my fouling a pistol on you."

"What I have said is true," Richard assured them when Gawin Todd had stopped, breathless. "You can think of it as you please, and call me everything that comes to you, but it must be met."

"Met," Gawin Todd repeated. "Did you suppose we wouldn't meet it? Tell him, Charles, that we'll be able to deal with him."

"Richard," Charles demanded, "is this just as you say it — that you have persuaded Lavinia Roderick to be in love with you?"

That wasn't, Richard Bale silently objected, what he had said; but he kept quiet; it was as good an explanation as could be hit on. "Answer me!" Charles insisted sharply.

"I've told you what happened," he replied, "and I am here for the reason you know — to give you the satisfaction possible."

"I knew it!" Gawin Todd's voice was practically a shout. "It's always been his reputation. By God, we'll have Lavinia here to kill his lying." Charles commanded him to sit down and lower his voice. "Of course, we can do nothing of the sort. Gawin, the pity is that it's not a lie. I don't see any clearer than you how it occurred, but it has. He's right, we must meet it. You'll have to decide, though, about that."

"The mangy hound!" Gawin Todd said. "The kennel nigger! The dirty dropping of a filthy army!" Richard met these terms with a set face. Once his mouth twitched, a hand opened and shut, but nothing more. Gawin would talk . . . for a space . . . and then be still. He was, the other went on, in a series of verbal explosions, a poisoner of women. "You're a coward, that's your secret, why you're always blustering — it's to hide what stinks inside you. But it will be torn out at last. Lavinia loves you! If I thought she had ——"

"Did, Gawin," Charles Todd quietly corrected him.

"I'd see her dead to save her soul," the other finished. "The army rake!" he cried. "The captain of camp whores!"

*

* *

A mocking bird was singing, imitating the limpid notes of a thrush, and nothing could have been more piercingly sweet. The rain had steadily increased; now it fell with an audible cool rush. Charles Todd was speaking again. "You realize, of course, what this means," he addressed Richard. "I have no intention of repeating Gawin's words, but I say to you, Mr. Bale, that I consider your conduct to be utterly debased, and that my family and I can have no further affairs with you. I can't even express a regret at this, you have so utterly outraged our hospitality." Still Richard made no reply; curiously he was more intent on the mocking bird's song than on what Charles was saying. Gawin Todd was about to speak again, but his brother stopped him:

"That's enough for the present, Gawin. What we'll have to discuss now must be private, for the moment. But there will be no delay," he assured Richard Bale.

" I'll have to ask you to act as though nothing had happened for a few hours more. But not, I think you will understand, from any hesitation on our part. The arrangements can't be as simple as you would like."

" Ask him how many people he has talked to already," Gawin Todd added. " He'd be quick to wear this black cockade."

" I have spoken to Mr. Dalney," Richard informed them; " it seemed to be necessary."

" He knew all the time," Gawin declared. " He helped you. He's the same kind."

Richard considered the wisdom of contradicting this, but he decided against it, since it would only serve to multiply words and incriminations. " Control yourself," Charles directed the other Todd. " Mr. Bale —— " He was standing, waiting for him to go, and Richard moved toward the door. " You will find me at my room," he said. He walked bareheaded into the rain, and suddenly, moved by an uncontrollable impulse to get beyond the sound of discordant voices, he continued on beneath the trees, over the lawn. Soon he came to the river, where he halted, watching the raindrops fret the surface of the water. There was a school of diminutive fish under the bank, and wild roses along the grass. But you must bring me oceans more! So far he had brought only trouble, but the future should make up for that. He would make the years to come pay in happiness for the misery of the present. Again and again and again. He stood gazing across the river, lost in thought, dimly conscious of the cool pleasantness of the rain. His clothes lay in a wet film on his shoulders.

What, he wondered, would Gawin say to Lavinia; he hadn't thought of the imminence of that scene; but, certainly, it would take place; probably it was going on now. Gawin Todd would make her suffer, he'd be brutally harsh: Richard was sorry that he hadn't been able to kill him before he saw Lavinia. Still, as he had reflected before, he couldn't hope to keep it all from her, however much he tried. And soon it would be over, it would be over soon.

The rain was running over his face, dripping from his hands; Henry Dalney, in the position before them, wouldn't approve of this; and Richard left the river, proceeded to his room. He could do nothing there but wait for Henry. If he could only send a word to her! William might manage to carry her a note; but, reluctantly, he gave this up — it would be highly incorrect. There was a distant break in the clouds; he saw that, by noon, it might be clear again; this, for the priming of pistols, was fortunate. He had behaved very well in Charles Todd's office: if he had lost control of his temper, resented the unendurable terms he had been called, the right of challenge would have been attached to him, and God knew what conditions and weapons Gawin Todd would choose.

Henry Dalney didn't appear and the time dragged insuperably; he could think of no reason for such a delay; and when, at last, he did come — it was past noon, and the storm was clearing away — he was largely unsatisfactory. The trouble, at first, had been with Jasper Robine:

" Even aside from Todd's attitude, he didn't want to

be drawn into it. He said he disliked it too much — Gawin Todd had evidently given him a very comprehensive account of you — but I showed him that it couldn't be avoided by either of us. After all, our concern wasn't directly with the cause, but with what followed. There could be no doubt about the standing of either of the principals; I mean their right to receive a challenge for such an injury was beyond question. He saw that. And then the difficulty with Gawin began. His hatred of duels is deeper than we thought. But, Richard, he had given up an idea that you were merely trying to get him into one. He had seen Lavinia Roderick. I gathered that."

Richard Bale nodded, with an ugly mouth: "He won't bother her long." Dalney continued:

"One thing developed that, perhaps, you overlooked — Robine assured me that if Gawin finally refused a duel, Charles Todd would take his place."

"But he can't allow that!" Richard Bale instantly protested. He fell silent in the memory of his long affection for Charles, of the years through which, practically, they had had an existence in common — their foxhounds formed a single pack, many of their race horses were owned together; their toddy had been held in one bowl. But all that, as well, he recognized, was swept into nothingness by his love for Lavinia. "There is this to be said for Charles," Henry Dalney proceeded: "he is a far better pistol shot than Gawin."

In that particular, Richard told himself, Charles Todd might be held almost his own equal. "It's bad," Henry commented; "but no one could say where this damned business might reach. You ought to have taken that into consideration, since you insulted all the Todds, dead, living, and to be born. But I can't believe that will go on," he admitted. "Gawin wouldn't kill himself that way. He's in the devil of a state, though. Do you know, Richard, it is in my mind that he thinks a duel would hurt him politically. I almost advised Robine to tell him not to bother about the future because his politics was about to be decided for him. Naturally I didn't."

"Well," Richard Bale demanded, "what am I to do now?"

"Nothing, absolutely. They insist that not a suspicion of the reason for this must ever be public. Only the two Todds, Robine, myself and you know the truth. Yes, and Lavinia. That was unnecessary, really, but Gawin lost his head with her. Yet it's certain she would have guessed. Jasper Robine is to see me after dinner. You are to go in to the table and it will be said that Gawin was called to the courthouse for a couple of hours."

When the bell rang for dinner, Richard Bale, his clothes changed, went rigidly into the dining room. After all, he realized, choosing his place, he would be unable to wear the tightly buttoned black coat. Its appearance was permanently ruined. It was necessary for him to present himself, on such an occasion, in the utmost nicety of dress, an appearance matching an ordered and determined calm.

Mary Todd was across from him, and she gave him a questioning smile. It had been in a world lost before this one was made that he had considered marrying her. How very pretty she was! Everyone was present but Gawin and Lavinia. Lavinia, Ava explained, had a slight headache, and Gawin was forced to go to the courthouse . . . he'd be back soon. Richard was glad, in a way, that Lavinia was absent; it spared her an unnecessary wretchedness and strain; nothing actually tried him; deliberately, with Henry Dalney's cautioning gaze on him, he made a pretence of eating.

*

*   *

Jasper Robine, engaged with the white figs of Todd Hundred, was occupied in his own thought; he spoke with an entire adequate courtesy to Richard, and then returned to his self-absorption. His dress, too, was sombre. Charles Todd was remote in manner and brief in speech: he had managed, Richard saw, to avoid noticing him, in what seemed a wholly natural manner. Ava, of course, had heard nothing, and several times she looked speculatively — obviously wondering about him — at her husband. She was, she finally declared, worried about the fate of her party, it had grown so gloomy. Didn't anyone like it? Charles Todd, with an effort at lightness, assured her that all the fiddle strings and satin slippers had been worn out.

"We'll get more from London," she replied.

"You'd better not let Gawin hear that," Bradlock Wiatt informed her; "he thinks we've had too much from England now; he's afraid his plain Western friends will have to pay for it."

" If the British sent back some of the servants they stole, we could have some more satin breeches," Henry Dalney asserted. Wiatt asked Richard if, after dinner, he would play whist. " No whist, to-day," Richard answered. He gave a slight emphasis to the word to-day for the benefit of Robine and Charles Todd. The former gave him a quick and unfavourable glance. " Not to-day," he was, it appeared, merely repeating Bale's words; " and to-morrow belongs to no one." Richard leaned forward: " I'll promise myself to you for whist to-morrow evening . . . at any stake."

" I have played in Russia for twenty pounds a point," Jasper Robine said to them generally, " but it was with very rich men. The limit with gambling ought to be easily inside the resources of payment. Thank you, Mr. Bale, but we won't decide the game so far ahead. It's possible one of us might have to leave earlier."

That, Richard Bale told himself, was very well expressed; compared to Robine, he was a clumsy talker; it would be wiser not to encounter him, not, at least, with words. For example — he didn't know whether Jasper Robine had insulted him or not. Certainly, his means of payment, the sums he chose to play for, were no one's concern but his own. It was his privilege to ruin himself by chance, by love, with Antigua rum, exactly as he preferred. However, the thought of Lavinia swept all that from his mind; he was thoroughly displeased with his fault-finding character. If this kept up he would find that some of the terms Gawin Todd had applied to him were justified.

He didn't want to fight, he told himself, but to live

in quiet happiness with Lavinia at Balisand. The first thing he'd do would be to put a roof over the end of the wharf, and then it would almost precisely resemble the spot at Todd Hundred where he had first talked to her. The interior of the house Lavinia would refurnish, change on the surface, as she liked, since fundamental change at Balisand was an impossibility . . . both in the house and in the Bales. Their inner qualities were fixed. For better or for worse. That, he recognized, was a phrase in the marriage service:

How fortunate it would have been if he could have seen Lavinia before Gawin Todd met her. Girls loved the music and wine and excitement of a formal wedding; that, with them, would be lost, for he was determined to marry Lavinia at the first possible chance. No one, Richard decided, would question his motives or doubt the explanation of the duel made by the Todds and him. Unless she wanted very much to travel, they would immediately return home. Trenton and Philadelphia, or New York, would come later, in October, when he went to the Congress . . . with Lavinia. There it would be very gay, and he'd insist on her going out a great deal. Richard wanted the world to see her young loveliness and realize her charm. He was inordinately proud of her, of his Lavinia, Lavinia Bale.

Once more dinner was at an end, the women had gone, and the rum was circulating on the bare polished board. He had fulfilled his obligation to be present, Richard considered: it would be better for him to go, to put no additional charge on Charles Todd's forced hospitality. He rose and bowed to the company, and, with Henry

Dalney, left the room. "It has cleared," he observed. Dalney repeated his own conclusion about a weather suitable to their purpose. "Late this afternoon." This was an opinion without exact assurance. "Damn it, Richard, he can't refuse us. I suppose you'll go back to the schoolhouse. Well, I'll stay and see Robine. I understand Gawin is on the place. This secrecy and the people here and the circumstances make our arrangements very difficult — Jasper Robine insists on the nicest form."

He had hardly mounted to his room before William appeared with a message from Ava — she wanted to see him at once. This was the devil of a situation, and he weighed sending her word that he couldn't come. Ava had guessed there was trouble; Charles, of course, would refuse to satisfy her; and she'd demand some part of the truth from him. To Ava — who probably already considered him promised to Mary — his conduct would appear no less than insane. But perhaps, in telling her that he was unable to ask Mary to marry him, he would keep her from the subject of his trouble with Gawin Todd. Anyhow, he'd have to see her, and return Ava's great goodness to him with lies. Then there was the other difficulty of accounting reasonably to her for his rapid change of mind. He must protect Lavinia:

He was on the covered way from the kitchen to the house, and he turned to the right, to a door which led into the pantry where she was waiting. "Richard," she demanded at once, "what is it?"

"What, Ava?" He tried, he felt, without success, to make his voice innocently surprised.

"I don't know. That's why I sent for you. I told Charles I would, and I have, although he positively commanded me not to. Commanded, Richard; you'll understand what that means with Charles. Somehow I got the impression from him that a ridiculous argument you had at the table with Gawin has gone on. But, Richard, I can't believe that, with Gawin just engaged and you interested in Mary. It is so senseless and childish." Suddenly he had hit on an explanation of his failure with Mary. It, too, was a lie, but that couldn't be avoided:

"Ava, you must realize that if Charles isn't ready to talk to you yet that I can't. But I'll say this — if you ask him he will tell you that there is no question of his letting Mary marry me. He won't hear of it."

"Richard!" Her tone and face were painfully shocked. "What stupidity! After all, he owes me a little. I won't let him interfere."

"I am afraid you will have to," he said gently, filled with his admiration for her.

"Then Gawin and you are going to fight."

Richard was silent, though that was as significant as a direct affirmation. The colour sank from her face, and she clasped her hands tightly. "It's you," she said, in a voice scarcely above a whisper. "There is something terrible about you. I loved you, but I have known it always, and I thought love and marriage and happiness would kill it." Well, he told himself, it would. "Then this is your honour and the reputation of the Bales —

that you will shoot Gawin out of nothing but your vanity, at any cost to us. At first I thought it couldn't be so, that the real reason, whatever the trouble was, had been kept from me. I didn't think you'd be capable of such cruel brutality. And I asked Mary to care for you." She moved away from him, her hands held behind her.

*

* *

After an uncomfortable pause he concluded, aloud, that he had better go. "Yes, you had better go," she echoed him, but her voice took on a note of doubt, a hesitation like a query. The sun was fully out, the air was soft and heavy with the odour of the banked roses. Time, in his room, passed slowly; but he tempered himself against impatience. Soon, now, it would be over. Once more seated at the window, above the bright colours of the garden, he reflected on the fondness for flowers that was such an anomaly in him. He always, but without special knowledge, noticed them; their scents gave him a profound pleasure. Yet, in spite of this, he had allowed the garden at Balisand to fall into a state of neglect . . . and that, too, Lavina would cure. In battle, his thoughts and memories proceeded, whenever it was possible, he had worn a green or blossoming sprig in his coat; he had come to regard it as a charm; and now it had changed into — what was Bradlock Wiatt's phrase? — the loveliest flower of Henrico County.

When Henry Dalney appeared, the sunlight had become a level golden flood, there were long luminous shadows falling on the white latticed summerhouse. "It's arranged," he said at once. "Gawin Todd was forced to agree to a meeting. But he is very bitter about it. Robine told me that it must be final. That may mean a number of shots: we'll finish the cartel to-night. But the time and the spot are fixed, very early to-morrow morning, back of Eagle Point, in a little field between the Point and Severnby. You can leave details like the distance to me. I'll say this for Gawin Todd, though — his objection to duelling was not because he was afraid of your reputation for coolness and as a shot. You'll find him adequate."

"The Todds aren't cowards," Richard commented. "Then, of course, he challenged?"

"Yes, and Jasper Robine wants to examine your pistols. I told him that they belonged to your family, and that you had never fought with them. It's my belief that Gawin has a right to try the set triggers."

"Take them with you," Richard Bale directed; "you will see about the charging. I suppose we'll have to go through with supper again."

"Naturally. Robine said that both Charles and Gawin would be there. He didn't mention Ava. I passed her at the office just now but she didn't see me. I thought it might have been on purpose. Somehow, women know things." He had the pistols out, side by side on the table. "There isn't a grain of difference," he asserted; "Jasper Robine will be delighted with them." He put the pistols away and stood with the box under his arm. "It isn't good for you to sit here and stare out the window," he added. "If I order a horse, will you ride?"

Richard replied that he wouldn't. "I'm not uneasy," he explained; "I haven't any nerves. It's that I like my thoughts."

He ought, he decided, to give some attention to what would happen if, against all his conviction, he were killed. Should, for example, certain of his servants be freed? There was London — but the Virginia law that made free negroes leave the State would be a greater hardship to London than the hardest service at home. Balisand was as much his home as it was Richard's. No, he could stay with the place — Henry Dalney must be informed of that. Yet it was unnecessary. He would kill Gawin Todd. Then he saw Lavinia; she was in the garden, on the grass by the cedars and river. She stood and gazed toward the schoolhouse; but he realized that the sun was in her eyes; she could see nothing. She wasn't as erect as usual, he made that out; her shoulders had a droop of weariness; her head, when she turned away, was down. An air of discouragement pervaded her.

Richard watched her with a passionate longing to be at her side; her oppression bred an immense tenderness in him; he was possessed by the tyrannical need to reassure her, to touch her hand . . . nothing more. She was beside the summerhouse now, and after a questioning regard, suspended in motion — almost, he thought, in breathing — she went inside. Very softly he cursed Gawin Todd. The honeysuckle hid her from him; for a long while she stayed out of sight; and then, suddenly reappearing, she went so rapidly toward the house that she was practically running.

"Lavinia!" he cried, on his feet in an agony of love and pity. "Lavinia!" But no one, fortunately, heard him. The only answering sound came monotonously from pigeons on the roof. Steps, later, mounting to his door proved to be those of William, whose expressed opinion it was that the time had come to dress for the evening. He would never own William, that was certain. No one else had ever shaved him so well. There had been another chicken fight, William informed him; and Stilley, the servant, so adept at gouging, whose rooster had been killed by the bird from Gloucester Point, had been set upon in the dusk, at the land entrance to Todd Hundred, and beaten into a red insensibility. William was certain that he would never again be useful in the fields. "Or in any other place. Nobody at the great house would want him around." He concluded that Fayson would patch him up and sell him at the courthouse. All the while he talked, he was putting the gold buttons in a waistcoat. He finished that, and was bowed over Richard's shoes, when he added he had heard, in the kitchen, that there was some trouble among the gentlemen at supper the other night. The negroes, Richard Bale recognized, knew everything that went on in all the departments of the plantation.

"Between Mr. Gawin Todd and me?" he asked directly. William glanced at him obliquely:

"Yes, sir, that was it. There was talk that you were going to fight and kill each other. The girl who came with Miss Lavinia — she's a light Richmond nigger — she was crying, so I judge Miss Lavinia knew about it."

"Mr. Todd and I had a difference over General Washington," Richard instructed him; "and it is possible there will be a meeting. Don't spread it around if you can help it, but if you can't, then remember it grew out of politics."

"Yes, sir, yes, sir," William repeated readily. He declared that the causes of gentlemen's troubles didn't rightly bother him. He stayed clear away from such fractious subjects. But, he was impelled to add, Mr. Gawin Todd was a bad man when he was mad. "Yes, sir." That phrase ran through all William's conversation like the ticking of a clock. However, he doubted if even Mr. Todd's badness would frighten an army gentleman, after so much shooting with cannons. In answer to all this, Richard Bale decided there was one thing which, with a semblance of propriety, he might do. "William," he said, "come here to the window. Do you see that bush of yellow roses? Well, I want you to pick one and give it to that pale Richmond girl for Miss Lavinia. No message. You are not to say where it came from . . . just the yellow rose for Miss Lavinia. She'll be in her room now, dressing." It was exactly the errand that a negro could best accomplish.

"You can leave me, I'm ready. And William, you are to have the gold buttons you put in for me. I'll write you a paper saying they were a gift from me because — because you were such an excellent servant." He watched from the window and saw William swiftly, with an instinctive caution, gather a yellow rose. He had, perhaps, exceeded the bounds of a flawless discretion; both Jasper Robine and Henry would have condemned him, but he didn't care. A rose . . . I send to you. Lavinia would know where it came from. She would carry it to Balisand, he thought. A memento. And to-night it would be either at her breast or in her hair.

*

* *

Richard Bale found most of the company at Todd Hundred in the hall, gathered and waiting without hurry for supper. Beverley Mathews, who had returned to Welfield, was again present, but evidently he had left Lucia home. Eliza Wiatt and Rose Ann Marable were talking together; Gawin and Charles Todd stood together at the foot of the steep circular staircase; Robine was with Mary, Delia and Sally; they were laughing a great deal; and Bradlock Wiatt was addressing Mathews in a manner that showed already the influence of the toddy bowl. As he was gazing over the hall from the doorway, Ava came down the stairs, and the sweeping turn from the landing on the second floor admirably showed the dignity of her carriage in an elaborate dress and pearls. Never had Richard seen in her a more impressive and handsome bearing; but her manner was cold, she showed no impulse to speak to anyone but Charles Todd; and then, in a clear measured voice, she merely explained that Lavinia had been delayed. "She will be down in a very few minutes," she ended.

The assembled party remained broken up into very definitely separated groups, and Richard hesitated before becoming a part of any one. At last, avoiding Wiatt's stupid reiterations and the small circle that included

Jasper Robine, he moved up to Eliza Wiatt and Rose Ann. " I am too young to listen to you, of course," he proclaimed; " and you ought to send me away at once, but I won't go." They said in chorus that it was miraculous having him with them. " With such a superior attraction close by," Eliza added. " He will come back to us later." This obscure flippancy proceeded from Rose Ann Marable. Richard Bale felt at a loss with her. Usually, in the women he encountered, there were certain recognized limits within which their comments ranged, there was a prescribed course for their pleasantries or indifference; but no one could be sure of what Rose Ann might say. She was looking at him now, with her impudently direct gaze; the absurd tilt to her short nose, that as much as anything spoiled her appearance for him, emphasized; and only God knew what her thought was. He asked her, with a satirical intent, if she had shared the toddy bowl with Bradlock, but she replied that she didn't like drinks with fruit and sugar in them. " I'd rather have Madeira or brandy," she admitted as simply as though she were choosing between a number of perfumes. Richard had never seen a woman of any pretensions drink brandy, and — but privately — he was very severe in his judgment of Ava's sister. If that was the habit on the James and Rappahannock, then so much the worse for those rivers. " It's still so Arcadian in Gloucester County," she went on.

He begged her to remember that the Tidewater was the oldest and most aristocratic part of Virginia. Such was the tradition, she agreed; but she mentioned the fact that, like everything else, aristocracy changed. " Even the minuet has become a little old-fashioned," she declared. However, that he dismissed as nonsense. "What do you mean by aristocracy?" he stiffly demanded. "The people at dinner," she answered inconsequentially. She was totally lacking in warmth, he discovered; her brilliancy resembled sunlight reflected on a windowpane — it seemed to have an actual flashing light, but it was no more than the glitter of glass. Richard infinitely preferred Eliza Wiatt, who said little and who was so satisfying to see.

Yet, compared with the vividness of Lavinia, Eliza was inert and meaningless; her charm was almost a mechanical device, or it was like a magnet, a mere force of attraction that had no individual poignant charm or meaning. The beauty in Lavinia was personal, inseparable, unthinkable, away from her; it lay in her every gesture, all the intonations of her voice, in the suspense of her pauses; and then her sheer young grace was matchless, the rare perfection of life for once in an equal loveliness of — of body. His thought of her body was without willingness, as though it were still a trespass against her inviolable purity.

"Richard doesn't like us," Eliza Wiatt announced. Rose Ann made a gesture toward Mary Todd. "But I told you," she said lazily; "wait."

"Then you think it's impossible to always love one woman?" Richard Bale couldn't suppress the temptation to ask that. "It has been done," Rose Ann replied; "but that was in the days of romance. Not in the present."

"I am sure to-day is as romantic as any of the past,"

Eliza insisted. "I'm glad it isn't more, because I couldn't stand it."

"She is thinking about the lost Mr. Garret," Rose Ann decided. Eliza Wiatt admitted that he was a part of it. "He was so desperate and he made such touching speeches about the desert of the future and a lot of things I didn't understand."

"Heavens, you don't think he'll go on loving you, do you?" Rose Ann laughed at her. "In a year he will be married to a pious Methodist and have a child every year for a generation." She grew increasingly outrageous, Richard considered. "Let him marry his Methodist," Eliza returned; "but he'll never forget me."

Again, Richard Bale wondered if that were true: he had a vision of Garret after a number of years, with some of the children Rose Ann had so indelicately mentioned, and a shapeless wife. Would then the memory of Eliza Wiatt, slender and tall and charming, come back to torment him with an old passion? But that he didn't put into words; it was an inquiry hidden in his subconsciousness, private to himself. "I'm starved," Rose Ann Marable admitted; "I wish Lavinia Roderick would finish dressing and appear." It wasn't necessary for her, Eliza added, to take so much trouble with herself.

"Now that she has been successful."

Richard stared disagreeably at Rose Ann. Women were allowed an inexcusable liberty in talk; it was a good thing that there were restrictions on the remarks of men; such, for example, as the pair of pistols, bushed with gold, that Henry Dalney had carried away. As he was thinking about him Henry came in; he was hurried and apologetic in manner; and Richard saw that there were stains of ink on his fingers. The cartel!

There was a faint stir from above, and he looked up . . . Lavinia was almost upon the stairs. The landing was dimly lighted, and he saw her features, her expression, the way her hands rested, by instinct rather than in reality. She hesitated, and the low tone of her voice, singing, drifted down to him:

> . . . I send to you.
> But you must bring me oceans more,
> Be true——

Richard Bale was dazed by his love for her. There was a blinding flash, like sunlight, in his eyes, and then he realized that the song had broken off with a sudden startled cry. He looked up and saw that, tripped perhaps by the flounces of her skirt, she was falling. She was plunging swiftly down; yet, in spite of the speed of her descent, every detail of her dress, her loosened hair, her bare arms, was pitilessly exact. She seemed to be suspended in air; then her body struck the central column of the steps; there was another and even swifter and jagged fall; and he heard the back of her head strike upon the oak flooring of the hall.

There was an instantaneous and absolute hush of sound, and, immediately after, a panic of voices. That was followed by a rush forward, stopped at the short commanding tones of Charles Todd. But Richard hadn't moved — he knew something that was yet hidden from the others. He realized it with a searing completeness which stripped him of all sight and other conscious being. Lavinia was dead. It was useless to send for hot water or to press anyone back so that she would be able to breathe. His hands caught together and his fingers interlaced; he looked up at the empty landing.

*

* *

There was a dragging at his shoulder — it was Henry Dalney. "You must get out of here," Henry said, and he half pushed Richard Bale out to the portico. But there he halted, undecided. "It might be better for you to stay. No —— " he returned to his first impulse: "there will be a confusion, and you won't be considered, or they'll think — you are not the family — that you were right going." Richard didn't answer him, he was incapable of speech; and Dalney conducted him down the stone steps and along the bricked walk to the schoolhouse. Then they were in his room.

"I'll go back at once," Henry told him, "and let you know as soon as possible. It was a terrible fall . . . full on the floor."

"Lavinia? She is dead," Richard assured him. He was at the window again, above the garden drooping with dusk, with the summerhouse before him. He repeated that final word, and he at once comprehended it and was totally unable to take in all its implications. Henry Dalney, he discovered, had gone. The greater part of his mind, yes, and his body, was numb: his hands were at once wet and cold; when he drew one across his eyes, in an effort to clear his sight, he had the sensation that it was a damp cloth. A feeling of shocked amazement possessed him, nothing more. He had seen Lavinia pitching downward through space, he knew that she had been killed; but those facts wouldn't form a whole, the sum of their horror he couldn't contain.

He moved slightly; his legs seemed to be wooden, his heels struck with a sound unrelated to his body. A wave of physical sickness, of nausea, swept over him. That was succeeded by a chill; he tried to stop it, to control his nerves; but he shook in a tremor that he thought must stir the room. This didn't stop. It went on and on, and he bit his lower lip until his chin was smeared with blood. He found it on his hands and transferred it in bright prints to the white-painted window ledge. All that he did was mechanical; he was, now, like a shape of tin which held an intolerable and agonizing fire. Henry Dalney returned, he stood silent while Richard Bale turned haggardly:

"Yes," he said, "she is dead. It killed her instantly. How in God's world —— "

"God's world," Richard curiously interrupted him, "God's world?"

"How it happened so quickly and fatally I can't understand," he finished his period. "No one can. It was fortunate I got you out of there when I did. Richard, you'll have to be reasonable until you are at Balisand again."

"I'll be reasonable," Bale agreed. "What does it matter who is or isn't? Henry, it was in the middle of a song. Did you hear her singing? It ends, But you must bring me oceans more. Be true. Be true. I only knew one verse. Goddamn it, why did I say that! With this —— "

"There is something else I am forced to remind you of," Henry Dalney proceeded; "it's necessary for someone to keep his head. What about Gawin and you? I couldn't find Robine, but I'll see him at once."

"It was politics," Richard reminded him: "do you think that will matter to Gawin Todd for a little? But you're right; we have his challenge; he may hate me worse than death. It's such a strange situation, Henry; here is Lavinia killed and Gawin and me — me and Gawin —— " his voice trailed into silence. "She was delicate." He spoke after a silence of laboured breathing. "Her head. On the oak floor. No one could catch her, it was so hellish sudden. You must have seen her on the landing, I mean when she was singing. I looked away, just for a second, and then she was gone. I don't think she could have suffered, but there was time for her to be frightened; you see, she did cry." Henry Dalney replied by saying that he'd send William up with rum. "Take the stiffest drink you can manage," he advised Richard. "Robine will have to stay until to-morrow, but we'll go home to-night. You came by the river but I suppose you will have to ride back. I don't think Charles Todd can object to your taking a horse. Anyhow, I won't ask."

He was gone again, with a quick agitated step, and the silence, the dimness, of evening, gathered in the room. Lavinia was dead, Richard Bale said to himself. Slowly this reality was being borne upon him; he was beginning to understand it. A frightful accident, that had nothing to do with Gawin Todd, had taken her away from him. She had already left Todd. Waiting, ready, to come to Balisand. He'd never know what she intended to say to him in the summerhouse. "Richard ——" he repeated aloud her broken phrase. Words that couldn't be finished. Words stopped by death. Yes, that was the end of the endless things they had had to say to each other. He had sent her away, then. "I wanted to save her!" he cried in a choked voice. "With so many people and Gawin Todd and Rose Ann. Not to go, Lavinia! Never to leave me!" That rang in his head as though the actual sounds had been thrown back from a wall. Never to leave me! Never to leave! The room darkened, and slowly, methodically, he lighted both the candles on the chest of drawers. Hung drying on a chair was the black coat wetted by the morning rain. William was a good servant and careful of his things.

Then it came back to him that Lavinia was dead — her beautiful youngness, her air of the absent-minded, her singing, was over, crushed out of being. And Henry Dalney had spoken of God's world. He laughed in a rasping contempt. How could anyone believe that now, ever again? "It's a lie," he asserted loudly; "a damned cold lie." Lavinia had been so warm, so richly alive. He started to curse God, but he was interrupted by the sense of its uselessness. There was nothing to curse, he had just discovered that. A joke. He had seen so many people die, black with cold or swollen with heat, shot and hacked out of all resemblance to humanity, that it occurred to him he might be steadier. But this was Lavinia. Lavinia. She was this; not Gawin Todd's; not death's.

A stir rose at the door, and, to his amazement, Gawin Todd accompanied by Charles, Jasper Robine and Henry, moved forward in a compact mass. "Mr. Bale," Charles spoke for them, "this will appear heartless in the face of what has happened; but it's Mr. Robine's judgment and mine that it was necessary. Miss Roderick has been taken from all that concerns us and it remains for us to keep whatever secret was in her heart. Your affair with my brother will not be followed a step farther by us. There is nothing else, I think, for us to say to you."

"Yes," Gawin Todd stepped forward, "you spoiled her life for her and her death for me. That ought to console you. But you lost her, and I'm glad. If you didn't understand what Charles said, it is this: never repeat Miss Roderick's name in public. If you do I will see that you are shot, out of your saddle or on the river or in the woods. Not a duel, an execution."

It was, it seemed to Richard Bale, all such a useless clamour. "Perhaps I lost her," he said, but more to himself than the others. "Of course, she's dead, but do you know what that means?" He was gazing at Henry Dalney. Then he collected himself. "It's enough to answer you, Charles, and you don't need an answer." People came and went so illogically; once more he was alone. He had been standing for a very long while; sharply, through its numbness, the old ache in his right leg recommenced, and he found a chair. The same mocking bird. A lilybud. His stomach contracted into a stone and tore its way up through his body to his throat. It was a sob. His head drooped on his arm, lying across the back of the chair, and his body was shaken with a gasping, dry grief.

II

PAST the middle of April, after a week of cold thin rain drenching the new white flowers of the fringe trees and dogwoods, there was a morning so still and warm with sun that Richard Bale lingered sitting over his breakfast in the dining room at Balisand. The only sound that came to him was the restless shifting of Diggery, the horse he usually rode, tied to the rack in front of the house. Diggery's hoofs struck sharply into the earth from which years of such trampling had cut away all the turf. Four foxhounds from his pack of six couples lay on the floor close beside him; their tongues were out, they were all watching him, and, whenever he moved, there was an answering beat on the oak floor from wagging tails. Perhaps half an hour before, Mrs. Patton had left the table to order and watch the affairs of the household. It was well enough, she had declared, for Mr. Bale to idle, since gentlemen had nothing in the world to do but ride over their plantations and talk all day, and drink and play hazard or whist all night.

There was a great deal of truth in this, Richard reflected; but there was a necessity, a responsibility, in such idleness that Mrs. Patton missed: he was, in a considerable way, the plantation itself, Richard Bale of Balisand. Without the weight of his authority, the force and prestige of his inheritance, the place would soon fall apart. The first Richard Bale in America had, in 1652, cut down the trees where the house was to stand and cleared the underbrush from the lawn; and, throughout the years that had followed, there had been a Bale in the direct masculine succession to maintain the unity, the integrity, of their home.

From where he sat, with the North River visible through the windows at his left, he could see the portrait of Richard Bale, the Cavalier, hung on the high dark panelling of the north wall. It had been painted in England, probably not long before the beheading of Charles I, for it showed its original to be already marked by the struggle which, fatal to the Stuarts, had ended for him in flight to the Colony of Virginia. Yet, in the portrait, he was young: he had been thirty when, after the final defeat at Worcester, he had sailed for America; Charles had gone to the scaffold in 1649 . . . he had been painted at twenty-six or twenty-seven years of age.

He wore a short jacket open for a drooping collar of lace, its strings tied at a gold ring; his loose breeches were ornamented by points of coloured ribbons; and his hair swept his shoulders in a careful disorder, a love-lock tied with a bow of blue. There was a full light on a thin face wrought, with the exception of his lips, by war into an expression of implacable determination. His mouth, however, had preserved the slightly sullen contours of the ease and petulant luxury of court life. But that hadn't affected his ability to found an honourable house in what was, generally, a primitive land. Immediately on his arrival at the Colony, he had met and married Lydia Morryson of Elizabeth City, who belonged to a family already established and important in Virginia; a family of soldiers — Richard Morryson had commanded the fort at Point Comfort — and at once they had made the foundations of all that Balisand became.

This, of course, was assisted by the fact that they hadn't lacked resources. Richard had brought a thousand pounds from England, a considerable sum then, and the Morrysons had both money and the influence of position. Soon even a large degree of the old luxury, but limited, naturally, to a few scattered plantations, had been possible; and the life they constructed followed, in its essential form and obligations, that which, in body but not spirit, they had left. Their son, Francis — the other children were girls — had been born in 1653:

It was that Francis who, it was evident, had not been in agreement with the wide opposition to Governor Berkeley which resulted in the rebellion of the younger Bacon. The freedom of the Colony under the English Commonwealth had bred a resentment to the Crown, against which the Bales of Balisand would have been arraigned by every personal and inherited quality. Francis Bale, certainly, had supported Berkeley throughout his long-disputed career in Virginia. He had been with him in the vain defence of Jamestown; and, when it was burned, accompanied the governor on his retreat to the eastern shore of the Chesapeake. It was said, too, that he had publicly asserted the necessity of the many executions which had followed Bacon's death and the defeat of his men. In 1680 he married Camilla Scarborough.

That was a marriage as fortunate in its happiness and connections as his father's: he settled into a distinguished and uneventful existence as a landed gentleman; and his third child and first son was, again, Richard Bale. For his part, in 1706, at seventeen years of age, he married Eveline Heyman, who was notably beautiful and a niece of the Peter Heyman, Collector of the Lower James River, who, humorously enough, had been killed on the vessel Shoreham in an engagement with a pirate, where he had gone as no more than a spectator.

This Richard, entering an imported horse, Rattle, against the celebrated Tryall and Colonel Taylor's Jenny Cameron in 1752, established the racing stable at Balisand. His first son, Morryson Bale, had never married, and now, in his seventy-seventh year, he was the companion of Richard, delaying at the breakfast table and thoughtfully studying the portrait of his ancestor. And his father, finally, the second son of Richard and Eveline Bale, again Francis, had been born in 1713 and put off marriage until forty, when he was wedded to Celia Tucker, but only to have her die at the birth of their child.

His life would have been different, the house at Balisand would be very different, if his mother had lived. Through his memory it had been a bare masculine place hardly tempered by a succession of housekeepers, paid or of the family. In that long train Mrs. Patton was immeasurably the best; yet she had been powerless, as at intervals he had noted, to soften the metal of the Bale existence. Still, her energy, her ambitions, were undiminished: probably at that minute she was attending to the comfort of Morryson Bale, who didn't appear until well toward noon.

Richard was very accurate in the memories and dates, the genealogical and personal facts, of his family; both because they had always engaged his pleasure and had seemed, other than as facts alone, to be extraordinarily present in him. He felt that he was a living repository of all that the Bales had been and must be; and toward this he kept a sense of importance together with a rigorously maintained responsibility; he accepted it all as inescapable, the good with the not so good, and made no conscious effort — it never occurred to him that it might be needful — to change and improve his nature or disposition.

He had had pancakes for breakfast, and one, he saw, was left — in the act of leaning forward there was a battery of thumping tails on the floor, and, with the pancake in his fingers, the foxhounds were riotously shouldering his knees. Richard Bale broke the cake into equal parts; but, in the lurchings that followed, a fight began between a hound named Bombo and another, Fife. He watched their vicious struggle for a little; with no intention of having either injured for fox hunting, he soon beat them apart. Suddenly impatient Richard drove the hounds into the hall; there the doors stood open to the lawn, and, from a window, he watched them stream across the grass. They set his horse, Diggery, into a fresh stamping and pulling at the halter. Diggery, the best race horse he had ever owned! His last race had been against Ancaster Stirling, owned by Bradlock Wiatt; Diggery had won — after setting a tremendous pace in the final, a four-mile, heat — but, Richard judged, at too great a charge upon his courage and endurance. However, in the three years before that, he had made close to five thousand pounds for the Bale stable.

*

* *

Time went that way, in an ebb like the North River returning to the sea; why, Charles Todd had been dead for more than a year! The fox hunt that, in effect, had killed him was in January, 1792, and it was now 'ninety-three. Charles had been thrown and, wandering half dazed in a frozen swamp, was discovered too late to be ever brought back to warmth again. A year and three months already; and it was nine years but a few weeks since Lavinia had — had died at Todd Hundred. He shrank from that fatal moment in a physical and mental pain which time, it began to appear, was powerless to dull. He ought to recover from that, he told himself — this had become a familiar admonition with him — and resolutely he put from his mind all thought of the past.

Instead, he began again to reflect on the curious and unpredictable situation then, specially connected with the foreign world, occupied by the United States. This wasn't, with Richard Bale, an abstract or political question, for, precisely to the degree that it affected the country, it formed and influenced him. Nothing more difficult, where he was concerned, could have been imagined: in effect, he had to choose an alliance either with French ideas or English principles. The problem of the

United States was presented to him in that sole alternative. Gloucester County was remote from the great world of Philadelphia and Boston and New York, news reached it but slowly; yet, in the present excitement and unrest, there were wide swift currents of rumours, of passions and fears, that bore with them an unparalleled circulation of facts.

He had heard, for example, almost immediately, of the landing of Genêt, the new Envoy from the States-General of republican France; and, though in that respect the Tidewater had been more conservative than the reports showed the rest of the country to be, there had been a flare, like that of a great fat pine fire, of enthusiasm for the triumph of the principle of freedom. The whole progress of the French Revolution, Richard remembered, had been followed in America with a natural intentness and approval. He had been, at first, one with this; but, at the execution of Louis XVI, the frenzied brutal murder which followed, doubts entered his complacent acceptance of the admirable similitude between the cases of France and the United States.

He was sure of this, however, that the Proclamation of Neutrality issued by Washington on the day Genêt had appeared was a necessary and heroic act. No one, he thought, had any conception of a separate and honourable unity for the States except the General. The neutrality, with the training of his military years and Federal convictions, he embraced; and he regarded with amazement and detestation the almost universal and wholly hysterical cry raised against the President; but the problems connected with that and the nation — if one could be said to exist — with himself, were far more involved:

He was, by tradition of family and old ties of blood, sympathetic with England. Nevertheless, he had, throughout the Revolution, fought the British with all the burning energy he could command. That had shown him, if it were further required, that he was, fundamentally, American; or rather, as he would have put it at the time, a Virginian. Richard had struggled for an independence from England; life had become unthinkable under all other terms; and such a liberty he had helped to win. That, too, was clear. He remembered, now, the indispensable services of France in the struggle of the American States for a sovereignty in common or divided; the memory of French officers of the highest courage and unselfishness filled him with admiration and gratitude. Without them, without their devotion and the money they had brought, it was conceivable that England would have been victorious ——

And that gave him what was, undoubtedly, an ungrateful thought: to what extent had just such a possible English defeat moved Louis XVI? Had he sent assistance to a cause of justice, or was it no more than a part of his policy in Europe? However, his forces had come, his best soldiers had fought shoulder to shoulder with Richard Bale; and the King himself had paid the last price of human fallibility. He was gone, his court and civilization were swept away in blood, and the States-General, the people, ruled in his place.

All that, of course, had been reflected, no, eagerly swallowed, by the United States. Mr. Jefferson, after his five years in France, had returned with an enormous enthusiasm for the French Republic, and this he had insistently spread. He was the head of the French spirit, the French party, really, in America; and that in itself, for Richard, served as a warning. It was Hamilton who had urged neutrality on the President, and, as usual, Jefferson opposed him with his customary obstructionist doctrines. Jefferson had declared that such a proclamation lay outside the powers of the executive but belonged to Congress, and he advised delay.

That was no more, everyone knew, than an attack on the President; and a deep pleasure, an increased affection and confidence, had possessed Richard Bale at the firm superiority of Washington. Genêt, certainly, had made a fool of himself; his conduct was small recommendation for the purpose he served. He had, for instance, been guilty of absolute impropriety, of insolence to the government, in making the French consuls at Charleston into prize courts, and fitting out there, with South Carolina men and supplies, two privateers. He had justified this, inevitably, by loud references to the 1778 Treaty with France, he had wept over the common cause of the people of France and the United States. But that treaty had been with the Monarchy and not with a set of savages in ridiculous caps with a new and bastard cockade.

Genêt was now on his way North, to present, at such a late hour, his credentials to Washington; but meanwhile he acted with every circumstance of an accredited ambassador. Yet this, Richard was forced to admit, had been thrust on him; the public, it appeared, had gone stark mad in their acceptance of everything that was French. And that alone had held Richard Bale away — he had little respect or liking for public opinion or the mass of the people. He avoided them and clung to the Federalism of General Washington. And, with that established, his position, his opinion, would have been secure if only the English were reasonably decent. But they weren't, their conduct was again — as though they had learned nothing from the late war — actually unbearable. The British, with their peculiar insular blindness, were as objectionable, in their arbitrary interference with American trade, as was Genêt.

Still Richard had to choose between one set of sympathies or the other, between the principles of Jefferson and his extreme republicanism or Washington's. There was, certainly, no question of Richard's individual preference, he didn't waver in his Federal allegiance; but there were aspects of the American situation unhappily transcending a personal or inherited view. It was no longer simply a question of Washington or Jefferson — a need had risen for him to make a decision from which all the old powerful supports had been cut. His independence had been created in 1783; but now, for the first time, he was experiencing the difficulties of a sudden and unprecedented isolation. His mind, and not his instincts, had been called into action, and he was far more familiar with the latter than with the first. The truth was that the French and English were equally impossible. If he denied the Republic of France — which in the end, he began to see, he must do — he would be cursed as an enemy to the race that had sustained him in the most desperate of hours.

*

* *

But, contrarily, to renounce what was so widely condemned now as a British sympathy would throw him into the company of all the ideas and men that by nature he distrusted. He had fought the English, he would be very willing to fight them again, Richard assured himself; with them the issue was clear — a struggle against tyranny and unlawful privilege; but God knew where any bond with the present French might lead. He was more at home, it seemed, fighting with England than he could ever be fraternizing with the republic in France. Such a debate was as uncommon as it was difficult, and he was very much relieved when he began to see that, for him, really there was no question, no possibility, or need of changing his fundamental convictions with a changed America. The superficial appearance of an English bias was, at bottom, an authentic allegiance to the United States.

He had moved out to the portico, where he was seated, squarely facing the North River, and, at a stir behind him, he half turned and saw Morryson Bale. His uncle, not a tall man, was moderately fat, with a large round head which seemed soft, indefinite in outline; and his face bore blotches of deep brown; a condition that, together with a constant irritability, came from a disturbance of the liver. His head, in reality, had the look of a slightly rotted apple; but his hands were small and finely made, though they shook in an extreme palsy.

"Diggery is tied too short," he immediately proclaimed, showing his age in an insecure step and by the cautious way he lowered himself to a chair. "You're not fit to have a horse as good as that was. Why can't you mend your niggers?" Richard, in reply, told him something of what, in regard to the affairs of France and England and America, he had been considering. "Citizen Jefferson," the older Bale commented with a snigger. This, it was plain, gave him an extended satisfaction, for he repeated the phrase with another name, "Citizen Madison. What have the men in Gloucester been saying about this damned foreign ragout?"

"They are Federalist, in the main," Richard replied; "I mean around here. But if you go only a few miles it's different. You might suppose that Richmond was Paris and the Legislature a States-General. This fever will have to die before we can see what's happened. The country's safe while we have Washington, but afterwards ——" He made a gesture of uncertainty at what then might develop.

"Liberty, equality, brotherhood," Morryson Bale persisted in extracting a satirical entertainment from the current celebrated phrases of men's freedom. "There is this to be said about the Colony — that men like Berkeley, yes, and Culpepper and Lord Howard of Effingham, had a government that could deal with such foolery. There was no Freneau or Bache with his filthy sheets while they were in power."

"That may be true," Richard answered abruptly, "but we can never get back to it." His uncle wasn't so positive that it couldn't be managed. "Hamilton would like nothing better," he declared. "And John Adams could endure a crown on his coach."

"Damn it," Richard complained, "you sound like a republican." The other objected to such a French term, but Richard Bale moodily explained that it was becoming American. "The Democrat-Republicans," he continued. "They are being organized as an opposition to the Federalists." Morryson Bale's opinion was that they would do as well to continue the former terms, Whig and Tory. "Everybody knows what they mean — Marshall's a Tory, and Madison, damn him, turned Whig. Edmund Randolph is a Whig at heart, and Monroe . . . and you're a Tory."

"I am not," Richard flatly contradicted him; "I'm a Federalist. You seem to have forgotten what has happened in the last twenty years."

"Washington is a Tory," Morryson asserted.

"General Washington is as free from England as — as Edmond Charles Genêt." Anger invaded him. "You talk like the damned old King's men you belong to."

"You are young," the elder Bale proceeded, "and things go to your head. You can't look back and so you don't see forward. How could you be a judge of conditions with a horse tied as short as that? You can't run your plantation rightly. No, and neither can that hell of a Quaker you've got for overseer. Is there a servant here who can polish a boot? There isn't. In my time you'd have been a disgrace to a fox hunt. Even in

Gloucester, then, a gentleman wore bags until he was on his horse. You have to get a woman to mix your toddy. And when you get it you're hardly fit to drink — with no more than a bowl you're as dull as a fish."

That, at any rate, Richard remarked, hadn't been a difficulty of his.

"I could drink," Morryson Bale admitted complacently. "I remember sitting down at dinner in the afternoon and getting up the next morning. Getting up! Yes, and then following the hounds. I could ride better drunk than you sober. And dance — I'd have danced with a wooden leg. If you lived in a society worth the name, never dancing a decent step, you couldn't get into the houses. I'm not surprised women don't seem to like you; I'm not, by God!"

An expression of pain narrowed Richard Bale's eyes and hardened his mouth. "Very well," he said, after a long silence, "we might as well let this go. I did . . . a number of years back." But Morryson Bale was indefatigable. "They let you go," he corrected his nephew. "We are an unpleasant family of men," he further observed; "I don't see any lack of that in you, I must say. But there's your mother in you as well as Bale. And Celia, Celia Tucker, had a character of her own. Quieter than us. We all thought your father would never marry, with waiting so long. But the day he saw her — I was with him at Williamsburg — I knew he was finished. There was a ball and almost all the boys from the college, and they sat together in a corner. A little girl with big dark eyes; small and fine but too sensitive. Not strong . . . not in body. With character. And it turned out she wrote verses. I had some for a long while. They were about love."

A packet sloop was sailing out into Mockjack Bay; there were, already, silver white buds over the Cherokee roses massed on a rockery at the left; the voice of a servant, a minor key, sounded from the hall.

"Less than a year," Morryson went on reflectively, "but Francis never had a mind to it again. A devilish silly thing with Balisand to look after. It wasn't that he kept away from women, if they would have let him; no, he was only polite. He might seem to be interested in one, but when she left it was like taking a light from the reflector — there wasn't a glimmer left. But he never mentioned her . . . I couldn't understand it.

"I happened to be with them when she died, a week after you were born. She just shut her eyes, only that, but Francis — he wasn't even near her — knew. He walked to a window and stood with his back to the room; early in summer it was and redbirds were singing. Yes, you ought to have them, but I put them away — where, I can't think."

"Maybe I have," Richard replied; "perhaps I have had them since then."

"How could you?" Morryson Bale demanded, exasperated beyond measure. "Didn't I tell you I had 'em? I ought to know. They were about love and eternity. Fancy ideas."

*

* *

It had never occurred to him, he said, that Richard himself would do no better. "But it seems you won't, though I can't swear it's not for trying. If I were a girl I wouldn't look at you." He made a vain effort to still the tremor of his hands. "That's from shaking the dice so often at hazard." Morryson was obviously chagrined when Richard Bale ignored his wit, and he repeated his phrase about a dull fish. "I'm told Gawin is at Todd Hundred. He'll go back to Congress, of course. Always a dangerous man and he is getting worse. You would have done the State a service if you had shot him that time — when was it? But the girl he was engaged to from Henrico County killed herself instead — a crazy sort of accident — and I suppose it put politics out of his mind."

"It was in 1784," Richard told him, "June. He comes down to Todd Hundred, I suppose, to look after its affairs."

"Now Charles is dead, I can't see why you stay away. With all you used to think of Ava. She didn't insult Washington, did she?"

"Charles made it impossible for me to go there. His death doesn't affect that; and then, as you've just shown, I might run into Gawin Todd. And that would be unfortunate."

"Then meet him in Richmond, anywhere, and have the business done with. Nine years! I wouldn't have let a man I was mad at get away for nine days."

"Gawin never, practically, accepts a duel; and holding an office, he wouldn't think of it; he'd be ineligible for everything at once."

"Then post him, damn it, post him."

Richard Bale descended the steps to the drive and

untied his horse; he gathered the reins and mounted. "Don't fall off," Morryson called maliciously after him. Diggery went into a trot and carried him around the end of the house; there he turned to the left, leaving the brick wall and low painted fence of the garden for the narrow lane that led from Balisand to the public road. It was cut, a sandy way, through brush and trees, willow oaks and elms and maples, flights of beech trees, with banks of rhododendron almost at flower, the white clouds of the dogwood and the beginning pink of Maytime shrubs. There was an occasional break, through which he saw his fields: once planted in cotton, with large expanses of barley, they were now sowed in corn and wheat. The negro quarters were scattered, negroes were ploughing, and, in sight of his entrance gate, he was brought to a stop by Thomas Ekkes. The overseer rode toward him, the horse's hoofs muffled in sand, slapping a bright bay flank with his broad hat.

"If you are going to the courthouse," he said, "and see Mr. Wiatt or any of the gentlemen, would you ask if we could hire a few likely hands — four or even six? And it had better be for a month, until after the planting. Two dollars ought to be enough for that. I was just going, but I'm busy, and if you don't object —— "

Richard Bale admitted that he might reach the courthouse. "I'll look around," he promised Ekkes. "But I don't like hired hands at Balisand. They have been treated differently, and make trouble." "Not Mr. Wiatt's or any from Welfield," the overseer explained; "and now that Dutchman's gone from Todd Hundred I expect they are all right there. But, I take it, you won't want them." Richard moved on without answer. The highway, he told himself, was hardly wider or harder than his lane, and there were deep slick holes, pools of water. On either side the woods were dense, and sweet with wild honeysuckle. He met no one until he had passed the ordinary with its steep-pitched roof and had come opposite the tavern, and there he encountered a small farmer, James Luke, whose place lay at the beginnings of Guinea. No one, certainly, would admit that he actually lived in Guinea, a locality with, for obvious reasons, a bad name; but Luke's acres were, practically, on Jinkin's Neck. However, it wasn't that which stopped Richard Bale.

"What have you got on your hat?" he demanded shortly. "You would know more than me," Luke answered; "one wouldn't hurt you, either. I'll willingly tell you, though — it's the new French colours and a good sign of liberty."

"You have been fooled with a lot of cursed lies," Richard informed him. "That is the badge of the enemies of America, the men who are attacking General Washington. What did they tell you — that if they were in power you wouldn't have to pay any debts? If you're owed a dollar you know what to think of that. I suppose they said the Federal Government was afraid of England, or that we were going to have one of the English princes here for a king. Lies! They are the men who tried to keep Virginia out of the United States, and who were abroad or in the Assembly talking through the war. Do you think General Washington was afraid of the British? By God, do you say I am!"

"No, Mr. Bale," the man on horse beside him was quick to answer. "Nobody in Gloucester would doubt that. But this is different, and perhaps a gentleman like you wouldn't have patience for it; he would be the last to." James Luke grew more assertive. "It is going to mean that all free men will be alike. That's the kind of a country we're bound to have. We won't throw away our independence now we won it. The people of France showed us where we were heading."

"All alike," Richard repeated, "you and any oyster thief in Gloucester Point. And the independence we won! Who the devil are we — editors and the farmers who fought nothing but the excise? I tell you this, I don't want to ride down a road so near Balisand and see the tricolour; for that reason I'll ask you to take it off."

"That's it!" Luke cried. "A man can't even wear a piece of ribbon if he wants. Soon none of us will be free. Things have changed already; and you can make what you like out of that."

"Take it off," Richard Bale repeated, in a level voice. What if he didn't, the other demanded. Richard drew his horse closer and reversed his whip, the lash caught in his hand. "Do you want me to take it off with a piece of your head?" he asked. He gazed directly, with an unmoved face, into James Luke's eyes. "You believe you're still in the army beating your soldiers around," Luke went on heatedly; "but the people will show you different."

"No," Richard corrected him, "in the army I'd have you shot." The cold sensation of his unpredictable temper invaded him: he swung his whip-stick across Luke's face, leaving it torn and springing with blood. The hat with the bright cockade fell to the road. He waited, easily seated on Diggery, restraining him with a light firm hand and a word. James Luke pressed a sleeve against his face. "Wait a little," he cried in a tone and fury blurred by his arm; "I'll have one of those ribbons over your heart and nail it there with a slug."

"If you got it anywhere it would be on my back," Richard Bale told him; "for that's where your slug would go." Suddenly the other kicked his horse into a gallop; blood was on his shoulder, Richard saw; then he was gone. Disagreeable but not serious. For periods of months on end embittered individuals had waited for opportunity, for the courage, to shoot him from cover. But not a trigger, to that end, had been pressed. The hickory of his whip was broken, and he pitched it into the bushes along the road. He had brought it from habit and not because it was necessary for Diggery. As he moved toward the courthouse he wondered, with a trace of a smile, if Morryson Bale would, for the moment, have approved him.

*

* *

The road, dividing at the courthouse to form the small green island of grass that held the brick buildings of the county administration, led him to an unusually large gathering of men for that season; the Clerk's Office, the door and windows open, looked almost as though court were in session. The preliminaries of a suit were being put in motion, and that and the warmth of the day had filled the narrow porticoes and immediate paths with interested or idle groups. On the bench reserved for that purpose a number of negroes, relaxed and sleeping in a lassitude of sunlight, waited to be hired; but Richard didn't like their appearance: they were gaunt and wretchedly clad; the man who had them in charge was scarcely better. Beyond, he saw, was Bradlock Wiatt, and he went forward with Thomas Ekkes' inquiry.

Bradlock, without certainty, thought that he could come to an agreement with Richard's overseer. "Tell him to ride over, anyhow. What's going on here? I just came." Richard Bale equally didn't know. "Bradlock," he proceeded, "I passed James Luke by the tavern and he had on one of the new French cockades. How could that get to Luke, back of Jinkin's Neck in Gloucester?" Wiatt delayed answering, and then, in a tone detached, it seemed, from whatever had gone, he said, "I saw Gawin Todd yesterday." Richard replied, "Then that's it. Yes, of course."

"But," Bradlock Wiatt continued, "what I want to know is how you did when you saw it."

"I'm afraid I knocked it off," Richard admitted; "and with a piece of skin." Wiatt was severe:

"I was afraid of something like that. I'll tell you again, Richard, that you'll have to do differently. You will, for a fact. The first thing you know we'll have a Terror . . . led by Gawin Todd. Damned if you appreciate the new feeling of the public. I'm afraid the old days — and you were splendid in them — are over. You're too young to be so stubborn; why, you might as well be Morryson. And there's this, too, as far as I'm concerned — things are better. Freedom is going to be more than a word. Say what you please about the French, we are in the same situation. It may be we'll have to support them."

"I ought to have brought the cockade along for you," Richard asserted. "This isn't France, or England either; it's the United States. My servant, David, tells me you have a fast horse in Grey Medley," he shifted the conversation to a less contentious subject. "By the best sire ever imported into Virginia," Wiatt declared; "out of Honeycomb. You know the blood — Medley and Jimcrack and Araminta. Jimcrack was by Cripple out of Miss Elliot by Griswood's Partner. There isn't another horse in the Tidewater that can stand in the stable with him, and nothing short of Maryland could hurry him."

"I've got a little mare, Careless," Richard replied; "we haven't, really, tried her yet, but we're not modest about her. She hasn't been worked enough; some time at the end of May or the beginning of June — what about it, Bradlock?"

"What about what?" Bradlock Wiatt retorted. "That wouldn't be a race. Listen to me, Richard — Grey Medley standing full is sixteen hands three inches, and his stride'll cover twenty-seven feet. By heaven, his barrel is so large that, when you are in front of him, you can see the ribs on either side. Don't back any little mare named Careless against him, if you want to save her from being eternally outfooted and outlasted. No, no, Bale."

" A little mare," Richard repeated, " in her fourth year. She's been on oats and cracked corn, and last week we tried her at two miles. Well, Bradlock, three-mile heats on the tavern course . . . for three thousand dollars."

" You are foolish, Richard," Bradlock Wiatt insisted; " and that's a stiff sum. If you had said two-mile heats it would have been more reasonable. I might have listened then. No, it's possible I'll take Grey Medley as far as Newmarket in May, have some real racing."

" At two miles I will make the purse five thousand," Richard informed him. Bradlock Wiatt considered him. " You would have it," he said finally. " I saw Diggery at the courthouse rail, and he took enough money from me to allow you a margin." He held out his hand. " It's arranged." Back again at Balisand, Richard Bale went to the stable. David was in the tack room, where the rows of bridles hanging from pegs, the saddles and saddle cloths and bright polished chains and bits, gave out a mingled subacid odour. " David," he proceeded, " I have arranged a match for Careless against Mr. Wiatt's Grey Medley. Two-mile heats. What do you think? " At once David asked, " How much for? " And, when he learned the size of the purse, he added confidently that they would soon have five thousand dollars in their pockets.

" No strange stableboys around," Richard warned him; " and we'll work Careless again to-morrow morning. Early. I'll come down." He then proceeded to the mare's stall; she was chestnut, a shade under fifteen hands high, with a delicate long neck, her head splendidly set, and, Richard maintained, the prettiest ears in the world. The best of knees, he told himself, neat pasterns, a perfect foot and a depth of chest no animal of Bradlock's could equal. But the other was right — five thousand dollars, as Wiatt had intimated, was a heavy bet for Richard.

However, the answer to that was he'd win it. Then, sending to Ekkes what word he had about field hands, he returned to the house, where, dismounting, he threw the reins to a waiting servant. Mrs. Patton had replaced Morryson Bale on the portico; and, as usual, her hands were employed, embroidering with an ornamental yellow thread initials on a number of linen pillow cases. She was a woman strong and graceful in body and a face strangely without freshness, her skin was dry and colourless and lined, her mouth older in appearance, Richard judged, by ten years than her age actually warranted.

"There is sangaree on the hall table," she informed him; "if you wait I'll have it carried out." She turned to the open door. "Nettie!" she called, "Nettie!" A slight pale girl, in a single slip, her head bound in a figured red handkerchief, brought the drink to Richard Bale. "I have come to the opinion," Mrs. Patton said, with a needle like quicksilver, "that Mr. Morryson Bale ought to be the housekeeper at Balisand. He tells me I haven't got a woman who can launder a sheet. As for these pillow cases, they are no more than bolting cloth or barley straw." Richard listened to her without comment, an admirable and restful woman with a notable readiness and point of expression. "But I found him some old bed linen marked Camilla Scarborough — that would be Mrs. Francis Bale — and that will satisfy him for one night, anyhow. It's early for sangaree," she commented, "but it was so hot, like June, and the limes were hard. I had to throw them all out. I can't get a person to understand how important the skin of a lime is. There's a kind of oil in it, and if they are dry ——" her attention was demanded by the sewing. "They are dry," she finished.

"I am going to match Careless against Mr. Wiatt's Grey Medley," he informed her. Mrs. Patton replied, "For some terrible amount, I suppose; and if we lose, of course it will come at the worst time, long before the crop is in. Well, if you breed horses for racing they must be raced, and if gentlemen are born to betting they'll bet." He declared that she had lived too soon. "In another generation you wouldn't have to be bothered by either," Richard predicted. That, however, with all the drawbacks of the present order, she didn't long for. "Richmond makes me dizzy now, with all those people; I expect it won't improve. It's so hot the thread sticks to my wet hand. Nettie," she cried, "come and get these pillow cases and lay them folded by the press in the upper hall."

*

* *

A soft grey veil of cloud, cloud like a sea mist, covered the afternoon sky; the river was grey and immaterial; the trunks of trees black with sap and water. A coolness penetrated the warmth of day, a pleasant change without a stir of wind; and Richard sat longer over dinner than he had at breakfast. The hounds, back of him, were asleep; Morryson Bale, sagging in his chair, was asleep . . . but when Mrs. Patton had gone Richard didn't know. With the removal of the cloth, probably, and the appearance of the rum . . . quickly and silently, on her endless errands about the house. It must be nearly five, he concluded; there was the beginning of dusk in the corners of the room. Outside, the grass was chemically green. A hound whimpered in his sleep. Then the dogs moved uneasily, they rose, one after the other, and stood in attitudes of attention, their muzzles lifted. Morryson woke.

"Someone is coming in," Richard told him. He heard the horses and the creaking of a carriage that stopped by the portico, and he went out. It was Ava Todd, and a maid; boxes. "Ava!" he exclaimed, hurrying forward. He helped her to the ground, as deeply stirred as she plainly showed herself to be. No Todd had been to Balisand in all that time, ever since Lavinia had died. "Is it anything serious?" he asked directly.

"Oh, yes, Richard," she told him; "you should guess that; but not to worry about." She deliberately adopted a lighter manner. "I have come to stay all night, and I hope you don't mind and there's a place for me. If I could have it, I'd like the little room over the portico." But that, he protested, wasn't large enough for her. Mrs. Patton would have the south chamber ready by the time she was upstairs. "No, the other," Ava insisted. "I've always wanted to sleep in it." Morryson

Bale came out on his insecure legs to greet her. "This is the only pleasant sign I've seen here for years," he announced; "nothing but foxhounds for company. Richard's about as entertaining as Thomas Ekkes, the overseer."

When she had gone up to the room she preferred — Morryson had vanished to dress — Richard Bale sat speculating on what could have brought Ava to Balisand. Serious, but he wasn't to worry. He was impatient for her to appear, to tell him all there was for him to know; but an hour passed, and then the greater part of another, and he remained alone. Twilight had fallen, it was dark under the broadnut tree close by the house, on the right, and supper was waiting, before she descended. She was still a beautiful woman, Richard saw; perhaps not, in reality, beautiful; impressive was a better word. She had grown definitely older; but that added to her charm, rather than detracted from it, now. Strangely, though he had known her all his conscious life, he had no memory of Ava as a child or girl, none as a young married woman; she seemed always to have been like this, detached and sympathetic and grave.

"I am going to upset your custom," she warned him, when supper was nearly over; "I'm not going to leave you to the bottle, but stay instead. I must talk to you, and I like it here, with the candles." She skilfully conveyed to the others that she wished to talk to him only; even Morryson grasped her meaning at once; and, with what was palpably an annoyed and adverse stare, he removed himself in the company of Mrs. Patton from the dining room. Yet, when they had gone, Ava was silent, lost in thought. "I've hated it all, Richard," she spoke suddenly, her face troubled; "but there was nothing I could manage. You would be the last to blame Charles. If I had only known, I could have insisted on a different way of doing."

"What do you mean, Ava," he inquired, "if you had known?"

"Gawin told me yesterday," she said with an utmost simplicity. "He didn't mean to; it came out in a burst of temper. A little of it like that and I made him tell me the rest. Richard, why didn't I see it then? It's so clear now; clear and mysterious."

Richard Bale sat stiffly, giving her no encouragement, no help. "I warned Gawin, when I knew about it, that I was coming to you. He had to be reminded that he wasn't Charles. Gawin isn't; he never could be; but he is my brother-in-law and honest; as honest as you are, Richard, and with that we'll let him go. Won't we? I don't even want you to talk, but you had to hear that — that at last I understood. About Lavinia."

He thanked her. "You mustn't do that," she objected; "you owe me more, and you used to be so fond of me. Listen to this, Richard, first; it won't be any easier for you than me. After . . . after it was over I undressed her, and I found a yellow rose. It was warm and still fresh and very sweet, and even then I put it away, to give to Gawin — you see, I thought it belonged to him. Then I forgot it, and when I went to find it later — in a box with some gloves — I couldn't. And yesterday, Richard, after nine years, there it was, among the gloves. That's how Gawin came to tell me—he destroyed it in a fury. I'm sorry."

William had been his name, Richard remembered, an especially good servant, a soothing hand with the razor; he had instructed him to carry the rose to Lavinia only a little while before her death. It had been dusk then, the rosebush stood under the window of his room in the schoolhouse, and he had watched William carefully gather it. "He destroyed it." Richard Bale repeated her words slowly. "Well, that doesn't matter. He isn't any more important now than he was to her then. The rose and Lavinia have been dead a very long while. I imagine, Ava, that when you found them the gloves were yellower than the flower. But you'll never think what a fool I was—I thought she would have the rose on her dress or in her hair. I looked for it, in the instant I had. Where is William?"

"William?" she asked. "William?"

"You wouldn't remember; he was a servant. It doesn't matter. Ava, and I can't help it if you do object, I must thank you for telling me this." She had had to, Ava replied. He had assured her that Gawin Todd was of no importance, neither Gawin nor his act of destruction, but he found he increasingly regarded him with an intact and measureless hatred. It seemed to him that Todd had desecrated the sole remaining trace of Lavinia on earth. But he said nothing of that to Ava; it had no concern with living women. A strong but unaccountable feeling possessed him that the moment was inevitable when Gawin Todd would make him a full payment.

The fullest. And this conviction bred a patience in his anger. "Do you want me to go on?" Ava asked. "Although there is nothing more, really, for me to say. I hoped you might be willing to; after being silent, lonely with it, for so long. You'd never think I was curious and just feminine."

At the impulse to tell her that he was equally without subject, there, for discussion, he was oppressed by a tyrannical necessity to explain everything which, as she had said, had been penned in him for years. He had sworn, under ordinary conditions, never to mention Lavinia in connection with himself; but this wasn't ordinary — Ava was, in a way, the same as Charles; and Gawin Todd had made speech possible. "There is nothing I could say," he admitted, "or so much that I don't know when I'd finish. All night, perhaps."

"Please," she begged him.

"And then, you said it was both clear and mysterious; that is true; except for the fact it gets more and more mysterious. You'd think it would be the other way round, and I would understand it better when I had had time to look back. But no. Anyone would suppose, too, that I'd change, my feeling grow less. No." His voice was sharp, loud, with rebellion and misery.

*

* *

The candles, for no felt reason, waved and fluttered, shifting the pattern of the shadows over the wainscot. Ava's chin was supported on a hand; in black, largely obliterated in the uncertain light, she seemed like a lovely mask created magically for his especial attention and encouragement. " There is so much of it," he insisted, discouraged at the difficulty of expressing all that he had sustained. " And what you must remember, perhaps more than anything else, is that we saw each other almost not at all. Once — it was dark — on the wharf, then in the summerhouse and again in the summerhouse. I saw her, yes, here and there, in the hall and the dining room, but I spoke to her only those three times.

" You'll think it's insanity. Well, I won't contradict you. We even disagreed on the wharf; when she walked away I am certain we were both relieved. Yet, the next day, when I met her at dinner I knew her, it appeared, better than I did you. Why? We went through the nonsense of an introduction, and she was furious at me, later, because she said I had been responsible for that pretence. Ava, when I saw her again she said I was detestable. There were a lot of people around, and we drifted out into the garden. She might have forgotten all about me, from the way she walked by the flowers, and then, without exactly knowing how, we were in the summerhouse. She wasn't cross any more; it was like a dream; the sun streamed through the lattice and dazed me. Ava, I never got over it."

He gave this assertion the emphasis of a long silence, sitting in an earnest alertness, regarding her, waiting, with a troubled and questioning gaze. She said nothing, she didn't move. Richard sighed deeply, as though a counted on assistance had been denied him. " I couldn't remember that she was engaged to marry Gawin," he resumed; " Lavinia didn't seem to have any connection with earth or men at all. She wasn't a part of Todd Hundred or of the minuets or whist or talk; she was there, but how I didn't know. I didn't think of her as going in or out of the rooms — she appeared and vanished and appeared. I can't even remember what she wore, except that once her hair couldn't have been covered, for I noticed it didn't stay where she put it, but slid across her cheek.

" And I had no sensation of time, Ava — a day might have been a year or a thousand, the world might have turned backwards; it was the same to me. I suppose the only word to use is love, but that's so dreadfully unsatisfactory, for it describes nothing. If I had realized that I was in love with Lavinia I would have left Todd Hundred while I could. At once. Nothing else would have been possible, and I give you my word I'd have gone. To say you are in love — no matter how inexact that may be — demands certain actions. Don't you see . . . love and honour. It's necessary for me to think I'm not insufficient there. But I had no name for it, I didn't recognize that it was what you would call a crisis, happy or unhappy or dangerous and perhaps fatal. I didn't think at all. I didn't even keep Lavinia consciously in my mind. I had been drunk, and a great deal of it I accounted to that. Then it got to be night and — and we were in the summerhouse once more. We went separately, and there, I'm obliged to tell you, Ava, I kissed her.

" But only once, only once. I've wondered about that

ever since; I wondered about it then. Once. And that, you'd suppose, would have waked me up; it did show me that she couldn't marry Gawin Todd; but all that part of me which had always been important never stirred . . . again. You see, no one could explain that, or the one kiss. Afterwards we sat down very quietly, and said some things about the future. Lavinia realized about Gawin; she saw what, we thought, must happen; and that, certainly, I wouldn't go on with. I hadn't a doubt about Gawin Todd — I knew absolutely, just as I know now, that I would kill him; but the other, Lavinia, the stairs —— " He broke off. Absently he picked up his narrow glass of brandy and held it against a candle flame, absently watching the brown liquid sparkle; then he set the glass back on the table.

"I don't understand, Richard," Ava told him, "and yet you make me believe it; oh, absolutely. It sounds like something that had happened in the past but would be impossible to-day. A state of the spirit, or of two spirits."

"One," he corrected her; "whatever it was, there was only one. We weren't separate and we were never together. Not really. Todd had no right to so much, to anything!" His voice momentarily rose from a low reflective tone. "I can't defend that or make it clearer; you'll have to accept it and have what opinion of me you will. The body is so much, Ava, but then, it seems, it's nothing too. And that has bothered me, for I haven't a trace of what you'd call religion. I don't believe that you have to die to live, I haven't any hope about a future after this; I'll never see Lavinia again.

Why, look, if I thought there was an eternity to spend with her, do you think I'd be what I am? Suppose I was religious, and I thought that death — the river — wouldn't bring me to her at once; that I'd have to wait for an appointed time, I'd be a miracle of energy and happiness and use.

"It's the past I'm lost in, never the present or future; June nine years ago. Nothing has been real since then. It's cold or hot, sunny or there is rain; I'm fox-hunting or racing horses or gambling; I go through with it all; and when the horses are running I'm interested; I like the hounds early in the morning; but when the post is reached or the fox holed, it goes out of my mind. As long as I'm active, say concerned with General Washington, it's well enough; but let anything stop for a minute, if I get alone on Diggery in the woods . . . shadows and dream.

"You must understand I'm not defending it; long ago it occurred to me that love might be a poison, a drug. When I went, that fall, to Congress in Trenton, I was like a dead man; that was natural, I think; and I got over it . . . but I never went back. I stayed here at Balisand, riding over the fields and drinking at the table. I used to be lonely and it seemed that marriage would be good for me — we spoke about Mary — but I'm never lonely any more, Ava. I don't want to be disturbed, or taken away. It's as I've said: my activity, the things I do, are no more than flares of anger, an occasional streak of lightning out of an indifferent sky. After all, the Bale inheritance is very strong. Put it this way, if you like, that I am ruined. I don't care.

You can say that — and once I was a soldier — I'm a deserter. It makes no difference to me. You'd even have some excuse for calling me a drunkard, but I don't get drunk, not in a way you would recognize, and I wouldn't contradict you. I've had letters from the President; men have been to see me from Philadelphia; they take supper and stay the night; the letters go into a box, and I'm glad when there's nothing to interfere with the other. What do you make of it, Ava? "

She smiled at him in a swift and tender compassion. " Anything I could say, the best, would be only impertinent, Richard. You've made it so plain you are beyond a human help. Why, you don't even hear the voices that speak to you. But I won't have you call it a poison. There are enough people to run the world. Too many. The mystery doesn't worry me now, either: it's a part of the tremendous amount we can't understand. I'm not very useful to you."

*

*   *

" Be damned to use," he replied. " Something she started to say to me was never finished. Richard, she began, but there was no more. She went away. I didn't know it then. If you are tired I'll stop; the important part, the most curious, I haven't explained." She made no reply to this; it didn't, she seemed to imply, warrant the dignity of an answer, a denial. Richard held up his glass against the light; it was empty, and he drew a decanter toward him; but he failed to take out the stopper, his hand remained on the engraved surface. "I got back from Congress, somehow, and I was just commonly unhappy, a man who had lost the only thing necessary to his life. Bitterness and cursing and Antigua rum and sleepless nights. The snow left, if there was snow; spring happened along with the usual flowers and birds; and I hated it all. But I did a few things — I built a cover over the end of the wharf, like the one at Todd Hundred. When it was finished, about noon I walked out to see if it was what I had ordered. A bright hot day, this morning exactly, and I was watching the tide draw down the river, against the supports of the wharf, when suddenly the sun got in my eyes; I was as dizzy as the devil." He paused: "I must be very careful so you won't get a wrong impression:

"I don't mean that I thought Lavinia was beside me, I didn't see her or hear the whisper of a skirt, there was no vision of Lavinia and heaven opening or promises; nothing like that. Lies and lies and lies. No, it was the same overwhelming feeling I had had standing with her in the sun . . . in your garden. I sat down, the wharf and water and land were pretty well blurred, and told myself that it would go soon. I didn't want it to, but that's what happened in my mind — I kept saying it will go at once, it can't stay this way. But it did for what must have been an hour or more. I won't describe it, Ava.

"Only, as I said, you can't dismiss it as a figure of the imagination. I hadn't been thinking about her, not all morning; it wasn't a picture of what you might call the senses. After a while it went away, of course; and it left me as much puzzled as anything. I was curious. What the devil! Dinner was as usual, and supper, and the next day and the next. Apparently that was all. I often went back to it, of course; but it seemed so extraordinary — I haven't made you see it — that I began to believe it hadn't happened. Just like the rest. Then, in November, I was out in the brush, along the river field, with a negro, yelping up wild turkeys. It was thick, no sun, the beginning of a pour of rain, when . . . I went into a mud sink, dazed by sunlight.

"Ava, I could smell the flowers of Todd Hundred, and hear the birds in the cedars, yes, by God, and the fiddles in the drawing room. There I was, in the cold mud, filled with the — the happiness of having Lavinia, of having her for the rest of my life. Just that — all hope and surprise and gladness. I got out of the sink and walked straight away, back to the house, leaving the best gun I owned. Little York hadn't seen it, and he kept yelping a turkey he had been tracking. He brought the gun in later, shaking with fright, for he thought I had gone down into the mud. Ava, tell me, had I? Was it mud? Am I drowned?"

"Drowned, Richard? Oh, yes; but I won't call it mud. In the sky, perhaps."

"I particularly want to avoid that," he asserted. "It wasn't poetic; very much the reverse. Nothing could have been more real, more physical. And then I began to wait for it, I wanted it to come back, and, at the same time, some of me was afraid. I dreaded it. Everything else stopped, went out of my head. I'll be in my room, on Diggery riding to the courthouse, talking with

Ekkes; it will all be as usual, as it should; and zing — Lavinia.

" I always have an idea that if I fought I could get over it; I look at it as a sort of weakness, yes, like rum, or gambling; I take the attitude that it's all wrong. But that doesn't last; I shove it in the back of my mind and wait for the next . . . what is it, attack? You'll recognize I'm not in the habit of thinking I am weak. That's not conspicuously a family trait."

" Don't you see," she cried, distressed, " that this couldn't happen to a weak man! Weak men sink, Richard; they sink and forget. But the ones who are strong swim a long long while, they stay up when it's hopeless, in spite of all the ocean." That, he replied, sounded very noble but difficult. " If you get disagreeable with me," Ava informed him, " I'll go to bed at once."

" This has happened to me," he further explained: " if you went to bed I would be sorry and I wouldn't. If love is a word with any meaning I could be said to love you. I'm conscious of that and it has no reality to me. You see, I have been robbed . . . empty, negative, no good. I mean underneath the skin."

" Richard," she spoke very seriously, " you must never marry. Promise me you won't make that mistake." But he wasn't certain she was right. " It might cure me," he proceeded; " just as I'm sure Mary would have saved me if I had married her at once. I'm Richard Bale of Balisand; I have a body; appetites; vices; and there might be a little good to cultivate."

" It would be criminal," she insisted.

" Then I can't be saved? "

" Is this being lost, Richard? "

" Very well — what is it, if you're sure of so much? " She couldn't tell him:

" We're agreed about the mystery. And, Richard, there's your father! " She was visibly excited at the discovery of the connection, the resemblance, between them. " Morryson, in a way, spoke of that this morning," he told her. " By accident, of course. Once he had a poem my mother wrote. He said it was about love and eternity."

Ava Todd rose, with both her hands pressed to her breast. " It frightens me now," she said.

Richard's only reply to that was a single and curt word, stuff. " I warned you," Ava backed away from the table. " I'm going up. I never could stand rudeness." He saw her leave moodily — the black velvet of her dress seemed to melt into the gloom beyond the candles. Well, she had asked for all he had told her. Women were continually a little remote from whatever touched other women. He knew that this was rank ingratitude: of all the people alive, Ava meant the most. In reality, she was the only one who had significance for him. She had come to him in an impulse of utter generosity and courage, and he had practically insulted her.

This ought to stop at once: Ava had showed him how far he had degenerated. With all his memories and affection for her, in a second, an illogical flame of ill-temper, or resentment, she was less than — than a servant. He filled his glass and emptied it, filled and emptied it. An exhausted candle went out with a flicker and an evil smell, and the darkness crept nearer to him. Soon another would be burned to the socket. If Bradlock Wiatt were there, they would have had their watches out, betting on the exact moment of the candle's end. A horse with a stride that covered twenty-seven feet. But no one other than himself and David and a stableboy knew how fast Careless was. A good name for a mare but better for him. Careless! Out of Celia by Francis Bale. That, however, wasn't very gracious. The second candle turned black and smoked. A yellow rose. Nine years afterward Gawin Todd had destroyed it. A pistol that lay in his hand like a flower, a rose on its stalk. When the third candle died, the night would be almost on him. Then the finality of the last and the victorious night.

*

*   *

It was still dark when, the following morning, Little York woke him; but when he was shaved and had dressed, the sky beyond the North River was bright with dawn. There was, yet, no breakfast, and he had a hard biscuit and a glass of brandy. On the left of the plantation, partly through what was called the river field and part beyond, there was an oval track with an exceedingly modest stand, some board seats laid across supports with a covering; the woods between that and the public way were so thick, so treacherous with marsh, as to be impassable; and there Richard Bale worked and ran his horses. It was sixty yards under a mile — they had exactly figured the deficiency for the purposes of timing, and all the track, practically, was visible from the stand.

David and Careless, the boy who was to ride her, and a very old negro, with an endless flow of soothing words for the mare, at her bridle, and Richard Bale, only were present. He had never, Richard concluded, owned a more beautiful animal than Careless. Diggery, nervously, impatiently, shifting from side to side, excited by the nearness of the track, had been a great horse; but he was big, as big, almost, as Bradlock asserted Grey Medley to be. Careless was, in comparison, delicate . . . but strong; and in an instant, it seemed, when she was permitted, she would be running like a streak of light. There was no perceptible space of transition from fast to faster; no whip, hardly more than the voice, the rein, and a touch of clear heel. " Benjamin," Richard said to his rider, " there's a hard race before you, but it only goes to two-mile heats."

Benjamin had seen Mr. Wiatt's horse. " We'll be in," he said, " before Grey Medley starts to jump." David sharply ordered him to stop his projecting, and gave him a leg up on Careless. " Not her best," Richard called. The sun rose over the woodland — lost now to Gloucester County — across the river; the river flashed into a simultaneous sheet of brightness; and Careless was off. She ran with the most extraordinary grace, the incarnation of a speed, apparently, heaven-born, without perceptible strain. She turned with the turning track, vanished behind a widespread black oak and reappeared. Richard critically watched her rider, coming in: he sat the mare well, perhaps a little too far up on her neck, but Careless liked it and responded generously.

He was entirely satisfied with the result: with the necessary deductions for distance, the additions for the comparatively indifferent track, always remembering that she hadn't been pressed. "Well, not far from two minutes," Richard told David, in a tone that reached neither of the other negroes. He laid a caressing hand on the mare's flank, he slipped his fingers under the girth and examined her bit. It was still early for breakfast, when he returned to the house, but Mrs. Patton was already active. Ava, too, was early — she showed traces of a wakeful night, the beginning lines of age — and, at the table, she said almost nothing. Leaving Balisand, she was obviously at a loss for an adequate wording of what she had to say. "I understand," Richard assured her instantly; "with Gawin around, it would be difficult for all of us." But she replied that it wasn't Gawin. "If Todd Hundred were his," she went on impractically, "I'd have you there as often as you would come. But it will always belong to Charles; now more than in the past." She held out her hand. "I don't feel as badly as I might, Richard — you don't need Todd Hundred, you don't need us." To that he could make no answer, it was indisputably true.

When she had left he thought throughout the rest of the morning about what had occurred the night before; he repeated silently all that he had said. Explaining it like that, so fully, to Ava, putting the strangeness of his feeling into words, had clarified it for himself. The special phase of emotion he had expressed seemed disturbingly like a weakness; he balanced what, to-day, he regarded as the vagueness of that past against what it had blotted out from his existence. The price was too high. He would never forget Lavinia; her memory would dominate his life to the end; but it wasn't necessary for him to remain in a state of besotted vision. No, he would become more reasonable, fight off the sun-dizziness that preceded his . . . but he didn't know what it was. A little later he might even try to re-enter public life, under the black cockade. Federalism was at an ebb now, the French enthusiasm had drowned everything else in its mad hysteria; but that was no more than temporary — Washington was still the greatest quantity in the States he had united; John Adams was an admirable and strong influence.

The first thing, after this decision, which occupied him was the race against Bradlock Wiatt's Grey Medley. Richard heard ominous rumours, statements, about the horse; he was, it appeared, as good as Bradlock had said, and he would represent the Wiatt stable at the Northern races, early in the summer. He might be fast, Richard thought, but Careless, at that distance, was better. Publicly he said very little about her, he was evasive with regard to her clocking, contenting himself with generalities about her condition and his hopes.

The tavern track lay between the public house and the river; it was a full mile, and the stretch was faster than the half and three-quarter poles. That was in the favour of Grey Medley, who would do his best running there; but Richard again counted on his mare's astonishing speed. The odds, naturally, were against him: at first, around the courthouse, the betting was five to two; yet his quiet secure manner and lack of assurances shifted his end to three; on the morning of the race some bets were laid at four to three.

Richard Bale had taken the longer odds to an amount he didn't care to contemplate. If Careless lost, the truth was, he would have to sell some of his best servants; a necessity which he regarded as a disgrace — no Balisand negro had been sold for a decade. Yes, if he lost he would be seriously short of money. That, however, was the hazard of races, of betting: without more up than he could afford, horse racing lacked interest for him. Damn it, that was the privilege, the duty, of his blood. The parsimony of the new masses would never have force in the ordering of his plantation.

The race, he found, had assumed the wide proportions of a county event; an hour before it was to be run, there were, Beverley Mathews assured him, a thousand people at the tavern track. Richard was standing with Henry Dalney, Beverley and, in riding habit, Lucia Mathews. Her interest in all that had to do with horses, he recognized, had increased with her years. She was now some months under twenty, but, except for an inevitable maturity of being, her appearance had changed singularly little since childhood — she had the same dark composed face and remarkable black eyebrows, the same straight shapely nose and firm large tranquil mouth. She rode continually in the fox hunts, a performance less common with women than formerly; and not even Doctor Ambrose, no longer the younger, was a more daring jumper or had less regard for the danger of woods.

"I haven't seen Careless for six months," she told Richard; "I haven't an idea what she can do — she's light compared to Grey Medley — but I remember her perfectly; and, Richard, I have confidence in her. I don't know why, and that's a silly thing for me to say about horse racing. It's almost feminine . . . you'll laugh at that."

"I hope you're right," Henry Dalney commented; "because if you're wrong I'll have to sell my pecan trees and ship in the West India trade. Richard," he turned, "have you seen Jordan Gainge? He's here with his Guinea wife."

*

* *

"Over there," Beverley Mathews pointed out, "just by that coach. They are coming up to us." Gainge was slight, a man at least sixty years old, but he moved with an undiminished spirit, the assertive habit of a master of ships. He had a small closely shaped beard, a penetrating gaze; he wasn't seen at a disadvantage beside the young woman he had married. No one standing with Richard knew her, and Jordan Gainge performed the ceremony of introduction in an assured manner that had all the ease of a more formal inheritance. Her name, Richard discovered, was Zena; she was no taller than Jordan; she was without special feature — except for hair that had the rich paleness of ripe wheat — but he found that he persistently noticed her. Appropriately dressed for her present situation, she showed nothing, at first, of her origin; and then he recognized that, beneath a determined calm, she was restless. It wasn't an uneasiness of embarrassment; she kept no sense of inferiority; but seemed quite like a thing of the wild in a momentary and forced constraint through which abruptly she must ultimately break and vanish.

He wondered how Jordan Gainge had managed to come in contact with her; the inhabitants of Guinea were a shy race, apart, in their lives and dealings, from the mainland. Jinkin's Neck, where mostly they lived, extended, between the inlets of the Severn and North Rivers, into Mockjack Bay; it was hardly more than a marsh, divided by an infinity of small tidal creeks; and the huts of the Guineamen, almost indistinguishable from the reeds where they were built, were held in a firm jealous isolation from all connection with the greater world. They were fishermen, hardy and courageous and intemperate, with even a speech — unintelligible beyond their scattered and united settlement — of their own; but that was the extent of public knowledge. The origins of their phrases, their hostility and stock, were only conjectural. Perhaps, Richard reflected, Gainge knew all about them now. But if he did, it would get no farther than himself.

Richard Bale was called away; the race was to be ordered immediately. Careless, standing quietly, was flawless in condition: her skin was elastic and glossy; drawn compactly into her muscle, she was yet lightly poised. Grey Medley, he admitted to himself, was dangerous; he was, it might be, a little short in the forelegs, from the knees down; his entire structure was a shade heavy for a blood-horse; but the whole long muscular sweep of the hind quarters was magnificent, the full equal of such extra weight. Beverley Mathews' voice was heard, "Saddle. Mount . . . and come up." There was the starter's drum tap. Careless was the quicker in getting away; she was three lengths ahead before her rider, with a hard pull, held her in to measure the pace of Grey Medley. The horse closed the distance between them to half a length; and, like that, they proceeded at a moderate rate over the first mile. The time was two minutes and seven seconds, slow for Careless; Richard burned with an angry conviction that the mare wasn't well ridden. More advantage should have been taken of the harder reaches of track. The pace was increased; it was fast, apparently, with no thought of the succeeding heats; Careless was running with the lovely smoothness of a waterfall . . . but she was being left. "Goddamn it," Richard exclaimed, "she's got more than that!" Careless was trailing a full twenty yards, and then, with a rush of her magical speed, she came up to Grey Medley, hung there, and passed him in the stretch, within a run of forty rods. Slower, but a clear length ahead, she led Bradlock Wiatt's horse to the post.

"Four minutes, thirteen seconds," Mathews asserted. "It looked faster, Richard. There's a chance that mare of yours — if she can last the distance — will make you some money this afternoon." Richard Bale offered him a thousand dollars in the opinion that she could, but Beverley declined. "You know well enough I never protect my bets." In spite of her preliminary success, Richard was bothered by the fact that Careless wasn't perspiring properly; she seemed swollen, too, in the loins; yet she showed no overmarks of distress; her spirit was excellent. The thirty minutes between heats passed, for all the members of the Bale stable, too quickly. The heaviness of the track had affected the mare:

Grey Medley, in the second heat, challenged Careless and passed her at the start; he was now superbly in his enormous stride — an animal with the appearance of a resistless wind — and the space between him and Careless widened hopelessly. Toward the end of the last mile Bradlock's horse had beaten Richard's mare by a hundred yards; but, almost at the winning post, he turned suddenly sulky, and, bracing himself, came to all but a stop. Careless sped up, with a fresh stirring courage; but the distance was too short — urged by whip and spur, Grey Medley was forced on . . . to win by a head.

Richard was grave; it was true the mare showed no signs of increased suffering; but she could hope to be successful only by showing a gait that even in her he hadn't looked for. But Grey Medley, he saw, was switching and flirting his tail in an obvious pain; he heard Bradlock Wiatt speaking in a harsh intemperate voice. "I tell you they were foul cuts, behind the girths; there's blood on his sheath." He was addressing Grey Medley's rider. "I had to get him in, Mr. Wiatt," the black boy protested; "Careless was right on our behind." The rest was lost. "How about it, David?" Richard asked; "can we do it?" If he didn't — David was speaking to their rider — he personally would see that there was another nigger on the new piece of stone road at Balisand. "You offer your foot in the stable yard again —— " Lucia Mathews came up. "Richard, I wish you could have a little more time. Careless might win, then." He thanked her. "This isn't all; I didn't mind losing the second heat; we rather expected to. Lucia, even I don't know how fast Careless is." Henry Dalney wasn't optimistic. "That thing of Bradlock's isn't a horse, it's got wings, like Pegasus. I can ship as a seaman, Richard, but what will you do? I have an idea how much you have up on this. You had better not let Mrs. Patton know." Richard stared at him, at his oldest, perhaps his only familiar, friend, coldly. "How far will you back your poetry? " he demanded.

Dalney ignored this, and Richard Bale turned to where his mare was waiting. But that, now, was at an end. Grey Medley, with title to the inside, again took the lead, and, closely followed by Careless, he kept it at what must have been the top of his rate. His tail was up again, in signal of acute suffering, but there was no perceptible break in his stride. The gap between them Careless seemed unable to close. It was, Richard thought, over; he felt, more than anything, a deep sorrow for the mare — he had entered her out of her class. Then David touched his elbow. "Before God, Mr. Bale, look at that Careless! " She was making her run as they entered into the last mile; they were, he realized, nose and flank. The mare drew ahead . . . it seemed that she was making a struggle to pass when, "Careless has the inside! " David exclaimed; and, with this discovered, a swift fear took possession of Richard — his boy had risked everything on that desperate measure, and it was possible for the other, in a momentary advantage of position, to rein in and force Careless against one of the poles. His fingers dug into his servant's shoulder, but his face was calm. " Now let her run," he said in an ordinary conversational voice. Run, run, run, he thought; and with every repetition Careless had the appearance of gathering a greater and more incredible speed.

But Grey Medley . . . Pegasus with wings. " Yes, sir, I told you." David was gone and he was facing Bradlock Wiatt. " Did you see where the whip cut him? " Wiatt stammered. There were answering assertions. " Your horse was beaten, Bradlock." He repeated doggedly that Grey Medley was the better of the two, and demanded another race. " Boy," Richard said to his rider, " if you ever take a chance like that again I'll — I'll set you free."

*

* *

His success with Careless, Richard Bale decided, was an auspicious beginning of an existence broken free from the tyrannical dream of the past. But he was, again, most careful to define his fidelity to the memory of Lavinia: it wasn't that his love was diminished: no, in the future it would be an accompaniment, like the sound of a harp, to his living, and not a music drawing him away from all life. That was the reverse of the effect he had described to Ava, but he felt suddenly confident he could bring it about, and already Careless had helped him. At supper he was uncommonly gay; Mrs. Patton was both puzzled and pleased; but Morryson studied him in a gloomy suspicion. The reason for this Richard fully understood — although, at long intervals, he was satirical at Richard's failure to marry, that, in reality, he dreaded, since he was convinced it would interfere with his present secret comfort.

"Winning a horse race, it looks to me, has gone to your head," he observed. "It doesn't take much, any more. But I would have thought your head was hard by now."

"If you could have seen the mare run," Richard replied, "if you had gone to the track, instead of saying horses were no good to-day, and you had any head left —— "

"He won't," Mrs. Patton interrupted, "if he doesn't stop drinking that Madeira."

"Ridiculous," Morryson Bale answered her inelegantly. "You can't call it drinking until after the third bottle. Though I can see that's been spoiled, too, with women staying at the table when the cloth's gone." This was a reference, in a stinging tone, to the night Ava had required him to leave the dining room. "I started to say," Richard resumed, "that Careless would have stirred anyone this afternoon. And here, at Balisand, I'll admit I wouldn't match her again with Grey Medley. At three-mile heats she'd have no chance." Morryson Bale proceeded with a rambling account of a twenty-mile race he had witnessed, when horses were horses. "Five heats," he asserted; twenty times past the winning post. The ones that finished were as fresh as ever the next week."

"The next year, perhaps," Richard commented. He saw that the wine was exhausted. "You must be trying to empty the cellar." Morryson exclaimed: "Cellar, cellar! If it's more than a closet I'll sleep in it." He wilted in his chair, made an unsuccessful effort to regain his erectness, and, collapsing, vomited. "I suppose," he managed to say, in a weak and gasping voice, "that upsets you, with the weak stomach you have."

"The weakness wasn't in my stomach," Richard concisely pointed out. Mrs. Patton, distressed, rose and helped a servant in the recovery of a decent order. "You're a damned absurd old nuisance," Richard went on, "and you might as well know it." Morryson Bale's reply was: "Nuisance yourself. That's a filthy Madeira . . . make your mare sick." His hands trembled so violently that he spilled the water from the glass he had lifted. He set it down and cursed, in a remarkably varied fluency, his palsy. "Shaking the dice," he declared, "that's what did it." Morryson thought he would go to bed — it was so dull in the dining room — and he moved, with a stiff tottering dignity, toward the door. He would have fallen but for Mrs. Patton; she walked beside him, an arm in his support, though he indignantly tried to repel her.

Actually, Richard admired him: Morryson had, to a rare degree, the quality of courage. He maintained an undismayed war on his increasing infirmities, his bodily decline. He cursed his palsy and he cursed death and, to him, the degenerate present. In Morryson the cantankerous spirit of the Bales had suffered no lapse. He was paying, without a voiced regret, for the years of his excesses. And he was right, to an extent, about the wine; it wasn't what it should be, what it had been. Madeira was slipping from esteem, its place taken by Spanish wines, Xeres and the pale sherries. Why, to-day, he had observed at the tavern track, gentlemen were drinking whisky, a liquor fit only for overseers. But someone, a long while ago, had spoken of that; he forgot who. Through his years, almost to the day forty, he had seen a new world come into being, and the old shift and fade. Change took place in a multitude of small things. Rum to whisky, Madeira to sherry.

He regarded Morryson as a part of the past, and he had no doubt the younger and different men looked on him, Richard Bale, as a survival out of humour with the times. But the times, in the sense they meant, were only misleading; they could wander, like a tied animal, around the picket; they couldn't get away from the centre and principle. The new world had come from the old; and yes, by God, America came out of England! That recalled his tentative determination to re-enter public life in the support of a federal government; he would speak to Beverley and Bradlock Wiatt; discover their opinions. In that case he'd have to end his present solitude: if there were a question of election, it would be necessary for him to come in contact with the electors.

Yet that he would never do in the modern servile

manner; he'd announce, where it could be heard by all, his political belief and intentions; attempt to conciliate nothing. Make it plain who were the dupes and fools and knaves! His treatment of Luke would stand as an example of his position toward such men. Bradlock had warned him against this, speaking of the people as a whole. But, hell, a rabble could never be a power; not even with the help of Jefferson's intelligence and unscrupulous energy. Hamilton had beaten him again and again and again — with the Assumption and Funding, the Bank, the Excise and now with the Proclamation of Neutrality. Federalism would always be triumphant. It wouldn't do, though, to underrate Thomas Jefferson and the mass with him; the present folly, the French fever, showed that. The Federalists, the President, were for the moment unpopular. All strong measures, and all strong men, were disliked by the mob. How clearly the war had showed him that. A passion for publicity was a confessed weakness. Humanity had to be ruled, marched in column; or, lazy, incompetent, they would straggle, the order and design of government lost.

Richard called for new candles; he had no disposition, to-night, to sit mooning in the dark. The thing to do with Careless was to save her for quarter races: at moderate distances on a fair track nothing could beat her. With the money he had won he'd repair Balisand, drain and fill more land into fields. And send to England for clothes . . . a better Madeira, a proper Bual. That brought him to the realization that he had decided, indifferently, not to go to the ball announced for the end of the week at the tavern. But, of course, he should be there; nothing could have better served his plan of renewed activity.

Probably Jordan Gainge would fetch his young wife. Did she, Richard speculated, regret the lost freedom of Guinea, where, probably, she had worn no more than the slip on the servant he saw about the house? She had preserved more than a touch of the bygone wild. But Jordan, with no inconsiderable wildness of his own to look back on, would be able to take care of her. Still vigorous . . . and grim. It would be stupid for her with Gainge — the women of breeding in Gloucester would meet her in politeness, but nothing more. A queer name, Zena. She dropped from his thought and Ava took her place in a dignity of black velvet. She went, too; and a fragment of song flashed into his memory:

A lilybud, a pink, a rose.

An involuntary pain contracted about his heart. Richard resolutely ignored it; the flowers of vanished years. A rose less yellow than the gloves it had been hidden among. Gone ——

*

*   *

The ball at the tavern opened promptly while it was still light, the stables and horse racks were full, and, when Richard arrived, all the familiar coaches of the county present. The music — it had come from Richmond — violins and a French horn, had begun, already the sounds of gambling rose from the cellar, and the taproom, crowded with men, was loud in greetings. He saw Robert Draper and Terrell, Wiatt Royston, Kennon Whiting, John Corwood and Hewit; Mordecai Cooke stopped him, Bradlock waved him toward a bottle; William Newsome, an adherent of Gawin Todd's, was formal in manner. Balantine, the tavern keeper, was pressed with twenty conflicting, simultaneous and impatient demands; and two tap men were performing prodigies of service. He stopped, finally, beside Wiatt and George Renolls, agreeing with their choice of brandy.

"As usual, you won't dance," Bradlock proceeded. "How's Careless? I hope not exhausted." Richard only replied by trusting Grey Medley had recovered from the whip. "If you take him North," he added, "a thousand dollars of mine will go with him." George Renolls thought that Grey Medley might well be the grandest horse of his generation. "But, Richard, I'd rather see that Careless of yours run than any other performance on a track." He explained his purpose of entering her in quarter races. "After the first," Renolls assured him, "you'll have to match her against her own time. You won't get a second heat."

"Gawin is here," Bradlock Wiatt told Richard in a low voice. "He came over with Beverley and Lucia. What is your feeling about him?"

"If you mean politically, he's a menace; why, hell, Bradlock, he's as dangerous as William Giles. But if you're asking me personally," Richard stopped to drink, "I can manage to get on without one at all." Wiatt replied, "Damn it, Richard, you're a bitter man. You give us a lot of bother — about what you might do."

"I'm sorry for that," Bale told him, "for I had just made up my mind to find out how you would take my going back to Congress. Would the men who know my record support me? And I'm not talking of my services in the war. I don't want a vote for them, I won't bring them up. It's my opinions I mean. I'm a Federalist, simple and pure. I haven't changed, where I stood I stand . . . for a strong government, Washington and Hamilton, and the devil with foreign ambassadors."

"That's your trouble," Bradlock promptly answered; "no one would question your integrity, and I am certain Virginia is Federal; the vote shows it; but you are not up on the minute; you antagonize too many people. Look here, we agree, you know; the truth is, the most we want is to live and race our horses in peace. The rest, so far as I'm concerned, is gabble, politics. You want to have everything as it always was. Well, it's just possible neither of us will be successful; and, if we are, it won't be by keeping on the way we have. You can't split heads open with your whip. Don't mistake me either — I'm not opposed to your sacred General. He has some of your drawbacks, but I'll back power in the government as far as both of you. What put this in your head, Richard? It's a good idea and bad at the same time."

"It is there, anyhow," Richard answered. A shift in the throng, confined within the close walls, brought Gawin Todd immediately in front of him. Todd was bulkier than Richard remembered him, a big aggressive figure with a heavy flushed face animated by a quick commanding look. "Good evening, Mr. Bale," he said clearly. " Mr. Todd," Richard replied, " good evening." There was, he perceived, a momentary curious silence around them; there was an intense unvoiced interest in their meeting; almost, it appeared, something arresting was expected. He was isolated, with Gawin Todd, from the rest of the world. But Todd, after a space, deliberately, without hurry, turned away toward the casks. Richard, before that, had decided to go in and view the dancing, but it was equally imperative for him to delay.

" Whatever we've said won't be final," he continued, to Bradlock Wiatt. " What you complain about you may come to depend on. There will be some bad years, and the men you can count on are not multiplying. The others are." He made a passage through the crowd and reached the ballroom in time to hear an address, delivered by Sewell Graveland, celebrated throughout the Tidewater for his practised skill in the conduct of dances and dancing, and the husband of Rose Ann, Ava Todd's sister.

" We have observed all the proprieties," he proceeded ornamentally, " and made our bow, in the minuet, to the past, and now it is my pleasure to announce an absolute novelty in Gloucester County. A number of us have been practising the figures of the French cotillion; and to-night, in honour of the Ambassador from France, Citizen Genêt, and of the Republic Français, we are going to dance it . . . as well, for your enjoyment." There was an instant ringing applause, hands were clapped, voices raised, the sticks of countless fans broken.

It would be for no enjoyment of his, Richard told himself savagely. Sewell Graveland ought to keep himself where he belonged, on ballroom floors. He was exactly the man Rose Ann would have married; and now, Richard supposed, where once she had drunk Madeira publicly, nothing short of rum would satisfy her. He was astonished to see men he had regarded as solid, safely Federal, as enthusiastic over the French innovation as those who couldn't be expected to know more. Even dancing had been spoiled: the nights gone when the managers, their hats under their arms, led ladies out to an acceptable music. The cotillion, directed by Graveland, formed; absurdities which, he gathered, were called favours made their appearance; women rose and danced and sat down; the figures had ridiculous French names. Richard Bale went back in the need of drink.

The taproom was emptied in the general curiosity over the cotillion; Balantine, drenched in sweat, was mopping himself by sections. "It's over soon," he observed. "What?" Richard asked stubbornly. "That new one. They were going over it this afternoon. It won't be fashionable to dance a minuet, any more, and God knows what'll happen to the congos and the reels and jigs."

"Not till we're moved to France," Richard contradicted him. "This won't last. You've seen enough people to understand them better." There was a repetition of the frenzied applause from beyond. "That doesn't sound like it," Balantine was sufficiently unmannerly to insist. "You are on the river at Balisand and a lot skips by you. Gentlemen like you will have to come around, Mr. Bale."

"To what?" Richard demanded. "To keeping taverns?" Anything but that, was the other's reply.

"I'll add this, though," he went on; "it's going to be better than it was. I can see that every day. Once every proper coach that passed was for Welfield or Todd Hundred or your plantation, and we could hardly afford to spread a clean cloth. Have you been to the Eagle in Richmond lately? It's as comfortable as you'd want. Gentlemen, and even parties with ladies, are often there."

"When I have to stay a night in a Virginia tavern," Richard Bale told him, "I'll know a Republican has been elected President; and that day I will give you a hundred dollars." Balantine turned and wrote with chalk on the wood wall. "Mr. Richard Bale of Balisand is agreeable to a hundred dollars when Thomas Jefferson is elected President of the United States." Richard objected to the wording. "Not when, if." Either way, the tavern keeper asserted, it was a good account. "You can't lose," it was Beverley Mathews, "but, by heaven, I don't want to see you win." The men crowded back; now, evidently, the cotillion was over. "If Mr. Jefferson is elected," this, Richard saw, was William Newsome, "you won't need his hundred. Honest men will have the money." This was humorously denied: "Not if the others own the fast mares." George Renolls, Richard recognized, had no intention of offence.

*

* *

However, he delayed in speech to consider Newsome: it might be necessary to give him an indication of the proprieties observable for public occasions and terms.

What he had remarked, about honest men, had, perhaps, an unacceptable flavour of the personal. But Bradlock Wiatt took his arm. " It's just as I say," he remonstrated; " here you are, looking for a quarrel before I had scarcely got done. You can't get into Congress with a pair of duelling pistols. Put that out of your mind. Do you think Lucia Mathews will marry Gawin? " Richard answered that he hadn't realized events, there, had gone so far. " It would be tremendously lucky for Todd," Bradlock continued; " endless money — he hasn't a fortune — for his comfort and political ambitions. I don't know about Lucia: I've hardly ever, in all her life, seen her off a horse. She rides like an angel. The truth is, no one, not even Beverley, knows her. But I can't wish him any success — it would be the devil to have him around here, stirring up trouble."

" If Lucia could ride to her wedding," Richard declared, " attended by foxhounds, she would marry almost anyone. I mean," he added carefully, " that one man has never been more to her than another. I can't imagine her in love; or being in love with her."

" You're going down to the hazard, of course."

" Later," Richard replied, " when the stakes are worth a throw." He walked outside, to where the tavern fronted the public road. There were couples promenading close by, in the drooping night; for the moment the music was still. He passed Rose Ann with Graveland. She gave him a brilliant smile and called back that she was waiting to teach him the French steps. " Thank you," he declined, " I have been drilled so long in the others." He saw Mary Todd; but she, too, was married . . . with four children. Marable Todd, her one brother, was palpably drunk; Sally was lecturing him severely. "It wouldn't be so bad, later," she asserted. "But now! Yes, I am ashamed of you." Marable, with a low bow, said, "Richard Bale of Balisand." The boy had been a long while in England; and his manner, the slight mockery implied in the complete politeness of his speech, brought Jasper Robine back to Richard's memory. Then, leaving them, Richard came abruptly on a solitary figure with an elaborate white dress and a bearing of angry rebellion. It was Jordan Gainge's wife.

"How long will it last?" she demanded. He replied, "Easily till dawn." The sharp stamp of a foot was perceptible. "I don't see why it must for you," he continued, "if you're tired of it." Jordan, she replied, judged it needful for her to remain. "A part of my education," she explained. "Perhaps you didn't know it — I am being educated so the Bales and Todds and Henry Dalney will have me to dinner."

The brutality of this assertion shocked him out of protest. All that he could manage to say, after an inexcusable pause, was that she would soon go wherever she wished. "No," she contradicted him, "and you don't believe that, either. But soon, if they keep like this, I won't want to. I think I hate everybody alive. Except Jordan." Even that, he felt, was a tardy modification. "Do you dance?"

"It happens I don't," he told her uncomfortably. "I haven't for years, on account of a bad leg." No one, it seemed, had taken her out on the floor for an hour. Mr.

Todd had danced with her, and Mr. Beverley Mathews, " all the old men. But the young ones — they are too damn afraid of the girls! "

Richard Bale was again shocked. " I'm not all learned yet," she said hastily. " It slipped out . . . the Guinea in me. I'm glad Jordan didn't hear me. Why did he marry me, Mr. Bale? "

" He loved you," Richard said inconclusively.

" Why did I marry him? "

" Indeed, I couldn't tell. It isn't what you'd call a general subject." She could see, she replied, that he was attempting to correct her. " I thought you would be different. I liked what I heard about you so much." Frankly curious, Richard asked what that had been.

" Why, in the war with England, all those battles; and then the way you've acted since. You'll fight — I think it's that, mostly. I was born among men who fight. It's the way they settle things, about girls and fish and voting."

" How do they vote? " he asked immediately.

" Oh, they don't agree with you." She was positive there. " You see, it's so free where I lived. No one likes to be told what to do. But they are only beginning to think of that —— " She broke off. " Why? " Richard urged her to continue. " I don't mind telling you," Jordan Gainge's wife admitted; " on account of Mr. Todd. He's been down among them explaining about the United States and what happened in France. He says it could be the same here, and the people have everything. Mr. Newsome is around more. They don't like you."

" No," Richard agreed, " they don't. I'd be bothered if they did. I could never get along with traitors and liars." She clapped her hands. " I love it when you say that." He gazed at her sombrely. " I wish they'd listen to me," he proceeded. " It's too late," she warned him; " you must keep away. They are even suspicious of me, now. I went home last week, and without Jordan; they treated me like I was strange. You don't want me here and they don't." Gainge appeared:

" It's good of you to talk to Zena," he told Richard; " we would be happy if you'd come to see us. Henry Dalney often does." He would get Henry, then, to take him, Richard agreed. " And you will have to visit Balisand. Though there won't be much there for Mrs. Gainge — we are out of the habit of entertaining."

Jordan Gainge's gratitude was at once evident and admirably contained. The old man was stiffly proud. " You ought to be in at the dancing," he addressed his wife. " Mr. Newsome has been asking for you."

When they had gone Richard thought at length about Zena Gainge. What an uncomfortable position! However, except for the dinner he had spoken of, he couldn't be responsible for her. Yet she stayed in his mind — not obviously an attractive woman, but with something indefinable. Perhaps it was the intensity of her spirit of revolt. A very different, Lucia Mathews, stopped before him. " That was nice of you," she commented. He disclaimed all right of approval. Then she asked about Careless. " You'll remember I thought she might win." He recalled the tone of his discussion of her with Bradlock Wiatt. " Lucia," he inquired, " do you ever think about anything beyond horses and riding? " She didn't answer immediately, but stood squarely regarding him.

" Why do you ask that? "

A devil of perversity entered him. " I was wondering if you were interested in Gawin Todd." That, he recognized, had been a mistake. " There are so many ways of answering you." Her voice was speculative, detached. " What made you think I would answer you at all? I can't imagine. It's so new and unexpected from a Bale . . . of Balisand. I believe I'll insist on your explaining how, or rather, what gave you liberty to demand that."

" Of course, I can't tell you," he confessed. " But I did, and I haven't any inclination to apologize. It wasn't an unheard-of question."

" I ought to be flattered," she responded, " but, do you know, I'm not. I like Careless better than I do you, if that could be called an answer. And I can see you've been discussing me with your brandy." Her tone was almost a drawl. Then, suddenly, she became quite cheerful. " Oh, yes, horses are much better. And foxhounds." He had invited it, he reflected; and he bent forward, inspecting her more closely. " Is it my hair? " Her hands were up, framing her face. " I was looking for the French colours," he explained; " at least, they are called that. The one I knew was white."

*

* *

It was exactly as Morryson had intimated, no, flatly declared, Richard recognized — women, in the main, he didn't get along with. What Zena Gainge had told him about Gawin Todd and Guinea took possession of his mind. It was nothing short of criminal to inflame the suspicions of Jinkin's Neck, to deliberately arouse an entire region against the government. Yes, traitor and liar were not too strong. Bradlock was afraid of his drastic manner, but his warning that such measures were necessary would turn out to be fact. It was no good to try conciliation with the present republican methods and men. The dancing had returned to a familiar form, a reel; the floor was crowded; Todd was with Lucia; and, annoyed, Richard went down to the cellar.

It was lighted with hanging lanterns, and, on the long table where the dice were being cast at hazard, there were supplementary candles. The table was surrounded, hidden, by men; but when he approached an opening was made for him. This, he well understood, was in recognition of the name he bore as a gambler. The two men immediately engaged were strange to him, but he saw that one was supported by William Newsome. The amounts chanced weren't large — the throwing was for the new ten-dollar gold piece. But Newsome indirectly greeted him at once. "Here's Richard Bale of Balisand, and he'll think we are children playing for buttons." Mathews put a hand on Richard's arm. "Don't let that rush you," he advised. "You can stand on your reputation." The immediate casting was over, and Newsome swept the dice toward them:

"Let Mr. Bale call the main, and be the caster, if we can find anyone to take his bets." Richard picked the dice up. "You've had so much to say about it," he addressed Newsome, " that some of us will think you had better back your talk." William Newsome was a tall man and thin, with a lower jaw that protruded in advance of his face and a habit of constantly raising and contracting his eyebrows. Of an inconsiderable family settled north of the Piankatank River, near the Dragon Swamps, he had been individually very successful in speculating with shares of the United States Bank — an institution it was now his profession to attack — and he was known to play for large amounts. "That's a way to put it I don't encourage," he replied; " but it can only be answered to-night with the dice."

"Try your luck, first," Beverley urged him, and Richard mentioned a hundred dollars. It was in his mind to call seven, since, out of thirty-six possible combinations, seven could be thrown in six ways; but, instead, he called eight and cast. He had thrown out — aces were turned up. The report had swiftly spread that he was engaged in hazard with Newsome, and the throng about the table multiplied. It was dividing, he saw, into two bodies — the men beside him were Federalists, supporters of Washington; those at Newsome's elbows were publicly French in sympathy, followers of Jefferson and John Mason, with some whose position was debatable. The game had turned into a struggle between the Federal party and the Republican. Richard lost a second hundred dollars, a third and a fourth; and then, impatient, he made his bet five hundred. "That is just what I've won from you," Newsome answered. " Take your money back . . . if you're able." Richard nicked in, with eleven. "Now I have it," he remarked,

"I'll let you fix the amount of your play." The other decided that, for the present, five hundred dollars was enough at a cast. Richard won again and again: once, when he was setter, by throwing ten, one of his chances; as caster with the number seven.

"Your thousand has bred another," he announced. "There is two thousand dollars up now." The whispering about him fell silent. "Eight," William Newsome called. "By God, he nicked!" a voice exclaimed. Newsome hesitated, with the dice in his hand: it was evident he was considering a momentous decision. "Four thousand dollars," he said finally, with his eyebrows in a knot. Richard agreed. He gazed curiously at the dice lying close together on the table; one showed a four, the other a five. Well, he had lost four thousand dollars. He thought suddenly of Careless and her superb running; compared with the mare, this was a petty business.

"Four has the look of an unlucky number for me," he asserted. "Five would be better; yes, five thousand." William Newsome was easy, arrogant, with the safety of his winnings. "I have an idea you're wrong still," he responded. "Five thousand dollars on a turn. That ought to satisfy even you. Mr. Bale, you are accommodated. To show you the delusions you're labouring under, to give you, and the gentlemen associated — shall I put it? — under the flag of a discredited monarchy, a last opening, I'll call the main at five, your own figure."

"Wait," Richard Bale interrupted him, "if you will allow us the definition of our position and loyalty: England is no more discredited with the United States than France is involved. America is free — your favourite word, I believe — from both. We, Mr. Newsome, the men back of me here, are not gambling with the fate of the United States; we are not content to let our country fall with a brace of dice or a turn of speech. Where you were in the spring of 1776, when Howe concluded to evacuate Boston, I have no interest in, but there are others with — shall I say? — better memories, and they will always be proof against schemes to debauch — well, the currency. Your friends have made this necessary. There was a time, hardly longer ago than yesterday, when the United States had hope of a single, a united, mind and heart, but you have split it in two; you have called up factions in the President's cabinet itself; God knows with what result. I am gambling with you, Mr. Newsome, but be sure we'll take no chances in higher affairs."

"I called the main at five," Newsome answered. "We are here for hazard and not to listen to shots out of old-fashioned cannon. If ever men gambled themselves out of an inheritance and power the Federalists did. Five!" he cried, and cast five exactly.

The four thousand dollars he had owed, Richard realized, was nine. Nine thousand dollars. Plenty. "I believe you are at Todd Hundred," he addressed Newsome, "and I haven't so much, in gold or notes, with me. But you will be paid, if it's convenient to you, by ten o'clock to-morrow morning. I'll give you the acknowledgment at once." Careless . . . running with miraculous speed. He'd have to forgo, for the year, the improvements he had marked out at Balisand. The throng broke into groups, low excited comments. For once Bradlock Wiatt didn't find fault. "That was splendidly lost, Richard. And not all lost either. The impression you made was very favourable. Justified gambling. It had dignity. It takes blood to lose."

"If you're at all embarrassed, Richard," Beverley Mathews told him privately, "I can put the money in your hand to-night."

"If you put rum I'd like it better," Richard reassured him. "I can get the other at once." They went up the stairs together and into the taproom. Outside, later, they discovered Lucia waiting to go home. "Gawin wanted to take me," she went on pointedly, "but I knew you'd be disappointed. Richard, I caught echoes of gambling at unheard-of amounts. Isn't keeping a tradition rather expensive?"

"Why, yes," he admitted; "but what else would you have me keep? The money? I'm surprised at your friends, though — drinking and gambling almost like gentlemen. And the trust of the people reposed in them. The plain people. The plough horses."

"I'll see that they don't in the future," she promised him. "Are you telling me that you should be congratulated?" As he was bowing, she turned sharply away. "I don't know where Lucia got her manners," Beverley Mathews complained: "unless it could be in the stable. We'll nick these Republicans yet, Richard; they'll throw a main out of turn."

*

* *

The following morning Richard stood on the wharf at Balisand and watched the canoe that held Thomas Ekkes and the money for Newsome swing out into the river. London, with the feeling that their passage to Todd Hundred had the importance of a mission, had taken four servants for the rowing, while he sat upright and severe at the stern. The negroes had begun a long-drawn song in minor key, but the headman stopped them. They were all, in the canoe, impressed with the fact that this was no ordinary occasion. Privately Richard Bale was chagrined at his heavy loss; he was exasperated at his bad luck: why, at the worst possible turn, had Newsome, and be damned to him, cast five? Still, this game was called hazard. He had lost before. He would win again. And Bradlock Wiatt had been encouraging about the few words he had had opportunity to say. Fifty men, anyhow, must have heard them; they would be carefully reported to Gawin Todd; actually, the whole affair, as he had hoped, had most happily brought him back into the world of men and politics.

His annoyance changed into a feeling of cheerfulness, of downright encouragement. He thought of Lavinia with a conscious impunity: how lovely she was with her song, a lilybud, a pink, a rose. The blindness of another chance had taken her away from him. Richard then shifted his thoughts confidently to his current affairs: he'd go around quietly first, see men and discuss with them the relation of the Tidewater, of Virginia, to Congress and the nation. The direct announcement of his intention could come naturally later. This proceeded, developed, as he had hoped. He made, in keeping with his temperament and convictions, no effort to meet the mass of voters — his wish to influence the Guineamen had been peculiar to that situation — his contact was with gentlemen and the more respectable of the small planters: the men, largely, who were familiar to him riding with the foxhounds.

He had been, during his renewed activity, twice, if not three times, at Welfield — Beverley Mathews was a warm supporter of his plans — and Richard had drifted into the habit of amusing himself with Lucia. They developed a verbal game in which, apparently, one was relentlessly, exhaustively, critical of the other. It had begun at the tavern ball, really, in a spirit of antagonism, if not dislike, but that had soon vanished. Richard, with an entire coolness, liked Lucia Mathews; she was, through years with her father and the management of the Welfield stable, admirably fitted to a masculine temperament. For the most part Richard Bale and Beverley discussed the feeling of the county, and Lucia, in clothes which no one ever noticed, sat quietly with her slim strong knees crossed and her features, more than ever those of an Indian, composed.

He went, as well, with Henry Dalney, to call on Jordan Gainge and his wife. They rode for more than a mile over a precarious way lying in a wide treacherous expanse of marsh grass before they came, at the end of land in that direction, to the small area of solid earth that held Gainge's house. The lawn about it was but roughly cleared, the grass was high and coarse in the shadow of a compact immensely old grove of water oaks. Nothing else broke the flatness of a horizon worked everywhere on its edge, it seemed, with the silver of the bay.

A pack of unmannerly hounds barked threateningly, crows rose with a harsh clamour from the oaks, and Zena stood in the doorway. "I'm glad you came," she said, facing Dalney, but the effect of her greeting she contrived to direct to Richard Bale. "Jordan is inside." They walked through a short gloomy hall, narrow and wooded like a way in a ship, passed a door on the left open to the side lawn, and entered a large room which, from the rigid order and bareness of its furniture, had a gaunt and inhospitable air. However, this was immediately contradicted by Jordan Gainge:

"I can't serve you with a fancy punch, but there is Barbados rum that won't be trifled with. I've heard it said it would kill a nigger. But now I don't get to sea, and servants and rum are so valuable, we won't waste it by finding out."

He was without coat or waistcoat, his white linen shirt open at the throat, but he took no care to repair this. Indeed, he was completely, pleasantly, indifferent to the niceties of formal attire. Gainge, Richard reflected, had a blood as old and vigorously defined as his own; not, perhaps, with exactly the same origins; yet — in the confusion of to-day — it was ancient, far more than respectable. He felt at home here, he told himself further; he understood Gainge and was a companion to his habits and preferences and speech.

Zena, wholly silent, sat at a small distance from the

men: Jordan had tried several times, without success, to draw her into the conversation. On a table, Richard saw, there was lying open a book of spelling; and he wondered if they had interrupted one of the lessons she had spoken of to him. His gaze wandered farther and encountered a pair of pistols exposed on the shelf of a mantel: rather, he corrected himself, they were small guns. The barrels must be a full sixteen inches in length, carrying an extraordinarily heavy bullet, of perhaps fifty-six calibre; they were heavily, expensively, mounted in brass, evidently their metal was superfine; but they were no match for the beauty, the delicate precision, of the pair at Balisand. The talk, now between Henry and Gainge, had to do with ships, and Richard definitely turned to Zena.

" I saw some flowers at the corner of the house as I came in. You planted them, of course. No true Gainge ever put one in the ground." Jordan laughed. " A woman's business," he answered for her. " You're right. Show them to Mr. Bale, if you like. The gentlemen inland on the North River spend a lot of time in their gardens." That assertion, Richard told him, had a strong flavour of salt. Zena was already up, leading him out to where a clump of day lilies were making a struggle for existence in a damp and inappropriate shade.

" You'll have to move them," he instructed her; " a sunnier place." That was easy said, she replied. " It's all gloomy here with the oak trees. I like the marsh, though; it's marshy where I lived. Mr. Bale, you must notice I don't call it ma'sh any more."

He complimented her. Why did she engage his interest? A thin young woman without one of the qualities he preferred. But she was amazingly quick, yes, graceful, in her movements, like the tall marsh grass she was at home with swaying in the wind. "Do we have to go back right away?" she asked. "I don't know. You must tell me. It used to be I could do anything. I wanted to go in the sea — the way I have — and Jordan all but died." Was it possible that she had meant unclothed? That was the only construction he could possibly put on her words, and it created, in him, a positive distaste for her. Still, she was so reluctant to return to the house that he forced himself to continue standing with her, gazing aimlessly at the lilies.

"I don't mind learning from you," she confided to Richard Bale. "I told you a lot that night at the tavern. We are brought up never to talk . . . to strangers. But you were so kind ——"

"You won't find many to agree with you," he replied unsympathetically; "I'm supposed to be the exact reverse." Illogically it annoyed him to be regarded as kind. "I know what they think," she assured him. "Don't you remember? I told you then. I wouldn't want you to be the way with others you are with me."

*

* *

Again with Dalney, on their horses, Richard silently dwelt on the fact that he hadn't, purposely, renewed his invitation for the Gainges to take dinner at Balisand. It would do another time, later; he had no present wish to entertain Zena Gainge. She hadn't, by a large amount, a proper reserve. At Roane's he parted from Henry, turning to the left, bound for Welfield, where he would stay that night with Beverley: Lucia was going to Todd Hundred . . . a party at Todd Hundred and it was again June. Would anyone be put in the room over the schoolhouse? There was, now, no need for a tutor. He recalled the passionate woe of Mr. Garret. Eliza Wiatt had married eight years ago and gone from Gloucester — a girl with a perverse and experimenting charm. It was after five when he rode into the lane at Welfield, but the day was still bright, clear and sweet with scents and the afternoon songs of birds.

The trees on the lawn were finer than those at Todd Hundred, finer than any others in the county; Richard could never remember all the variety of their names: the maidenhair tree he knew, and, of course, the myrtles and magnolias, the beeches and varnish trees and yews . . . he must get Lucia to go over them again. She hadn't, he found, left for the Todds' yet. She was on the paved terrace above the falling garden — there were four terraces, at the bottom flowering almonds and mock oranges, arbours with white jasmine and cloth-of-gold roses; there was a grape walk and greenhouses; and beyond, in place of river, a far sweep of cultivated field, acre on acre closed in by the distant forest. The upper terrace was cool with shade.

"He'll be down any minute," Lucia explained, in connection with her father. "I should have gone long ago, but I didn't; I won't bother to tell you why." Richard begged her to take no pains on his account.

He selected a deep low chair, and a servant put a jug of sangaree beside him. "You will be very gay," he spoke over the rim of a glass. "On the contrary, I think. It would be quiet under the circumstances." Of course, referring to Charles Todd's death, a scant year back, she was correct. "Gawin is here again, and, I imagine, his friend Newsome."

"I don't know about Mr. Newsome," she answered. "Rose Ann with her husband and the young person from Baltimore Sally is going to marry." That, he considered, the smallness of the affair, practically a family party, made Lucia's presence more significant. For two months rumours of her engagement to Gawin Todd had reached him, and he studied her with a renewed interest: the Mathews had long been intimates of his, and, he told himself, he didn't want to lose Lucia. A marriage with Todd would come to that — he would soon find it awkward, even impossible, to frequent Welfield. He disliked, as well, the thought of Gawin Todd successful with her; with anything, candour obliged him to add. Her remarkably straight fibre, the simple directness of her mind, would be warped by his circuitous nature and life.

This he was willing, no, anxious, to prevent; but he was uncertain how to proceed. He had once been mistaken in the manner of his reference to Gawin and her. He couldn't beg Lucia to let Gawin Todd go by and he couldn't warn Beverley, who, very rightly, would regard such a liberty as totally unwarranted. "I am sorry you are going," he said, without much attention to his words; "it's pleasanter when you're here."

"Richard Bale!" she exclaimed. "I never listened to anything more futile. You never know if I'm in the room. You never speak a word to me, except the nonsense I'm sick to death of. Why, you are not sure, always, if I am a boy or a girl. And then, then, you pretend to be melancholy because I'm leaving! You've been drinking — I mean more than usual."

"I have," he acknowledged; "some heavy rum at Jordan Gainge's, but that's ridden off. Good heavens, Lucia, can't I make a decent remark without bringing a storm?"

"It's so late," she replied; "you must remember I am not used to it, from you."

"I'm too old for a string of compliments," he told her; "that's not the Bale manner. I thought you understood us. You ought to. I will repeat it, that it's too bad you are leaving. I wanted you to go over the trees with me again. I keep forgetting. Now you'll pretend I've never had an interest in them." He had always liked such things, she admitted; but he was stupid about names. There would be other days for that.

"Will there?" he asked. He hadn't intended to say so much, and he waited in considerable doubt of her reply. She ignored his question entirely. "You ride to Welfield once or twice a week regularly, and the next time will be devoted to botany — but that's not the name for trees — instead of to the damnable state of the nation."

"I want to come often," he said, relieved. "I find I can't get new habits or any new friends at all. Even now when I'm stirring around more. It's supposed to be a drawback. Perhaps. I can't help it——" Nonsense, she interrupted him, he was proud of it; she knew the Bales well enough to be certain of that. "We have opinions," he acknowledged, "and we hold to the past; but I'm told it isn't wise to-day, that I am being left, since everyone has discovered that he is as good as everyone else."

"That's true," she admitted; "but I won't agree." He recognized that she was referring to conversations with Gawin Todd. "In my heart I admire what you are. Besides, you can't, as you say, help it. I added the other — that you didn't want to. I listen to more of your talk at dinner than you imagine. There is nothing to take my mind from it. Father, naturally, agrees with what you say; and I do but I don't. I don't but I do. What I am does and what I think disagrees with you. Wouldn't you know from that my name's Lucia?"

He decided to be more exact. "You are coming under an influence foreign to you," he declared; "you are being talked into a position. No one is more aristocratic than you, and you'll never escape from it. Thank God, you won't! The people, generally speaking, I dislike you'd dislike. Why, you will judge a man for ever by his seat on a horse or if he overrides the hounds. You belong to the party of Washington, to the Mathews and Bales. You'll never follow Madison's example."

She sat very quietly, following him with a clear gaze, and, it appeared to him, there was a little pallor through the dark flush of her cheeks. Only her hands, locked under the sweeping fold of a riding skirt, moved. Then, "Are you very sure, Richard?" she asked. "Are you sure for me? It could be very serious, what you've said."

"Entirely." He spoke calmly, but, within, suddenly, there was a small nameless tumult. After all, was he serious, and seriously speaking in utter good faith? A feeling that he was merely petty, and therefore contemptible, possessed him. But he repeated his assurance, at length, with even a more decided inflection. All that could be measured was in his favour. Beverley would agree with him. "A line has been drawn between this and that," he proceeded, "through no wish of ours, and it's more and more important which side you stand on. A line," he exclaimed, "a gulf we couldn't shout across, Lucia." He modified his voice; "we'd never see each other afterwards."

She rose, gathering up her skirt, and Beverley appeared from the house. "I thought you had gone an hour ago," he told his daughter; "a horse and the carryall have been standing ready longer. Now you'll miss supper." Ava, she was certain, would keep supper for her. It was a short ride. "Richard has been scolding me; he's afraid I may be getting — what did you say, a little common?" Richard Bale cheerfully denied even the shadow of such an intention.

*

* *

With Lucia gone the two men were, without speech, idly intent upon the wide prospect before them. There was a sound of bees in the jasmine, the faint call of partridges from the fields; a lavender-coloured twilight gathered along the border of the woods and slowly pervaded the open. The pitcher of sangaree had been replaced by a bowl of toddy. Richard, however, was kept from a complete enjoyment of the tranquillity by an uneasiness, a self-blame, following all he had said, intimated, to Lucia; the thought of her sudden gravity returned to trouble him. He had deliberately taken the responsibility of influencing her feelings, perhaps her acts: there was no possibility of escaping the recognition that, at last, she had put some dependence in him; she had begged him to be careful in his advice.

But, on examination, he was convinced that it had been, quite aside from a personal element, sound. His thoughts were directed to Gawin Todd; and, where he was concerned, a curious and familiar patience supported him. Events, he was sure, would take care of Todd. How different Gawin was from Charles, how immeasurably his inferior! Yet, Richard Bale was forced to acknowledge, not altogether inferior: Gawin, however he might disagree with him, had more energy, stronger convictions, broader interest, than his dead brother. He was — but of a new and not praiseworthy type — a fighter; he fought with phrases, in committee, by intrigue. Yes — the new art of politics. His thoughts were interrupted by a stir within; Beverley rose, and Jasper Robine walked unexpectedly out upon the terrace.

" This is agreeable," he announced, in what was, for him, a tone of cordiality. " Your daughter told me you'd be sitting here, like this, and — Gawin was so occupied — I rode over." He would, of course, Beverley asserted, stay until to-morrow, but Robine begged him to let that rest on the progress of the evening. "It would be very improper," he explained, "when I am really stopping at Todd Hundred."

Three chairs were arranged around the toddy bowl, fresh glasses provided, and, in an easy state of comfort, Robine related the circumstances which had made it possible for him to stop, on his way North, at Gloucester. "The truth is," he admitted, "that I have been to New Orleans on a private and official errand; or public and unofficial; but we needn't bother with that. Damn the Mississippi River," he added, "since we're not in Kentucky. There's no reason why we shouldn't discuss actual conditions; if you will be good enough to remember that I am by birth, anyhow, one of you." That, Richard Bale realized, was very gracefully said; he was exceptionally glad to see Robine again — a man he instinctively approved of and admired. He had, as far as possible, followed Robine's career; superficially he was well enough acquainted with it: at the requisite moment, it was palpable, he had dropped his allegiance to Virginia as a State for a national activity. Elected to the First Senate as a compromise between aristocratic and more liberal tendencies, he had been drawn into the second class, and was retiring — without effort to be retained — this year. He was still considered a man of importance, one destined to high office; but nothing to warrant that had yet been publicly shown. The nine years which had gone since Richard saw him last had deepened the lines at his eyes, turned his month in, secretively; he had rapidly aged.

"We'll have to send an army South," it was his opinion; "and not without you, Mr. Bale. The Spanish are intolerable — they have a whole system of robbery called passes and duties. On the levee at New Orleans there is a duty of fifteen per cent, and then the cargo can't be sold. It must be immediately shipped back at a charge of six per cent. Kentucky is in an uproar with its demands on Congress — practically a challenge to fight the Spanish or them. But even that isn't the kernel of the affair — Genêt is organizing a French expedition down the river; two, really, from Kentucky and the Carolinas. A most ambitious young man." Richard corrected him, "A damn dangerous nuisance." Jasper Robine replied:

"You can say that here, in the Tidewater, but not in Philadelphia. I assure you there you'd meet with violence. The French, the saviours of mankind!" He put in his tone the contempt screened from his words. "I went to one of the dinners given to our noble allies, the citizens' dinner, where Biddle presided. There were artillery salutes and songs no one understood and tears, tears, kisses, of brotherhood. I'm told the Republican dinner, a week before, was worse. Anyhow, we all wore red caps; and I can imagine what the President thought of it. There was no need to imagine what we thought of the President. I've always been convinced of the ultimate futility of the Federal party, but, by God, Freneau almost drove me back into it. A filthy business."

Richard Bale listened with an intense interest — Robine baffled him. Report had him woven closer than ever into the fate of Jefferson and the new party; the

National Gazette, the paper Freneau had been brought from New York to conduct, was the official Republican voice; but Robine, in a characteristic and transparent spirit of mockery, was condemning his own associates. His face, it began to appear, was stamped with discontent. "You have been very courteous," Richard said, "and I wonder if you will satisfy us about this — we get only rumours here — does Freneau write the attacks on the government, on the President, really? To be honest with you, we hear they are inspired, or even direct from a more celebrated pen." Jasper Robine studied him, frowning:

"To answer that as a separate question would be unjust. A great deal would have to be explained before you were equipped to judge. And then, with all the facts, I'm afraid you couldn't be persuaded. Mr. Bale, if you will allow me, I'd like to think you were bigoted. There is something about your bigotry that would refresh me. Still, on Mr. Jefferson's part, I ought to undertake at least an explanation." He set down his glass. "I'll ask you to listen to me without heat. Well, in the first place, you can't, here, appreciate the change over the country. You are free to distrust it, or think it's only temporary — I don't — but it must be met. We spoke of this, you'll recall, that other time at Mr. Charles Todd's:

"The people, Mr. Bale, the people, and now, in 1793, a damned sight more so! You believe in strong men and measures, you regard the mass as a quality to be dealt with in mass, and between that and your leaders there has been neither sympathy nor communication.

I think I am justified there. You made the mistake of putting all your dependence in a single man; for you're safe only as long as Washington lives. When he dies, or when his influence goes, the Federalists will go too. John Adams isn't the same. We can never look for another Washington. Thomas Jefferson is totally different. When that happens, then, you must ask yourself, what next? Why, the people. Jefferson saw that long ago and he persuaded Madison of it. Astute men, Mr. Bale, but not naked of ideals. Supporters of the Constitution;" a fleet smile touched his lip. "Strict Constructionists. They would be — it made them possible:

"When the government became national it dealt with individuals and no longer with States; that's an axiom. I can assure you of it because there, until it happened, I was mistaken. The executive, except for Jefferson's influence, is Federal in your sense, but the House is Republican, it is the mass. The Senate —— " He stopped, arrested by thought. "I could never be a success in the House," he finally declared. "Gawin Todd is the man for that; a perfect agreement and opportunity." What all this had to do with the National Gazette Richard Bale couldn't yet see.

*

* *

"New times and new methods." Jasper Robine addressed this directly to Richard. Was it the answer he had requested? Regarded as that, it was a complete admission. "The party, the public, has to be reached,"

Robine went on, "instructed; or, if you'd rather, led; and it isn't, as you've suspected, exclusively made of superior intellects. A mass . . . but you have had it to deal with. The common good! That is the National Gazette, it isn't the only one of its kind and it isn't the first. Freneau is a translator in the Department of State — Madison recommended him — but he is a poet, too, and the historic license, don't you see? We have a gigantic problem to solve. Gigantic," he repeated. The ladle struck against the bottom of the toddy bowl; it was empty. A servant opportunely appeared. "We will have supper here," Mathews informed him; "whenever it is ready." Fresh toddy arrived.

"You should regard the attacks on the President in this light," Robine insisted. "With all your coldness, politically you are sentimental, provincial. A chapter or two of Machiavelli would be useful. I see Hamilton and Jay often, we are at the same houses, and, personally, on good terms; but politically — they are traducers of the sacred cause of American liberty." He spoke in imitation of a florid public orator. The toddy was again consumed; supper, with Madeira, disposed of; and brandy supplanted the rum. As he continued to drink, Jasper Robine's satirical comments grew freer. "Yes," he repeated, "Gawin promises to be a later Patrick Henry; and, while you're damning Madison, don't forget Henry turned Federal.

"Todd was fortunate — coming into the third session of the First Congress. He missed the fight against Assumption but was there for the Excise Bill and Hamilton's Bank Measure. With Giles he practically led the

Southern opposition in favour of the Virginia farmer and not the fox-hunters. There are so many more farmers. And then, this January, they brought in the resolutions against the conduct of the Treasury. In case you haven't guessed it, that was planned to drive Hamilton out of the Cabinet."

"There was a rumour about the author of them, too," Beverley Mathews observed.

"My dear Mathews, expediency! Would you let your overseer draw a petition for you, for example, to the courts? There were five resolutions, you will remember, and a beautiful time in consequence: as you hinted, it was Jefferson — and the people — against the government. They wanted the dates and drafts of foreign debts; a statement of the balances with the Bank . . . but you are familiar with all that. In February the charges against Hamilton were specific — he had violated the Constitution by spending money without permission of Congress. By heaven, your representatives were on their feet then! Fisher Ames, for a sick man, was remarkable. Smith, from South Carolina, with a speech Hamilton wrote — I'll get you to notice that — made an impressive racket until Jefferson had him charged with a fortune Hamilton had thrown his way in speculations."

"But the resolutions were discredited," Richard added; "no measures ever had a quicker death. I understand only seventeen members supported them." They were put aside, Robine admitted; for the while. "The St. Clair business helped Todd, too. They very near had that accounted to the Treasury; and think of the opportunity to baste the British — the Indians led by Joseph Brant, half English and the son of Sir William Johnson. We know better, among ourselves; but the public, I must remind you of their taste for dramatics. And when Burr came in, from New York . . . you'll agree it took a French tone." Richard Bale replied, "Anything but American; thank God Virginia is still Federal. We have some power in the Assembly again." Robine repeated, "For the while."

The far rim of forest, the fields, and then the lower terraces, had been veiled by night; a glimmer of fireflies showed in the grass; the new moon low in the west had grown brighter only to vanish. "But if you've missed some of this in Gloucester, John Adams is no better in Philadelphia;" it was Jasper Robine again. "Every time he drives out in state with that coach of his, he cools popular enthusiasm. The old method. It will be good, perhaps, for another ten years, and then the Democratic nag. I'll be goddamned," he exclaimed, "if I know whether I'm a Republican or a Democrat! It's come to a mixing of both. Jefferson can't keep the name Democratic-Republicans. Theoretical. I tell him that and he talks about architecture. But Marshall bothers him. Marshall ought to be recognized, he's sure; a sharp young lawyer; but why, with Fauquier County behind him, do you suppose he is blind to the people?"

"Marshall ought to be rewarded, Robine: I hope, some day, he will be elevated to a position equal with his talents, his legal talents. Relieved of politics. Patrick Henry, Jasper, is burned out, a squib; but Aaron

Burr will knock open the windows. Mathews," he asked, at a tangent, "do you get this rum from a river?" His hand, with the ladle, was unsteady. "Genêt worries him, too." Obviously he was still concerned with the Secretary of State. "He'd like to be rid of him; the private fact is we all would. The public run mad. I'll add this, Bale; you can't see it now, but Genêt will be a blessing for the Federalists."

He was, Richard observed, cursed well disguised. "Wait. I tell you he is a keg of powder under the Republicans, the Democrats, the Democrat-Republicans. He'll blow us up . . . but we will come down again, in office. The people! This is the hell of a big country, bigger than you'd ever reckon; and there will be more people than you could count in a lifetime; individual men will go for nothing. But the system will do it, unless it breaks down; and then there will be a French omelette. One big yellow hell of an omelette. You gentlemen have had things your own way for a long time, with your plantations to hunt over; but they are going to be cut into little farms for the people; and you will have to be good and join the Baptist or the Presbyterian Church. No Church of England. You can't expect to eat nectarines, and the people with only potatoes. No, by Jesus Christ!

"The nectarine trees will go, and the apricots and bowers of jasmine. Bale, you were a fool not to contrive to get killed at Yorktown. Richard Bale of Balisand. It won't do! You ought to see that. Yes, killed by your old friends, your own family, the British. The army will be put under Congress, under the people, where it can be kept democratic . . . no nonsense from Citizen Bale or drilling for free men." An acute unhappiness had crept into his voice. Only the whiteness of his face and his hands delicately white against his beautiful attire were visible. At last, Richard realized, he was drunk.

"Perhaps that is enough." Beverley Mathews rose in an evident intention to keep Robine from saying what, later, he might regret. "It is so thick here we would be better in at a table." The two men followed him into the house, and Mathews had candles brought to the drawing room. Jasper Robine turned morose, silent. The drinking steadily went on. Richard Bale was blurred, uncertain, in his thoughts and movements. He attempted a speech in return to what Robine had told them, a song, and a detailed eulogy of Gloucester County, all without success. One broke, trailed into the other, and returned to the first. He felt tremendously sorry for Robine, and, with a hand on his shoulder, expressed his affection. "Come back to the Tidewater," he begged him, "where gentlemen are not cut up in sections and the ministers are fed on apricots. Come home to the Northern Neck — nectarine." This moved him to gusts of self-approving laughter. He explained his humour to Beverley. Northern Neck, nectarine. "Never try to be funny," Mathews advised him; "it's not in the Bale character."

*

*   *

The morning, thin and grey, flowed into the drawing room: Beverley Mathews' face was swollen and inanimate, as though from hidden ulceration; shadows, fleeing from the room, seemed to adhere like cobwebs to Robine; Richard Bale's disturbance moved from his head to his stomach; his emotions sank to a cold distaste for all living. Jasper Robine, contrary to every expectation, had been — in his own troubled comprehension — a failure; that was privately the truth about him. Why, Richard couldn't penetrate. Perhaps what he intrinsically was came inescapably in conflict with his ambition; yes, that was it — he had set out to use the power of what he called the people for his own end, and it had retaliated by using him. He wasn't astute enough to compete with a mind like Jefferson's. What he had intimated about John Marshall's future, it was clear, he had applied to himself. Richard walked out on the terrace:

The east was flushed with the coming of the sun, the colour of the dew-drenched roses below him; partridges were whistling from every cover. He went on, passed the circular white-painted brick ice house, and, finding a servant, ordered his horse saddled, determined not to return to the house. Once he broke through the hands of the negro helping him to mount; the lawn rocked, the trees, in the stillness of the morning, bowed; but, on Diggery, his feet engaging in the stirrups and the bridle in hand, he was steady, automatically competent.

His thoughts in the days that followed — June became July — often returned to Jasper Robine; but not so much to the individual as what, in effect, he had predicted. No one knew the veritable condition of the United States better. If he had been certain of the impending collapse of the Federalists, equally he was sceptical of his own party: the burden of his speaking had been the people, the people, and every time he referred to them his voice had grown sharper, his distrust more apparent. Militiamen! Yet there seemed to be no limits to the popularity of Genêt and his cause. The Proclamation of Neutrality, where the French Ambassador and American public were concerned, had, it appeared, no existence: Genêt addressed aggressive letters to the government; the ships of the States-General continued to bring prizes into United States ports. The Little Sara, conducted by the French Ambuscade into Philadelphia, was rechristened the Petit Democrat, and, fitted as a privateer, put to sea down the Delaware in express defiance of the Commonwealth's Secretary. Washington was temporarily at Mount Vernon, absent during this; and Jefferson had withdrawn himself, in an inopportune — or opportune? — fever to Belmont.

But, for Richard, there was a more immediate and local, a threatening, development of Genêt's activity. He gathered, in scattered phrases and conversations at the courthouse, that a Democratic Club was being formed in Gloucester County. Only a few men here, he was certain, would have any part in such an organization . . . outside Guinea and the poor whites. But the French tricolour appeared in increasing numbers. It was impossible now for Richard to beat off with his whip the hats to which it was pinned. The men who wore it, he observed, regarded him with a concerted unmistakable enmity. Once, when he had utilized a favourable opportunity for a seemingly impromptu public expression of his political opinion, he was interrupted by jeers from those outside the group before him.

Richard Bale stopped abruptly and went forward in search of the disturbers; but he met only a sullen anonymous silence. "Your trouble," he announced, "is the trouble of all crowds — it's made up of stupid cowards, men too lazy for the least success or any kind of thought. You can't think and you let others, unfortunately not so stupid, attend to it for you. I have this to say to you — somewhere at Balisand there is a black cockade. It was worn in a time you know nothing about. And, when I go home, I'm going to find it and wear it. And if anyone has a contrary word to say I'll kill him. Repeat that to your Democratic Club." From behind him came an assertion: "The British colour." He wheeled and identified the speaker:

"Not here, in Virginia; but the colour of the Continental Army; where it wasn't white. And there is another fact for you — the Democrat Club in Pennsylvania was a political trick to re-elect Governor Mifflin. Dallas managed it. If that means anything to you." He walked contemptuously away to the horse rack where Diggery was tied, mounted without a backward glance. "Wear it," the shout followed him, "and we'll cure you like a hog!" A serenity of mind enveloped him riding home over the narrow way filled with the hot peace of midsummer. There would be a pleasant air drawing down the North River, cooling the afternoon, the portico, at Balisand. He recalled where he had put the cockade; it was in a table drawer in his bedroom; and he requested Mrs. Patton to sew it, firmly, on his hat. Morryson Bale appeared while she was busy with this, and he asked if Cornwallis were back of the woods. "Nothing so admirable," Richard replied; "a few citizens behind trees." Mrs. Patton was uneasy. "I don't know why," she confessed, "but this black upsets me. I'm sure you're being contrary again; and when you are, there is a lot to pay."

He advised her not to worry . . . about him. Let the Guineamen do that. His thoughts swung to Zena Gainge: she was, he realized, increasingly apt to occupy his mind. His dislike of her had shifted again to curiosity. A very remarkable woman in the strangest of circumstances. On account of her birth, her antecedents and associations, he considered her with more freedom than his habit was with women. She seemed totally different from all others, aside from them. He must, he told himself once more, have the Gainges to dinner. First, however, it would be better for him to see them again. He found that he was looking forward to it. At this he tried to examine himself, and his motives, in connection with Zena; but, of the latter, there were none he could identify. He wasn't — damn the word — in love with her. That he was certain of. Zena Gainge was married. Richard couldn't, either, discover the presence of an inexcusable physical desire; he wasn't open to such vulgarity.

Yet Zena persisted in engaging his speculations; and, riding to Jordan Gainge's — it was past three o'clock and their dinner would be over — an anticipation which was almost excitement engaged him. The tall marsh grass was bronze-green, its blades like a sweep of swords opposed to the shining water. Gainge had gone out, across the Severn to Sadler's Neck. "He'll be back for supper," his wife continued; "you must stay."

He couldn't do that, he reflected, studying her. She had been unprepared for visitors — they were so rare, she added — caught by him, really. But he preferred the simplicity of her dress to her more formal efforts. "Don't let's go in the house," Zena Gainge said. "It's so cold in there and full of lessons." And, in response, they sat where the side of the house sheltered them from the sun. "The day lilies are all flowers, now, after you told me how to do with them. Perhaps that's what's been the matter with me." Incautiously he asked her for an explanation.

"When you came here it got sunny right off." This gave him an uncomfortable pleasure. It was one of the admissions her training hadn't taught her to repress. "It's only that you are getting used to it here," he corrected her; "you're more at home, Mrs. Gainge." Her name, she instructed him, was Zena. "Say it." Richard Bale repeated it, "Zena. That is very pretty." She was, warmly, glad he liked it. When Jordan Gainge's wife smiled she was almost charming. Superb teeth white in the intent brown of her thin face.

*

* *

She talked intimately, at random, rehearsing the incidents of her empty days; and he listened more conscious of her personality than of her words. Her throat was informally bare; he was surprised at its sound smoothness. But she was all, he saw, made that way: the appearance of thinness was a deception. He grew annoyed at himself for such thoughts — inadmissible in the manner he had expressly disclaimed. Damn it, how did the woman affect him? He didn't — always a danger — feel sorry for her. With her, he thought, rather, about his own sensations. In a manner, he realized, he had been starved of warmth; his life might almost be called abnormal. It was so easy here, with Zena, to be sympathetically appreciated; she soothed the customary harshness of his mind. She wasn't unlike the sun — bringing out qualities in him long dormant, unsuspected. If her existence was empty, why, so was his; nothing but the troubles of servants, planting, Thomas Ekkes, Mrs. Patton and Morryson. His uncle was becoming more difficult every year; nothing satisfied him; he was, with his eternal comparisons, not in favour of the present world, making him, Richard Bale, sick of the past. "You weren't listening to me," Zena complained; "but thinking of some other woman." That, he assured her, was an impossibility: none other was — was alive.

"Do you mean it?" she demanded. Their chairs were close together, and she touched his arm. The brief contact of her hand stirred him. "None," he repeated positively. "That isn't much better, for it includes me." He was forced to admit in that case he had been wrong. "I do think of you. Without quite knowing why." She swayed toward him, and then rose swiftly — Jordan Gainge was coming across the lawn.

"I call this friendly," he declared. "Zena would

never move a foot to get you a drink. We can soon mend that." He joined them, bringing with him the celebrated Barbados rum and glasses. "It was hot over the river. Now you're here we'll keep you for supper: you'd better not cross the marshes before morning. There's no reason why you can't stay." His gaze encountered Richard's hat, on the ground. "A long while since I've seen that cockade. The badge of the Georges, once." Zena demanded an explanation. "The ribbon on Mr. Bale's hat is a sign of war," he told her, a gleam of humour over his set face. "It's a challenge." She scarcely heeded him, but turned to Richard and, in an indiscreet concern, exclaimed that he mustn't expose himself to harm.

"It was his trade," Gainge continued; "it's what he lives on — the chances of harm and toddy. Men do . . . used to," he corrected his tense. He was looking at Zena, Richard observed, whenever her attention was diverted from him. A stabbing metallic inquiry. His good humour vanished. A servant called them into the house, and, as the men waited for Zena, her hand, as she passed him, touched and caught at Richard's. Involuntarily he glanced at Jordan Gainge: the elder man's face was like a carved figurehead from one of his ships. She was an idiot, Richard thought resentfully. He felt damned uneasy — he was the idiot. She continued to treat him with a positively indecent care; Zena hardly replied to her husband; at times her shoulder was turned squarely upon him. "We ought to have Madeira," she told Richard; "I'm sure you drink it at supper, and not horrible currant wine made at home." He replied that what they had was very agreeable. Gainge suddenly stood, moving back his chair. "You'll excuse me for a little," he addressed Richard; "there is something I want to do, and then I have to see about the reaping to-morrow. You won't miss me." He nodded to Zena and quitted the room.

"I don't know why he did that," she said; "he wouldn't let me. It doesn't matter, though, does it? And he was right — I won't miss him." However, Jordan Gainge's informal departure didn't serve to lessen Richard Bale's growing disturbance. It was strange rudeness, for Gainge well knew that it was his wife's place to retire. He became awkwardly silent; Zena smiled enigmatically at him; and, when they rose, she frankly took his hand, leading him into the room beyond. "No one knows who is behind you in the dark," she explained. A pair of brass lanterns, on the walls, had been lighted; but for them the room was empty; she stood before him with her face lifted.

He was conscious of a sudden constriction at his throat; and, independent of resolve, in the grip of an urging need, he was bending over her when the waiting stillness of her face changed into an expression of dread. "Look," she whispered, pointing to the table at his back. He saw at once what she indicated: one of the pistols that had rested on the mantel-shelf was placed where the light was brightest. Richard picked the pistol up, examining it — the hammer was cocked, the flint exact, powder in the pan. He stared at it, and then, detaching the ramrod, tested its length in the barrel.

"Loaded."

He had spoken without volition. Zena was pressed against him, but no longer in dread; her whole being was charged with a vital eagerness. "Jordan left it, for us. It's exactly what he'd do. A hateful old man!" To Richard Bale's amazement her arms were around his neck. "Take me away, Richard," she implored him. "It's no happier here for you than me. Richard . . . where we'll be free together. You knew how I felt, that night at the tavern, when you were so good to me. You've always understood when no one else did. You can have all of me; for ever." Her mouth was on his, her cheeks transferring the wetness of her tears to his face. He released himself violently:

"You are mad," he declared; "Jordan may be anywhere and see us."

"No, he wouldn't," she reassured him; "he'd leave a pistol and he would kill us, but he wouldn't hide behind a door now."

Richard Bale was infuriated at Zena, at himself — he had been betrayed into an utterly ridiculous, a criminal, position. In the heat of his temper he spoke brutally, with no regard for the feeling of the woman moving slowly back from him. "I can't imagine how you came to do this, and it's evident you're not used to even decent social custom. I'm not in love with you; if I were such a — a thief, I'd expect a rope and not a bullet; and nothing in life could take me from Balisand. If I'm to blame for this it doesn't alter the facts."

She was against the wall, shrunken together, with her hands pressed to her throat. "Oh!" she said, with a sobbing breath; "oh!" Then, before he realized her intention, she was across the floor, at the table. Zena Gainge was incredibly quick, but, instinctively, he was quicker; and he broke the pistol from her grasp. "Two murderers," he said, unexcited. "But I'd rather face you with a pistol than without." He laid the weapon down, in an exact care, on the table. "Tell Mr. Gainge," he instructed her, "I found his suggestion, but didn't need it. Say to him that, from his place, I acknowledge the justice in his action. I ought to ask you to forgive me, and I do. I'll wait outside, since you won't want me in your house, for my horse."

"You're more hateful than the women," she spoke, through a concentrated labouring passion, with difficulty. "I can't tell you how I —— " Words failed her. "I hope you sink in the ma'sh. I'll never say marsh again. Not while you do. And the others. Gentlemen! Oh, God! There isn't a drop of fit blood in you. I'd like to cut your horse in strips and choke you with them." She sank beside the table, a crumpled heap, crying with the abandon of a child. He lingered a moment, distressed. He could say nothing further, nothing to stem the great injury he had done her. Yes, he was guilty. Yet nothing remained but to get his horse.

*

* *

The return to Balisand had all the aspects of a flight. Indifferent to the precarious road, he galloped Diggery away from the Gainges', over the marsh, through the later heavy dust; and when they reached their lane the horse was in a lather of sweat. Richard went directly to his room, where, half clothed, he sat in a gloomy physical inaction. His mind, however, went at a furious pace: he was appalled by what had occurred at Jordan Gainge's, what — so nearly — had happened within himself. The inescapable fact was that he had very practically kissed Zena; he had led her to believe that that was his intention, his desire. All he could find in his own defence was that he had been in ignorance of what was occurring to him. He didn't want to kiss her, and yet, all the while, he had been moving steadily toward precisely that. This progress against his will, in opposition to his fundamental being, disturbed and frightened him; it gave Richard a sense of insecurity, of harbouring qualities capable of betraying him.

Women, for him, were divided into two classes — what he had come to call camp women and all the rest; he had had absolutely no experience in any mingling of those separate worlds. Rumours came to him of different conditions on the estates along the greater rivers, of scandals at Court; but his law operated with those as well — there were bad and good, none other. He held himself, too, as responsible for the maintaining of this: if a woman, through him, fell from heaven into hell, he became too low for life, for ever unfit for decent associations . . . and that, very nearly, had happened. But there he was wrong, unjust to whatever propriety was in him; no such accident had really threatened them, Zena and him; nothing more than the bare beginning. As soon as he had realized the possibility descending on them, he had killed it. As he thought about Zena he blamed her less, he increasingly regretted the tone he had instinctively taken with her:

She wasn't bad, he concluded; she was lonely and unhappy, and then — the Guinea blood. Actually, what she had hoped for was as direct and courageous as any act of Jordan Gainge's. Yet Richard couldn't forgive her attitude toward her husband: marriage was absolute, a duty to be discharged to the last minute of life and at every cost. Yes, the fault was largely his, he had suffered from a strange lapse of all that he was.

Curious glances, about the courthouse, followed the black cockade on his hat. Bradlock Wiatt, as usual politic, peace-loving, advised him to remove it. "Why do you dig all that up?" he demanded. "Let it sleep. It will end by killing your chances for election, if you should run." Richard Bale replied that, contrarily, it was his announcement of campaign. "Everyone will know where I stand." If he remained standing, Bradlock dryly added. "Look here." He led Richard to the board on the courthouse where notices were fastened, and pointed to an announcement of the organization of The Democratic Club of Gloucester County. It proceeded: "Citizens! What is despotism? Is it not the union of executive, legislative and judiciary authorities in the same hand? This union, then, has been effected. What has become of our Constitution and liberties? We have reason to presume . . . monarchical ambition . . . not long be permitted to enjoy a Republican government."

Richard Bale deliberately tore the notice from the board and dropped it on the flagging under their feet. Wiatt exclaimed, dismayed, "This is the courthouse!"

Richard asserted, "It doesn't belong to a party or any few men. No one, if I can stop it, will use it for such a purpose." Riding away from the group of county administrative buildings a large stone whirled closely by his head. He didn't draw Diggery in or turn; but, home once more, he oiled and loaded a small pistol which he continued to carry in a pocket.

Beverley Mathews, as well, spoke about what he chose to call Richard's exaggerated conduct. "Why can't you live quietly, like a planter? You did for a while. And now, at the worst time, you come out with this damned insult — that's what it is called — and get us all in trouble. I'm beginning to think a soldier can't be cured."

"It's splendid," Lucia contradicted him calmly. They were seated in the hall at Welfield, the wide doors on either side open. "And I agree with Richard — they won't really do anything. Besides, it shows them where they belong."

Beverley was amazed. "Them!" he exclaimed; "where they belong! That's a new song for you. I understood you were hot for the people and their wrongs." She answered serenely, "Oh, never. You must have misunderstood." To this he could only oppose a disparaging generality about women and affairs outside the kitchen. "I mean the stable." It was plain he was annoyed. Lucia smiled. "Beverley had it in his head I was going to marry Gawin Todd," she went on. What a remarkable girl she was! "Probably he wouldn't consent," Mathews' temper rapidly returned. "You ought to marry one of the great Northern stables."

But she said nothing further. It was cool, ingratiating, at Welfield, and Richard reluctantly rose to go. Lucia's tranquillity, her dark still face, were very engaging after his late unfortunate experience. How little she had changed since early girlhood: slim and straight and impersonal.

Again at Balisand, Thomas Ekkes came up to the house, looking for him. "I met Jordan Gainge on the road," he said; "and the old man is failing at last. You wouldn't know it from seeing him; it's his mind. He sent you two messages without any sense to them at all." Richard listened with an uncomfortable attention he was careful to hide. "He advised you to keep a few extra men near the house. I asked him why, but he wouldn't say; and, when he was going, he wanted you to be told that he had drawn the charge from some pistol or other." What was meaningless to Ekkes, Richard Bale fully understood. The first message was interesting to him from the probability that Jordan Gainge had taken its suggestion from his wife. Zena, who hated him; Guinea; the threats that were frequent! However, he would do nothing about it: he'd ride and live in his usual custom; the need of men to guard him and Balisand he laughed at. Yet he was glad to have been informed about the pistol. He had a great respect, a strong liking, for Gainge — a man in the old mould, old steadfast metal. What, he wondered, had happened at the Gainges'? It was fairly evident that Jordan had made a revealing discovery about his wife. He would abhor anything — as Zena had acknowledged — connected in the smallest way with treachery.

The Democratic Club, limited by the traditional Federal sympathies of the Tidewater, yet managed to progress. Its proclamations appeared at the tavern, the ordinary at the edge of Gloucester Court House, on trees and fences. And, whenever Richard passed one, he tore it down. They were very much the same; and, with creases where they had been folded, had evidently been sent into the county; probably from Philadelphia. The denunciations of the President, in them and the papers of widest circulation, were now virulent: there was scarcely any name he wasn't unhesitatingly called . . . for the ends Jasper Robine had indicated. They might, Richard perceived, be impersonal — though he doubted it — with minds, for purposes, like Jefferson's; but the attacks bred an actual enmity for Washington among the ignorant, the envious and the venal. Robine had intimated more — that the power they had created, the people, might, in the end, corrupt and destroy the Republicans. It would, Richard never questioned. And soon. The French bonfire must exhaust the flimsy material of its flames. Sanity would return. But he was obliged to add that he saw no sign of this — the term sovereign had been resurrected: Genêt and the sovereign people of the United States; it was a stubborn article of faith with him.

*

* *

It grew clear that, for the present, his political activities must be deferred. The Federalists were quiet, with the exception of Hamilton, who, at a meeting of the cabinet, demanded Genêt's recall. Richard Bale learned that a statement of the Frenchman's conduct had been prepared, to be forwarded to Morris, at Paris, against the protests of Randolph and Jefferson. They — now — charged that it would make the President the head of a party and not of the nation. The old treaty with France was again brought forward, the familiar cries of American ingratitude. Genêt, arriving in New York, was met with a salute of cannon and address of welcome. "Henfield was acquitted," Richard informed Morryson Bale. He flung the paper away from him. Who the devil was that? Morryson asked. "Another citizen," Richard told him; "an American prize-master on a captured British ship. If I'd had him before a court-martial —— "

"Richard," his uncle interrupted him, "a canoe came into the creek then." They were on the portico, Mrs. Patton was seated in the doorway, and Richard gazed toward where, hidden in flowering bushes, the thrust of water and sand, from which Balisand had its name, ran in to the right of the lawn. "You must be wrong," he replied; "a canoe would stop at the wharf." As he spoke a man emerged from behind a clump of althæas, where Richard had been looking. He was, he recognized, strange; but, without hesitation, he walked deliberately across the grass. "Why," Morryson exclaimed, "there is another, and another; a hundred of 'em!" From all the quarters visible a small mob was coming together in front of the portico.

Mostly they were unfamiliar, but some Richard had often seen on the roads and at the courthouse; inconsiderable figures, holders of unproductive lands, of no land at all. He turned to Mrs. Patton. "There is no need for you to receive these visitors," he said quietly, and, with her, he went into the house. There, from the hall table, he secured his hat with the cockade — it settled in customary military arrogance on his head — and returned to where he had been sitting. Morryson, in a high thin anger, was speaking:

"What you're doing here, a dirty rabble, at Balisand, no one seems to know." He had been walking with a cane, and he stooped, painfully securing it. Then he went, as fast as he was able, down the shallow stone steps, up to the compact and silent, the menacing, crowded men. He shook the stick in their faces. "Rabble!" he cried. Richard Bale was beside him, cold and alert. His mind operated in a swift precise order. Morryson, he saw, was incorrect — this wasn't, in the ordinary sense, a rabble. There were too many determined, weatherworn faces for that. The fishermen of Guinea. On one hand he identified John Bage who, like himself, had fought throughout the War with England.

"Bage," he said, "you are in bad company."

But, he recognized, it was no time for words: the quietness, broken at any unpredictable movement or sound, might well become fatal. A number of dark faces, uncovered heads, had flaxen pale hair. They could, easily, be Hessians. Others were obviously Latin. He regarded with a careful deliberation all those he could individually mark. Someone, the pivot of hostile intent, was there. He must find him. A diagonal scar on a cheek arrested his attention . . . James Luke. Perhaps.

Luke met his gaze with a vindictive triumph. All life was a chance, the chances of death were invisibly balanced. Luke was in the front rank, the French tricolour caught Richard's eye.

Three paces carried him forward, a hand in his pocket: with an entire steadiness, a selective and calculated aim, he shot James Luke where his nose flattened into the bony ridge of forehead. Aware that there was no need to survey the effect of his shot, he turned shortly and took Morryson's arm. With their backs to the throng the two Bales returned slowly and erect to the portico. Morryson, though, had difficulty with the steps; his weight hung crookedly on Richard's arm. In the hall he was exhausted; but if he had a glass of rum, he was certain, he'd recover. "You walked back to the house so fast," he complained. "It looked like we were running away." He would have said more, but his voice failed him. Half carried into the drawing room, he fell, practically, on a sofa. The veins in his neck were swollen, leaden lids closed over his eyes.

A negro appeared and Richard sent for Mrs. Patton. Towels twisted in cold water, wrapped about Morryson Bale's head, brought him to a degree of consciousness, but he was unable, at last, to speak or to more than partly move. Borne up to his room, Richard sat there while the elder man was undressed. He spoke once, asking if Ambrose had been sent for. A man of courage, he was thinking of his uncle. From a window he could see the lawn — it was empty; out on the North River a canoe had pointed upstream. He was bare of sensation, stripped of exultation or relief; feeling had stopped in him. Later, in an introspective curiosity, he searched his emotions at the killing of Luke. He had, himself, been totally indifferent to what overtook him. He faced death with its own impersonal demeanour. This wasn't to his credit; indeed, it was a criticism of his mode of life. Yes, empty.

The danger he had met had hung upon the correctness of his judgment, nothing more. It had lain in his hand; he had been merely under the necessity of not making a mistake. Again he recognized that he hadn't encountered a common mob; the element of hysteria was negligible. He might almost say that an adequate act had procured his safety. His, but not, ultimately, Morryson's. After Ambrose had arrived Richard waited for him below. "The Democratic Club made us a call," he said briefly, in response to the doctor's question. "The pleasure was too much for Morryson." Ambrose, glancing keenly at him, asked nothing further. "A great deal too much," he repeated Richard's words. "Morryson is done with things. A month or so and then — another Bale with those outside the garden wall. Damn it, Richard, I hate that. You must marry."

"It was Morryson's idea no woman would look at me," Richard replied. "I'm going to miss him. It will be like a punch without bitters. Too sweet. Tell me," he demanded, "are we as hard as I hear?" Ambrose smiled, "Harder," he assured him; "but I didn't know women disliked that. Not a woman you would marry." There was a tone in his voice that Richard Bale instantly challenged. "Do you hear, in the county, of any special one?" The other deliberated. "There is no reason why I shouldn't tell you," he decided: " You are thought to be a great deal at Welfield."

" Lucia! " Richard cried. " I've never considered her that way. On the contrary, I keep thinking what a child she still is." Ambrose reminded him that Lucia Mathews was near twenty. That was a fact, Bale admitted. " You'll believe doctors are meddling old women," he was at the door. " However, don't remember Morryson too exactly. It's the Bales of Balisand, Richard; I'm afraid I wasn't interested in you then."

Through the evening, as he had expected, he was depressingly lonely without Morryson. In another moment he would have been beating the heads of the Democratic Club with his cane. Not altogether an unfortunate ending to a gentleman's, a Bale's, existence. How far, he speculated, did times, generations, make their individuals? How limited, in spirit and fact, was each man to his period? Morryson, for instance, had been stranded, lost, in the present; he might as well have been carried into a totally different and foreign land, among people who had hardly more conception of him than he had of them. Yet, he had gone the distance . . . to the finishing post.

*

* *

A large part of Mrs. Patton's time was spent upstairs, with Morryson Bale, and Richard was even more alone than customary. However, as this progressed, he didn't find it monotonous: it seemed to him that the events of his life had come to a pause. Very shortly he would take them up again — they would both be the same and very different — but for the moment he drifted, as though he were in the canoe with the oars lifted, at rest. Every afternoon, following the heat of day, there was a violent thunderstorm — he sat quietly watching it, the silver of the river turned to lead by the pall of cloud, the gathering gloom, and the smashing reports falling simultaneously with the lightning striking into the woods and water. Sometimes he could hear the splintering of trees; there would be an immediate plume of smoke from the burning wood. Echoes of past battles returned to his mind, the flash of powder . . . when they had any. He rode to the courthouse in his old raked hat and black cockade aware that he had gained still more reputation for his special quality of — of reckless assurance. Individuals who had been sullen were now obsequious, a condition he disliked more than at first. However, on several occasions he tried to meet the men of Gloucester County in the spirit of the times; but he recognized that invariably he failed. The truth was that he had neither interest nor patience with views which — idiotically — differed from his own.

When he followed the advice of Bradlock Wiatt and Beverley he was wrong: such as he was he must endure. But there was, as always, no humility in this conclusion; Jasper Robine had admitted that he would, soon, be justified. And, together with their urging, he saw that his friends were coming to regard him as incurable. On this plane he began to afford them a quiet amusement: they expanded the subject of lime toddy until he almost gave up drinking it. The black ribbon once taken so seriously was treated with humorous references to its antiquity. His clothes had become old-fashioned.

He got, from the North, all the papers possible, and, on the portico, treated them alike — he'd unfold them hurriedly, begin reading, and then fling them away unfinished, cursing their rabid falseness. There was, practically, no Federal press. Such as existed — Fenno's Gazette of the United States — he discovered totally inadequate: no reasoning or decency of expression could be effective against the Republican flood of abuse. One thing, however, was increasingly clear — once more Robine was fore-wise — even in Gloucester: Genêt's influential friends were unobtrusively dropping away from him; he was solely dependent on the public; and, in consequence, his periods and acts were growing wilder and more extreme. Gawin Todd had suppressed the vigour of his French sympathies; in Virginia, Richard inferred, he was welding the Republicans in a greater solidity. Todd had acquired a broad reputation for speaking. He could be suave, he was always fiery, and his insistence on men's rights had all the persuasive force of Paine's writing.

Richard considered him individually, for, it appeared, in his new composed attitude toward past and present, his enmity for Gawin Todd should vanish. It didn't, a fact that often surprised him. But, he reflected, Todd remarkably gathered in his person all the beliefs which he most disliked: Gawin Todd was his opposite in almost every particular. A nuisance to the country! His thoughts shifted to the pistols, set with gold, in their polished case upstairs. The supreme answer to all argument, all sound, all disagreement. The finality that had overtaken James Luke! He revolved again the accusation, made against him more than once, that war unfitted men for civil life and peaceful affairs. It left, certainly, its influence — war was no minuet — and that, more than bloodthirstiness, was a breaking of the attachments to humanity. There was its actual, probably most unfortunate, result: it killed small easy affections, made contacts insignificant, if not impossible to form.

The Republicans, at least, were right in this, that soldiers had small place in a government of the people; they might support such a state; perhaps they alone could make it possible; but they lay outside all the fiddling community of popular interest and occupation. But wasn't that almost as true of birth? Breeding, in men, had a peculiar democracy of its own. For example — he, Richard Bale of Balisand, was on terms of intimacy with a score of stablemen, of oyster fishers; yet between him and a more established, self-respecting society there was absolutely no intercommunication. He would ride and talk through a day with the driver of a stage, yes, drink from his bottle; but for casual passengers, well enough in their worlds, he hadn't a word. It was remarkable, he didn't pretend to solve it, he was simply, proceeding to Welfield, busy with the fact.

However, he had begun by considering himself in connection with Lucia, Lucia together with him. There was an increasing possibility that he would ask her to marry him. If he decided that, in justice to her, he might. He had been subjected to a great deal of battering, mentally and physically. His heart, his love, was not fresh. Richard considered, for a short space, the advisability of telling her about Lavinia Roderick; but, he concluded, he was bound by his old engagement of silence. It had been different, unavoidable, with Ava. Then, at the thought of her, he recalled that she had begged him not to marry; she had insisted that it must be disastrous. But Ava didn't understand his feelings and need.

This much, in himself, was beyond all question — he would be completely faithful to whomever he married. Faithful, that was, in every sense. It was his inheritance, his conviction, his pleasure. The Bales had never, in all the long history of their descent, been in serious difficulties, complications, with women. His brief affair — hardly more than an unresponded-to minute — with Zena emphasized more than disproved that. The Bales were masculine, consorters of men and the bottle, of gambling and racing and wars . . . of no infidelity to their blood. A memory, rigidly limited, couldn't threaten that. He was free, innocent in the past. Yet these, perhaps, were only negative virtues; negative qualities impressed women little if at all. They wanted — what was it they wanted? Oh, yes, love! That, for them, covered every imaginable fault and omission. Whatever it was.

But there — if Lucia listened to him at all — he was, in her, fortunate, since she wasn't the ordinary sentimental girl. He'd be damned if he really knew what she was. Although a coolness was evident she couldn't be deficient in feeling; that, anyhow, he was sure of. Her slow reflective voice wasn't cold, but deep; the tone of a strong body. She had never, in his memory, been tired. He came, sharply, on a characteristic which, until then, he had overlooked — Lucia loved babies. A fine maternity would be part of her strength. This — a strange connection — together with the late unhappy episode with Jordan Gainge's wife led him to the recognition that marriage had become a physical, a natural, necessity for him: quite aside from his duty to the Bales of Balisand. Yet that, in its turn, created a fresh tragic difficulty, an obscure denial, within him: it brought back, why at first he couldn't make out, an appealing and lovely and immeasurably sad vision of Lavinia. Lavinia dead, for ever without the children, his children, it would have been their supreme joy to have had. A conviction seized him, like fingers at his throat, that no others were possible. He had thought this satisfied, stilled, when here it was alive in him, striving to dominate him, again. A brutal and grim struggle, the familiar sense of horrible murder, swept over him. He was forced, Richard almost cried out to the vanished and insatiable past, to keep it, in his mind, separate from his life. The past receded, dropped slowly from the easy progress of his horse.

*

*　　*

A servant came forward to take his bridle, leading the horse, without instructions, away from a temporary place at the rack to the stable. In the hall he was met with the assurance that his customary room was prepared; the toddy bowl was placed near him on the shaded terrace,

The Mathews, he learned, father and daughter, had gone to Blundering Point to inspect a litter of foxhounds. Why, Richard couldn't think — Lucia must have thirty hounds now. She was talking of importing more from England. He thanked God that, while his walking was impeded, his riding, even to her, was sufficient. However, Beverley returned alone:

" Lucia will be disappointed. She was persuaded to stay at Shelley. A party to celebrate the news. Why you're respectably sober is a mystery." What, Richard Bale demanded acrimoniously, was the reason for that comment. Beverley gazed at him in amazement. " You haven't heard," he said. " Wait, there is a copy of Louden's Diary in the house." He returned, with the paper, in a growing excitement. " There! And if you don't, at once, understand all it means, I'll have you disqualified for voting." The paragraph he indicated, Richard saw, was signed jointly by John Jay and Rufus King.

" Certain late publications render it proper . . . to inform the public that a report having reached this city . . . that Mr. Genêt said he would appeal to the people from certain decisions of the President; we were asked . . . whether he had made such a declaration. We answered that he had; and we also mentioned it to others; authorizing them to say that we had so informed them." The paper fell on Richard Bale's knee; he gazed incredulously at Mathews.

" This," he managed to say, " is the end of Jefferson's scheming." The sweeping importance, the consequences, of the official announcement of Genêt's contemptuous bearing toward American government confused him with the multitude of its inevitable results. "It will kill the Republican opposition." Beverley agreed, "Exactly. Every charge against the President will have to be retracted. We'll see them all, all of them, crowd into hiding behind the national flag. It's the end of French influence in the United States. But I'm not sure you're right about Jefferson: he always has the people — you'll remember Robine — to fall back on."

"Beverley," Richard declared solemnly, "they have lost the next election. John Adams will be President." The other assented, adding that the Democratic Club of Gloucester County would have a short life, and required Richard to give him a concise account of the invasion of Balisand.

"It was well organized," he finished his description of that event.

"But if you had coughed, or stumbled over a rough place in the lawn, what would have happened?"

"Everything," Richard answered. A feeling of exultation possessed him at the public, the final, triumph of Washington. He was surging with delight, a feeling of renewed power; and, in a rush of affection for all his world, he told Beverley Mathews that he hoped to ask Lucia to marry him. Mathews at once grew self-contained, uncommunicative. He sat staring at a terrace stone before him. It was a long while — Richard Bale grew thoroughly impatient — until he spoke:

"In many ways that would be undesirable."

"Very many," Richard agreed.

"You are too old."

" I am."

" You drink too much."

" Entirely."

" Damaged."

" One leg might as well be wood."

" You fight all day."

" — most of the night."

" A hundred people hate the sight of you."

" A thousand."

" As usual," Beverley Mathews concluded, " you know everything. No one has ever been able to tell a Bale the smallest self-evident fact. I understand your family as well as it's possible, and a more disagreeable lot of men never existed. How they managed to get such charming wives I can't imagine. And now here you are, the worst of all, with pretensions as large as any. And you may succeed. But I'm not speaking for Lucia. If you think I could, you'd better say no more about it. I'll admit this, though, Richard, the litter of foxhounds was very promising; Lucia's in a good humour." Here, Richard perceived, was an admitted encouragement. Beverley's spirits, however, rapidly dwindled. It was plain that, confronted by a future, a house, without Lucia, he was illogically appalled.

" It had to come, from somewhere," he said later, with a lame philosophy. " And — if it does, why, Balisand isn't far away. Just up Ware Neck. I'd break yours if you married her and kept up your gloomy and disreputable habits. You have never ended your difficulty with Gawin Todd," he commented.

" Never," Richard Bale answered coldly. " I am not

a man who changes. You'd have to accept that, if it touched Lucia, as in my favour." Mathews damned him for a contentious menace. "I never suggested she wouldn't be safe with you. A Bale of Balisand. Hell, I want a drink! Between us, and without a word from Lucia, we've got her married. Well, I can't influence her, if that's of any service to you."

"I believe," Richard said, "since we're as far as this, I had better ride over to Shelley." Mathews protested vigorously against being left deserted. "You're not twenty," he warned Bale, "but forty. And after such a long wait you can last till to-morrow." But Richard was invaded by a dread of any delay; he wanted — if he were to have it — the assurance of Lucia's consent to their marriage.

In the dusk, although August was almost at an end, the heavy foliage, after the constant rain, was a deep glowing green. He rode at a rapid trot, without a plan other than his sheer purpose, toward Shelley, and when he arrived he tied his horse unassisted before the house. Supper was over, there were voices from a porch beyond, facing the York River. If he joined that company, exhilarated by drinking and the Federal success, he wouldn't soon have a chance to speak to Lucia.

Richard went, instead, still undiscovered, into the wide dimly lighted hall, and there he found a servant. "Ask Miss Mathews to come outside," he directed. "A message from Welfield." That wasn't, strictly, true, but it would serve better than an announcement of his name. He waited on the grass, by the great door, and moved forward to meet Lucia.

" Oh, Richard! " she exclaimed, in a voice half inquiry. "You weren't home," he proceeded; " and I wanted — no, I had to see you."

" Yes, well —— " She waited. He was conscious of a tension, almost a frightened suspense, in her. " I've spoken to Beverley of this, Lucia. He complained, naturally, but he isn't opposed to it. Lucia, I'm asking you to marry me."

" It's so strange, here, this way. Listen to them." The sound of gay high laughter rose from the porch. " I know it is hot but I'm cold. My hands —— " She held them out to him. " And — and yes." He kissed her in a happiness that was suddenly calm, measured, determined; but all her reserve left her . . . for a moment. " Don't come in," she begged him; " I couldn't bear it. Everyone would see. It would be too terrible. And I'll come home early to-morrow. Early in the morning, Richard. We'll ride together to Balisand, where I am going to be with you, for the rest. Richard, kiss me again. Now go." She held him away from her with spendid vital hands. He led his horse carefully, noiselessly, from the house and laughter, from Lucia.

III

IN August, on the eighteenth, to be exact, there was a party at Balisand for Flora, the eldest of Richard and Lucia Bale's three children. She was six; all three were girls; and it was the year 1800. These apparently widely separated facts Richard, at that moment, viewed as one: he was amazed that Flora was so old, chagrined because there was, yet, no masculine heir to Balisand and the Bale blood and tradition, and, generally, surprised at the imminence of a new century and — yes — a new time. The old would be gone in hardly more than four months; but, until it had been impressed on him by Flora's years, the absence of a son, he had given that but little thought. A great many events at once — so characteristic of him — detached and personal had served to obscure the succession of one year to another. The death of Washington had occupied him with memories, and then they had been routed by the actuality, the extreme peril, of what had come to be called the political situation of the United States.

But, for the present, abstract questions were given no place in his consciousness. He was seated in a customary chair on his portico, the cane with the assistance of which he now walked — it had been Morryson's — beside him, and Flora was demanding his immediate and whole attention. She was, it seemed to Richard Bale, even more mature than her advanced years warranted.

Flora was small, her face, lighted with an eager charm, was almost meagre, eclipsed nearly by the cascades of bright chestnut hair that fell and spread upon either thin shoulder. Flora's colouring was his, rather than Lucia's, and her temperament, vivid and impressionable and withdrawn, resembled, as well, the Bale character. Lucia, no less remote, was far more reasonable; but not for the sake of reason — what had the form of a perfect consideration was, in her, a genuine indifference to most people and ideas. He, personally, resented twenty things in a day which she regarded as having not the slightest importance. Flora was pounding his knees:

"Camilla Scarborough ate Nancy's gooseberry fool. Nancy put it for a little moment on the steps and Camilla picked it right up." Without, immediately, grasping the enormity of Flora's declaration, he yet realized that it was serious: as a name, Camilla Scarborough was used only on occasions of grave misdeed. "Your mother will be out in a minute," he told her, avoiding any responsibility of judgment. "But that won't bring the gooseberry fool back," his daughter insisted. "And there isn't more in the bowl." Nancy Ambrose, with a napkin, was wiping away individually the large tears that threatened to fall too fast for such a particular care. Camilla, Camilla Scarborough Bale, a diminutive but exact replica of her mother — Indian colouring, straight nose, wide calm mouth — faced him with an admirable and disarming candour.

"I had to," she said in brief explanation.

She was, Richard announced, a greedy girl. Even Flora's hope of an adequate recognition of Camilla's fault was satisfied by this. Nancy Ambrose stared at him fascinated, an incongruous tear left stranded from her previous emotion. Three other little girls shrank together, merging the starched whiteness of their party dresses; and Flora, in a shocked and triumphant tone, repeated his words, a greedy girl. Camilla merely reasserted that she had had to. She wouldn't, he knew, cry; but he was suddenly aware that, inwardly, she was acutely miserable. Still, her conduct had been inexcusable. "I hate for you to behave like that," he continued, "without any manners at all. What will Nancy Ambrose think of you and Balisand? Why, Mr. Ekkes' children would know better."

"Mr. Ekkes is the overseer," Flora announced to the young impressed company. It was evident she didn't want a word of her father's condemnation to lose a trace of its full darkness. Camilla said nothing further in her own defence, but she remained standing, meeting his gaze. A sense of profound helplessness descended upon him — it was ridiculous of Lucia to leave him with all those children. Their attention, in a breathless silence, was centred on him. A failure now, any fall from the clouds of his mature estate, would, he felt, be simply unthinkable. Happily, what promised to offer him an escape from his critical position came to his assistance:

"I am sure it would be only right for Camilla to offer Nancy Ambrose her glass of orgeat."

"I don't like orgeat," Nancy answered. "Flora finished mine." He had never before, he admitted, even heard of a girl who didn't care for orgeat; gaining, in spite of the prolonged elaboration of his period, no more than a moment or so in time. Flora pressed back her hair from her cheeks; clearly she expected an opinion of an absolutely devastating finality. His mind, however, betrayed him, and he was obliged to resort to an arbitrary, low, exercise of adult parental authority. "Say to Nancy that you are sorry," he directed. But, for a totally inexplicable reason, it developed that that was exactly what Camilla couldn't do. "Then you are a bad girl," Flora added.

"Anyhow, why don't you play on the grass?" Richard Bale asked inconsequentially. "Break the Pope's Neck is a very good game."

"That's mostly for boys," he was uncompromisingly informed. One child had been expressly cautioned against it by her mother, "when I'm fixed up."

"Nancy," he was reduced to saying, "I am sorry Camilla Scarborough ate your gooseberry fool. I hope when you come to Balisand again she will behave better." At that point, to his great relief, Lucia returned with Alice Ellen. "What is it?" she asked at once, setting their youngest child on her feet.

"Camilla Scarborough ate up Nancy's gooseberry fool and she won't say a thing about it."

"I had to," Camilla repeated to her mother.

"If you had to, if that's it," Lucia calmly returned, "there is no use talking about it. Instead, go in to Mrs. Patton and tell her I said you must be put to bed. It doesn't seem to me you'll need any more supper."

At this Nancy Ambrose began again to cry, but Camilla turned silently and went into the house. "Don't be silly, Nancy," Lucia Bale commanded. "Take Alice Ellen down on the lawn." This, greeted with cries of delight, at once emptied the portico of the birthday party. "You are so undecided with them," Lucia commented. "It's not me," he objected, "they are so damned severe. But it was hardly necessary for Camilla to go up to bed alone, to-day."

"I'll manage Camilla," she told him serenely.

"You ought to understand her, since she's exactly like you, except for horses." Lucia called to have Alice Ellen kept in the shade of the house. "I ought to have a cap on her if it wasn't so hot," she spoke aloud but, obviously, to herself. Then, "About Camilla — she isn't all me, Richard. You must admit I'd have apologized. Yet, stubborn as she is, sometimes, it isn't Camilla but Flora who gives me trouble. She doesn't mean to, it's her disposition. Flora is so sensitive. I was never that. What is it in you, do you suppose?"

"I am what I am," he replied definitely; "I can't go hunting around inside of me for bits of thread, like a woman. So long as Flora is well and happy and comparatively good, I wouldn't bother. Lucia, tell me, is that child with the red hair Mary Todd's?" She was, his wife informed him. Mary Todd, with a daughter older than Flora! Once it had been his intention to ask Mary to marry him; long, long ago; sixteen years back. He spoke abruptly. "Lucia, I have been very fortunate, married to you after so much — so much trouble and war and bitterness. No one could have predicted it. Here we are, so peaceful at Balisand, with the children ——" he broke off as sharply as he had begun.

Lucia glanced at him quickly; when, in a tranquil voice, she replied, she was looking out over the lawn, at the North River. "Of course, why not? There is nothing strange about it: we've known each other all our lives. You're not composed enough, Richard; you don't take enough for granted. You speak, sometimes, as though this weren't entirely simple, as though it weren't safe and solid. Flora again. I should have married you years before I did. We always said, at Welfield, you were too much alone. But I won't have that in your head now, you hear me."

*

* *

The day was hushed with a still full heat, the air appeared to have an amber glow of its own, aside from the sun, as though the floating richness of perfumed pollen held an independent radiance. There wasn't a visible ripple on the river; no sign of movement; its transparent blackness was mirror-like, flawless and empty. Far to the right Mockjack Bay met the sky with an edge that might have been solid indigo. The intermittent treble voices of the children, Richard thought, were pressed down to the sod by the weight of summer. He counted them: with Alice Ellen, there were seven. Two, Catherine and Vera Fanning, who lived higher up on the North River, drove daily to the school Richard Bale maintained at Balisand for his own children; Mary Todd's daughter presented an arrangement in bare awkward knees and elbows supporting a consuming blaze of hair;

Nancy Ambrose, with her father's vigorous movements, was attempting to conduct Alice Ellen through the process of a courtesy. That, he reflected, was a mistake. Simultaneously with his thought came its justification:

Alice Ellen, flinging herself on the sod, raised an outcry of inarticulate fury accompanied by a frenzied drumming of her heels. "I expected that," he remarked, both annoyed and, secretly, a little amused. Flora hurriedly climbed the steps to the portico. "We didn't do anything to her," she breathlessly announced. "Mother, we were dreadfully careful; but Alice Ellen just cried. I reckon you'll have to come down and spank her hard."

Lucia, on the lawn, picked her daughter up and held her unmindful of a fresh accession of crying and kicks. "Good God, Lucia," Richard called, "the child is purple in the face. Can't you stop it!" She replied that she couldn't now. "Three or four hundred years ago would have been the time for that." It was fortunate, he told her, that she had the Bales as an excuse for all that upset life's peace. "Your bad temper is famous," she replied. "At least you didn't say infamous," he commented. Alice Ellen had managed to turn so that she was kicking her mother. How admirable, Richard Bale realized, Lucia was. A nurse appeared from the house. "You take her, Easter." The coloured woman assumed charge of the youngest Bale. She was, she said, in a voice like a low singing, surprised at Alice Ellen, she was for a fact. Crying that way! Beating around with her feet . . . the same as ordinary people. Her, Easter's, baby. The child subsided, soothed to a drowsy acquiescence, borne out toward the slumberous river. A trace of Easter's opinion — that it had been the fault of the obstriferous Ambrose child — floated back on the afternoon.

"What will we do now?" Nancy demanded.

"You will have to go home soon; perhaps it would be nice to sit quietly on the steps," Lucia suggested. "Worse than the militia," Bale added.

"I don't know what that is," a Fanning admitted. Flora instantly addressed herself to the explanation:

"When General Washington was a general and had to fight with England no one would help him but father ——" This the Fannings indignantly interrupted, stamping it as utterly false. Their father, they recited, had been South, fighting like anything; and their uncle Alexander, who was only sixteen years old, was killed at Great Bridge.

"You mustn't stop me," was all Flora interposed to this. "Nobody at all hardly wanted to fight, and mostly they were militia. And once when father told them not to go to town two did, and he made them get fifty apiece, with a cat-of-nine-tails, tied to the gun."

"Richard," Lucia demanded, "when did you tell Flora that? It's an outrageous story for a little girl; and, when you remember her disposition, it's inexcusable." He thought she had overheard it, he couldn't remember directly telling her of such an incident. "Yes, but you did. I can recognize it easily. And I know what was going on in your mind — you thought the girls ought to understand about the Republicans and the Federalists. I'm sorry there isn't a boy; but, after all, the politics will keep a little longer."

" Fifty what? " Nancy Ambrose inquired.

" Fifty lashes," Flora returned. " And when it came time to meet the enemy the militia went home to their homes and left father and General Washington. And General Washington said to father: Captain, we must turn a flank, and they turned it, a whole flank." That, however, wasn't so hard, it was pointed out, since a flank was no more than part of a horse. " Not the one I mean," Flora insisted, " because the militia ran away from it, and I don't believe even they would do that with a horse. You ask me things and then tell them yourself and that isn't polite. Well, General Washington said to father: Captain, we got to turn a flank, and they were practically Hessians with their faces painted black to frighten everybody —— "

" I don't believe that." This, as well, was a Fanning objection.

Richard, without invitation, entered the controversy. " The Hessian Jägers," he asserted, " did, when they went into battle, smear their faces with black pomatum." Flora proceeded dictatorially: " And father said to General Washington: General, we will, and goddamn the militia anyhow! "

" Richard, positively," Lucia was really angry, " it will simply come to this — that I won't let you talk to your own children. Flora, never, never, say such a thing again. It's too naughty for words. If Camilla wasn't there already I'd send you up to bed. And, another thing, while your friends are here — your father didn't fight the entire War with England. There were hundreds of gentlemen from Virginia and everywhere who did quite as much. He didn't say he did, of course, and I won't have you. Here, I arranged the nicest party for your birthday and Camilla was bad and Alice Ellen cried and now you are swearing like I — I don't know what."

"They asked me about the militia and I had to tell them," Flora answered; "and if I make up a little it doesn't hurt and General Washington did talk flanks with father."

"Yes," Richard Bale supported her, "once he did, and Flora's copy of what he said was mild, very mild." Flora concluded, "that's what militias are."

"What?" the insatiable Nancy Ambrose asked.

"Mother won't let me tell you any better." Richard laughed and Lucia rose. "It's time to go home," she announced. The children followed her into the house; and, when the Fanning carryall vanished, a silence fell on the Balisand portico: Richard gazed out across the Bay, Lucia sat in the composure that was her special invaluable property, and Flora, intense and still, was on the bottom step. "I wish you would look at the hounds, Richard," Lucia presently said; "they are scratching themselves ragged. It's that disgraceful kennel. At last I am going to rebuild it, with a run, no matter what you say about the past."

"If you like," he agreed; "but I have always had good foxhounds. You keep them too close." The truth, he realized, was that the racing stable at Balisand Lucia was changing into a fox-hunting establishment. After marriage his interest in racing had lessened, but hunting occupied almost as much of Lucia's thought as did her family. On a horse, fox hunting, he recognized, she was in a world peculiarly and appropriately her own: quietness, decision and courage distinguished Lucia. Never sick, she was indifferent to the rigours of winter ——

" I prefer a trencher to the dining room," she replied. " But the negroes used to steal near all that went out to them." The hounds, undoubtedly, were healthier under her care. The next thing, he continued, she would be improving the breed of red foxes. " Why not? " she inquired. " Isn't it a part of a hunt? Flora, you'd better not sit longer on that stone. The sun's been off it from noon. Your skirts are up, too."

" I wanted to cool myself," Flora explained. " It's awfully hot underneath." She rose and came up to them. " Wasn't it almost a lovely party? Even if Camilla did eat Nancy's gooseberry fool and Alice Ellen screeched."

*

*   *

At supper there were now, in addition to Mrs. Patton, Lucia and Miss Howlett. Miss Howlett, taking the place of a tutor, sat with the two elder children at a smaller table. She was an excellent English governess, and, passing through the black insurrection in the French West Indies, she had left there, almost overnight, all traces of youth. In that she was Mrs. Patton's opposite, for the housekeeper, no longer young, still preserved her elasticity, and the governess, who could hardly be thirty, tall and spindling, seemed to have lost every atom of physical vitality. Her intelligence, however, had not been impaired — she comprehended Flora, Lucia maintained, to a remarkable extent. With Mrs. Patton, Richard discovered, Lucia agreed splendidly. When he had brought his wife to Balisand the housekeeper was, with half-concealed tears, preparing to depart; but they had insisted on Mrs. Patton remaining.

"Really," Lucia said privately to him, "I'd be lost if she went. You remember Beverley told everyone I was more around the stable than in the house. And, in the season, I've got to hunt. I'm sorry if you're disappointed by me. I can do it, you know; I am willing to try; but you'd be happier with Mrs. Patton. I'll take the responsibility, of course, with the keys and supplies and the negroes; but I'd like her to help me if it's only with the lime toddy."

He had thought, from what he had heard and suspected of women, that such an arrangement wouldn't, in all probability, last; there must, he was persuaded, be a collision between authority and habit; but he had been wrong. His mistake was due to a lack in his early understanding of Lucia. In very many ways she was different, superior he thought, to other women of breeding. She had, maternally, an immense active vigour and ability; it was a common opinion that her children were beautifully conducted; but for the smaller phases of feminine daily occupations, the measuring of rice and the locating of flagrant dust, she had no application. Lucia, he supposed, couldn't be called neat — when she took things off she forgot them, a broken ornament in the drawing room she could ignore as successfully as any shiftless yellow girl; she spent no days in the preserving-kitchen. But those details were Mrs. Patton's delight, and Lucia, with a complimenting candour, begged her to retain her control of them.

She didn't, either, frankly, like the company of women, and took no part in keeping stirred the local feminine rumours and gossip. She never talked much, outside the fundamental interests of her existence; Lucia danced indifferently; and, altogether, she freely admitted that she was without social talents. But that, Richard added for himself, was nonsense: she was, in the simplicity of evening dress she affected, a personage of notable appearance and manner. Still, he was forced to admit, she was more commanding in riding habit. Her management of the whole body of servants, too, was superior to Mrs. Patton's; she was miraculously successful with the negroes. Lucia established a strict command over their cabins and life; she treated their sickness with a tonic sharpness and ability; their exuberance she met in a wise restraint; their dilatory character she urged into quick performances. The men about the stables, naturally, accepted her with a fanatical admiration. Whenever, with a single keen glance, she found that a duty had been neglected, an audience of stableboys and grooms and hostlers gathered with half-suppressed approving laughter to hear her exposition of the just currying of a horse or of the wrapping of a swollen tendon. Once Richard had found her assisting in the remedying of a quarter crack, burning out with an iron the damaged hoof.

The years with her father had taught her, as well, the art of living among men. While the foxhounds no longer depended for food on casual favours, they still, unrebuked, occupied the hall and dining room; the horses continued their destruction of the grass at the rack on the lawn, and she was entirely philosophical to any excesses of drinking. She drank rum herself, when they were together, after a cold day's hunting; and more than one glass; yet, except for an increased flush under the smooth darkness of her cheeks, it had no effect on her. Lucia took it, the truth was, in a frank enjoyment masculine in quality. With all this she lost no trace of a charm always feminine; he would have been immediately critical of that — Richard recalled his old dislike for Rose Ann Marable — and his objection to it was fully shared by Lucia.

She was what her being and life together made her, and the result was beyond any fault he was aware of. All the wives of the Bales of Balisand, he reflected, agreeing with Beverley Mathews, had been extraordinarily fine and charming women; all, by pure coincidence, not only highly born but rich, and two were famous for their beauty. He, rather than descend from this plane, had lifted it. It wasn't a fact that tended to reduce the arrogance of the Bale men. Their character had been largely supported, justified, by such marriages. With the approval, the confidence and love of Lucia, his inattentiveness to any general adverse attitude was rendered absolute.

Miss Howlett, with Flora, rose, and, at a slight bend of her head, asked to be excused. Flora kissed her father, then her mother, and they left. "I think as much of Miss Howlett as you do," Richard observed, "but she is too dismal. I need another bottle of wine to get over her impression on me." He remembered Mr. Garret, years ago, at Todd Hundred, reading in the failing light a book of sermons, or some such thing, in Latin. "I suppose they're all that way. God knows, it's not a gay profession." Lucia's answer, that he needed no governess as an excuse for a third or even a fourth bottle, was obvious. "I always heard that you drank so much more than you do. It used to be the story that you got drunk with your Uncle Morryson every night of your lives. Or, perhaps, I contradict Miss Howlett's influence."

"Morryson would try it." He smiled. "Mrs. Patton, do you mind that time, not long before he died, how he got sick at the table?"

"Mr. Bale, I don't," she admitted. "There's been so much drinking on and off, young and old, at Balisand. But I must say," she turned to Lucia, "he didn't deserve all that was told about him. I must. The Bales have a bright anger, and he has a taste for my lime toddy, but no more." Lucia gazed at him speculatively. "I've never seen you really angry, Richard. You haven't been since we were married. I suppose you will some day. You get excited over politics, but everyone does that, don't they? Gawin Todd was always in a fever. I've thought a great deal about Gawin and you. He used to be very uncomplimentary, half the things he said about the Federalists I'm sure were at you; and you are icy if I happen to mention him even now."

"He's on his way to ruining the United States," Richard Bale declared; "and, by God, it looks as though he might succeed. Beverley spoke about that when I told him I wanted to marry you, and all I could say was that I don't change. I've been hammered too much, the metal in me is too hard, to turn or bend. I won't put myself in Gawin's way, I haven't since — since the old trouble, but if I ever have the slightest difficulty with him again, Lucia, I'll kill him."

"I can see that isn't only a threat," she said in an equable voice; "you mean it. I hope such a time will never come, I'll tell you this and then never refer to it, never try to influence you again: don't, Richard." Her words, never loud, came to him on a sudden passionate intensity of feeling. She smiled at him, a smile warm with love. "I don't want for you to think I'm afraid, or that I'd have you not be you. But don't . . . Richard."

He made no reply; there was none. His hatred for Gawin Todd, he told himself, was intact, impervious to time. He might die with it like that, probably he would, but it would go down into the earth with him. Why, he didn't know; he didn't understand the essence of his cold destructive animosity.

*

* *

Nothing, no one, could have so well suited him, Richard concluded: his life, the customs and prejudices of Balisand and the Bales, hadn't been interrupted; no, the pleasure in them was increased. He couldn't imagine, he announced to himself, any other woman so perfectly in keeping with what he needed. At this a swift feeling of discomfort possessed him, a fragment of young song echoed in his memory: but you must bring me oceans more, be true, be true. The tender and beautiful image of Lavinia returned to his thoughts. He hadn't, since his marriage, consciously or subconsciously, dwelt on her. He had been swept into the deep reality of Lucia's passionate feeling, occupied by the fresh vitality animating all the plantation. Richard had no impulse, he was certain, to consider Lavinia emotionally now; but the phrase he had used about Lucia's unique suitability to him challenged everything which he had deliberately granted to the past.

Richard Bale repeated that word — deliberately — for it, he insisted, described and limited his allegiance to the dead. The dead! He recalled the long explanation of a strange returning emotion for Lavinia which he had made to Ava Todd, at Balisand. However, that, he was persuaded, at last was over. He could think of Lavinia with a steady mind, realize her incomparable sweetness, and address himself contented, more than contented, to the present. Richard tried, experimentally, to see Lavinia at Balisand; he pictured a very different set of events from those that had actually happened: a duel with Gawin Todd, successful, and then at the plantation.

But he was, against his best effort, unable to visualize Lavinia at Balisand. He tried to see her standing on the portico, at the dinner table, in the room above with its pointed windows; but she constantly slipped away, remained isolated and apart, from such familiar backgrounds and settings. He couldn't even re-create Lavinia perfectly, not her whole presence, her entire charm — she stayed a little blurred, indefinite, veiled almost in her very loveliness. She might have kept his house magnificently, he didn't know; there was so much of her that had been lost — immediately — to him. The conditions which had separated them had equally made it impossible for him to go to Henrico County and ask interminable questions about her, touch what she had touched, see what she had seen. Their love for each other had been their sole shared existence.

Through the years that had followed his loss he had been certain that his love, lasting till the end of life, would make all other loves and attachments impossible. In reality, first, he had regarded such a possibility as detestable, an absolute act of infidelity; but that conviction had subsided, vanished. He was married to Lucia in every sense of that inclusive term. Yes, and he loved her. He was falling back on that word, Richard realized, a great many times; and he knew no more of its meaning now than formerly. Yet, to others it seemed clear enough. He tried a definition — it was the feeling a man and woman had for each other leading usually to marriage, children and a life together. An obligation of honour never to be departed from! It might be, it sometimes was, where happiness was concerned, a failure: it might lead to years of disagreeable wrangling or frigid remoteness — in those cases love would have fled — but that had no bearing on the inescapable complete acceptance of a single duty. Here a difficulty entered the simplicity of his inherited belief — somehow love and marriage had parted. However, in that event, they had damned well better be joined again. He was annoyed at the direction his thoughts had taken. His definition was correct.

But that, to his surprise, left him precisely where he had begun — with, he discovered, an unanswered need to understand his feeling for Lavinia, or, rather, his feelings for Lavinia and Lucia. He had never, with his wife, approached the sharpness of ecstasy brought him by Lavinia: the attacks of blind longing for her — he could think of no better description — were infinitely stronger than any present. With Lucia he was happy. That was it. If Lavinia had lived:

Yet she could never have possessed half of Lucia's actual vitality of emotion — Lucia was jealous even of losing a second of the agonies of birth. A woman of the very old times, he thought. That was birth, a high strain of blood, in its finest sense. Richard Bale was carried away from the subject of his doubt by the thought of Lucia's reality and strength. A further conviction seized him, a renewed certainty, that only such women, such fulfilment, were, in the end, admirable. The others were no more than a tune on a fiddle, a verse ——

A lilybud, a pink, a rose.

Somehow Lavinia contrived to remain outside of what, he recognized, was a condemnation. The tragedy of death had robbed her of all that, without question, she would have been. And the fact that he could consider her so reasonably, proved to him that his memory of her was what he would have most desired. He hadn't solved the mystery of love, but at least, he had arrived at a splendid knowledge of himself.

He wondered what Gawin Todd felt toward all that had occupied himself; the trace of a smile, without humour, set his lips at the realization that Todd had tried to marry Lucia. He recalled the day when Lucia had left Welfield to go to the party at Todd Hundred, when, from no very laudable motive, he had tried to influence her against, well — the Republican Party. Gawin Todd, probably, would never hear that. He hadn't married since. At intervals he came to Gloucester, to assist the affairs of Todd Hundred; Richard saw him on the road, at the courthouse; when it was unavoidable they spoke, briefly; only that was left of his familiar connection with the Todd family. After Lucia married him her long association with Ava had come imperceptibly to an end. Ava never returned to Balisand.

Richard didn't confine his entire questioning about Lavinia and the past to one occasion; that was a subject he came back to; for it seemed to him he hadn't wholly satisfied it. He accused himself, in his pronounced opinion of what was looked on as the poetry of living, of ingratitude toward all she had been to him. It occurred to Richard Bale that Lavinia had been like a flower, a yellow rose, which he had held in his hand, and then . . . dropped, allowing it to wither unattended. But it was the property of flowers, individual bloom, to die. Yet that reasonable conclusion was suddenly, unaccountably, interrupted by the curious speculation if, actually, Lavinia were dead. He grew impatient at this, at himself: she had her proper place in his memory, just as Lucia had in his life, and, where he was concerned, that was the whole extent of Lavinia's continued being. Too much thinking, he told himself, was making him morbid.

At this he began to reflect on the disturbing quality of not war but peace, inaction — it left the mind free for so much nonsense. He wasn't — and this, too, troubled him — completely absorbed in the affairs of Balisand, he couldn't lose himself in them and the attending life of Gloucester County. In 1793, when he had determined to go back, if possible, to Congress, he had married Lucia instead; she had said, plainly, that she would not move North for the Sessions of the House; and this had resulted in his staying on the plantation, the permanent severing of his actual part with the Federal Government. But his interest in politics and the county was as bitterly alive as it had been when Jefferson first threatened Washington's ideal.

*

* *

In this manner a vague discontentment ran parallel with Richard Bale's complete appreciation of Balisand, his unquestioned allegiance to all that the plantation and his fortunate engagements expressed. But with the progress of summer, the approaching election of a President, he was drawn further and further into the local agitations and party rivalry. He viewed this, mostly, from a largely traditional — Bradlock Wiatt called it an antiquated — position. Richard had never been reconciled, at ease, with the extreme developments of party organization. He insisted that, with things as they were, the voter — after shouting that only the Democratic-Republicans could ensure his freedom from tyranny — had become no more than a machine: he would cast a prepared ballot, in the coming election, for electors already chosen in the State legislature; and the electors, in turn, rather worse than better, must vote for candidates previously selected by Congressional caucus. That was the full extent of his new liberty.

For this, though, Wiatt reminded him, he had his own party to blame: it was Hamilton who had conducted secret nomination committees, and there had been a conference in the Federal Senate chamber for the purpose of forwarding Adams' interests. " The Republicans only followed our example," Bradlock asserted. " But I'm not like you, I don't object; it's necessary, Richard; the country can't be reached to-day with local methods. And, we might as well admit it, Jefferson is ahead of us. Damn it, look at his supporters — Madison, he came back to the Assembly to take care of his party in Virginia, James Monroe, Sam Adams, Gallatin, George Clinton, in New York, Franklin. Perhaps Marshall is as good as any, but he hasn't the support here he'll need. Those Richmond circulars in March that Franklin signed did us a lot of harm. Why, the one on the vindication of the General Ticket Law carried the list of proposed Republican electors everywhere over the State.

" We've had no such meeting as the one in January

where they had near a hundred members of the Virginia legislature, and every prominent man they could get, at the capitol. There isn't a Federalist as loud as Giles or as skilful as Samuel Shields. By God, they appointed committees for everything — to interview the electors for the party, to notify the counties of the answers; they have special men to see voters they may influence; and, not satisfied with that, they have a standing committee in all the important sections. I've heard 'em. Don't you think they're letting the Jay Treaty get out of sight! Copies of the Virginia and Kentucky resolutions have been sent to every excuse for a village. I don't know who wrote them, but it was no clerk. The Alien and Sedition Acts were never popular, Richard; we know why they were framed, to take care of Genêt's friends and editors like Freneau and Bache; but that's all been forgotten. It's the Federal Government again oppressing the people."

"Are you preparing to follow Madison?" Richard Bale demanded. He stared with disagreeably narrowed eyes at Bradlock Wiatt. "No, I'm not, you be damned contentious Tory, and you know it. If you insult me I'll shoot you with both barrels of one of these new French guns. It's just that I'm not blind." They were standing outside the tavern, where a meeting had been called of the leaders among the Federals of Gloucester County. There was a stamping of tied horses, a great activity among the hostlers, a hum of voices from the taproom. "It takes more energy than I have to convince you of anything," Wiatt proclaimed; "I'll have to have brandy." They went in to the familiar crowded space, sharp with the odour of strong spirits, and a concerted laughter met Richard Bale.

He was led, ceremoniously, to where, written in chalk on a wall, was his engagement with Balantine, the landlord: Mr. Richard Bale of Balisand is agreeable to a hundred dollars when Jefferson is elected President of the United States. "How much," he was asked, "will you pay to have that wiped out? What will you settle for now? Fifty dollars?" That amount was met with jeers. Ninety? Ninety-eight! "I am at the wrong meeting," he called above the friendly tumult of voices. "This one is to propose Page as an elector. I'm looking for one to nominate me." Henry Dalney cheered.

"Listen to them supporting each other," Bradlock cried; "the old musket and the venerable hull. Why, they think it's still winter in 1776. My dear Henry and Richard, follow us carefully—the law of 1792, when elections were viva voce and held by the High Sheriff, is no more. The Act of 'ninety-nine has taken its place. You must now proceed in a decent and orderly manner, and endorse the names of your choice."

"Or make their mark on the printed ballot." That was greeted with prolonged applause. "In addition," the instruction was continued, "the clerk of the county will be at the polls to see if your taxed land is proper and right."

"Taxed land, I'm told, would disqualify me," Richard answered. "To have anything to-day, a plantation, a house, a servant——"

"A fast horse," he was interrupted.

To own anything," he proceeded, "is to be suspected of designs against ——"

"Thomas Jefferson."

"That will do as well as another," he acknowledged. "And I'll say this — the country may go to hell with him, but Balisand won't; every friend I have can turn Republican, but there will be no Republicanism at Balisand; as long as it stays where it is by the North River, as long as there is a Bale alive, it will keep the way it's always been, with a bowl of punch on the table and a horse to carry the black cockade. It may be a small horse, or even a mare, but I'll back her to beat any grey Pegasus ever foaled."

A renewed shout rang through the taproom. Everyone present emptied a glass in the honour of Careless. "But this black cockade," he was asked; "we don't appear to remember about that." A chorus rose eager to repair the fault of memory. "Richard's grandfather wore it riding, and whoever passed had to get off his horse and stand at attention, or he had a whip broken over his head." Dalney said to Richard: "It's getting pretty drunk. If the meeting isn't called soon there won't be one."

This, Richard Bale saw, was true; but he replied that if it were necessary to stay sober in order to preserve the Federal Party, then, at last, it had vanished into thin water. "No gentleman can make his mind up about a candidate, any more than he can fox-hunt, without the resources of Antigua," he said. "An election can only be floated on rum."

"If that's so," Dalney replied, "and true of meetings,

the anchor is up and you are already far from shore. It's a good thing you have a safe harbour up the river." The noise, generally, was subsiding; the tone of the assembly grew serious; solemn voices, absurd plans and pretensions, took the place of the former lightness of humour. Richard Bale was suddenly depressed, his confidence in the ultimate, if not immediate, triumph of Federal principles, diminished; he felt almost helpless in the face of an increasing spirit that he couldn't measure or understand. In the past there had been a specific issue, a designated man, to meet; but now no place could be selected for attack. It was useless even to declaim against Jefferson, for he had withdrawn himself into the organization of his ambitions. Washington, and, it seemed to Richard, the example of Washington, was gone. He was obliterated in a featureless and shallow praise. Hamilton, who was popularly supposed to have prompted and led the President, was an infinitely smaller man . . . and so were all, all, the others.

*

* *

The meeting, in the main room of the tavern, was called by James Fanning, who proceeded, briefly, with a review of the local situation and its part in the approaching national crisis. "As we have found out," Fanning went on, "the local conventions we have been holding were very unsatisfactory. They hadn't any authority, and the delegates they sent to Richmond couldn't bind their districts. They were held whenever called and at any time of the year, and each year had to be completely reorganized. Sometimes their instructions were followed and sometimes not, and, if one or another wasn't satisfied, he was free to nominate himself and split his neighbourhood twenty ways. In addition, what we've been hearing of as the correspondence and conference system, though it was an improvement on mass meetings, isn't a great deal better for the simple reason that the local committees are too loose and narrow — I'd like to say ignorant — in their sittings. We're too content with ourselves, that's plain.

"I have seen, in our committee room, a dozen circulars asking for our preference in candidates not even opened. That, however, will soon be over, because the general elective privilege of Virginia is slipping away from us, since the Legislature is taking on itself the nominating power. Well, we can't complain about that, for we brought it on ourselves; but we can, if it isn't already too late, come to a common agreement and act with one informed mind. I do not, personally, think it is too late; but the situation is dangerous. We're carrying too much old baggage, relying on the special virtues of our past, and if that continues it will mean the destruction of Federalism."

Richard Bale, increasingly irritated by all that Fanning said, and recognized by the meeting, rose. "Before I came into this room," he said, "I was pessimistic about the future of the principles we firmly believe in; and, again before that, there was a certain amount of laughter at the mention of a black cockade. My temporary dejection, I'm certain, was from that misplaced though happy humour. Mr. Fanning thinks that we are at fault; we have, he says, no organization, no party integrity; and he makes it clear that he'd like to call us, in his sense, ignorant. For one, I am totally willing to accept that charge — I am highly ignorant of all but a few things; and, as I hinted in the taproom, when they pass away and are no longer valid, then I shall be no longer valid; there will be no Bales at Balisand.

"With your permission, and the assurance that they hang directly on the issue of the gathering, I shall repeat them. The first is that the United States is a nation independent of all other nations, and, together with this, you will recognize the undeniable truth that the business of the separate integrity of a country lies exclusively with the central Federal Government. We will not pause here. The second fact for your notice is that, practically speaking, what independence we have was won for us by a small, a pitifully small, group of men guided by Federal honour and principles. They were strong men, and, I am willing to admit, moved by prejudices. Even General Washington — I like best that title — had certain views upheld with more emphasis than, perhaps, was warranted. These, then, obtained our freedom; and, through a bitter period of doubt, they were ceaselessly attacked by what, I believe, is known as the people. Every law passed for our proper safety, every measure for our mere life, was fought by the public and the leaders of the public. I needn't, now, recall the outrageous conduct of the Democratic-Republicans through the summer of 'ninety-three. That soon enough collapsed, broken down and dispersed by the character of the President. The Jefferson party has made you so familiar with the Jay British Treaty that I won't subject you to further details; except, it may be, to remind you that it was a compromise measure.

"I repeat that every move which has resulted in the high engagement of the United States, each with each other, came from the determination and wisdom, yes, the prejudices, of a strong individual. Our county, once, bred strong men — but where are they now? We have drifted into a modern and lax state comparable with the beginning of Rome's collapse. We were founded on individuals, I shall say on gentlemen, and if we are to continue, it must be by that means. The weight of Mr. Fanning's remarks, as I took it, was against this. He didn't, in my estimation, keep before him the fact that we were, we are, and always will be, Federalists. He discourses on the need of sinking our personalities in schemes and circulars and bodies of voters; he is discontented with the conference and correspondence systems; both, I have found, efficient and admirable.

"In other words, he wants us to copy Jefferson, and that, with the help of God, we will never do. The place, in any war, of an officer, is ahead and not back of his line. We will never put forward the mass of voters and manipulate their coat-tails from some comfortable and convenient plantation. We'll never hire blackguard and vilifying pens. Better, a thousand times, the pistol than the pen. Death is not always, universally, an occasion of mourning. I do not like bribery or the smell of corruption, either in the corporal body or the body politic. I do not like compromises. I do not welcome servility in the face of inferiors. Nor do I endorse buying even freedom at too great a price. Too much forgetfulness is among us, traditions needed for our very breathing are in danger of being discarded."

He paused a moment, by no means at the end of what he intended to say, but a voice cut sharply in upon him, asking that the business of the meeting be resumed. Richard Bale glanced, in a growing chilled anger, from man to man through the assembly. Dalney nodded in friendly encouragement, Beverley Mathews applauded him by a silent gesture; but the majority, he saw, had been waiting with only a politeness of silence for him to finish. There wasn't a comment, an expression of approbation, upon all he had so — so carefully said. His anger sank before a return of his depression. Now he was certain the Federalists were hurrying to destruction. Why, damn it, the men about him didn't know the causes that had brought them, the business of the meeting!

A sudden binding realization, a resolution, really, came over him — this was the last time he would ever speak politically and publicly. The present didn't want to hear him, it had neither interest nor knowledge in his experience and convictions. He was no good, now. He smiled — the familiar twist, without gaiety, of his mouth — at the memory of past scenes, the commanding men of his generation, dead or old and weary. All that, it seemed, had gone for little: crude efforts in the early crude days of the republic. But the contrary was true — this was the crude time. Francis Bale, clearing the river front of Balisand, was a figure of infinite fineness compared with the men of to-day. It took time, acres, leisure, servants, privilege, to make a gentleman; and only he could be wholly free from threats, fear, influence, dependence on mobs. What, once, had been concentrated, invaluable, a standard for conduct, was being diluted and spread out and lost for ever in the mass. Without leaders reflecting in their persons the qualities which alone made life acceptable, there could be no victory or peace.

He was on his horse, riding slowly back to his plantation. The temper of the meeting he had attended, its resolutions and arranged future, were all in direct opposition to him. The gift of oratory, he told himself, had fled. Balisand. The wooded sides of his narrow lane closed in on him; soon he could see, between the trees, the sparkle of the North River; he passed under the spread limbs of the broadnut tree and turned to the left; a negro took the bridle from him.

*

* *

He confined himself, thereafter, where public affairs were involved, to remarks and discussions in the immediate surroundings of Balisand and of his familiar close associates. The remainder of summer had, for him, the aspect of a disastrous forced encampment in the middle of hostilities. The Federalists gave the impression of activity; there were repeated meetings, legislative party councils at the capital, gatherings at the courthouse and the tavern; but they were only, he continued to think, a weak and unavailing copy of the enemy's tactics. He was obliged to admit that the Democratic-Republicans pressed the last possible good from everything that was to their advantage. Jefferson made a national concern the carrying of legal action from the State to the Federal courts; Monroe, a candidate for Governor of Virginia, was elected on a wave of popular sympathy following his recall from Paris. And, during these subversive plots and movements, the Federalists — owing to their damned futile methods — were scarcely more than holding their ground.

"It will result in Virginia electing the whole twenty-one Republican electors," Richard declared to Beverley Mathews. He replied that, against such a possibility, Massachusetts was solidly Federal. "And North Carolina, probably. New Jersey will be for Adams, and Jefferson have no sweep in Maryland." Lucia interrupted them to say that there would be fox hunting in another week. "I'll be thankful to hear something beside scandal about Mr. Burr. Richard used to talk to Flora of the war, but now it's the election, and his language isn't a particle more careful than it was." Flora added, "I like it." They were in the south room at Balisand; the afternoon was darkening early; the glow of the soft coal burning in a grate visible on the oak floor.

"I've never known the oysters to be better," Beverley remarked. "There is one thing here — you're directly at the river and you can sit on the wharf and eat them as they're brought up. But you can't stand in the garden and shoot partridges." Richard said, "London broke his arm early in the spring, and, for all we've done, it won't mend. I'd almost as soon break my own."

London, Mathews recalled aloud, was Richard's head-man. "I suppose I'll have to choose another, and that will near to kill him. Beverley, even the negroes aren't what they were. By God, if Thomas Jefferson could, he'd have them vote."

"Nonsense," Beverley Mathews replied. "Look here, Richard, actually, what difference will it make to us in Gloucester if Jefferson is elected — I mean aside from the hundred dollars you will have to pay? Once the Tidewater was important, the coast of Virginia and New England. We were, it's just to say, America. But hasn't that changed? At one time we commanded the colonies, when we were young; and now, comparatively speaking, we're old. Giles, in a way, is right — we are like England. In our lives we have seen the current of the United States set away from us, run uphill to the mountains and beyond. We are as unpopular with the body of the States as they are with us. They just let us exist, if we don't try to interfere with their plans; that's about the extent of it. And it won't improve.

"This will horrify you, but I don't believe even Jefferson started the movement he's head of; I think he was swept away by it. We had it all, Richard, and it got away from us. Your daughters, for instance, will marry into another world. And you spoke at the tavern of Balisand staying always as it was. Impossible. When you die, let me tell you, half of it, more, will go with you. A son won't help that . . . born in a new era. You forget how much you have seen shift and break. Remember Morryson; he was convinced that you and Ekkes were letting everything go to the devil. To-day, that's your song. The truth is we can't keep up with the truth."

"Father," Lucia objected, "it's right enough for you to be reasonably venerable, but I won't have you making Richard out so old. Everyone does, and I can't understand why. After all, he is only forty-six." It wasn't his age, Mathews replied, but his inheritance. "His cursed stubborn blood. There isn't a shade of difference in his looks from the painting of Francis Bale in your dining room. He'd only have to let his hair grow and tie it with a ribbon you'd give him. I'm proud of him, really, I look on him with admiration; but you can't expect the rabble at the courthouse to agree with me when he shoves and damns them aside. My dear Lucia, there is a pistol bullet in his remarks."

Flora Bale gazed at Richard with a speculative surprise. She came close to Miss Howlett. "Does father talk pistol bullets?" she demanded in a low agitated voice. "He means," Miss Howlett explained, "that Mr. Bale speaks with great decision. It was only a way of putting it. When little girls talk it should be like a happy song." Camilla, freshly dressed, came into the room. "Alice Ellen is mad again," she announced proudly. "That's three times yesterday and once today," Flora observed. "The Bale temper," Richard remarked; "we're not only getting out of fashion but out of favour. Together with other things. Now duelling ——" he turned to Beverley Mathews. Lucia addressed the governess: "Please take the children into the hall, Miss Howlett. Richard, I never get over being amazed at you." He continued:

"I don't want to seem inhuman, but there is something to be said for it. The custom does this — under it every man is directly responsible for his acts and speech. Anyone who will back his opinions with his life, holding his name higher, can never entirely lose his honour. Where the protection of women is concerned, a duel is sometimes absolutely necessary. A man who slanders a woman, or has any advantage of one, should be shot. In the army, too, it can't be escaped from, even with the greatest impropriety to discipline. It's the one final answer, Beverley; the shot of a pistol settles all question and difficulties. I have said this before: if any man of sufficient standing to demand attention throws the shadow of a doubt on the honesty of my words or intentions, I will, if I'm able, kill him."

"There," Mathews agreed, "duelling might be defended. The trouble is that it breeds an intolerable class of professional and vain murderers continually looking for more notoriety. The affair of what they call their honour! There are times, of course, when an individual shouldn't be allowed to live. But that is what the law's for. And this in itself makes you wrong. I know how you feel and what you are — a Bale of Balisand — and there are moments, when I reflect you're married to Lucia, that frighten me. Professional murderers. Perhaps it wasn't the same in the past, but that's what duellists are getting to be to-day. Newspaper editors and shady political colonels." He couldn't, Richard observed, be held responsible for a present misapplication of the code. "I'll add this," Beverley said, "if, with your family, you ever engage in a formal duel and survive, I will never again, in any manner, recognize you."

"Father," Lucia said quietly, "isn't that an affair of mine rather than yours? I understand Richard better than you ever can, and I know exactly what you're referring to; but I married him, all of him. I hope, I think, he wouldn't put us in danger from just bad temper; but if it happens differently . . . we might as well be quiet. I'm sick of having Richard perpetually blamed; I was serious about your talking as though he were a — a relic of the ark. Nobody, any more, remembers that he was a soldier; it might be regarded as disgraceful; something to be kept hidden. I asked him once, too, never to fight; but I think it was impertinent. I'm sorry I did. As I told you, I married him. And that's enough of that."

"Indeed, Lucia," her father returned, in a mock humility. "I regret that I spoke that way of your young man. If you could get Richard to say a word about his soldiering I'd be indebted to you."

*

* *

The balloting for Presidential electors, at the beginning of November, fell on a day in which, it appeared, the sea had taken symbolical possession of the land: a great salt fog had moved across Mockjack Bay and up the Gloucester rivers; its grey density alternately thinned and thickened and there were diagonal gusts of rain, an erratic violent wind. The air, the fog, was pervaded by the sound of waves: Richard Bale had a vision of the white raging water along the coast. He was riding to the courthouse to vote, wrapped in an aged cloak he had worn in the army, a soft black silk scarf about his throat. The rain beat squarely on him and ran in streams down the sides of his horse; eddies of fog swept through the trees and enveloped him; the trees were but insubstantial and agitated tracings. He wasn't, except for the sharpened pain in his leg, troubled by this — his experience had included weather so much worse than it could ever be again — but he wondered if, in effect, the storm would drive Federal power away from the Tidewater, its peculiar and proper home. His thoughts returned to something Beverley had said, about the general world, the United States, turning regardlessly from Gloucester County, leaving it without interest, almost without comment, to its different past. That Richard didn't, he couldn't, agree with; but there had been a substance, an excuse, for Mathews' assertion. Yes, here was the truth — at one time, during even his memory, the Gloucester of tidal rivers and early plantations had been individual, a locality with a spirit and air of its own. It had been jealously apart from the newer Virginia of the high inland counties; the men from it cherished it and their inherited lands; they upheld the Tidewater against all other regions. That he had had from preceding generations, from its first isolation; and it was gone.

Locality by locality, district by district, State by State, the country was losing its separate identity; men were losing their characteristics; the land, at last, was beginning to assume the solidity Washington, in another sense, hoped and demanded for it. Under his hand, Richard saw, the political body of the United States had changed more utterly than he had known. In a way, now, he, Richard Bale, was opposed to the development of the Federalistic ideal. At the beginning the men who had become Republican fought the Constitution — the Constitution had been forged as a Federal document — but to-day the Democratic-Republicans supported it in its absolute form; and he was in sympathy with the arbitrary interpretation of Hamilton.

It was the devil of a humorous situation! He recalled — how long ago it seemed — that Edmund Randolph had carried to the Convention of 1787 the Virginia plan from which, ultimately, the Constitution had been formed, and that Randolph, persuaded that the Federal Government was arrogating to itself a limitless privilege, had finally refused to support his own proposals. Gawin Todd had declaimed against the Constitution at every conceivable place and time — Todd, who was now its champion in the protection of the rights of the people! And those were the politics, the convictions, of the present. It was natural that such men, such measures, were in opposition to any tradition or memory whatever.

He had fought for a united country, but, God knew, not one united from the present undesirable materials. His fundamental belief, that a happy arrangement of government lay in the administration, by a few capable minds, of an obedient and industrious people, was now only laughed at; and yet that had always been, it must always be, the religion of his party.

The conclusion of this, certainly, was that his party was vanishing; perhaps it had vanished. He had seen the Whigs and Tories go with all that once they had so passionately contended for; he had seen a small country actually brought out of war into existence by Federal effort. The reaction, after the death of Washington, had grown increasingly powerful — past motives and needs and battles forgotten — and now the colour of events had again shifted. The people, which he had regarded as an undisciplined mob, at which Jasper Robine had jeered through a long night of his drunken discontent, were mounting to a greater and greater magnitude. They had taken the words of the Constitution for their own.

There was a wet morose crowd of men in the court-house; the voting proceeded rapidly and silently; the lists of twenty-one candidates, Federal or Republican — some previously signed by the voters and some hurriedly endorsed at the polls — were folded; the County Clerk checked name after name against his register of taxed lands. Bale found himself beside James Fanning, and a short conversation followed in relation to Fanning's daughters and the school at Balisand. "I saw they had arrived safely," Richard said; "and Lucia will keep them all night, certainly. Fanning, I used to know every man at an election, but there are fifty here I'm sure I've never seen. Or do you suppose their faces have changed too?"

"It's the opposition vote," the other explained; "Gawin Todd has them all out in spite of the weather. Do you remember the old elections, when the candidates sat in a row and you made your bow to the one you preferred? " Richard did. " And argue with them, too, if you were a candidate," he added. He told Fanning a little of all that, coming to the polls, had been in his mind. " You're right and wrong," James Fanning declared. " We won't lose the party but drop out of it the men and ideas not in keeping with the times." Richard supposed that had happened to him, but Fanning had left him, forced away by the movement of the crowd.

The rain, Richard found, had ceased, the wind gone down, the fog suddenly settled in the hollows of the road and woods. Above, it was lighter; there was visible a diffused radiance of the sun. The booming of waves in the air had sunk to a low far murmur, soothing and reflective and melancholy. The impersonality of Richard Bale's thoughts grew personal; his leg ached with a vindictive persistence; and he was impressed by the fact that, in a very short while, he would be fifty. That wasn't exactly young. He didn't actually feel this, at no moment had he been conscious of a change from youth to middle age; it was only a mental realization; a thing he told himself. It had created a state of mind in keeping with the November day; one seemed appropriate to the other. Richard looked back in amazement at the hardship he had, with hardly more than a curse, survived. He recalled the parties, his idiotic performances, in the past. Remarkable! The amount of drinking hadn't lessened, but the manner was not the same. Why, damn it, Madeira was old-fashioned now; the habit of drinking port was vanishing. The tradition of toddy had been lowered, diluted.

Dropped by the party! Yes, that was what it amounted to, with this difference — the party was no longer strong enough to hold itself together. It would go. It would go. He wished that he might have Robine to talk to, but Jasper Robine was dead; he had died on a mission in Spain. A gentleman who had, at heart, been unable to conform to a present. It was a question with Richard if a man of complete breeding could. His thoughts were never widely projected, they returned to the same few conditions and ideas; and he said to himself, very positively, that breeding in men was one of the things a universal party, the equal people, were casting away. It insulted, contradicted, their pretence of equality. This, he thought later, was the last thing Washington would listen to. It was December, and the result of the election had been announced from Richmond: Virginia had chosen twenty-one — her entire number — Democratic-Republican electors. To that result Richard devoted a night of wine and rum varied by toddy. He sat alone, except for the portrait of Francis Bale, in the dining room; and the candles, one by one, flickered, sent up an evil smoke, and went out; yet they had been renewed, and it was dawn; but he was impervious to nights and days and calamities.

*

* *

Definitely he was drawing back into Balisand, to Lucia and the children; there change might come, but not until he had followed Morryson Bale to the walled enclosure by the garden. His days became what, in the past, the life on his plantation had been: the school bell was rung in its regular rotation, it marked the school hours, controlled the movements of the negroes, called the house to the dining room. Another headman was appointed in the place of London — who became an unofficial but increasingly tyrannical power — and the new man, Jacob, stood at the foot of the portico steps to drink the glass of whisky which was the public recognition of his new importance. Every day, practically, he fox-hunted with Lucia and the neighbours. They rose early in the cold dark of their room — a servant had started the scarcely perceptible fire in the grate — dressed hurriedly, had a breakfast with rum, and rode with their hounds and an informal kennelman, through the brightening morning, to join the day's hunt.

There were hounds from Balisand and Welfield, from plantations on the Severn and York Rivers, with Bradlock Wiatt and the Fannings, partly merged in a pack that, Lucia constantly protested, could not be properly handled. She had very decided, and revolutionary, ideas about fox hunting. For example, she disliked the competitive running of single hounds; that mad chase, she insisted, spoiled hunting. Her dogs were trained to hold together. In the Tidewater such hunting was mainly an affair of the fastest hound killing the fox; and Lucia was so contrary, Richard declared, that she was actually relieved when the fox escaped.

"Of course I am," she acknowledged. "We're not just ridding the farms of foxes." They were trotting past Roaring Springs, toward the Cow Creek Pond and Balisand after a long hunt. Lucia was ahead, with an easy looseness of seat but a ready hand for the holes in the way. "I'll say this, too," she added: "I wouldn't allow any cur dogs in the circle. But a lot of the riders are no better. They go yelling through the woods by every possible path as though they were chasing negroes. Half the horses aren't fit for what they make them do. I positively ordered one back to-day." She was, Richard Bale said, more dictatorial than himself. Fox hunting was for everyone, the high and the low, but principally for the low. She paid no attention to this.

In their hall they sat for a minute, weary but keen from excitement and the rush of cold air. Lucia had taken off her hat: her hair lay always in a flat black sweep, he thought. It was lustrous and orderly, and that brought to him the memory, the softness and perfume, of hair very different, light and in a waving disorder. It was stronger than a memory, an emotion, dark with regret, longing, and touched by pain. Nothing like that had happened to him for years, and, after drifting into its mood of agreeable sorrow, he recalled himself brutally. Lucia was gazing at her hands, abstracted and content. A feeling of anger took possession of him; he was infuriated at a weakness which, he silently asserted, he had as well as invited.

His wife rose, went upstairs, but he remained sitting; his anger turning into what, almost, was panic. He had conquered Lavinia's swift invasion of his life, but an echo of it, like the falling vibration of a clear bell, lingered within him. Nothing now was as desirable. That, of course, was absurd, a sentimental delusion. Nothing now . . . so sweet. "Absurd!" he spoke vigorously aloud. But, against his decided manner, fear again brushed him, fear and a sense of guilt.

Abruptly he followed Lucia and changed his clothes; it was still the middle of day, and, explaining that he must see Thomas Ekkes, he mounted a horse at the rack. He wanted to be alone, not even — not most of all — with a mere memory, a shadow. At any rate, he told himself, what had happened to him wasn't as full, as strong, as it had been when such seizures were more frequent. It had gone, retreated, almost at once. Probably it would never come again. Yet, for the briefness of its duration, he had been filled with rapture. To recall it brought back the insistent vibrations of his joy. The trouble was he didn't understand what had happened to him — his mind wasn't yet at rest about Lavinia. The whole thing had been so fantastic, and — good God — sixteen years ago.

Where Lucia and he were concerned he had no doubts — he was hers, his body and his spirit and his thoughts. Yet, sitting before her, while she gazed idly at her hands, he had been filled with — with love for another woman. The word love came independently to him. It wasn't that, however. He loved only Lucia. But merely to say that didn't help him. If it were something else, then what was it? He had no will to deny his old passion for Lavinia; that he had put away, not disclaimed. It came over him that he was needlessly exaggerating the importance of his feeling. No one could perfectly control his mind, his thoughts, put out of memory all that had passed. Yes, that was a reasonable attitude, a just conclusion. Purposely he thought of Lavinia as a yellow rose that, once, had made lovely a minute of his existence. His emotion, consequently, was one of gratitude.

With this he should be satisfied; but he wasn't. He could argue as long as he pleased, but the fact, the thrilling reality, remained: Lavinia, who was dead, had given him a moment of ecstatic happiness. But what, particularly, shook his confidence in life's safety and proprieties, was not the past, not even the troubled present, but the future. What if Lavinia — that, for convenience, was the way he put it — came back still again? It was evident that his logical trust in the preserving attachment of his marriage had been destroyed. Even Lucia hadn't been able to control, to banish, the charm of an old June. Damn it, there she had been, peaceful and intent on her capable hands!

This much, however, was certain — the past might overtake him in flashes, but, at the end, he'd put it out, extinguish its fragrant flame. Not entirely because he wanted to, but because it was his simple duty. And in this he was assisted by what Lucia, supremely, was. His duty and his happiness were absolutely one. Richard didn't find Ekkes, he hadn't looked for him; and, since it was the hour for dinner, he rode back to the house.

"You look tired," Lucia told him; "the run this morning wasn't long or hard. Richard, are you quite truthful about your leg, are you certain it doesn't hurt more than you say?"

"I'm not," he assured her; "and my leg is all right when the weather's reasonable. It was fine to-day."

But she wasn't satisfied; he was conscious of her gaze upon him in moments when he seemed to be occupied. The following morning Lucia wouldn't let him hunt. "I'm not certain you're honest," she said; "there is no use in your objecting. I won't have you along. But be careful what you say to Flora. Miss Howlett complained to me that Flora insisted you told her that her history lesson was a lot of lies and nonsense, and you had decided to teach her things that were useful and true." Some of that, he was forced to admit, he had said, "I wanted her to understand what was going on now, and about France and England in the United States." He was, Lucia answered with a light despair, incurable. She was at the front door, and, suddenly, he was reluctant to have her go . . . to leave him alone. But already she would be late——

A breath of fear — yet which might have been the cold from the opened door — touched him. He couldn't go on like this; probably he was sick — fever accounted for so much. Really, he was inclined to laugh at himself: Richard Bale afraid of a memory, of a lovely and fragile shape dead sixteen years. That was all he had to do — repeat the bare facts of what concerned him.

*

* *

His confidence in himself and in his circumstances slowly returned; now that Lavinia's invasion of his contentment was over, he again felt that it hadn't been as strong and unsettling as, at the time, he had thought.

Anyhow, it was ridiculous to magnify it into a voluntary or involuntary infidelity. It had nothing, nothing at all, to do with his life. Richard asserted this silently, but emphasizing each word. At last he was convinced that what had happened was merely trivial: he had walked to the wharf, and, indifferent to the cold, was looking out over the dull tide to where his oyster beds lay. A marking pole, he thought, had been dragged from its mooring; it lay almost parallel with the water, a possible danger to his canoes. It must be replaced. There was a flash from the surface of the river that utterly blinded him; and, dazed, grasping at the support of the wharf covering, the winter was swept away in an illusion of full summer, a garden of flowers and trees with mocking birds singing in their leafy branches. It was the perfection of the year, with nature bright in the tender promise of fertility; the sky and river were a distant idyllic blue; the sun a gold veil thrown over the earth.

His happiness, his joy, grew more and more complete; it seemed to be advancing graciously toward him; as it drew nearer he thought he must choke with rapture. The impersonality of his emotion gave way to the realization that this was Lavinia. Not, certainly, Lavinia herself; nothing to hold in his arms, to kiss; and yet that, in sensation, exactly. Richard sank down on the bench fortunately beside him, his eyes open, but seeing no winter, his hands tightly clasped. He thought he said her name, again and again, Lavinia; his lips moved; but no sound came from them. Waves of triumphant delight passed over him; he was submerged in a sense of utter fulfilment.

It left him slowly, no less entrancing in retreat than when it had overcome him. Richard Bale sat bowed forward, cold and empty and shaken. He must go back to the house, he recognized, and he rose, moving with a stumbling tread and the uncertain dragging assistance of his cane. He found a fire — where it didn't matter — and huddled over it, trying to set in order the confusion of his shocked mind. What, specially, he combated was the impulse, the temptation, to return to and dwell on the passionate loveliness of his experience. It had created an immense desire in him, yes, a hunger of his defrauded love; he wanted to take it up from the interruption by death and follow it to the end.

This struck him — the beauty of his vision, if it might be called that, was like whatever he had known of Lavinia, preliminary, a miraculous beginning. Just as their summer was unfolding it had been halted, suspended; it hadn't, after all, been killed. Flowers, it appeared, could escape death. His thoughts, then, turned outward, to the room about him and Balisand, to Lucia. He was appalled at the knowledge that, for a space however short, her reality had been less a substance than the texture of memory. He couldn't help himself by denying it. No, what had happened to him was too serious to be disposed of in empty conventional phrases. His situation was precarious. A hatred for what he had participated in began to rise; but it didn't include Lavinia. How could it? The weakness was his alone, a secret fault being made increasingly clear to him.

This, as well, was plain — for all his thought, his logical conclusions, he knew nothing about his emotions where the two women of his life were implicated. He might as well give up his speculations; he'd be forced to, Richard saw, since the sheer struggle before him would require determination and not argument. The gathering peace around him had been suddenly shattered. There was no question of what he must do, of what, at bottom, he desired: nothing could destroy his attachment to Lucia. That took the form of a challenge . . . but addressed to what? The room where he sat was familiar, reassuring, actual with the materials of his existence; a horse was stamping on the lawn; a sudden barking came from the hounds left at the kennels. Lavinia wasn't present in any of this, she had never had a part in it; nothing here was hers. Even now he still couldn't imagine Lavinia at Balisand.

Yet she had been here, on the wharf, wrapped in tender love and June. But to think of her in such terms was an act of faithlessness; it was, in effect, to pray her to return, to stay with him always. Damn him, damn him into hell! He deliberately, in turn, re-created the images of his family: Lucia, splendid and strong and dark; Flora, so curiously, in a totally different mould, like himself; the candid and sturdy Camilla; Alice Ellen, flaming with the impatient temper of the Bales. How engaging, how warm and superior, they were; how fortunately his. Every aspect of his life was favourable to him, to what he regarded as the success of his honour. His problem had grown simpler, direct, at that second when he had ceased trying to solve it. The obligations of duty he fully understood. This was what confronted him:

He must disentangle himself from the memory of the past, keep his mind rigidly on the need, the happiness, of what he had, so that Lavinia could not intrude her loveliness into his whole commitment of being. Richard felt relieved at once. For seven years Lavinia hadn't dominated him, and, now that he was so armed against her, it was probable that she would fade back into the past. Now that he was armed against her! Against Lavinia. A cruel phrase in connection with her. He didn't, exactly, mean that; it was only her measureless charm, her perfection, which he was forced to combat. Her very beauty made it imperative for him to guard himself. This, his explanatory thought, his silent apology, took the form of a remark addressed to her. Almost he was begging her to forgive him. He was asking for a release, a peace, like that of death — imploring Lavinia to accept the fate which had overtaken them.

He would have to cultivate a sounder mind, Richard determined; he wasn't sufficiently normal; but neither was there any trace of insanity in him; no Bale had ever been threatened by that. A race of soldiers, a supporting fact. Born to fight, he would continue, with necessity, to the end. He was grimly entertained by the ironic humour in that: now, in the serenity of Balisand, the apparent tranquillity of his middle age, he was, perhaps, entering into a struggle more desperate than any in the celebrated warfare of his youth. If Lavinia came back! With this, when he thought of his wife, he was conscious of an increasing dislike for himself, for his body and thoughts. It seemed to him, somehow, that he had been — well, contaminated. A little of his arrogance in the face of the world, his severity of judgment, had gone. He was allowing for pressures, temptations, in men that formerly he had dismissed with contempt. By God, he was getting soft!

That, with the loud clangour of a warning, sent him upright on his feet. If this grew impossible, he told himself, if he couldn't conquer it on the land, he would sink it, cooled for ever, with all that it included, in the North River. Better that than a slow corruption. He'd give Lucia no half allegiance, he wouldn't live with her and fall into shuddering delights at the vision of Lavinia. Richard went into the dining room, to the long high table that held the decanters, and drank a glass of brandy. There later Lucia found him. " That was full when I left this morning," she observed, of the decanter. " Only part of a half cask is left. You will have to send to Norfolk or Welfield for more."

*

* *

At supper Richard Bale, sombrely dressed, was self-contained, silent. " Miss Howlett, have you told the children what to-day is? " he asked. His demand was so uncompromising, he had addressed her so severely, that she was wholly confused. " I'm afraid not, Mr. Bale. If I should have remembered I am sorry." He replied that it was the first anniversary of General Washington's death. " Never again, in my house, let that be forgotten by anyone." Lucia objected to his peremptory tone. " But, Richard, you said nothing about it sooner."

He had been preoccupied with something else, he explained briefly. A sudden appreciation of the simplicity of his years in the Continental Army, the Virginia Line, possessed him. The difficulties, the abject privation, seemed to have been immeasurably less than the reward, the reward not of recognition or public applause or payment, but the sense of victory over the body, of accomplishment with no thought of price. That time had been best suited to him of any in the degenerate present. And how various it was, how many different scenes and countrysides and services he had passed through. The War with England was an affair of scattered engagements, long retreats, forced marches, North and South. Only a little group of men, about Washington, knew how many times their cause had been potentially lost; how many times from defeat, imminent ruin, they had at least preserved a few troops with which to fall back.

Winter and summer and winter again; they had stopped keeping track of seasons, of years, except to remark that January always overtook them when most they lacked clothes. It was in the fall of 1776 that, with a captain's commission, he had recruited a company in the Tidewater. They had joined the 6th Virginia Regulars at Williamsburg, and drilled there through the winter. Even then there were objections, muttering in the line, against an indispensable discipline. What training his men had had, in addition to ornamental and really disorganizing muster days, had been in open marches, through the woods, against Indians. Each held stubbornly, ignorantly, to his individual freedom. Yet, when they marched North, into Pennsylvania, they formed able if unimpressive troops. They crossed the Delaware above Trenton; there was a town . . . what was it? Perth — Perth Amboy. And, almost at once, they went into action, under General Lee, covering Washington's retreat. They began that way! His men had held a bridge across the Raritan River while Washington withdrew his army and stores beyond the Delaware.

He, Richard Bale, was particularly fortunate, since he had been with the force that, hurried across the river, had beaten the Hessians at Trenton. Then, for a while, he was attached to the staff at Princeton — his company already had been decimated, left, for the most part, on the bank of the Raritan. However, what he had experienced was nothing to the bloody and often single-handed fighting at Middle Post. Forays at night, outposts surprised, quiet slaughter. That had lasted well into June, and then he joined the main army under Wayne. At the Brandywine he was in Wayne's division, with the 3rd Virginia Regiment on the left of the American line. Across their front meandered a narrow creek, and beyond that slight interruption Knyphausen had had seven thousand men. All day the German assaulted, but without success. How many times, Richard wondered, had he closed in the gaps in his company. But, at sunset, with the right of the army turned, Wayne had been forced to fall back. With Colonel Marshall, he, Richard Bale, had removed to Chester.

Again over the Schuylkill they had tried, without avail, to save Philadelphia from the British; but not because Philadelphia had shown any great desire to be saved. That city had the appearance of a cheerful reconciliation to its occupation and fate. The echoed violins of its balls, the genial sounds, almost the savours, of its dinners incessantly reached those who were supposed to be its defenders. Then came the disaster at Paoli, when, at the Warren Tavern, they were surprised by the British rear guard. He had fought in the dark, trampling through the guy ropes of his marquee, with — his sword lost — a detached bayonet he had been lucky enough to catch up. This finished, Wayne had demanded the vindication of his conduct by court-martial, and Richard had testified, with a reprimand for his contemptuous bearing toward the ignorant malice of the charges.

When was it Washington had held the general conference of his officers for the purpose of considering a proposed attack on Germantown? Toward the end of September, for the engagement took place the first week in October. The discussion, anyhow, had been at the White Marsh encampment, and Wayne recommended the action. A dark morning of fog, through which the noise of the gunfire was less noticeable than its red streams of flame. The left wing, with Greene — Richard paused to damn him into the last hell for faithlessness — never came up, and Wayne and Sullivan, on the right, took the whole stunning weight of the English attack. Yet, mainly with the bayonet, they had pushed them back — by God, a full three miles, when they had mistaken Greene for British reinforcements and retreated.

And then winter; with no shoes; he had had no baggage since the Brandywine; winter with cursed little to eat and less to burn. Disconnected memories came back to him: a fife and drum corps on a January day, a hard, brilliant, glittering day, with their bodies more naked than clothed in rags that had never even been uniforms; his company too weak to drill or bear muskets; details through the New Jersey pines in desperate search for cattle not sent in to the English, to Philadelphia. But, for encouragement, Von Steuben, the incomparable drillmaster, had arrived at Valley Forge, and worked the miracle of his energy and military science. Richard could hear him now, shouting in a German that men without German yet contrived to understand.

But, if Valley Forge had been cold, Monmouth was fought on the hottest day he had ever experienced. That, too, had opened with defeat, with General Lee's failing to obey his order. June, that was. Richard had been with the advance post, in the famous Monmouth orchard — famous, that was, once — and engaged the English guards under Monckton. The best blood, the best troop, in England! He had fought body to body with radiant English youths, beautiful boys with fair hair, in a welter of stabbing and tripping and strangling . . . splendid boys from the green serenity of England, the fashionable drawing rooms of London. He remembered their desperate efforts to recover Monckton's body! In the end they had broken and killed them, left them, impressive in uniform, at the trunks of the apple trees.

Lucia, he saw, had gone from the dining room; Mrs. Patton and Miss Howlett, with the children, had withdrawn. For the moment they seemed immaterial, like a dream in the profound weariness after battle. Lucia,

Lavinia, were figures far away; it was as though, in place of gazing into the past, he had been enabled to see the future. Lavinia was like an infinitely small cloud on the horizon; it wasn't conceivable that he would get himself involved in a net of women and sentiment. Not he, a Bale of Balisand, not Richard Bale of the Virginia Line! Yet the war was long over; this was an anniversary of General Washington's death. He drank without rising, with no show or form, to his commander. He had, once, directed Gawin Todd never to disparage Washington to him, but that had been only an act of bravado, a drunken mood at dinner. Now he disowned any such conduct. He recalled the vileness of the Republican prints, Jefferson's papers. The death at Mount Vernon had silenced even them, made unnecessary the continuation of such abhorrent political expedience.

*

* *

What followed those celebrated engagements was very different. He was a major — this dated from the fall of 1778, but he hadn't been able to secure his new ranking until a year later, when his captain's commission was rubbed to a paper shred in his pocket — yet he performed the duties of every grade and separate service, almost, in the army. Richard had returned to Virginia — it was now 1780 — where he was aide-de-camp, for a number of months, to General Nelson. Indeed, his employments had been so various that he couldn't recall them in proper order. He had had charge of the magazine and laboratory at Westham, above Richmond, but how long had that been after Monmouth? When was it, exactly, that from the heights at Rocket's, below Richmond, he had cannonaded General Phillips? Then, certainly, he was attached to artillery. Such guns as had been available! Every possible military resource Virginia commanded had been ordered South for the support of General Greene.

After that he moved the Westham magazine across the James River by Brittan's Ferry, and a devil of an undertaking it was; yet, no sooner, hardly, had he succeeded than it must all be brought back. He had sunk his cannon in a creek and left his stores at Point of Fork. Colonel Tarleton, about then, crossed the James near Charlottesville and drove away the Legislature. Richard had watched the Dragoons galloping over the mountain side, looking for Jefferson. Thomas escaped, he told himself; yes, he got away; the country, America, the United States, might have lost him! Again his mind, his memories, were confused. He had marched a uniformed detachment over the mountains with colours flying and beating drums; and, everywhere, they were mistaken for the British — the only Virginia troops the countryside knew wore hunting shirts. He rather thought it was on that occasion his men had mutinied. No pay! Anyhow, they had appeared at the General Beat without knapsacks, and he had been forced to run a sergeant through the body with his sword. Upon that he had set the barracks on fire — they couldn't, he saw, have been on forced march — and, though it was evening, removed the command to a situation eight miles distant. He had fought a duel, in addition to all the rest, with a relation of Nelson's.

A ridiculous affair: he had been late to roll call, and, not wholly sober, had explained that he preferred lateness to appearing in a dressing gown and slippers. Slippers and a dressing gown had, on that occasion, adorned the General's relative, and the duel followed. Neither had tried to hit the other. He had reached the summer of 1781; early in June, Wayne, with some eight hundred men, had — in place of proceeding to South Carolina — joined La Fayette at Fredericksburg. Two battalions were formed, and to them was added a third, Virginians under Colonel Gaskin, with Richard bringing seventy-five soldiers.

He was quartered with General Lawton's brigade; they had one cannon, a six-pounder; and he remembered a small operation with a vidette corps of dragoons under Larkin Smith. Somehow he was in a skirmish at Hot Water, with Butler and the rebellious Pennsylvania Line. But the purpose of this campaign was to harass and check the English raids sent out from the headquarters of Cornwallis at Portsmouth, which the British had made into a fortified magazine for the supplies of the fleet. Together with this, too, the meagre American force had to keep Cornwallis from moving into North Carolina. The English, mostly, operated through the region between the James and York; and Richard, with an insuperable amount of marching, was intermittently engaged with the enemy's rear guard.

He had fallen into the habit of attacking at dawn, when resistance was lowest. They would sleep at brief moments, in the closeness of the woods, or on dignified lawns by a river; and, in a weariness too deep for cursing, again move on their inconsequential and important purpose. He had spent, that way, informal nights in formal, stately, drawing rooms, eaten hurried suppers past midnight on tables of old magnificence and renown . . . a figure of shadowy passage, of muted orders, indefinite men, constantly, needfully, alert. He must have been a haggard night visitor to those historic plantations; haggard but welcome; and, God, how strong, how young, he had been; how little sleep he had required. No thicket of forest, of wild grape vines and brush, or treacherous marsh, was too difficult for his course, no stream too swift to ford, no river so wide but that he crossed it somehow.

Yes, that time was best, better than the present, even with Lucia and their children, at Balisand. Then he had thought with longing of the peace of his plantation by the North River; all he wanted was to return there; and now he was envious of such a desperate past. Yet, not that — he was regretting himself, what he had been, and his supreme privilege. Such years, he felt, would never come again; there would be other wars, of course — probably they'd never cease — but not quite the same. Not such a pure incentive; and never a second Washington.

It was in July that Cornwallis, moving along the James, had sent a small detachment across the river, and the report carried to Wayne that the British force was cut in half. Richard Bale, himself, had seen the negro who brought them that false intelligence, just before Green Spring was fought. He was with the advance — an insignificant number that had passed over the causeway of a swamp — which had suddenly found itself opposed to the greater part of the English army drawn up in battle array. But they escaped, orderly they withdrew across the swamp; and then, to avoid the ruin of panic, Wayne had charged the overwhelming forces threatening to surround him.

Soon after, Cornwallis was driven back into Yorktown, where he was fortified; the French fleet under de Barras, the French ships from the West Indies with Saint-Simon's troops, arrived; and the finish drew near. They were a different French from those who, under the States-General, had been their successors — the Republic had actually thrown La Fayette into jail — and Richard recalled them with affection and gratitude. Together they had sung a song, in French . . . from an opera then in great favour. Lucille, it was called, and the name of the composer came back to him, Grétry. Some words, as well, returned to memory; and, uncertain in air, with no possible reference to their part in a strange language, he half sang:

"Où a-t-on plus de bonheur
Qu'au sein de sa famille —— "

He had had no active part in the final attack on the Yorktown redoubts; in the main an affair of siege-guns; and on the seventeenth October the enemy blew the chamade.

That call, proclaiming the end of English dominion in the American colonies, had, as well, sounded his,

Richard Bale's discharge from war. Or had it been from peace? He couldn't determine which. Cramped from long sitting, he rose, still enveloped in the heroics of the past, and, forgetting the weakness of his leg, he nearly fell. Where had he laid Morryson's cane? As he went around the table, limping from the room, he met the painted supercilious gaze of Francis Bale, the Cavalier; but not even he had seen a more desperate or honourable service. And Charles had been beheaded, the first Charles; and then the Second: the revolution that had freed America beginning in Great Britain! "—— on plus de bonheur," he hummed, slowly mounting the stairs. The candle he bore cast a pale and isolated light around him; there was a flicker of shadow, Richard Bale, on the wall; he nodded to it and it nodded vaguely back, a dark insubstantial confirmation of their joint approval.

*

* *

The immediate result of his extended and special memories was that, with a refreshed energy, he applied the precepts of a more than civil discipline to Balisand and himself. It seemed to Richard that he had fallen into a disorganized indolence in itself dangerous. And, obstinate to the shrinking of negroes from the cold, he undertook improvements to the plantation long ago designed and put off. He had the marshland back of his informal race track drained and filled and the trees cut out. Once before he had begun this, but he had been forced to stop after a particularly heavy loss of money at hazard, in the tavern cellar, to William Newsome. He supervised the labour from his horse, closely wrapped in the worn cape with a martial history. He must be occupied, Richard told himself; employed, when he wasn't fox-hunting, throughout the day. A part of his conscious strategy against the invasion of his security by Lavinia. The political situation was, very temporarily, completely quiet: the vote of the electoral college wouldn't be opened until February; but there was a general conviction that the choice would lie between Jefferson and Aaron Burr. Adams, though the general acrimony of the late contest had died, was submerged in a petty and vindictive quarrelling with his cabinet. Gawin Todd, it was reported to Richard, in a probable event of a Jeffersonian victory, would be very suitably and publicly recognized.

His life, it appeared very clearly to Richard, had been divided into two utterly different periods: formerly it was vivid, concerned with events, and later it had grown contemplative. The second part began with Lucia — or had it been with Zena Gainge? — and Lavinia belonged to neither; she inhabited a sphere of her own, unreal and compelling, disembodied and enchantingly present. There, he felt, his panic had shifted to a philosophical willingness to accept the evil with the good in what yet awaited him. A single reflection troubled this — the realization that, when he wasn't overcome with his strange late passion for Lavinia, he couldn't credit its potency. Free from it, and in the warm presence of Lucia, it seemed fantastic, no weakness of a Bale. But, in connection with that, he recalled what

Morryson had told him about his mother: a small, quiet, oversensitive girl, Morryson had said, who had written a poem about love and eternity. And when, within a year, she had died, his father had never married again. Richard Bale vainly wished that he had asked Morryson more about that — it might have a bearing on his own experience. Lavinia, for example, was like a poem. Poets, he gathered, chose just such subjects for their lines. There was his mother! He, Richard Bale, since the forced pages of his early instruction, had read nothing; he wholly distrusted extravagant books and sentiments.

In that, he now recognized, he had been right. The habit of indiscriminate reading was responsible for a great deal of harm . . . among other undesirable things, the Democratic-Republican party: Jefferson was an acknowledged friend of literature. The people got hold of printed subversive promises and lies, and, as a consequence, lost their grasp on the plain indispensable facts of existence. The Bible was, for such reading, sufficient; and it was well to have it chained, written in Latin. This he repeated, at length, to Lucia. Miss Howlett, with Camilla, was in the room, and she became so patently distressed that, against her painful reluctance to being noticed, she finally spoke. "Mr. Bale, I have such trouble with the children now, making them listen when I read, and if they hear you I might as well go away."

Lucia laughed. "I have just been arranging for music lessons," she told Richard; "for the first time in the children's lives it's possible; and what will you say to that?" Music, he asserted sharply, was as dangerous as poetry. She grew serious. "Richard, you've never talked this way before. What is it? And Miss Howlett is right; we can't let you interfere with her. It would be decidedly better if you went back to explaining Federal politics to Flora, even with the cursing. Actually, you sound like the people at camp meetings."

He wasn't, Richard replied, to be taken so literally. He had only tried to say that he wanted his children taught the solid and undeniable facts of life. "It isn't religion at all, but as far from that as possible. They must be like you, Lucia." For that — she was standing — Lucia gave him one of her rare public kisses. She pressed it, cool and reassuring, on his forehead. "Then send them out to the stable, since you and Beverley insist that's where I learned whatever I know."

He wasn't, unfortunately, able to describe his feeling. The truth was that he didn't want his girls to inherit or be encouraged in any of the nonsense that had upset him. It had occurred to him that a measure of it might have come from his mother; for, if the habits, the very appearance, of the Bales descended from generation to generation, why wasn't it possible, as well, that he bore within him the influence of the other?

Entirely a poetic affair. Poets, he continued, were individuals who got along notoriously ill with actual events. In that they resembled unhappy women. He was alone, Lucia was at Welfield, the children were with their governess, and he proceeded to the case of books standing in the hall by the door to the east room. They had been there since the time of Francis Bale, not later than 1680; one or two volumes, at least, had undoubtedly come with Richard from the disaster to a Stuart England; yet a number of them, he rigidly decided, no longer should have a place in his house. Hakluyt's Travels he ignored, Wisdom in Three Books he left undisturbed, but a romance concerned with Cleopatra he unhesitatingly condemned. He passed by Aristotle's Problems, a religious book by Diodati, another called Boanerges and Barnabas, An Observation on the Turk's Government, a Jure Maritimo, and then came on a slender volume of Virgil's poems, which he removed. The Cure of Gunshot Wounds he approved, as he did Directions for Planting Mulberry Trees. A Discourse Concerning Comets and what seemed to be a medical work, The Birth of Mankind, could demoralize no one; but Homer's Iliad, a book by Ben Jonson and Donne's Poems he added to those he had condemned.

Unhappy women and poetry! That chance phrase stayed in his mind. Music and trouble — he heard, from the garden at Todd Hundred, the low singing of the violins. Lucia might mock him as she pleased, but he'd be damned if the Methodists weren't justified in their opinion of — of such traps for the heart. Poetry and women who were dissatisfied, cut off from their desire. He elaborated this into the tentative and highly unpleasant theory that what he chose to call beauty rotted like apples when they were left on the tree. It might be that the whole loveliness of a woman kept from its purpose, the simplicity of birth and its attending business, grew into a poison. This wasn't a new thought; somewhere, long ago, he had been familiar with it.

If he could convince himself of the truth of that all his indefinite dread, persisting, he found, hiding, at the back of his logic, would be vanquished. But merely to announce it wasn't enough: he knew this, that his problem was not of the head. Mentally he disposed of it a score of times in a day. Lavinia had never appeared to him in a sensible light. She had come to him, as a matter of fact, through the dark, a voice . . . with pauses. Almost at once, after a moment, a flash of sun, she returned to darkness, and there, really, she ought to stay.

*

* *

With, privately, the destruction of such volumes of poetry and imagination as he could locate, Richard made no further efforts or comment in that direction. Lucia would have been very decided in her objection to such an apparently arbitrary interference in her plans for the children. Her placidity there wasn't indifference. And, as it was, Miss Howlett, he saw, had grown frightened of him. His natural severity was increasing; but with it his affectionate interest in Flora and Camilla and Alice Ellen had expanded. He asked for them more frequently: he was specially tender with Flora; Camilla impressed him by her early ability to look out for herself; and he was, very much in secret, amused by Alice Ellen's bad tempers. At the slightest provocation she would screech — he always returned to Flora's word for that — as energetically as Von Steuben at drill. She required more attention than anyone else at Balisand.

Camilla largely went her own way, a way almost as satisfactory to others as it was to her. She got her lessons more easily, remembered them better, than did Flora, but her curiosity never extended beyond them; she never, Miss Howlett reported, read a line other than necessary. Flora, however, overtaken by eagerness, would neglect the studies set her for the infinity of possibilities they suggested. She had to be restrained, her history lesson shortened, for more than once it had made her ill with excitement.

Lucia, he thought, was inclined to be impatient with her; impatient, that was, for Lucia; in another, probably, her bearing would have been a model of consideration. "I don't understand Flora at all," she admitted. "She hasn't a single Mathews trait, and try my best I can't see you in her. Unless I don't know you. All the Tuckers I've met are different, too. I don't want to be unjust, but, unless she changes, I'm afraid she's going to be unhappy. Flora is too intense. But then you are that. Sometimes I think you're beyond me, Richard; I didn't used to, but I do now. Could you be a little different, do you suppose? It's not your leg, I've given that up. Are you worried, Richard? You would tell me if you were, wouldn't you?" He wasn't worried, he replied, justified in what was, at times, very much a lie. "What is there to bother me?" he demanded. She didn't know, she couldn't put a finger on it. Beverley, Lucia continued, had spoken of this, as well. "He thinks you seem thin." Richard managed to laugh at the mere suggestion of a fat Bale.

"Richard, I haven't disappointed you?"

Here he was free for the expression of all he felt: "How could you do that, Lucia? You are so perfect that at times I forget to mention it, I don't notice . . . Balisand is like a heaven with you." She nodded. "That's all right, then." Thank God, she hated sentimentality as much as he did. "You haven't known it but we're going to Welfield over Sunday, all of us. Christopher and Amalie will be there, and maybe Garland." That, he said at once, would be pleasant; a change of scene do him good; perhaps it would shake him out of the mood she seemed to have noticed. Christopher Mathews was Lucia's brother. He had married Amalie Lagné of New Orleans, where he had lived for the past twenty years, getting very seldom to Gloucester County. Richard would be glad to see him, and then, too, Beverley would have the latest news of the vote for President.

For a while it had been thought that the Federal Senators of Pennsylvania had, in Richard Bale's sense, saved the country; but a corrected report from South Carolina exploded that hope. Yes, Adams was already defeated; however, a new possibility, in which Richard found nothing to commend, had developed: there was a strong Federalist current turning toward the support of Burr. Anything, the cry was, to beat Jefferson! A rumour spread that the New York Republicans might refuse him their vote. Jefferson, it was asserted, to combat this, had offered a cabinet position to one of the Livingstons.

At the tavern a Republican celebration was held, where the liquor consumed, the proprietor assured Richard, would have almost done credit to a gathering of Federal gentlemen. Gawin Todd made an impassionate address of confidence in the future and ridicule for Adams and the reigning families of the past. About this Richard Bale was cold, but he heatedly denounced the efforts of his own party entirely to defeat an election by the forced choice of a temporary president. He came to the conclusion that, in the old, the correct, meaning, he no longer had a party. He had denied this to Beverley Mathews, but it was true. Yet it was, at the same time, equally true of Jefferson and James Madison: those iron constructionists of the Constitution now, dismayed by the growing strength of Burr, proposed that the two candidates for President join in summoning a new national Congress. A humiliating situation.

December had gone in that way, and January, and — waiting for the carryall to bear them to Welfield — it was February. The balloting at Washington was under way. The entire Bale family, however, were, just then, indifferent to the political crisis: Alice Ellen was absorbing all their attention. She didn't want to leave Balisand, and, in her usual manner, she was making her objection clear. "Let her stay on the floor and kick," Richard advised them; "she'll have to get tired."

"Perhaps, then," Flora added, "we will be here, just like this, for a week." Camilla thought not. Mrs. Patton was solicitous, Miss Howlett declared that her nerves could not last at this rate; but Lucia unceremoniously picked Alice Ellen up, turned her over, and applied a succession of loud firm spanks to her youngest daughter. "She can't make any more noise," she observed. Flora was transfixed in an agony of attention. "She is though," she announced, "twice as much." Richard agreed with her. "I don't know why you take her," he protested; "in the future if she goes anywhere I won't." He was thoroughly exasperated. Miss Howlett's attitude fitted him exactly. Lucia begged him to remain calm, since none of the trouble actually rested on him. But he was in no mood for calmness or his ordinary — concealed — entertainment at Alice Ellen's outbursts. He called for a servant, ordered a horse saddled, and expressed surprise that he should have considered driving with a cursed nursery and mob of women. "Indeed," Lucia retorted, "I'd far rather not have you. It was your own suggestion to go in the carryall. And I'd be glad if you weren't so unreasonable before the whole house. You have been too strange lately."

A vision of Balisand with only Morryson and himself there, except for the tactful Mrs. Patton, returned to him, and he viewed it regretfully. He had no talent, it appeared, for living with women, none for a family. "If you would take care of your children, instead of riding all over the county behind a pack of hounds, you might be able to manage them," he incautiously asserted. Lucia gave Alice Ellen to a servant. "I don't like quarrelling in private," she said evenly, "and I certainly won't descend to it here. If you think I oughtn't to fox-hunt I'll stop, of course." He was, now, infuriated at himself: all that his temper had betrayed him into was the precise reverse of what he felt. How handsome Lucia was! Damn it, he was degenerating into a woman.

Flora's eyes were filled with tears and Camilla's mouth was open, Alice Ellen silent in the negro's arms. "If I am going to ride," he spoke lamely, "I shall have to make a change. Go on, Lucia, and I'll catch up with you." How handsome she was, how correct in manner! He mustn't subject her to another open scene; by God, Richard recognized proudly, she wouldn't have it. Not Lucia! His cape settled about him with a familiar comfort. Bradlock Wiatt owned a horse she admired; and if he happened to be at the Mathews', and would sell . . . the perfume of a June garden illusively enveloped him.

*

*   *

The gathering at Welfield was larger than he had expected, with Christopher and Amalie Mathews and their daughter; Eliza Wiatt Cozzens; her husband, a Philadelphian; Bradlock; Sally Todd — Richard couldn't remember whom she had married, he wasn't there — and Marable, her brother. The house was very gay, with gentlemen by the bottles in the dining room and ladies ornamentally spread about the fires of the drawing room and hall. The Bales occupied the room which had been Lucia's, with the exception of Alice Ellen, who, fortunately, had a space together with her nurse. Lucia, dressing for supper, was completely silent, and Richard was careful to avoid the mistake of any attempted apology or hasty reconciliation. It was best to let her proceed as she liked, to refer or not to what had happened.

Christopher had many of her traits, but, while Lucia was undoubtedly growing heavier, he was thin to the point of gauntness; and, to a natural darkness, had been added the dusky burn of a Southern sun. He was a great deal on a plantation, Richard had heard, experimenting with sugar cane. Amalie was small and ugly, yet her ugliness had the charm of authentic personality, an air of seductiveness graced her; and Garland, their daughter, as old, he thought, as Lucia when he had married her, had a pale mysterious beauty, like an earthly and fashionable nun.

Eliza's husband, Frederick Cozzens, was at least twenty years her elder, approaching sixty, evidently — his manner was dogmatic and his apparel faultless — a man of import. And, after sixteen years, Eliza had hardly changed; the petulant attractiveness of her youth seemed as fresh, as unspent, as when, in the past, she had filled Mr. Garret with the wretchedness of an unreturned love. Richard sat between Amalie and Sally Todd — what the devil was her name now? — and he found that Sally, too, was very much what, as a child, she had been. She resembled his daughter Camilla, with an added sense of humour. In that, while Lucia possessed a quiet appreciation of the ludicrous, the Bales were largely lacking. Bradlock Wiatt's face was tinged with the purple of his living; his heavy cheeks had grown noticeably looser, his hands shook quite as Morryson's had; but his voice had lost none of its arrogant assertiveness. After supper, but not too long after, Richard must approach him about the hunter. Christopher Mathews, he discovered, was explaining the present complicated relationship between the Spanish in New Orleans and the United States, or, more particularly, Kentucky. Jasper Robine had once been on a mission to Louisiana, and Richard recalled his uncomplimentary remarks about Spain:

"In the end Louisiana will be taken into the United States." Christopher was positive about this. "It's inevitable — the Mississippi River flows down, to the Gulf, and not up. If that doesn't happen soon, Kentucky will leave the United States and make an alliance with France. You hear of the Spanish at New Orleans, and not the French, and there you miss most of the situation. We have very reliable advice that Louisiana may be ceded to France. And, if this continues, then you would see Kentucky under Napoleon fighting America at the mouth of the river."

"It would be a warm day for Kentucky," Bradlock declared; "even with a Republican President." Christopher Mathews admitted that the chance of this was slight. "The Kentuckians will hardly live under what government we have, and I can't imagine them ruled by Manuel Godoy, from a boudoir. No, we have already taken the Mississippi Territory, and we'll add the rest to it; Florida, too. I hope it will all be friendly; it should be, now Lopez has restored the American right of deposit at New Orleans."

"We don't need Louisiana," Richard entered the discussion; "we have too much now, too much land, too many people, too many political divisions. We can force a decent treaty out of Spain or France, it doesn't matter which, and that's all we require. There's a sort of insanity of adding to the United States, and every time a new piece of woods is taken in there is new trouble. All these rebellions have come from the West. If they didn't like the government I'd let them go to the devil with the Indians. They're no better. Why, we can't manage the territory we have now; it's a question if you could get out to most of it with your life. Kentucky, specially, has always been a nuisance: first it wasn't content with being Virginia, and then its Resolution —— "

"It depends where you live," Christopher reasonably observed; "things are seen differently." Cozzens nodded. "We have an agent in New Orleans," he told them; "the business there with Philadelphia is growing every week; I'd be glad to have an American Louisiana."

"Merchants would," Richard agreed ungraciously; "but others must be consulted. What are we going to be — a government or a selling house? I'll admit it looks a lot toward the last; but I'm surprised to hear you defending it, Christopher. You talk like a Boston trader. You're a crop, in New Orleans you are that, and not a manufactured thing. Or maybe, that distinction's gone, too." At this there was a wide laughter. "The country is falling apart like a handful of straws," he said heatedly. "George isn't here to hold them together," Beverley spoke solemnly. "The United States should be smaller and not larger," Richard Bale persisted. "In another generation we will have twenty nations."

"You must visit Louisiana and us," Amalie told him; "then you shall see." The politeness of his reply barely concealed the fact that he had no taste for travel, toward either foreign lands or ideas. There was nothing to be gained from a jumble of theories or people; as well try to associate Turks with Chinamen and Americans with Persians. His private opinion was that Louisiana was Turkey or China, and, therefore, of no importance to the American Federal Government. It couldn't be considered with an equal gravity. How could anything serious be expected from a man named — as the Governor of Louisiana was — Gayoso de Lemos?

But it was different about women, they were universal; he liked Amalie very much, Amalie with her Cape jasmine of a daughter. Sally Todd was nobody's jasmine, however — a tremendous big girl with a deep voice and a mischief in her grey eyes. The spirit of Charles. His affection for Charles Todd had been as strong as his feeling for Henry. Men of another generation. To-day even gentlemen were sharper, in a greater hurry . . . traders. Cozzens with his agent in New Orleans! They drank less, too, Richard noticed: probably afraid of muddling their wits. But he didn't observe this in Bradlock, who preserved a tradition as venerable as Bale's own — long sitting over the bowl, gambling in great sums, the sport of horse racing. The Bales of Balisand, and before Balisand, had served too continuously in armies, they were too attached to kings and parties in adversity, to grow comfortable and fat. Yet he had owned some good horses, Diggery and the mare, Careless. He had had his moments. Eliza was speaking of Philadelphia:

"It's like a chestnut burr, you have to be inside.

Then it is delightful." Beverley interrupted her. "Richard will tell you that the only Burr he's familiar with is filled with worms." The talk, among the men left at the table, inevitably returned to the election of a President. An irregularity had been discovered in the Georgia vote. Jefferson had announced that the election was void. The balloting — a post rider bore the news — first gave eight States to Jefferson and six to Aaron Burr. A nineteenth effort to obtain the necessary majority had been made at midnight. A representative of North Carolina, denouncing the proceeding as ridiculous, carried his delegation for Jefferson, but without decisive effect.

*

* *

When an opportunity arrived Richard said to Bradlock Wiatt: "You were on a strawberry roan one morning last week." This, Bradlock acknowledged, was a fact. "But possibly I won't hunt him again." Richard asked why not. "Isn't he sound? Can't he jump?" Wiatt was appropriately annoyed. "When," he demanded, "have you seen me on an unsound horse or that couldn't jump? I'd trust him over a solid board fence in the rain. He's as sound as we used to be. No, I'm sending him to Maryland, for a wicked price." That wasn't an encouraging opening. "I rather wanted to get Lucia a new hunter," he continued indifferently. "But certainly it won't be necessary to pay what you call a wicked price. What'll we do now — whist?" Wiatt believed so. "Christopher will play, and Beverley. A thousand or twelve hundred dollars," he added.

"I'll ask you again, when you're sober," Richard replied to the sums mentioned, the strawberry roan implied. "It's for Lucia, and I might be willing to pay five hundred." Bradlock owned a horse he might have for that. But not the roan. It wasn't for the carryall, Bale reminded him. To the suggestion that Lucia try the horse in question Richard objected. "I want her to find him at the rack," he explained. "Five hundred dollars is ridiculous!" Bradlock returned; but Richard knew it was. "It's a present," he pointed out; "that's why I'm willing to pay so much." He, personally, didn't like a roan, but his wife was indifferent to that. "Greys are not much better," he went on. "They're not!" The other was exasperated. "Grey Medley wasn't much, then; selected out of all Virginia to run against the North. If he hadn't been foully whipped in our race you would have been a joke."

Eliza came up to say that there would be dancing, and, with her arm within her father's, she bore him away. There was a preliminary discordant scraping of fiddles; an increasing uneasiness settled over Richard Bale. It was the music, he decided, and Eliza, looking, in the candlelight, exactly as she had in the past, at Todd Hundred. The whist, he perceived, was interrupted. He couldn't make up his mind what to do: not sit and watch the dancing, certainly; the fire had been allowed to sink where he was; the hall beyond was crowded with flowered skirts, humming with the fiddles. A faint disturbing dizziness touched him, a swift instinctive fear. One thing must not happen — a falling back into the spell, the seductiveness, of Lavinia.

Fiddles and a minuet and a garden bright and scented. But this was February, no roses were in bloom, the mocking birds had gone; without knowing why, he went up the stairs to his room. It was totally dark, but not still, for he could hear the regular breathing of his children asleep. That, more than any other sound, would control him; and, careful not to make a noise, he found and sat on the edge of a chair. Camilla's breathing was stronger, slower, than Flora's. There was a small suppressed gasp, which he recognized as his eldest daughter's. But even here, with the door shut, the music was audible, low and stirring. It dominated the rest, rose triumphant over all sleeping children, all honourable engagements. A joy enveloped him that came closer and closer. It wasn't Lavinia, yet it was laden with what, supremely, she brought him. He still fought his tyrannical emotion. He could hear himself saying over and over, this mustn't happen. It's done with. It must not happen . . . done with. His contrary determination was like an island in a flood tide: the perfumed, the rapturous, sea reached higher and higher. It closed over his head.

How long he was submerged, when his passionate delight receded, Richard didn't know. The palms of his hands and his forehead were wet; there were flashes in the darkness before his eyes. That was Camilla — Camilla Scarborough — and that Flora. Flora was moving restlessly in her sleep. God, he had been faithless to them and Lucia, to himself, again! This time he had been wrapped in a greater, a more profound, happiness than he had ever known. Before it he was abjectly helpless. The dangerous conviction held him that he could now, whenever he wished, summon Lavinia to him. He had that to struggle against, as well. He wanted her, he wanted to let the earth fall from him, and ascend to her eternity of young beauty and summer. Imperishable youth like a fire consuming and unconsumed. He took that thought exactly as though it had a material substance and cast it from him, waiting a moment to hear it strike on the floor. In a few minutes, he told himself, he would be normal again and able to make a necessary final decision; now . . . he couldn't.

Slowly he grew steadier, resolutely heedless of the imploring, the weeping, fiddles. It seemed to Richard Bale that his perceptions returned one by one to a numbness of mind and body. That was it — he lost possession of whatever he was: Lavinia claimed him for hers. Well, he wasn't! He let her know that. He was Richard Bale of the Bales of Balisand, married to Lucia Mathews, and sitting in the room with two of their children. He was faithful in every particular; he loved them with every instinct he possessed. I loved you, Lavinia — his thought had the agony of a desperate cry — and I put you away in my memory. Hadn't he once compared Lavinia with sweet lavender? I said good-bye to you and what used to be. Don't you understand, it used to be, but never again. It's different now, not less, yet not the same . . . more, the way things turned out.

What, he wondered, whom, was he addressing — a girl dead or himself? And he couldn't stay here much longer. He'd be missed; Lucia come up, looking for him. His face, he felt, was drawn and white; that, too, would be commented on. Why hadn't he stayed in the dining room with the rum! He had been cold before. Perhaps if he were drunk for the rest of life —— Pleasant for Lucia. The old excuses, the familiar plans and resolutions, had left him. They were useless. Reason and logic were no good. Character, blood, went for nothing. He couldn't kill Lavinia. At that he was shocked — there was a duty to her. However, she showed little enough consideration for him. But, among other things, he'd have to stop thinking of her as a present warm being. It was a bad, an upsetting, habit. He moved the chair, sharply, forgetful of the children, and there was a stir of bed-clothes. Flora spoke in an unnatural tone:

"I'm frightened."

So was he, Richard thought; but instantly he reassured her. "It's me, Flora. I came up just for a second and I'm going back right away. Go to sleep again." But he had to touch her, rearrange the bed and smooth her pillow, before she was quieted. Camilla continued to sleep magnificently. Richard did, in reality, find a flask he had in a drawer. Brandy. However, it might as well have been water. "Go to sleep, Flora, and have a pretty dream." She murmured that sometimes they weren't.

Below, he avoided Lucia, and soon he was at whist. When it was over, and he was at Balisand, an all-important decision lay before him. Now he didn't see how, but it must be accomplished; and not with vain self-promises and empty imposing conclusions. At last he would bring his unbearable situation to an end; some end; it didn't matter what. His desperation, before that certainty, approached indifference. Consequences to himself. Unimportant. A depression, mental and physical, made all living, all objectives, valueless. "Game," Beverley announced. Richard shuffled. The incessant fiddling began to exasperate him. "Damn that racket," he said unguardedly. "Richard, Richard," Wiatt reproved him, "that's youth. Don't be so impatient. Dancing youth. Christopher's girl is marvellously well at it. Christopher's girl, Beverley; and Lucia has three. But I have a strawberry roan horse to cherish, unless Bale can find seven hundred dollars."

*

*   *

The work at Balisand, Richard's presence on horseback, silent, his face muffled, continued. He was exacting and harsh, not only with the negroes but at the house as well. This was the result of a necessity to compel an interest and attention in the affairs of his plantation. Days and voices dragged interminably. What went on was meaningless, purely casual and without weight — a field filled or marsh, what did it matter? Holes in the lane were holes in the lane. Sand was sand, shifting, eternal, sterile. And after all Jefferson was elected, following the usual expedients and compromise, the universal political faithlessness to engagements and previous convictions. Bayard, of Delaware, who had the Federal course in hand, had failed to get Burr's assurance of future support, and turned his energies toward securing the Federal vote for Jefferson, who had agreed to preserve the navy, keep the army of Federal office-holders intact, and make good the public credit; but not until the thirty-sixth ballot had this been successful.

A great deal, Richard Bale told himself, was, for him, drawing to a close. In the main, events went on unremarked until they accumulated to a point where they showed what, unsuspected, lay beyond. That, again, had happened. Where Lavinia was concerned he had arrived at no conclusion. The truth was that, in his present lassitude, he was incapable of mental action; what energy he had was exhausted by the small round through which he drove himself. The strawberry roan horse he bought from Bradlock, for seven hundred dollars; and Lucia was obviously pleased. She found the hunter, as he had planned, waiting for her at the door. And, with her skill, he had performed splendidly. Richard was conscious that she was still unobtrusively watching him, puzzled. How strong her recognition of their bond of flesh and spirit was. He had a feeling that there were whispers around him, inquiries, feminine anxiety, whenever he wasn't present, when he was uncommonly abrupt or peculiar.

A drift of warm days, a premonition of spring, followed an excessive cold; buds made their appearance with an effect of the instantaneous: the earth was soggy with water. Richard Bale, riding to the tavern, was aware of the sun on his hand. The score against him had been chalked on the wall of the taproom seven years ago; then, he would have been willing to bet a thousand dollars against Jefferson's election to President. That was the night the French cotillion had made its bow to Gloucester County. Its popularity had grown, too. Other forms of dancing, developments of the faster quadrilles and reels, were taking the place of the minuet. That required dignity and grace, attributes of breeding and leisure. Garland Mathews' dancing, applauded by Bradlock Wiatt, had amazed him with its boldness. He couldn't imagine, when his girls had grown up, what they would be about. He'd have something to say there, however: if women were universal they should, equally, remain always the same — a beginning innocence of childhood, a later nice gaiety of youth, and then their husbands, children and the duties of plantations.

He dismounted at the tavern, finding another horse, a heavy but admirable chestnut, in the shed, and he instinctively paused for inspection and approval. Richard didn't know the animal; he was not a familiar on the local roads. Balantine was in the taproom, and Richard passed through the door from the main place of general assembly. He went forward without attention and discovered himself to be facing Gawin Todd. There was an instinctive pause, a stiff interruption of movement, through which the tavern keeper watched with a close curiosity. Todd spoke first:

"We might as well acknowledge that we are both here. There's no harm in that. If it's agreeable to you, Bale, I'm glad of a chance to speak to you in what we would call private." Richard assented in a short adequate phrase. "We have been enemies, political enemies, a long while," Todd went more easily on. "I had as little confidence in your principles as you had in mine. You had a full opportunity to see the results of Federalism, and now, whether you want to or not, you can watch the Democratic-Republicans. I believe we are right, I believe in Thomas Jefferson; but the proof, one way or the other, will come along. You ought to be willing to meet that fairly."

"Where I'm concerned," Bale replied, "one now is as rotten as the other. You speak of the Federal party as though it were still alive, but it isn't. The Federals and the Republicans have allied, and a bastard is the result. That doesn't excite me. I have retired from political heats. I don't mind saying I've been retired." His animosity for Gawin Todd, it was impressed on him, was unabated; he meant animosity in its minute individual traits — tone and clothes and bearing. A strange brother to Charles!

"Bastard is not the word of a man without heat," Todd remarked. "But it was allowable once, politics was spoken of that way, and it needn't make fresh issue here. Our trouble is so old, so buried, it occurred to me we might drop it altogether. Don't misunderstand me; it isn't in my mind we'd ever be companions. That's not necessary, since I'll live in Washington and you at Balisand. No, we'll hardly ever see each other; but that's no reason why we shouldn't speak decently on the road. And, if only on Ava's account, I should appreciate it if you would stop at Todd Hundred and see her, when it is convenient . . . for us."

"When you are not there," Richard said sharply. "Did it occur to you that I might leave by the back door when you came in at the front? Is it your idea that Todd Hundred is yours? It belonged and belongs, for me, to Charles, and he told me never to come back.

What I have lost with Ava, and it was a great deal, I must do with. So far as our speaking on the road goes, I'm not aware it has ever been interrupted. We are speaking now, and you admit more than that is undesirable. I can't understand what the devil you are after."

"I said speak decently," Todd repeated, "and your what the devil and bastard does not come under that. Even with the fullest allowance for your habit of cursing." Richard's coldness of anger began; he had, within him, the sensation of water congealing into ice. He turned away, to Balantine. "I came to discharge my debt — a hundred dollars if Jefferson were elected President." He gave the money to the proprietor of the tavern. "You'll perhaps remember, Mr. Bale," he remarked, "that I said when Jefferson is President, and not if. But you would have it the other way." He picked up a wet cloth and wiped the engagement from the wall. He was, he said, sorry to see it go; he'd gladly pay back the money to keep it there. "The talk over it sold many and many a glass of rum," he asserted. "And it was a part of the old times, when the cellar was lively with gentlemen at hazard and cards. It's dark now more often than not. But I won't complain — I'll make you my compliments, Mr. Todd, that to-day, for taverns, is better. You said it would be. The other is just a natural regret, for years when Mr. Bale of Balisand didn't have to walk with a cane, when he'd see a hundred silver pounds roll away with the dice, yes, twice that, and not a blink of the eye."

*

* *

A sudden thought animated him, took him to the back of the taproom. "I have an anker of old Charente brandy," he explained. "It was here before me. The spigot hasn't been opened on it for ten years." He returned for two glasses. "If you will allow me." Richard Bale deliberately surveyed the drink put in front of him. Gawin Todd was revolving the other undecidedly in his fingers. "I am obliged," Bale finally addressed the tavern keeper; "I'll drink your brandy to the friends and enemies of America." Todd frowned. "If I join you," he asserted, "you will have to make your meaning clear. Friends, enemies — which are which?" Where Richard was involved, he said negligently, those definitions never changed.

"Is that personal?" Gawin Todd asked.

"The friends and enemies of the country," Richard repeated. "How personally you take it, will depend on your attitude toward America. If it is personal, it is, simply, that. But if the United States is only a field for ambitions and schemes, then you can drink as comfortably as possible." Todd's face was red with anger.

"In other words, this — if I'm a damned rascal! I don't happen to be; your opinion can't make or affect that. I was a fool, besides, to offer you any civility. I might have known how you'd take it, blind with vanity. You had it correct the second time, you were retired. Even the Federalists couldn't get along with you." As Gawin Todd became more excited, Richard grew frigid.

"Certainly you haven't had to make the effort," he remarked. "And your beginning now is as useless as it's late." This, Richard realized, was the appropriate moment for him to go; yet his annoyance, a disagreeable pertinacity of being, a reluctance at even the appearance of retreat, kept him staring directly at Todd. "You can forget that," the other told him; "I as good as never said it. I'll put something else in its place: once, but for a calamity, you would have forced a duel on me; though it was Charles as well as you. I didn't believe in duelling then and I don't now. There is no need for me to be insulted by you. I could just as reasonably get mad at the shade of Governor Berkeley. Go back to where you belong, the seventeenth century and Balisand."

"You have a charming sentiment for your brother, for Charles," Richard's voice was measured. "But we must remember that honour never had a place in you. Really, you were bought to attack it." The proprietor of the tavern protested, "Gentlemen, gentlemen." No attention was paid him, and, after a visible hesitation, he abruptly quitted the room. "Charles is dead," Richard Bale went on; "fortunately, I think, since he is beyond the influence of what you've helped to bring about. Charles is dead and so is Lavinia —— "

He hadn't intended to speak of her; her name had come, on the sweep of his hatred, out of his subconscious preoccupation. "Long back," Todd reminded him, "I thanked God she was safe from your hands. But you killed her for me, too." Richard smiled into his face. "You never had her," he answered. "Lavinia made a mistake, for a minute, about you." He added, at what was purely a venture, "After that first night at Todd Hundred you never had a finger on her dress." It was, he saw, from the whiteness which had succeeded Gawin Todd's flush, true.

"One at a time," Todd said, "even with Lavinia and you." Here, finally, Richard knew to what he was addressed: Gawin Todd he was determined to kill. "That was deliberate," he asserted quickly; "no one can say it to me, to Lavinia, and not pay its cost."

"I won't be dragged to a duel," Todd repeated. "I can damn you without standing up to be shot at, and my reason's impersonal — the Government of the United States."

"The United States, the Government," Richard echoed his phrase satirically. "Oh, yes, you'd be out of a place if you fought. How can you tell you would need it? You might be provided with one for — for life. I've heard you're religious. Perhaps I could get you a higher preferment. I'd be willing to at the price of a charge of powder and lead. It's worth no more."

"Between us, you are the worthless," Todd returned. "I see nothing to be gained standing and accepting your abuse." Richard asked, "What would insult you?" Gawin Todd drew away, toward the door to the yard. "Nothing human." It was Bale, persisting. "I got Lavinia from you with no more than a cursing . . . and Lucia. You didn't quite realize that. It was almost too easy to be worth while. You impress girls with your noise, until they're beyond hearing you."

Todd came heavily back to where Richard Bale waited, leaning slightly on a table. Todd's breathing was hoarse, his face congested; his rage was so oppressive that he stuttered inarticulately. This was more promising, but Richard wasn't prepared for the heavy glass of brandy Todd threw into his face. The shock staggered him, flung him across the table. Recovering, blinded by the liquor in his eyes, he fumbled for his handkerchief. Wiping away the brandy and blood, a phrase automatically returned to his mind — time had taken care of Gawin Todd.

He was, yet, unable to speak; with his vision cleared, he saw Todd, trembling violently, staring in an abject horror at the consequences of his lost control. "I don't know how it happened," he said impotently; "I couldn't have — by heaven, I've ruined everything I was! You, out of hell!" Once more he was choked with emotion. "You're nothing," he said, after a struggle for words that clenched and knotted his hands; "life was done with you, it had kicked you out; you didn't matter, except to women and children; but I let you get me into a trap. Because I offered you a friendly word. My God! And now what'll happen? — a filthy publicity, and what I worked for all my life gone. I let a decayed shell, a thing without a heart, rob me."

His speech, to Richard Bale, was nothing more than the twistings of a venality at last brought to a corner. If Todd wasn't afraid of death, he dreaded the loss of his material chances and possessions. But Richard said nothing: speech, now, was highly irregular. A cut on his chin continued to bleed; on the whole he had had a fortunate escape. The glass of brandy offered him was still half full; and, with a steady hand, he lifted and drained it. There was one thing. "Mr. Dalney will call on whom you may select," he instructed Gawin

Todd. "The arrangement must be final; but, beyond that, everything will be in his hands." Todd made no answer. He stood with a lowered head, loosely and appalled.

Again on horse, Richard avoided the direct road to Balisand; it was necessary to get his thoughts, yes, and his face, in better order. The blood dripped sullenly from the worst of the cuts. It was, if anything, warmer, like April. Two needs of equal importance occupied his mind: to get word to Henry at once and tell Lucia what was before them. He must manage to communicate to her his feeling that the meeting would be disastrous to Gawin Todd. Richard considered the fact that Todd, who had been challenged, had the choice of weapons; yet, between gentlemen, in Virginia, only one — the pistol — was allowable. He would have, too, the right to select the ground; but to Dalney belonged the fixing of the distance. It would be soon certainly and not far . . . across the North River would serve admirably. But he couldn't, with what lay ahead of him, ride over the county the entire afternoon. It would be difficult, telling Lucia. With other women it would have been impossible. Lucia wouldn't faint or cry, or even try to restrain him; she'd suffer quietly. That he bitterly regretted. Yet, before the code, he had no alternative; the responsibilities of his birth, position, she shared.

*

*   *

Lucia was quieter by far than he had anticipated. He had found her in their room, dressing, and at once, laughing at the appearance of his face, she had accused him of falling off his horse. But an end had been quickly brought to her light humour. "I have a feeling that I ought to apologize to you, and to the children; but you don't need it. You know how I think of you, and about Todd. Nothing else can be done." She came over to him and, swiftly and unexpectedly, put her arms around him. She held him so tightly to her, her embrace was so intense, that it quite cut off his breath. Then she resumed her occupation before the mirror. Her back was toward him. "This has been coming a long while," she said presently; "now it seems to me that I have always expected it. You have never explained your attitude toward Gawin, Richard; and I understand that something has prevented you. But it isn't politics." Lucia's hands were raised in the fastening of her dress, she had sent a maid away. "I always thought your hatred for him went back to that Miss Roderick who was killed at Todd Hundred, when I was a child. I'm not asking you, and we'll say no more of it. If you are not getting Henry already, I'll send down for a man to go to Piping Tree." That, he replied, had been seen to. Richard was both amazed and distressed by Lucia's instinctive recognition of what had begun his quarrel with Gawin Todd. It was purely feminine; but her restraint, the fact that she had never questioned him about Lavinia, that she said nothing now, transcended not only feminine but universal human qualities.

It would take Henry Dalney, if he were home, an hour to reach Balisand from the upper York River, riding mostly at a gallop. Richard was calculating this the moment Henry entered. Lucia rose and, briefly welcoming him, left the room. "Henry," Bale proceeded immediately, "once I asked you to do a service for me, and you then agreed. I wonder if you'd do it now." Henry Dalney replied without hesitation, "Yes. What is it?" Richard spoke two words: "Gawin Todd." The other was grave at once. "I noticed your face as I came in," he said. "Then it's serious — a blow." A glass of brandy in the face. Dalney went on with what Richard had reviewed. "He'll have to choose pistols, and I will insist on your pair. There are no better in the Tidewater. The Irish code, of course; and I hope he'll have someone who can draw up a cartel. You won't, of course, be bothered with the general arrangement, but we will have to decide about the distance. What is your idea, Richard?"

"I have only one," Richard Bale answered.

"Then you ought to be close, but not too close. Anything under eight paces would throw away what advantage you might have as a shot. Ten occurs to me. It's the best, everything included, under the circumstances. But the rule for firing isn't explicit: the pistols may be held down until a word is given, and then either shoot as you please; or, fire, one, two, three, stop, can be said; but you know better than I do. I should think you'd prefer the second. And I hope — you heard this before — you haven't been eating a great deal, Richard."

"I can add this," Bale told him, "the right of another shot may be demanded by Mr. Todd or me. In any case, Henry. If you are able to fire is the only condition there. Draw that so it can't be escaped from.

I don't want to meet him limping around the county for the rest of life." Dalney studied him curiously. "We've both seen stiff men, Richard, but I believe you're the stiffest alive. I want to say a little about the consequences of this, too. I mean if you are successful. Duelling isn't as well thought of as it has been. The laws are getting tighter. What a fool Todd was: on one hand, to bring you down upon him, and on the other, public disgrace."

"He mentioned that," Richard grimly observed.

"I'm certain," Dalney continued, "that a Gloucester jury wouldn't convict you, and you haven't an ambition left for Congress. Well, I'll see Todd, or his second, to-morrow, and bring this along. You won't care to wait. Three or four days of consideration might shake his hand, but then, probably, it would get out and become generally a mess. I should be back here before noon. Lucia, of course, was wonderful." She was, Richard assured him. "I'd almost rather have had her in hysterics. But I'm very confident." So was Henry Dalney. "You wouldn't spill a grain of sand from the barrel of your pistol. The weather, I'm sure, will hold." He asked once more for the details of the meeting at the tavern. "And Balantine quitted the taproom —— "

"A good thing, there were some names to be heard." Henry said, "Lavinia Roderick."

"Tell me," Richard asked, "I'm not a judge: was she very lovely?"

"Yes, decidedly," Dalney answered after a thoughtful pause. "A little hollow in the cheeks, perhaps, not a high colour, but lovely. Absent-minded, I remember.

I believe that's what killed her — she hadn't an idea she was near the steps. I danced with her, and I noticed she'd begin to talk and than not finish what she was saying; she trailed off into a kind of stare. Richard — if it's the last thing I say — she couldn't compare with Lucia. More ornamental, I suppose; perhaps more disturbing. Not against Lucia, though, not at a distance race. I think I'd say disturbing instead of lovely. She stirred me, in a minuet; I'll gamble it was the same with all the men who came near her. That would have gone on till eternity. And here I am — how long ago was it? — seeing her as clearly as any woman of today."

It was the same, Richard Bale moodily admitted, with him. "I can't make up my mind about it, either; I mean her; what it was. But it doesn't affect my appreciation of Lucia, nothing could do that." Dalney acknowledged his full recognition of this. "I'll take the pistols," he said absently; "they ought to be tried. It's disagreeable, but I'll have to touch on it: how are your affairs?"

"So simple they'll hardly need a laywer — all to Lucia absolutely. She has so much more than I have, outside of Balisand, that that's only a form. But Balisand is a lot, Henry; we've held it together pretty well, man and man. It hasn't changed. Richard and Francis and Francis and Richard. War and the plantation and then the United States, only those. Not bad. I have the damnedest feeling, now and then, there are flowers around me, roses blooming." He grew silent. The perfume of tea roses and delight, but he fought them off.

Not now! Henry, returning to the principal object of their meeting, asked if he could stand solidly without his cane. He could, Richard assured him. "Particularly if it isn't wet or very cold. Moving, I catch it." Henry Dalney spoke of the days of Lambert Wickes and his service in the British Channel. "We fought under the English cliffs, lashed bulwark to bulwark, and a whole town, maybe, watching us from the land as though we were a piece at the theatre." Peter Heyman, Richard related, was killed through just such a curiosity. "That was Eveline's uncle. She married my grandfather."

To the end, Dalney answered, Richard Bale would be a genealogical chart. The opportunity was decreasing, Richard dryly observed. "It is something of a novelty." That, Henry replied, was satirical rather than true. "Damned if you're not a tough and twisted old root. It was no favour to you when you were dug out of the past." That, in turn, Bale denied. "The children are green enough shoots; charming little blossoms, Henry."

*

* *

The windows were grey with beginning dawn when Richard woke. Lucia was up, moving about the room. "I thought we would take the hounds out," she said. "Not the hunt; you and me." An excellent idea, he assured her. He had been conscious the instant of waking of what lay before him. It seemed, until activity came to his assistance, depressing. Then he put the duel out of his mind. A whip for the hounds would be enough, Lucia decided, downstairs. Soon after, there was a confusion of barks, a preliminary excited baying, from the lawn. The negro selected to accompany them was holding the pack together with a long flexible leash, and they trotted slowly out the Balisand lane. It was too warm for comfortable hunting; before they had crossed back of Ware's Neck the horses were sweating. They passed by Roane's, skirted the woods of Welfield, and turned up, riding parallel to the rivers.

There was, certainly, no question of finding a grey fox, but they agreed to wait for the chance of a red, since, Lucia pointed out, they were not hunting foxes in the trees. He was very happy, with Lucia, in the bare sunny woods, on the soft winding roads and paths. They kept together, where it was possible, but said practically nothing; their brief speech was limited to the present purpose, to occasional comments on what they saw. Yes, Lucia was noticeably heavier, Richard thought; she needed a horse like the strawberry roan. The hounds yelped, lost to sight in covers; they cast out in wider circles, and found a grey fox; but, after a great deal of trouble, they were headed off that scent. The negro asserted that as soon as the hounds began their racket he could tell the colour of the fox. Suddenly Lucia stopped. "I'm tired," she explained. Richard gazed at her in surprise. "As long as I've known you," he answered, "this is the first time I've ever heard you suggest that." Probably it was the weather. Yet, now that she had spoken of it, he realized her usual erectness of carriage was lost in a drooping of her shoulders, of her whole body. The horses, standing, shifted restlessly from foot to foot; the hounds were plainly disconcerted.

They were at the edge of a thicket, in a small clearing by a narrow, deeply rutted sand road. From beyond, the barking of a dog answered the pack, partridges ran with a faint dry crackle of dead leaves. A cloud like a dark hand shut over the sun, and then, as though at the heat, let go hurriedly. Lucia took off her hat and pinned it to the skirt on her knee. She hadn't slept, Richard told himself: even against Henry's council he should have stayed awake, with her. His sleep had been deep and dreamless. But that, in the interest of their future together, he must not regret. Lucia had never talked much; he discovered that they lived with practically no chatter; he was absorbed in his speculations and Lucia in hers. What were they? The children, he knew, himself, but what else beyond hunting? "I'd like to hear the things in your mind." She looked up, startled. "I was remembering my childhood," she admitted; "and when I first realized you were you. I was wondering, too, if I had done as well as I might. But that couldn't be helped; I can't even promise myself to be different." Why should she, he demanded.

"If you changed I'd be lost. But that is impossible: we were this way before we were born and we'll stay the same till we die. I can't remember a man with more enemies than I've had, but I couldn't let that influence me. If I tried to be this and then something else — if it were possible — I'd end in nothing. What I really want, now, is to be happy and peaceful with you at Balisand. But I can't buy peace or happiness at some prices. I have a feeling that an obligation or a privilege, call it whatever you choose, was given to me, and that I must always keep it safe. It may be lucky or unlucky, there it is! I wish I could put it more clearly for you. For instance, a thing I am convinced of I'd follow at any cost to — well, to even you. If it were right or wrong wouldn't matter so much as how I supported it. I might easily be wrong, from ignorance, but I'd have to be firm. It's better to take the chance of sacrificing everything than to fall back in disorder. There was Wayne at Green Spring! And then, Lucia, I must be free to say what I believe: I don't mean if your dress was unbecoming or a bottle of Madeira, away from home, bad; but about principles. The Bales, perhaps you have noticed, aren't diplomats.

"Then, at all times, I am responsible for myself, what I say and do and think. Without excuse, you see. No question of avoiding the result. This isn't an apology, it's an explanation; I believe the first I have ever made. I'm anxious for you to think as well of me as you can, Lucia." She smiled at him in an assurance that had no need of words. "I was a good officer, and yet I was hated there, too; not by the soldiers who took the fire. There we were together, in the ordinary way of duty. For the rest ——

"There isn't much rest. And what I've told you isn't new. Only there is a satisfaction in saying it. God knows that's unusual enough, though, for me. Even Henry and Beverley curse me for having no feeling, except, perhaps, for Balisand; but I couldn't be attached to the plantation without understanding that it was more than a place by the North River. It's part of the responsibility I spoke of; yes, and the affection."

"Thank you, Richard." Lucia's voice was glad. "I did know that. But it was beautiful, your telling me. I can't do it; not even now. It's so simple you won't need me to. I want, more than anything in the world, to tell you how much I love you. I can't! Words won't come. It's because I live my life instead of thinking about it. I'm duller than you might admit. I've hardly ever, all my life, opened a book. I'm frightened of Miss Howlett, and of Flora, they are so intelligent. I have a — a sort of talent for attachments and for horses. But what else? Perhaps for understanding you.

"What you haven't said is what I'm mad about . . . in you. Honour. Of course it is disagreeable. How could it help being? People don't like to see the reflections of their own failings. We want to hide behind a tree now and then without having you drag us out. Perhaps I can speak, if it's you. I took it so for granted. Richard, the only quality I care for is courage. Do you hear that? Courage. And you wear it like that old black cockade. I don't think I want to talk any more, Richard. Can't we hunt?"

He spoke to the negro, lounging on his horse a short reach away, and the hounds were called together. They went on until there was a high concerted yelping that deepened into the steady cry of a chase. The huntsman called that a red fox had been raised. Richard followed Lucia over a fence and up a precarious path, a path with no secure footing and where the branches met across their way. A field lay before them and a hill to climb. Beyond, the running was open. A sudden stream but a fair bank. Fences and a farmhouse. He saw the fox, red and swift, flattened along the ground. The trouble at his heart, the confusion in his brain, was left far behind. To-morrow didn't matter. His horse was in a lather, but the roan was faster. Lucia, with an arm upraised, left him. She vanished into a sharp ravine, reckless and superb. A cascade of loose stones followed him down the slope to where she had mounted breaking through the underbrush, free.

*

* *

It was late in the evening before Henry Dalney returned. "I had the devil of a time," he reported. "First waiting for Newsome — Gawin Todd sent to Richmond for him — and then with the conditions. They accepted the pistols, but for a long while William Newsome wouldn't agree to the right of a second shot. He said that his principal was fixed in that. Finally I had to tell him that if he persisted I'd make the distance five paces instead of ten; and, after a conference, they came around. I chose the place, as it happened; he didn't know the country: across the North River, about halfway between Todd Hundred and Balisand. I was able to speak to Ambrose, too. He'll be ready as early to-morrow morning as the light will permit. The rest was all satisfactory enough, no more than conventional. Newsome seems to have had experience. I thought he rather looked forward to the show. I can't believe Todd does."

Their talk left the duel for a general conversation, and — Dalney was plainly weary — they soon went upstairs. Richard's room was dark, but Lucia, he discovered, a shawl over her preparation for bed, was seated at a window, looking out toward the river. There was a moon, veiled in warm haze, faintly reflected on the water; trees on the lawn were visible as bare uncertain shapes. As he entered she rose to meet him in a voiceless abandon, an illimitable burning richness, of passion. When he woke Lucia was sleeping. There was no light, but he felt that he should get up — he ought to be on the river at daybreak. As he moved she sat upright, her face a vague white blur in the cloudy blackness of her hair.

"Not so soon!" Lucia protested. Kneeling, she lighted the fire, and then, propped with a pillow, she watched him dress. "Your scarf," she reminded him; "it will be cold going." He took the military cape and square of soft black silk; and, beside her, he was once more at a loss for words. "Don't be long, Richard," Lucia begged. She kissed him with the pure lips of a child. "Come back soon. I've had some eggnog made for you; there's more in it than the rum." Still he was speechless. All, finally, he said was thank you. As he went through the doorway she sank down into obscurity. Dalney was already below.

The eggnog Henry approved of. There was a quantity for both; and, disposing of it, they moved out to the portico. The new headman was waiting, but Richard, in a sudden impulse, sent for London. When the negro appeared on the wharf Richard Bale said, "London, I am going to fight a duel with Mr. Gawin Todd, and I want you to take me over the river." It was easy, taking him over, the servant replied; what he'd be busy with was to bring him back. The long canoe slid noiselessly away from the land; the oars took the water together. A streak of light mounted in the east; it expanded and showed a mist hovering on the river. The mist lifted, floated away, as the brightness increased. At their back the objects of the shore grew visible, but the further bank was still formless. Richard was cold; he wrapped his cape closer about him, glad that he had the warmth of the scarf at his throat. Henry Dalney had charge of their direction, and, at intervals, he spoke to London in a low voice. The canoe drew up by a wooded point. "This is it," Henry announced. A second canoe was beached. "They are here."

Richard Bale walked up a steep rough ascent, through bushes, to an irregular open space enclosed by trees. He studied it critically. The length ran east and west; and, at the east, away from the river, there was a break on an expanse of low sullen cloud. Above that, however, the sky was clear. Gawin Todd was standing alone, Newsome was walking shortly up and down, and Ambrose was with them. He came forward immediately. "This is an unfortunate errand, Richard. I wish we were all out of it. A wicked destruction of the body; and, having said that, I'll say no more." They were interrupted by Newsome. "Mr. Dalney," he called. The seconds stood together, looking up at the morning. "At any rate," Henry decided, "we can load." Richard's pistols were taken from their case, the hair triggers set, the powder and balls rammed in. A coin spun flashing in the brighter air, and the choice of weapons fell to Newsome. "I shot them both," he admitted, "and there isn't a fraction of difference. Do you think it is light enough for us to proceed?"

"Perhaps after another five minutes."

The buds had multiplied astonishingly, Richard saw, the bushes and trees were tipped with vermilion and green. But the winter wasn't over; they would be killed. He was quiet, without a tremor; he had neither fear nor regrets. What would follow he had been powerless to avoid. He dwelt, for a second or so, on the manner by which, undoubtedly, he had forced this on Gawin Todd at the tavern. However, as he had in effect told Lucia, Beverley, he was what he was. For that he would apologize to no one. There was a sound of quick steps and he looked up: Todd had moved to the middle of the opening. "I call you to witness," he said in a loud voice, "and I call God to witness, that I loathe and detest what I am about to do with every instinct I have. I was brought into it by an act of my own, and I'll go through with the consequences for the reason that I am a coward. Whatever feeling I had against Mr. Bale is gone. I have only myself to condemn."

"Gentlemen," William Newsome spoke, "there is now enough day for firing. Mr. Dalney has won the toss for position, and he preferred to place Mr. Bale with his back to the river." Then, accompanied by Henry Dalney, he took ten deliberate steps. "Those are your places," he went on. "Mr. Bale, Mr. Todd, you will please take your positions. The cartel covering this meeting fits, we think, every possibility. The words, ready, fire, one, two, three, stop, will be pronounced, and between them you may shoot. In case either principal is able, and demands a final shot, it must be allowed. Until the word ready you may stand as you like except that the pistols cannot be in the line of fire."

Henry Dalney gave Richard a pistol and Todd took his from Newsome; but, when they reached the points where they were to stand, Dalney stepped quickly between them. "There is an irregularity I won't allow," he announced. "The cartel directs that the pistols are to be held in the right hand. Mr. Todd's is in his left. It isn't just to have his heart exposed to Mr. Bale's fire."

"I'm left-handed," Todd told him simply.

Henry Dalney was unconvinced; he wouldn't, he insisted, permit his principal to engage in that way. "We give you our oath Mr. Todd is incapable of shooting with his right hand," William Newsome replied. "It's my mistake and I regret it wasn't dealt with before."

"Enough, Henry," Richard's voice was low.

The seconds moved away, and Richard Bale, with a swift measuring glance, saw with exactness how Gawin Todd stood against the east. Beyond, at one side, Ambrose was watching him with a corrugated brow. "Gentlemen," a voice said, "are you prepared?" There was no answer. The pistol Richard held, cocked by his second, was held at a patch of green by his foot. "Then, ready, fire, one, two, three —— "

The instant his arm swept upward in a short smooth arc, the sun poured over the low clouds and fell with a blinding directness into his eyes. His pistol exploded impotently, and a shocking blow in the chest drove him, with a violent half turn, backwards.

*

* *

Above even the racing agony of his wound he thought, I must stay on my feet; but, with that in his mind, Richard found himself on the ground. Dalney was over him. "Henry, I tried to stand firm, but I couldn't." Ambrose was there, too, with a hand on his body. "How . . . serious it is?" Richard Bale asked; then he had fainted, for he heard no reply. He wasn't concerned with the injury to himself — a dogged will possessed him to finish the duel. By God, he would get up. "Be quiet," Ambrose commanded him sharply, but Richard moved up on an arm. "Mr. Bale is unable to deliver a second fire." It was the doctor speaking. His lips stiff with blood, Richard said, "I demand another shot." Exhausted by the determination of speech, his arm failed him; he collapsed on the coldness of the ground. A struggle took place within him, between his outraged physical being, alternate numbness and pain, and the tyranny of his need to again face Gawin Todd. He would collect himself for that. Henry was down beside him. "It's over, Richard," he insisted. "Another shot," Richard Bale whispered. "You can't get up or stand." He coughed. More blood. "I will . . . soon. Long enough." Newsome and Gawin Todd had joined Henry and the doctor; Todd was looking at him with a drawn face. “It was the sun,” Richard articulated slowly; “my eyes.”

He made a prodigious effort, and, from his hand and knees, actually rose; but only to collapse into Dalney’s arms. “You’ll have to wait,” he gasped; “in justice to me. I have a right —— ” Todd directed, “Force him to lie down. This is a crime.” Henry replied, “I am responsible for Mr. Bale; kindly retire a little with your second. Give it up, Richard,” he implored him; “you couldn’t hold a pistol or mark an object. Every honourable requirement has been met. Ambrose must look after you at once.” Holding himself erect by Dalney’s shoulders, Richard repeated, “I demand a second fire.” His vision was dull, but he found that, by setting it on a single object, he could still see. What he was intent on was a small tree in the opening. “The scarf,” he spoke with an enormous difficulty. And, quitting Henry Dalney, he stumbled in a suspended falling over the rough grass to where the sapling offered him support. From far away he heard Gawin Todd protesting in a shaken voice:

“I won’t! Nothing can force me into it. I tell you to take Mr. Bale in charge. If you don’t I’ll accuse you in the highest court I can reach.” “The scarf,” Richard reiterated. Dalney had it. “I’ll show you it’s impossible,” he agreed. He passed Richard Bale’s black silk neck covering about his body and, carrying it beneath his arms, knotted it to a limb of the young tree. “The pistol;” Richard’s eyes were stony. Once more Newsome was before him, critical and detached. “If he brings up his arm,” he declared, “Mr. Todd will be obliged to give him satisfaction." His fingers closed about the familiar pistol butt; spasmodically he raised his hand until the barrel pointed away from him. There was a succeeding confusion of talk.

"Very irregular. Guess at the distance. Mr. Todd will have to stand ——" He lost what followed. Then Ambrose was speaking. "In my opinion, no matter what he will pay, he is able to sight and fire. I am obliged, by Mr. Bale's conduct, to admit this against my professional inclination." The disturbance was renewed by Todd. "I won't shoot at him." Henry Dalney was curt. "The code specially forbids that: no dumb firing or firing in the air is admissible in any case." Richard Bale muttered, "Henry." No one heard him. His arm had fallen; it required a hideous power to keep hold of the pistol. He fastened his gaze on the woods before which Gawin Todd would appear. Henry returned to him and wiped off his face. "Richard, even I didn't understand the spirit in you." William Newsome again interrupted them:

"Doctor Ambrose has decided, over our objection, that a second fire is possible, but the conditions will have to be changed. Mr. Todd will take his place at what we judge the correct distance in the front of Mr. Bale, and the shots are to be made at will, after the word present." At last Todd appeared before him; the woods, the ground, faded; only the body of a man, a purpose, remained. A fear assailed Richard that he would miss the last signal, there was already such a tumult in his ears.

His response, however, was automatic: a double report and Gawin vanished. The pistol fell, his head drooped. Weariness, weariness more than suffering. Ambrose passed him, hurriedly, but he came back almost immediately. " Nothing to do there, for me. Instantaneous." He skilfully laid back Richard's coat, cutting away his linen. I had better see it, Richard Bale thought, and he looked down. A glance was enough: he was so accustomed to wounds, to death, that he fully realized the meaning of such an injury, of the bright bubbled blood. It had come to him as it must to all men! He was staggered at the greatness of the fact settling upon him; he wondered, under the administrations of Ambrose, if that were fear. A distasteful thought which he put hastily from him.

A liquid, not unpleasant, was held for him to swallow. The pain sank into an indifference toward all that had happened to him; he was comfortable rather than not; and sleepy. Green buds on the trees! But they would be black, frozen, soon. He had been fatally hit in a duel, by Gawin Todd. That old indebtedness, then, was discharged. Duels were final. Laudanum, that was it — the pleasant-tasting drink. Henry was seated beside him, and Ambrose straightened up. Richard said:

" I should like to go back to Balisand."

" The negroes are coming," Dalney replied.

London first reached him. " The sun came into my eyes," he tried to explain to the servant, but he wasn't sure that he had pronounced the words. His negroes carried him across the clearing, down the steep bank, to the canoe; wrapped in his cape, he was settled into the stern. He was returning, as he had required, to Balisand. Henry Dalney was with him; his arm was around

Richard's shoulders. "I never believed he would do it," he managed to say. "I thought of it differently. Gawin seemed like a target to me: Democratic-Republican. Henry, I know about this, in my chest." An idea, a desire, came over him. "Tell London . . . the men are to sing." The Anabaptist hymn swirled about him like audible memories; it swept out, a minor key, over the water, God's children lost in the land of Egypt.

His boatmen were the best in the Tidewater, they rowed with never a break. But London was getting old; with that injury to his arm, there would have to be a new head of the servants, taking his whisky at the foot of the portico steps. A lassitude drooped over him, but, dreading its result, yet, he fought it off. "I never thought that Gawin was dangerous," he repeated. "Henry, listen to me, I believe I was right. If I was wrong, then wrong was right for me and the end was just." He was fretted by the obscurity of what he had said, the need, struggling with his exhaustion, to express his final belief in the articles of his faith. "Don't talk," Henry answered. He listened, instead, to the negroes singing salvation, relief from want and miseries and toil. They had beautiful voices. "I mean," his tone was very much fainter, "when they say . . . hard things about me, Lucia and you will know how it has been with the Bales. Always. I defend this — this morning absolutely. Are we near Balisand?" Soon, Henry Dalney told him, they would be there. Richard slipped further and further from reality, he lapsed into the imagery of dreams.

* * *

Yet the images were more logical than dreamlike, his thoughts were consecutive, at the sleepy ordering of his mind. Rather, his mind had been detached from the needs of his body; it was no longer utilitarian; and, through it, there was a sense of the river, broad and shining, an expanse of serene light, and of remote singing. All else was forgotten. People came and went in his mental pictures; but they only appeared as the figures of his own creation, the visible signs of what, on earth, he had experienced. He went back to his childhood, to the days when Morryson hadn't palsy and his father was alive, a man very much, on the exterior, like himself, but — secretly — gentle within. The only Bale Richard knew of with patience. But he, too, had been a decided man; his invariable courtesy, his willingness to listen to anyone for apparently any length of time, possessed an aloofness of its own. He could deal perfectly with Morryson, Richard recalled; as a younger man, Morryson had offered difficulties; he had regarded the resources of Balisand to be inexhaustible, and acted accordingly — clothes and hazard, astonishing amounts of liquor and witless bets. But he, as well, decrepit with age, had raised his cane, contemptuous of result, against the invasion of his dignity and privileges.

Balisand was the same through his childhood as now: the round deep ice house whitewashed in the identical way of the present; the Cherokee roses grew in unrestrained freedom by the river; the gardens and negro quarters were identical; the graveyard, except for three comparatively new headstones, was still adorned by what flowers grew from the chance seeds carried there by the winds. The oaks were little older in the span of his years. Trees that lived slowly, a hard wood, a rough bark. The fields lately cleared, the roads bedded with fresh stone, made no difference, not in the persistent whole. The rooms stayed without a chair shifted; a table repaired, braced, was put back on the spot where it had worn the boards of the floor. Shingles were replaced, one by one, but their brightness soon merged into the quiet of the mossy and weather-beaten roof. Everything attempted was drawn back into the old harmony of Balisand plantation.

The very negroes looked always alike, a reasonable fact, since in many cases, they were the children of men and women born, living and dying, there. A small black mob was perpetually eddying about the gates, scandalously naked in summer, and in winter covered with the gay ends of nothing; the young girls sat on the doorsteps of the cabins at evening, a laughing murmur ran from door to door, broken by deeper, more serious, masculine tones; the windows glimmered with candles in the darkness. Refrains, falling inflections of song. The house servants came and went with an air of superiority, of elegance, moving disdainfully aside from the field hands.

Balisand had never, like Welfield, been celebrated for its fruit; there were no wall gardens of apricots or grape walks; the garden itself couldn't compare with the one at Todd Hundred; none of the women here had specially cultivated flowers — not Lucia; his mother had scarcely walked through the paths bordered with box; Eveline, the wife of the second Richard in America, had been herself too flowerlike to be concerned with other blooms; Camilla, who had married Francis, was a creature of drawing rooms; Lydia had had Indians rather than mignonette to think about. But even as a boy he had lingered in the garden, inside the vine-covered brick wall with its low crowning fence. He had been a great deal alone; once for a year without a tutor; and, never very imaginative, he found a pleasure in positive colours and scents. The garden and the broadnut tree! One to linger in and the other to climb. The broadnuts, resembling the oak trees, were hard; it took a large stone to crack them, but they were sweet inside. He preferred them to softer and more luxurious fruit——

The field hands singing; the bell for dinner!

Above all the details of the plantation, there was a single binding atmosphere; no other place was quite the same. Richard was aware of this as soon as he turned from the public road into their private lane. He couldn't identify it, it escaped recognition; when, purposely, he sought its peculiar quality, it retreated, like a faint wind lost over the river. Now, however, he saw that it was in him as well as about him — Balisand was made from its trees and acres and grass and water together with what he felt toward them. It wouldn't have that effect on anyone from the outside; he doubted if Lucia — but this was in another existence — were actually conscious of it. When he stood on Balisand he was like a tree with its roots in its own, its appropriate, soil. There he was home. It was strange how men, long gone, remained; how what they were stayed in stone and wood and earth.

Eveline's loveliness was a part of Balisand; the ironic silken manner Richard Bale had brought, in 1651, to America, a mask of silk worn by a soldier, was woven into its texture; a chain of lives forming the plantation and formed by it.

The best of it, Richard thought, he had inherited; the instincts and objects and traditions had come to him in their full power. In him the old Balisand, it might be said, had culminated. He was too deeply involved to hold himself lower than the rest; he couldn't be disentangled from it. All that it was he was. That he had said often, in different ways and to different people, but the meaning never varied. What others, who had no Balisand, felt, he was unable to imagine. His later service in the war, his allegiance to a beginning, a scarcely hoped for America, had had its being in his ground on the North River: his love for one had expanded by necessity into love for the larger. Balisand, his plantation, the place of his integrity and blood and happy freedom! Yes, they were inseparable, the thing and his perception of it.

What that threatened, of course, was that when he was gone, when the Bales were gone, the plantation must, in a true sense, cease to exist; it would equally overtake the country; it, too, would be no more than miles; it didn't matter how many they were or how rich. That, he discovered, but too late, was his attitude and conviction toward all the political animosity which had so often torn his equanimity into shreds. Men, like trees — he relinquished his thought. It was better to be back in an older time.

A profounder drowsiness assailed him; he was borne on a contentment like a soundless river between far placid banks. A short distance to Mockjack Bay with the sea beyond. The North River was tidal; it ebbed and returned; but the Bales of Balisand, each in his moment, went down it for ever. Into deep water. They left the oyster beds and the duck settled on the rivers in November, the terrapin in the Guinea marshes, the wild turkey and brown partridges; they left the toddy bowl and the sparkling decanters; they fell out of the hunt, leaving the high running cry of the hounds, the notes of the horn; those who danced deserted the minuets and fiddles. Down the river to the bay, like a packet making for the horizon, a sloop with the properties of Balisand on board. Dreamlike images and quiet coloured thoughts. A flickering pain restored a dim sense of actuality. Henry Dalney shifted him to an easier position; London had the immobility of a carving in black wood. He was still, Richard realized, going to Balisand.

*

* *

He became more directly concerned with the present, yet he surveyed it as a difficulty from which he had been released. For this he was glad; he was, he found, at last weary of contention. Although apparently he had had so many tranquil days, Richard was surprised at the amount of fighting he had been involved in. His youth had merged abruptly into the war with England, and the echoes of that had never died. He had been always opposed to something, struggling against contrary men and ideas. It would be truer, perhaps, to say he had been contrary. But his principle was to attack the things he didn't believe in, to fight with all his resources what he hated and distrusted. However, now he was tired of it, relieved that it was over — the brilliant English guards and Guineamen and glasses of brandy where they had no business to be.

It was peaceful with Lucia; she was, herself, like a peaceful day; after, maybe, the summer was over. The summer . . . that was Lavinia. However, what joy was in his remembrance, the loveliness of June, was blackened by the realization that Lavinia had, in the end, destroyed him. She had been fatal to Gawin Todd; for, without her, they would never have cherished the bitterness which had finally brought them to their ultimate duel. She had always returned to him in a commemorative and blinding flash of sunlight. Yes, Lavinia had killed him, but that carried, rather than resentment, a fresh accession of serenity. It freed him: she was now, for Richard, only a dead rose.

A vision floated before him of a tree with golden apples; they were shining in the sun among leaves as green and glittering as emeralds. He broke one from a dry metallic stem; a heavenly scent clung to it; but, suddenly wise, he threw it away, cleansing the odour from his hands. It was dead, evil, enclosing a dry perpetuity of sterile seed.

Lavinia.

That understanding had brought to a conclusion his last and most dangerous strife. What was left to him,

Richard Bale, she couldn't steal. He had paid extravagantly for this release, yet not too dearly. If she had lived, and married him; if their love had been satisfied, she too, like Lucia, would have been happy and natural. He made an effort to see clearly the river, the canoe with his men, but the morning was so bright it blinded him. Henry spoke, "Do you want to sit up higher?" He shook his head, no. He had been sitting up, standing and riding, long enough. Richard tried to smile, and wondered if he had been successful. It was an unusual effort for him, a sombre man, to make. He hated a show of emotion, in the past; all hatred, all opposition, had left him. Henry Dalney, though, a strong man, was more demonstrative. Sailors, he had heard, under their thick storm jackets, owned a marked sentiment. He thought it to be the result of long loneliness on the sea.

Still concerned with his comfort, Henry folded Richard's cape closer around him. "I am very warm." It was the movement of his lips, more than the sound, that Dalney seemed to attend. He, too, had fought, on ships. In times of peace they were laughed at together. He wished that Ambrose hadn't given him laudanum, for it was that, he was certain, which made it so laborious for him to talk: there were some things Richard wanted to say to Henry Dalney. And he must be alert to meet Lucia. It wouldn't do to frighten her. Then, when they were alone, in their room, he could tell her, himself, the truth. She would take it marvellously. It was so warm the windows would be open on the lawn and the river; perhaps he'd stay with her until evening; and he'd ask her to dress for dinner . . . watch her arrange her smooth black hair with quick strong fingers.

Above all else, he wanted to reassure her about himself: it wasn't too terrible. He wouldn't have chosen it then — not, with her, for a long long while — but time, where they were touched, mattered very little. It couldn't be divided into days and years. Fifty years more would have gone like a flash. The seven years of their marriage had been an eternity. There was a depth in love that obliterated time. He'd lie still now, gather his strength for the wharf; perhaps, with a little help, he could walk the short distance to the portico. "I'll walk, when we get to land," he said. Henry Dalney bent lower. "Walk . . . on land."

"By God, Richard, I believe you'd walk on water," Henry asserted, profanely.

His mind turned to religion, he was thinking about the negroes and their implicit belief in heaven; but, at this, he cursed himself — he would rather trust to his ignoring of any God in the past than limp before Him now, with his fatal wound. What if it, the legend of an eternity of punishment or praise, were true? This was a speculation in the spirit of his peculiar and satirical and rare humour. The Bales weren't noted for humour. If it were a fact, there would be no hesitation in the disposal of him, Richard Bale of Balisand.

He tried to speak again — he wanted Henry to dip a handkerchief in water and wash his face, for Lucia; the cape would hide the other. But Henry couldn't make out his desire. He laid a band of cold wet linen on Richard's forehead. That, however, was refreshing; it served to stay the effect of the drug. He might, he felt, contrive to live into another day. Lucia would hold him against the passionate vitality of her body, in her vital arms. The children she'd send to play at Welfield; he had no anxiety to see them.

His children, except, perhaps, Flora, wouldn't suffer from their loss; they'd only understand it when they were older and he had become a memory to them. That was safely trusted to Lucia. The canoe had changed its direction; they were coming in to the shore. Richard began to be fearful of the narrow steps up to the level of the wharf; even with help he doubted if he could manage them. They were difficult when he had been merely drunk. The sun was in his face, and he slightly and heavily moved his head.

They ought to be under the shore, but he couldn't see the bank. Where were the branches of the trees? But he wasn't impatient or rebellious; he'd be there soon. The sun wasn't so bright. He was glad of that. It was so warm that it must rain. Rain clouds. They darkened rapidly. The boatmen would hurry to get in before the storm. That was what had stopped their singing. The pain returned and he moved restlessly. Henry shifted him once more. "It's cramped, here, Richard," he explained. Richard Bale knew his canoe. Naturally, with him stretched out on the bottom, it was crowded. But it was almost time for him to sit up, to prepare for Balisand. Already the feeling of its nearness was coming over him. They would float, with lifted oars, up to the steps, and London stop their progress with a hand on the wharf. Henry lifted him higher.

Through a gathering dark he saw the familiar landing; the house was farther away than he had remembered it; Balisand appeared infinitely big and shadowy, as it had in his earliest impressions. Someone, he felt rather than saw, was on the wharf. "Who is that, Henry?" he asked. It was a long while before he heard the answer, "It's Lucia." They must be quick to reach her before the storm. He leaned forward to escape the coldness swiftly overtaking him. "I will never get there," he said with a clear voice. Then, in Henry Dalney's arms, he died.

* * * * * *

BRYAN UNIVERSITY LIBRARY

2113

THIS BOOK MAY BE KEPT